Praise for bestselling author
Jennifer LaBrecque

"*The Big Heat* showcases Jennifer LaBrecque's
big talent...she gifts us with great dialogue, hot
sensuality and characters I adore. I'm a fan!"
—*New York Times* and *USA TODAY* bestselling author
Vicki Lewis Thompson

"LaBrecque writes her characters
to jump off the pages."
—*The Romance Reader*

Praise for bestselling author
Jo Leigh

"Heart-stopping action and adventure twists
with romance and sex...the excitement is endless."
—*RT Book Reviews* on *Relentless*

"Excellent excitement, tension, sex and mystery
combine to make *Closer*...a book that flies by
as your heart pounds."
—*RT Book Reviews*

After a varied career path that included barbecue-joint waitress, corporate number cruncher and bug-business maven, **JENNIFER LABRECQUE** has found her true calling writing contemporary romance. Named 2001 Notable New Author of the Year and 2002 winner of the prestigious Maggie Award for Excellence, she is also a two-time RITA® Award finalist. Jennifer lives in suburban Atlanta.

JO LEIGH

has written more than forty novels for Harlequin and Silhouette Books since 1994. She's thrilled that she can write mysteries, suspense and comedies all under the Harlequin banner, especially because the heart of each and every book is the love story.

A triple RITA® Award finalist, Jo shares her home in Utah with her cute dog, Jessie. You can chat with Jo at her Web site, www.joleigh.com, and don't forget to check out her daily blog!

JENNIFER LABRECQUE
Barely Decent

JO LEIGH
The One Who Got Away

HARLEQUIN®

TORONTO • NEW YORK • LONDON
AMSTERDAM • PARIS • SYDNEY • HAMBURG
STOCKHOLM • ATHENS • TOKYO • MILAN • MADRID
PRAGUE • WARSAW • BUDAPEST • AUCKLAND

Recycling programs
for this product may
not exist in your area.

ISBN-13: 978-0-373-68807-4

BARELY DECENT & THE ONE WHO GOT AWAY

Copyright © 2010 by Harlequin Books S.A.

The publisher acknowledges the copyright holder of the individual works as follows:

BARELY DECENT
Copyright © 2002 by Jennifer LaBrecque

THE ONE WHO GOT AWAY
Copyright © 2004 by Jolie Kramer

This edition published by arrangement with Harlequin Books S.A.

For questions and comments about the quality of this book please contact us at Customer_eCare@Harlequin.ca.

® and TM are trademarks of the publisher. Trademarks indicated with ® are registered in the United States Patent and Trademark Office, the Canadian Trade Marks Office and in other countries.

www.eHarlequin.com

Printed in U.S.A.

CONTENTS

In memory of Carol Mann Arnold, who loved Howard, her family, Hannah Banana, pinochle, golf, hickory taters, pink dogwoods and life.
You taught me to believe in angels.

BARELY DECENT

Jennifer LaBrecque

PROLOGUE

"I DON'T CARE if he did ask you to the prom, he's just trying to get in your pants. Bobby's a player." Ryan Palmer stood in front of his best friend, Phoebe Matthews, his arms crossed over his chest, his chin jutting at a stubborn angle, a classic case of the pot calling the kettle black. Except it had never occurred to Ryan to try to get into her pants, and Bobby wasn't a player— just a quiet guy who'd developed a crush on her.

"According to you, they're all players or dweebs or punks or something. Anyway, he invited me to the prom, not a hotel room." Heat crept up Phoebe's face as she toed the swing into motion, forcing Ryan to step back or suffer a whacked shin. She felt like whacking him upside the head. "For crying out loud, Ryan, all he did was kiss me and ask me out."

She was probably the only eighteen-year-old girl in their entire school—possibly the entire planet— who'd never been kissed until today. Mainly, she figured, because outspoken, tall, flat-chested brainiacs didn't exactly have boys lining up to kiss them. But also, because Ryan had taken on the misguided, self-appointed position of watchdog over her virtue. And because her best friend, Ryan, was the chief eighteen-year-old boy *doing* the kissing. And best friends didn't kiss. Did they?

So Phoebe had come up with a plan, and when Bobby Richmond had whipped out his ChapStick, primed his lips and laid one on her, she'd been ready. Kissing Bobby had been a little waxy—actually a lot waxy—but okay, until thoughts of Ryan had popped in her head and she'd wondered if kissing Ryan would be more than okay.

Phoebe studied Ryan from where she sat on the swing. Average build. Stocky. Sandy blond hair. Jade green eyes. Ryan wasn't the best-looking boy in school or the smartest or the most athletic, but he possessed something far more potent. Aunt Caroline called it charm and charisma. Whatever "it" was, he had it. Girls had been dropping at his feet since elementary school.

"I'll have a little talk with Bobby Richmond."

"Do it and die." Phoebe swung a little harder. "Don't get all bent out of shape about a kiss. A kiss is nothing when you consider there are girls in school having babies."

"Phoebes—"

A little shock was good for him now and then. "I don't want to have a baby, you nut. But a kiss and a date to my senior prom don't seem like too much to ask. Thanks to my flat chest and your 'talks' with every guy who even looked my way, I'm blooming plenty late without any additional help from you."

She handed him the perfect opportunity to pull out that charm he plied all the other girls with—curvy, busty, petite, cute girls—and insist that her flat chest and gangly legs weren't important. She awaited his response, her heart pounding far harder than when Bobby had laid his ChapStick-coated lips on hers.

"But, Phoebes, you don't know guys the way I know guys." Ryan shoved his hands in his blue jean pockets and looked everywhere except the vicinity of her chest. Had the subject of her nonexistent chest embarrassed him, the King of the Casanovas? Was that what had brought on this awkward tension between them?

She looked past him to the azaleas blooming outside the screened porch, embarrassment radiating through her. Toulouse, one of Aunt Caroline's numerous adopted stray cats, sunned himself by the porch steps.

Slightly bruised, her heart slowed to its normal rate. So much for the silly notion Ryan might see her as more than a friend. She was just feeling uncertain with all the changes looming around the corner. High school graduation. College in the fall. Would she and Ryan remain close? Or would he meet some girl at college and no longer need her friendship?

"Sure I know guys. You're a guy. I've got the inside

scoop on that dark hole known as the male mind. That's why I had to come up with a plan."

Ryan groaned and ran his hand through his cropped hair. "Not another one of your plans?"

So, once in a blue moon her plans went slightly awry, like that fourth grade science experiment. Ryan needed to get over that. His hair had only been pink for a day or two.

"Plans make perfect sense." Plans were important. Phoebe had already planned the next ten years while Ryan was still trying to decide on a college major.

"You've got to learn to go with the flow, Phoebes."

"If you make a plan, you should stick with it." She glared at him, daring him to disagree.

The front door opened. Aunt Caroline stepped onto the porch, the two calico cats, Lilly and Millie, trailing behind. "Sugar, I'm running up to the store. I want to make that chocolate torte you like so much for your graduation party and we need cat food. Uncle Frank's in his studio. He's having a hard time with this piece of stone, so you might want to steer clear."

In the twelve years Phoebe had lived with them, she'd learned not to disturb her uncle when he was sculpting in his studio. Give Uncle Frank—a nice, reasonable man—a chisel and a stone slab, and he morphed into Mr. Hyde.

Lilly twined between Ryan's legs. Millie found

Phoebe's lap and kneaded before finally curling into place.

Aunt Caroline blew across the porch and out the screen door, letting it slam behind her. "Do you need anything? Ryan, are you staying for dinner?"

"I don't need anything." Phoebe absently scratched behind Millie's ears. She double-checked the driveway two houses down. "Your dad's not home." Ryan didn't bother to look.

"Sure, I'll stay for dinner." Ryan seldom turned down an invititation. Mostly because he never knew whether his father and his father's latest girlfriend would be around. But Phoebe knew he joined them more for the company than the food.

Caroline paused on the last stone step, looking at Phoebe. "Lynette called this afternoon." Phoebe's stomach lurched, as it always did when anyone mentioned her mother's name. "She and Vance can't make your graduation, after all." Caroline's voice carried, soft and apologetic, in the spring afternoon, the same as every time she broke the news that once again Phoebe's parents would be no-shows.

Twelve years ago, Phoebe and her parents had driven to Nashville from Florida, where they lived from town to town. Lynette and Vance had dropped their daughter off for a "visit" with her aunt Caroline and uncle Frank. Phoebe hadn't seen them since. They'd never came back. Phoebe lost count of the number of times they had promised to come and never showed up.

Relief warred with anger. Relief that she wouldn't have to see them. Anger, once again, that they had passed her on like a useless piece of furniture. She kept her expression neutral and her voice steady. "I didn't really expect them. But thanks for letting me know."

Aunt Caroline paused and then jammed her sunglasses on over angry, sympathetic eyes. "I won't be gone long." She hadn't walked out the door without uttering that reassurance since the day she'd given up her job as a flight attendant after six-year-old Phoebe had freaked out over her two-day absence.

Desperately trying to swallow the lump lodged in her throat, Phoebe watched her aunt climb into her car. Dammit, she'd thought that since she was valedictorian, just this once her parents might... Couldn't they ever follow through on anything? "It's important to make plans and stick with them."

Ryan dropped beside her, setting the swing in motion again. He pulled her close, his hand smoothing her hair in a familiar gesture of comfort. The same way he'd comforted her twelve years ago when he'd found her crying in the woods behind his house, when she'd finally figured out her parents weren't coming back for her. The same way she'd comforted him when he'd told her his mother drank herself to death months before. "They're idiots, Phoebe."

She looked at him. Her tears, held at bay, blurred his features. She recognized the pain rippling through him. Every time her parents let her down, Ryan lost his mother all over again. She repeated the comfort they'd offered each other throughout childhood. "We can't choose our parents, but we can choose our friends. And I choose you."

She settled her head against his shoulder and squelched the shiver of girlish longing that chased down her spine at the contact. Boyfriends came and went, but friends were forever.

CHAPTER ONE

Twelve Years Later

"SO, WHAT DO YOU THINK?" Phoebe pushed the glossy, trifold brochure across the pub-style table-top. She already knew what Ryan would think of the photos promising white sugar beaches, clear blue water, more aqua sports than she could count and sizzling tropical nights.

Ryan pointedly glanced out the restaurant window at the slushy sidewalks and heavy gray skies.

"The temperature in Nashville's barely going to crawl above freezing for the rest of this week." A slow grin revealed the dimple that had broken hearts since grade school. "Sun, sand and sex. What's not to like?" He flicked the brochure with his finger, "What's the occasion?"

"It's a celebration of sorts." She paused, smoothing her hand over her red suit jacket. "You are looking at the new marketing director for Capshaw and Griffen. It comes with a window office and a nice fat salary increase."

"Hot damn, Phoebes. That's great. You got it." He

high-fived her across the table. Genuine happiness crinkled the corners of his eyes and pulled his dimples into full play.

Even after all these years as friends, her heart pounded a little harder when he smiled that way. "I couldn't wait to tell you." She'd forced herself not to call him on her cell phone, wanting to share the good news in person.

"You deserve it. You've worked your butt off for eight years and you're brilliant. They're damn lucky to have you. How'd Charlie take it?"

Poor Ryan. How many weekly lunches had he suffered through her trials and tribulations with her nemesis, Charlie Langley? About the same number she'd suffered through his change of girlfriends.

"Charlie didn't take it well." Phoebe nibbled at the end of her bread stick. "He and Skip Griffen were Lambda Chi brothers. He pretty much considered the promotion his for the asking. He resigned this morning when they made the announcement. Good riddance, if you ask me."

"Damn straight. He made your life hell for the last couple of years. I'd like to have met him in a dark alley more than once," Ryan grumbled, always ready to champion her.

"Nah. It was much sweeter this way. He should've never underestimated a woman with a plan." She forked her olives onto her bread plate and slid it across the table to him.

"A plan and a competitive streak a mile wide make for an overachiever. Let me guess, you're the youngest marketing director in the history of the company."

She couldn't suppress a grin. "By two years. And you're one to talk about overachievers, Mr. Top Salesman in the southeast for Rooker Sports Equipment."

Ryan devoured the olives, taking her comeback in stride. He knew his accomplishments meant as much to her as her own. "This fat salary increase…how fat?"

"Do I make more money than you? Is that the question?" She shook her head, teasing. "I'll never tell."

"You know I could catch you with your shoes off and tickle it out of you."

"You'd be a dead man. Let's just say I'm catching up to you fast. So, do you and a date want to come to Jamaica with me and Elliott?" She lined up the proper balance of lettuce, tomato and feta on the tines of her fork. "Come on. It'll be so much more fun if you're there. By the way, who *is* the girlfriend de jour?"

"Her name's Kiki. And she's a very nice girl."

"Uh-huh. They all are." And they were. Even after he moved on to the next one, they remained friendly. One big happy harem. It never ceased to amaze and annoy her. "You change girlfriends the way some men change ESPN channels."

Ryan quirked one sandy eyebrow, devilment lighting his pale green eyes. "There's lots of good sports,

Phoebes. You stay on one channel too long and you miss something on another one."

That was no way to approach a relationship. Phoebe shook her head. She worried about Ryan and his steady stream of vacuous relationships. "What do you talk about with these nice, but let's face it, not very bright women you tend to favor?"

"Are you saying a smart woman wouldn't want to date me?"

A sexy, captivating man with the attention span of a gnat? He made a wonderful friend—considerate, caring, dependable, fun—but she'd watched him over the years, and he didn't extend the same effort as a boyfriend.

"Absolutely. No woman in her right mind would go out with a man who changes channels as often as you do."

Ryan's smile qualified as wicked. "Maybe I've got a really impressive channel changer."

A purely feminine response shivered down her spine at his sexy suggestion, setting off a clamor of warning bells in her head. No way she'd ever tell him she'd wondered about his channel changer on the odd occasion, late at night, in the privacy of her bedroom. Channel changers, impressive or not, didn't belong in a friendship. "Don't go there. And don't try to switch the subject." Phoebe stabbed her fork in his direction. "What *do* you talk about?"

Actually, she was terribly curious. What allure did

these women have other than the obvious physical appeal? Sex only carried a relationship so far.

Ryan shrugged. "Stuff. I'm not looking for deep conversation from a girlfriend—"

"Good. You'd be out of luck." Well, that sounded nice and bitchy. Even if it was true.

"If I want to discuss world peace, I've got you."

Sometimes they talked for hours on end about everything and nothing. And sometimes they spent hours together with only comfortable silence between them.

"I've been thinking about it. I've decided you're emotionally retarded, and I think I'm an enabler." She was only half teasing. Was their friendship part of the reason he drifted in and out of relationships? If she were a male friend instead of a female one, would he look for a deeper relationship with some of the women he merely skimmed the surface with? It was a painful thought.

"I'm a guy. I'm supposed to be emotionally retarded."

She hated it when he refused to take her seriously. "You do a good job of it. Go ahead and laugh. One day someone's going to break your heart. Big time."

"Nah. It'll never happen."

"How can you be so sure?"

"You change the channel before you get that interested in the outcome of the game." Ryan sliced off a neat quarter of his stromboli and shifted it to an empty salad plate, stringing melted cheese along the way. "Anyway, in the unlikely event that transpires, I've always got you to pick up the pieces, Ms. Enabler."

Just as she'd always been able to count on him. Phoebe brushed aside the niggling thought that a part of her liked the fact that he never had a serious relationship with another woman.

He shoved the plate across the table. It dinged against her water glass. "You sure Kiki and I won't cramp Geek Boy's style if we tag along to this couples-only resort?"

Her mouth watered as steam rose from the cheese-and spinach-filled dough. She preferred the stromboli, but the salad made her feel better about her waistline management. So each week she ordered what she needed, and Ryan parceled out a portion of what she really wanted.

"I'm sure *Elliott* won't mind when I mention it." And it would be so much more fun with Ryan along. And Kiki.

"He doesn't even know yet, does he?" Ryan laughed and shook his head. "You're something else. You'll just set everything up and then give him the dates he's supposed to show up?"

"Something like that." Ryan often razzed her about her take-charge personality. "He's close to tenure now and very busy."

"Do the two of you ever discuss anything *other* than world peace?" Ryan turned the tables on her.

An associate professor of Greek and Roman literature at Vanderbilt University, Elliott took himself very seriously.

"Occasionally." Actually, Elliott was so reflective, a touch of frivolity would be nice. "We both need a break." She hoped the break jump-started their stagnant relationship. He was sweating his upcoming review, and she'd been working her buns off to land this promotion. A little R and R should do them both a world of good.

Naomi, their regular waitress, stopped by. "The stromboli okay?" Ryan gave her a thumbs up. "Good. You two splitting a baklava today?"

Beach? Bathing suit? Baklava? "No."

"Yes. One baklava. Two forks," Ryan countermanded. Naomi grinned as she walked away.

Ryan affected women that way. Young. Old. It didn't matter. He charmed them all. She thanked the powers that be—and not for the first time—that she fell under the best-friend immunity umbrella.

"One bite." She'd allow herself a taste of the honey- and walnut-filled pastry. "Stop me at one bite." Phoebe eased back on the wooden seat, fairly sure how Ryan would receive her next piece of news. Sometimes she thought she knew him better than she knew herself.

"Okay, I'll stop you at one bite." He leaned back and crossed his arms over his chest. "Now, what gives? You've got that look."

"What look?"

"That I've-got-a-plan look."

"I do, in fact, have a plan." Phoebe operated with plans. She'd had her fill of surprises and changes when her parents upended her world when she'd been only six. She liked plans. In accordance with her long-term plan, she'd devoted her twenties to building her career. Right on schedule, she'd realized a major career goal. Now it was time to work on her personal life. "Having a plan isn't a crime."

"Let's hear it. What is it now? Vice presidency within two years?"

"Well, there is that, but this is a little more personal."

"You're going to start yoga classes?"

"No. But maybe that's something to consider." No easy approach to the subject presented itself. "I want to check out Hot Sands as a potential honeymoon site. Elliott and I have been dating for almost a year. Once he makes tenure, we should consider getting engaged."

"Engaged? Honeymoon?" Ryan choked the words out. She'd expected surprise. He looked positively stunned.

"Do you need me to Heimlich you?" Why did she feel so guilty? As if she'd somehow betrayed Ryan?

"You'd really marry *him?*"

"Don't you like Elliott?" Well, that was a stupid question. Since her first prom date at eighteen—no, actually since her first crush on Gary Pelham in middle school—Ryan had always found her boy-friends lacking for one reason or another. Of course, she couldn't say she'd cared much for the girlfriends who flitted in and out of Ryan's life, either.

"He's okay. But not to ma-marry." Ryan stumbled over the word. "Why do you need a husband?" He appeared genuinely perplexed and sounded close to desperation.

"I don't *need* a husband. I *want* a husband. You and I just turned thirty this year. I want to grow old with someone."

"Remember when we pricked our thumbs and took a blood oath when we were nine? We promised we'd always be friends. *We'll* grow old together. Look. We passed thirty. We're already getting old."

Phoebe studied his earnest expression across the table. Could she make him understand this void in her heart that ached to be filled, the desire for the one thing always denied her? "Not like that. I want a family."

"But you've got your aunt Caroline and uncle Frank."

"Yes. And they're wonderful, but they've been my family on sufferance." She held up a hand to stem his protest. "Loving sufferance, but sufferance nonethe-less. They graciously stepped up to the plate when my parents dumped me on them, but we aren't a family by choice. We're a family by obligation. My parents…

there's nothing left to say there. I want to build my own family."

"We're like family," he stubbornly maintained.

Ryan's entire life was built around the short term. He leased his sports cars, trading them in for a new model every few years. His sales career brought new faces and new conquests on a daily basis. His girl-friends…well, they'd covered that. The only perma-nent, long-term fixture in Ryan's life was Phoebe.

She bought her cars and drove them past the point they were paid for. Her job required months on long-term projects. She'd worked with Capshaw and Griffen since she graduated college. For all that Ryan knew her better than anyone else, he didn't seem to understand her craving for stability and a family to call her own.

"Yes. We are like family." Phoebe's connection to Ryan ran soul deep, but she wanted more than friend-ship. "But I want a ring on my finger that symbolizes commitment. I want a husband to come home to every night, and in a few years a baby. I want the family I've never had."

Naomi plopped down a baklava between them and stopped to finger the Hot Sands brochure. "That looks like a good time. You two going?" She glanced from one to the other.

Ryan sighed. "Phoebe thinks it has honeymoon potential."

Naomi clutched at her blouse. "I feel faint. You two

have been coming here once a week for what? Seven, eight years? Every Thursday at twelve-thirty? Finally. Finally the two of you are getting together."

Phoebe tamped down an odd flutter at Naomi's comment. Naomi wasn't the first person over the years to speculate that she and Ryan felt more than friendship for one another. But they were wrong. "Pull yourself out of that faint, Naomi. We're just friends."

Ryan swallowed hard and pasted on a smile. "I'm helping her check out Hot Sands for a honeymoon with another guy. What else are best friends for?"

JUGGLING WONTON SOUP, beef with broccoli, dragon chicken and a six-pack of beer, Ryan knocked on Phoebe's door. He figured he might as well kill two birds with one stone. They could catch the hockey game on TV and he could try to talk some sense into Phoebe about this crazy marriage thing.

The bitter cold wind sliced through his jacket. Jamaica couldn't come too soon. He hoped Phoebe would come to her senses before they left so he could enjoy his week of sun, sand and sex—and not necessarily in that order.

He knocked on the door again.

"Hold on." Locks turned on the other side, then Phoebe threw the door open. She wore her usual Sunday afternoon attire—old sweats, fuzzy socks and a baggy T-shirt. His shirt, in fact. His T-shirts had a funny way of winding up in Phoebe's closet. "Hey, you. What'd you bring? I'm starving."

"Chinese." He hefted the cartons.

"Good deal." She stepped aside and reached for the six-pack of beer. "Come on in. I'll get this in the fridge. You can put the food on the coffee table."

Ryan placed the cartons on the newspaper-littered coffee table. He shook his head at the mess and smiled. For all that she was the queen of efficiency at work, Phoebes was something of a slob at home. He tossed his jacket on top of hers in the armchair.

While she rounded up paper plates in the kitchen, he flicked on the TV and opened the cartons of steaming food. A fire crackled in the fireplace. Phoebe's place always felt comfortable.

"You want a beer now?" she called from the kitchen.

"Sure."

Bridgette, Phoebe's pound-rescued border collie, ambled over and laid her head against his leg. "Hey, girl. You're not fooling me. I'm old news. It's the take-out you're interested in." She regarded him with solemn brown eyes. "Forget it. This isn't good for dogs."

Phoebe padded in, balancing plates, napkins, silverware and two beers. Her easy laughter washed over him like the familiar waters of a cool stream. "Watch it. She doesn't know she's a d-o-g." Bridgette settled on the floor between the couch and the coffee table.

"She's smart. I think she may have figured it out." He settled on his end of the worn sofa. Phoebe sprawled on the other end, helping herself to the wonton soup. Ryan dished up some dragon chicken. "What're you doing with Bridgette while we're in Jamaica?"

The dog who didn't know she was a dog lifted her black and white head off her paws at the mention of her name.

"Aunt Caroline and Uncle Frank are keeping her. They can't say no to strays." A hint of melancholy tinged her smile and flip comment.

"I don't think they consider it a hardship to care for things they love." His sweet Phoebe—would she ever realize how much Frank and Caroline loved her for herself? "Bridgette'll be happier with them than in a kennel."

"That's what I thought, too." Phoebe turned to the TV. "Now are we gonna watch the game or not?"

"Five bucks says the Rangers take the Flyers." They always bet on the games.

"Point and half, and you're on."

Throughout the first period, Ryan enjoyed Phoebe's animation more than the game. Give her a bit of competition and she positively glowed.

"Did you see that? Did you see that move? He should've whacked that guy." She was a bona fide hockey nut and bloodthirsty as hell. Her sherry-brown eyes sparkled with outrage. Her blond hair stood on end where she'd raked her hand through it.

Ryan laughed. "You're a scary woman."

"Yeah, well, don't forget it." She rolled her eyes at him and went back to the TV.

He was on the verge of bringing up Elliott when she spoke. "So, Keely's all set for Jamaica?"

Damn. It was uncanny how she precipitated him in changing the subject sometimes. "Kiki. Her name is Kiki. And yeah, she's psyched about the trip."

"So what does Kiki do for a living?" she asked without looking away from the game.

"She's a rocket scientist." He dropped the info casually and sat back to enjoy her reaction.

"Yeah. Right. What does she really do?" Phoebe scooped up a piece of broccoli and popped it in her mouth.

"She really is a rocket scientist. Degree in quantum physics." He hadn't known that when he met her at the car wash—only that she was hot with a capital *H*. He hadn't known until he'd bothered to ask last night when they went out.

"You're not kidding?" The absolute shock on Phoebe's face was priceless.

"Degree from MIT and she speaks five languages fluently." He didn't particularly care. He wasn't looking for a long-term relationship, and Kiki was fun with or without her job description, but it seemed to impress the hell out of Phoebe.

"Oh."

Ryan shrugged. "I guess there's at least one smart woman willing to date me, after all." Her comment at Thursday's lunch had crawled under his skin.

Phoebe narrowed her eyes. "What's she look like?"

"Former Miss Texas."

"Oh." Phoebe sat a little straighter on the couch. "Well, then, I can't wait to meet her."

"She's looking forward to meeting you, too."

Phoebe glanced at her T-shirt—technically his T-shirt—and her sweats. "Uh-huh."

"You clean up okay."

"Thanks. I think."

"I'm just teasing. I think you look great just the way you are now." With her soft, messy hair and wearing his shirt, she had a tousled, morning-after look that suddenly struck him as inappropriately, inordinately appealing.

He reached across the space separating them and brushed plum sauce off her lower lip with his thumb, lingering far longer than necessary while a slow heat spiraled through him. "Kind of sexy."

She stared at him as if he'd lost his mind. It was a distinct possibility. He yanked his hand back, disturbed by his reaction to her. This was Phoebe, after all.

Something flashed in her eyes. Caution? Awareness? In an instant it was gone.

"Right." She diffused the tension between them with her flip dismissal, yanking them to the safe path of friendship. "There's plenty of beef and broccoli, if you want some."

"Sure." He plopped a spoonful on his plate to cover the awkwardness he'd introduced. He'd meant to pay her a compliment and wound up damn near making a pass at her. "So, Elliott doesn't mind if Kiki and I come along on the trip?"

Phoebe shrugged. "He was distracted but fine with it when I talked to him on the phone."

"Have you thought through this potential thing—" he couldn't bring himself to say marriage "—with Elliott?"

"Of course I have. I'm fond of him. We get along well together. He's stable. Dependable. I think it's a good plan." The obstinate tilt of her chin echoed her defiant words.

Crap. If he didn't do something, Phoebe'd wind up married to Elliott just for the sake of seeing her damn plan through to fruition. And Elliott was all wrong for Phoebe because...hell, Ryan didn't exactly know why, he just knew Elliott was.

If Phoebe really had her heart set on a husband, Ryan would help her find one. Later. Maybe when they returned from Jamaica. Someone who appreciated her beauty and wit and her multitude of good qualities, but not so wimpy he couldn't stand up to her strong, take-charge personality and fierce competitive streak. That someone wasn't Elliott.

Ryan sighed silently into his beer. He'd have to figure out a way to convince her, because friends didn't let friends marry the wrong person.

CHAPTER TWO

"WELCOME!"

Phoebe smiled at the young man who greeted her and Ryan at the restaurant entrance.

"Two?"

"Four. We're expecting two more."

"Certainly. If you will come with me, please."

They followed him along the covered walkway to the dining area. Of all the resort brochures Phoebe had looked over, the resort's smaller, intimate size and this restaurant had sold her on Hot Sands. The open-air restaurant, supported by stone pilings and covered by a thatched roof, jettisoned over the sparkling aquamarine waters of the Caribbean.

They wound past a number of tables until the maître d' stopped beside a round one next to the rail, overlooking the translucent blue-green water.

"How is this?" He pulled out a fan-backed rattan chair.

"It's perfect." Enchanted, Phoebe sank into the cushioned seat.

"Your waiter will be with you in a moment."

"We'll hold off until the other two arrive," Ryan said, taking his seat next to her.

Phoebe sighed with pure pleasure as she looked around and absorbed everything. Straight ahead and to her right the calm expanse of water, a kaleidoscope of tranquil blues, continued until it reached the sky. A smattering of white clouds floated above the horizon.

To her left, a pristine sugar-sand beach stretched along the shoreline, bordered by lush, tropical jungle and windswept palms. She glanced over her shoulder, past the restaurant and the colonial Spanish architecture of the resort, to the faraway rise of the verdant Blue Mountains, home of some of the best coffee in the world.

Shouts from a distant beach volleyball game underscored the rhythm of calypso piped in over discreetly placed speakers. The gentle lapping of the sea against the rocks drifted up from the pilings and mingled with the murmur of conversation from other tables.

A warm Jamaican breeze shifted against her skin, carrying with it a mixture of salt air, coconut oil and Ryan's familiar scent. Overhead ceiling fans lazily stirred the thick, tropical air into an exotic blend. Utter contentment stole through her.

Impulsively, she reached for Ryan's hand. "Isn't it beautiful? I'm so glad you're here." It wouldn't be the same if she couldn't share this perfect place with him.

Phoebe wound her fingers through his. Surely her heightened senses led her to imagine the fleeting shock when his fingers curled around hers.

Ryan's green eyes held a slightly bemused expression. "The brochures don't do it justice." His fingers tightened around hers. "Everything's brighter. Bolder. You can't feel that breeze in a brochure, can you?"

The warm wind slid over her skin. "That's exactly how I feel—more vibrant and alive." That explained the irrational leap of her pulse earlier. "This is a perfect honeymoon spot."

An image popped into her mind. She was wearing a simple white dress with her veil blowing in the breeze and the shift of fine powdery sand beneath her bare feet, feeling the steady clasp of her new husband's hand in hers and seeing the heated promise in his green eyes…. Urk. Her fantasy ground to a halt.

What was Ryan doing in her fantasy? Elliott belonged there. She took a deep breath to calm her racing heart. No harm done. Just a little brain spasm brought on by the beautiful setting and Ryan's proximity. Absolutely nothing more.

She freed her hand on the pretext of lifting her hair off her neck. Now seemed like a good time to focus on Ryan's near-perfect date. "When will Kiki be down?"

Ryan shrugged. "She was on the phone checking on a project. She wasn't sure how long it would take. What do you think of her?"

Phoebe rearranged her napkin on the white linen table cloth. "You've hit the jackpot." Which proved the old adage, be careful what you wish for because you might get it. She'd worried that Ryan would continue to flit from relationship to relationship. So why did she feel disconcerted by Kiki's near perfection? An insidious voice inside her head whispered to her. *Because she's the first woman you feel threatened by. Because you can see her displacing you in Ryan's life.* "She could be the one."

"The one?" Ryan stared at her as if Phoebe had spoken in tongues.

"You know, the one you can't resist. The one who breaks your heart." She should be very happy for him. "She's beautiful. Great body. Brains out the wazoo. A degree in quantum physics. Speaks five languages fluently, three of which are dead. I think that about covers it."

"I'm glad you like her."

Phoebe thought it best not to correct him. She *should* like Kiki. There was no reason not to. Twofold guilt ate at her. First, she'd imagined herself on a honeymoon with Ryan, the woman's date. And second, she couldn't quite get past a niggling dislike of the other woman. Guilt urged her on.

"I feel like a flat-chested Amazon next to her. I'm at least a head taller and a cup size smaller than she is. And she has beautiful orthodontia, as well." Phoebe ran her tongue along the small gap between her two slightly crooked front teeth. She'd grown boobs since high school, but nothing of Kiki's magnitude.

Ryan laughed and took stock of her while she groused. His gaze swept over the bodice of her sarong-style dress and up. Laughter died in the back of his throat. His eyes darkened.

"There's nothing wrong with your orthodontia." His gaze dropped to her breasts. "Or the rest of you."

A shiver chased across her skin. Something dangerously akin to sexual attraction blossomed inside her, a woman's response to a man's appreciative look. Except she was the woman and her best friend was the man and there was no room for looks and responses like that between them.

Confusion filled her. "Ryan—"

"Hi, guys." Kiki slid into a chair next to Ryan.

Phoebe blinked. The tension binding them disappeared like an ephemeral whiff of smoke gusted by a strong wind. Had she imagined the last minute? There was something about this place. She'd make sure she didn't fall prey to further flights of fancy about Ryan.

"Sorry I took so long," Kiki apologized, stunning in a short jungle-print dress that showcased her curves to full advantage. Her dark hair was twisted into a sophisticated chignon.

Strands of hair clung to Phoebe's sweat-dampened neck. Kiki looked fresh and chic and sexy. Phoebe felt rumpled and sweaty in comparison.

"Not a problem. We were just enjoying the spectacular view." Ryan nodded toward the expanse of beach, ocean and sky. "Everything okay at work?"

Kiki ignored the view. "They're managing without me. Barely. It's amazing the level of people the space program settles for these days. I'll need to check in every evening before the west coast office closes." She eyed the empty seat at their table, a near predatory look sharpening her features. "Where's Elliott?"

Elliott and Kiki had gotten along like the proverbial house on fire during the two-hour ride from the airport to the resort. Both had completed undergraduate work at Loyola. And it turned out that Kiki occasionally visited Vanderbilt as a guest lecturer.

"He wanted to unpack before he came down. He should be here in a few minutes," Phoebe said. She bit back disappointment that Elliott had shown more eagerness to put away his underwear than explore the resort.

"I unpacked while I was on the phone." Kiki nodded as if she completely understood Elliott's compulsion. She looked past Phoebe. "Here's Elliott now." She turned on a sixty-watt smile. "We were just talking about you," Kiki said, welcoming him.

"Sorry I took so long." Elliott dropped into the empty seat between Phoebe, and Kiki, a lock of dark hair hanging over his forehead, his dark eyes brooding. Phoebe and Elliott had both been busy with work. Aside from a snatched lunch one afternoon, they hadn't seen one another for a few weeks. But now that the right man had arrived, Phoebe was ready for some island magic.

"You're here now, and that's all that matters." She leaned forward and pressed her lips to his lean cheek, eager to embrace the magic. No shiver. No quiver. No magic.

Phoebe sat back, nonplussed.

"All unpacked and settled in?" Ryan asked. His smile wore a faint edge of sarcasm.

Elliott frowned. "Almost. I ordered extra towels and pillows from room service." He twined his fingers through Phoebe's, his touch cool and antiseptic. "How about a drink to celebrate being here?" He glanced around expectantly.

As if on cue, a waiter appeared. "Hello. I am Martin. I will be your waiter." His lilting accent brought a smile to Phoebe's face. "You have just arrived in Jamaica today?"

Ryan laughed, "How can you tell?"

"You do not yet have the sun-kissed look of relaxation." Martin returned a ready smile. Maybe that was it. She needed sun-kissed relaxation. "Perhaps I can bring something to drink? Our house specialty is made with a local rum, which is most excellent."

"And what exactly is in that drink other than rum?" Elliott asked.

"We begin with pineapple juice and blend it with coconut milk, some of our local rum and a touch of grenadine. It is a favorite among guests. Quite potent."

Elliott and Kiki both ordered the house special.

Although it sounded yummy, rum left her with a headache, and she wanted to savor every moment of this vacation. Phoebe opted for a ginger beer, and Ryan ordered a Red Stripe lager.

"Very good. I will return shortly with your drinks." Martin hurried away.

Phoebe picked up her menu, aware that breakfast had been a quick piece of toast several hours ago. "I'm ravenous."

Casual conversation floated around the table as everyone looked over the menu. Within minutes Martin arrived, dispensing their drinks with a flourish.

"Very good. Might I suggest a *boonoonoonoos* platter for lunch? It is a sampler of our local dishes, an excellent introduction to Jamaican food."

"Let's have that," Phoebe said, eager to try the local cuisine.

Elliott turned up his nose. "No, thanks, I'll have a turkey sandwich, shaved not sliced, on whole wheat. Light mayo, Lettuce and tomato on the side."

"The last thing I want to do is come to a foreign country and get sick eating the local food. I'll have a turkey sandwich, as well," Kiki instructed Martin.

Phoebe shuddered at Kiki's rude comment. Despite the relaxed, open-air structure, they were dining at a four-star resort, not eating from a street vendor's food stall.

Ryan caught Phoebe's eye and shook his head, reading her indignation as clearly as if she'd voiced it. "We'll try the sampler platter."

Martin left, their orders in hand.

Phoebe tasted her drink, inhaling the fragrant aroma of ginger, savoring its cool, refreshing bite against her tongue. "Delicious."

Determined to tap into the island's underlying sensuality with the appropriate person—her date— Phoebe ran her fingers along Elliott's forearm. The only thing she felt was the soft smattering of dark hair beneath her fingertips. "How's the house special?"

He pursed his lips—sculpted, full, Phoebe had thought his mouth sexy from the first time she'd seen him—and considered his drink. "A touch more coconut milk, and it'd be superb."

Martin arrived with their food. "How are your drinks? Is everyone enjoying?" He placed a steaming platter, fragrant with exotic spices, between Phoebe and Ryan and served Elliott and Kiki turkey sandwiches prepared to Elliott's exacting specifications. "Is there anything else you desire?"

"Fresh ground pepper on my turkey. Please," Elliott said.

Phoebe brushed aside a flicker of annoyance. Elliott knew what he liked and liked what he knew. She should view it as an asset, a measure of his stability.

Having peppered Elliott's sandwich, Martin gestured toward the food on the table. "Enjoy. You may want to take a siesta after this. We have a saying in Jamaica. The days are long, but the nights are longer." Martin retreated with a good-humored laugh.

A siesta. A few hours in the cool, quiet intimacy of their room. Perhaps a relaxing hour in their private pool or a soak in the whirlpool tub in their sumptuous marbled bathroom. The idea left her flat. Here she was in one of the most sensuous, romantic places on earth with a handsome man, and the strongest emotion she felt toward him at this point was annoyance.

Ryan shifted in the seat beside her, his hair-roughened knee brushing against her leg. The brief contact sizzled up her thigh. She jerked her leg away. Ryan appeared mercifully oblivious to her errant hormonal reactions.

Something was terribly amiss. Elliott's touch left her cold, while Ryan's sizzled through her. Maybe she'd suffered some weird form of jet lag, although Nashville and Ocho Rios were in the same time zone. Or maybe she desperately needed that siesta to get her head screwed on straight.

Determined to put her inappropriate responses to the two men at the table behind her, Phoebe spooned a sampling from each dish, her mouth watering from the exotic aromas. "I spent too many hours this month behind a desk. This weather's fantastic. Let's make a plan for this afternoon."

Kiki caught her enthusiasm. "What about Jet Skis? We should be able to get a few hours in." Kiki nodded toward two couples on machines racing across the blue-green water in the distance.

Ryan nodded, his green eyes alight, always ready for fun. "It'll be a blast. What do you think?"

He looked from Phoebe to Elliott.

"Sounds good to me. It was one of the things I wanted to try while we were here," Phoebe said.

"You've never been on a Jet Ski before?" Did Phoebe imagine that note of condescension in Kiki's question?

"Neither have I," Elliott confessed.

"Oh, my. Two Jet Ski virgins," Kiki drawled. She arched her brows at Ryan. "Did you know we had two virgins here? We'll definitely have to initiate them into the pleasures of wave riding, won't we?"

Kiki's heavy innuendo mingled with the exotic spices permeating the air.

Ryan's mouth quirked in a smile. "Phoebe, you could ride with me—"

"And I'd consider it an honor to initiate Elliott," Kiki interrupted.

"Only if you promise to be gentle with me," Elliott protested with mock innocence.

Elliott had a sense of humor? He'd never displayed even a hint of playfulness with Phoebe.

"Trust me, it'll be so good, you'll beg for another

ride," Kiki promised, skimming one of her long red nails down his arm.

"How can I turn down an offer like that?" Elliott capitulated.

"What do you think, Phoebe?" Kiki asked.

She thought she could vamp with the best of them, that's what she thought. Kiki had Elliott all but drooling in his turkey sandwich. Phoebe glanced at Ryan from beneath her lashes, "I can't think of anyone I'd rather be with my first time."

His eyes held hers. "I promise you'll enjoy it."

A slow flush ran over her, through her. "You don't think my inexperience is a problem?"

"All you have to do is hold on and leave the rest to me. I'll make it good for you. I've had lots of practice."

She didn't doubt it for a minute.

PHOEBE DREW THE DRAPES over the French doors, plunging the room into cool shadows. The glazed tile floor was warm beneath her bare feet where the mid-afternoon sun had slanted in. As she retreated into the room and approached the four-poster bed, the tiles grew cooler against her soles.

She wrapped one arm around the wooden post of the footboard and leaned into it. Elliott presented a spectacular specimen of manhood stretched out on the bed. How appropriate he taught classical Greek and Roman literature. He possessed striking, classical looks. Aquiline nose. Chiseled lips. Hooded eyes with a sweep of dark lashes. At five feet nine inches, she was no shrinking violet, yet he topped her by several inches. His legs, while not particularly muscular, were long and lean.

"You need to grade *all* those papers?"

He glanced up from the stack before him. "Uh-huh. I should be finished in a couple of hours. In time for Jet Skiing."

Instead of disappointment, relief washed over her. They'd drifted farther apart in the last few weeks than she realized. They needed a little more time together before she was ready to climb into a whirlpool tub with him.

Tonight, they'd enjoy a few glasses of wine over a romantic dinner—how could it be anything less in Jamaica—and things would feel different between them.

And what about Ryan and Kiki? She bet no one was grading papers in their room. How many girlfriends had Ryan run through in the course of their friendship? She'd lost count long ago. So, what chemical imbalance in her brain rendered the prospect of Kiki and Ryan together bothersome now?

Phoebe shoved away from the bed. She'd find something to do other than watch Elliott immerse himself in paperwork and speculate on Ryan and Kiki's sexcapades. They'd arranged to meet at the Jet Ski dock. She'd be there.

In the meantime, there were things to do. Places to explore. Phoebe slid her feet into a pair of sandals. "I'll see you at four."

"Hmm," Elliott murmured, engrossed.

She slipped out of the room. She doubted Elliott even knew she'd left. A restless energy propelled her along the walkway skirting the lush, barely contained jungle garden. She paused, transfixed by color-splashed parrots perched in the dense foliage.

"They are beautiful, yes?" Startled, Phoebe looked around to find their lunch waiter, Martin.

"Yes. They are beautiful. Everything here is." Martin wasn't wearing his white waiter's jacket. "Are you through for the day?"

"It is my break before the dinner hour begins. I will bicycle home to see my wife and children. It is only six miles from the resort."

Twelve miles round-trip to see his family, before returning for another shift? "How many children do you have?"

"A boy and a girl. Seven and five. They are most excellent children. Very smart. They must go to bed early for school. They are asleep when I finish with the dinner hour." He pulled a worn photo from his back pocket.

A boy and a girl, wearing school uniforms and Martin's smile, flanked a tall, slender woman with long braids and kind, laughing eyes. The three stood before a sun-yellow cinder-block house. "They're lovely. They look like you. That's your wife?"

"Yes. Mathilda." He pointed to the boy and girl. "Terrence and Louise. I am a very rich man."

The light in Martin's eyes brought tears to hers. They both knew he didn't refer to material wealth. His obvious devotion to his family intensified her resolve to have the same. "Yes. I think you are a very rich man. Thank you for sharing your family with me."

He tucked the photo into his pocket. "You do not wish to have a siesta?"

"I think I'm too excited to siesta." It sounded better than, *My boyfriend is busy grading papers and I'm in a green-eyed sulk because my best friend is cozying up with Kiki.*

"Perhaps you have a bit of the native in you." He tilted his head to one side and considered her. "I hope you do not find me forward, but have you ever thought to wear braids?"

"Like Mathilda's? No. I never thought about it."

"You possess lovely bones of the face. It would be a most excellent choice for you. If you decide to try this, go to the salon here at Hot Sands. Ask for Katrina. She is my cousin and the best braider in Ocho Rios. Tell her Martin has sent you. She will do quite an excellent job for you. I think you will be most pleased."

No one had ever mentioned before that she possessed lovely bones. Martin probably received a nice fat kickback from Cousin Katrina for any business he sent her way, but Phoebe couldn't possibly begrudge anything to a man so enamored of his family.

A head full of braids struck her as just the thing to do. And it would look sexy, to boot. Perhaps her problem wasn't Elliott as much as it was her attitude. Braids offered a more sophisticated, sleek alternative to a ponytail or having hair cling to her sweaty neck.

"Thank you, Martin. I'll look Katrina up right now. Enjoy your family."

"That I will. I look forward to serving you during the dinner hour."

CHAPTER THREE

RYAN CHECKED HIS WATCH. Again. He'd made it his personal philosophy to never worry, but worry niggled at him. And it was Phoebe's fault. While Kiki lived by the fashionably-late code—she'd nearly missed the flight this morning—punctuality almost qualified as a religious principle for Phoebe.

She was officially thirteen minutes late meeting them at the pier. Elliott, who said he'd been grading papers, was clueless as to her whereabouts. How could Phoebe, who had so much going for her, possibly consider tying herself to this guy until death—or, more likely, divorce—they did part?

Nothing had happened between him and Kiki, but they hadn't been dating for ten months, either. Kiki had sequestered herself in the bathroom for a facial and a pedicure.

He'd spent his time trying to get Phoebe's flirtatious teasing out of his head. *I can't think of anyone I'd rather be with my first time.* How many times and with how many women had he engaged in the same meaningless innuendo? But never with Phoebe. She'd never slanted her almond-shaped eyes at him in invitation until today. Her voice had never dropped to that husky octave and wrapped around him like a lover's touch. And if he'd had any damn sense, he'd have seduced Kiki during the siesta and forgotten all about Phoebe.

"Check her out," Elliott said.

Ryan glanced up. A sexy, braided blonde strode across the white sand. *Wow.* For a second something struck him as vaguely familiar about that self-confident stride. *Right.* That fell into the wishful thinking category. For the first time, he felt a kinship with Elliott—ill-begotten, lust-ridden admiration for an incredible pair of legs and a sexy swagger.

"You're not kidding." Hell, he could barely breathe. "The braids and those legs that go on forever…" In the span of a heartbeat, his mind had her naked beneath him with those luscious legs wrapped around his waist.

"Actually, I meant Kiki. But, yes, Phoebe's definitely got nice legs."

Phoebe? *Phoebe?* What the— Ryan whipped off his Ray-Bans and squinted against the sun. Hell's bells. No wonder he recognized that walk. Ryan shoved his sunglasses on and belatedly noticed Kiki next to Phoebe.

The women passed a beach volleyball game. A guy playing front net position turned to gawk at them, his mouth hanging open. A spiked ball caught him square in the back, throwing him to the sand. Served the clown right.

"Sorry we're late." Kiki linked her arm through his.

"Kiki and I ran into one another on the way out." Phoebe smoothed a hand over her head. "So, what do you guys think?"

Beaded cornrows brushed her shoulders, the style accentuating her high cheekbones and the fullness of her mouth. A thin white cotton T-shirt offered a teasing glimpse of her bikini. Since they'd arrived in Jamaica, he'd noticed all kinds of new things about Phoebe. And he had no business responding with fantasies of her beneath him, that's what he thought.

"It's definitely different." Elliott considered her with his head cocked to one side. "But it suits you."

"Why in the hell did you go and do that?" The minute the words left his mouth he realized he sounded like an ass. He just wasn't used to this sexy, fantasy-inducing version of Phoebe.

"Come on, Ryan, why don't you tell me how you really feel about it?"

Damnation. He'd hurt her feelings. His earlier fantasy flashed through his head. How he really felt about her at this point would scare the hell out of her. It did him. "Sorry, Phoebes, I'm just used to you the other way. It looks great."

"I think it's awesome. Wish I had the bone structure to carry it off," Kiki said with a pout.

Elliott flashed a cavalier smile and eyed her brimming bikini top. "There's nothing wrong with your structure."

Kiki preened, and Phoebe's eyebrows arched above her sunglasses.

Elliott was an idiot, Ryan thought. Why was he flirting with Kiki when he had a gorgeous woman already?

Phoebe planned. Ryan seized opportunity when it stared him in the face. Kiki and Elliott. If the professor kept putting the move on Kiki, Ryan wouldn't have to worry about Phoebe walking down the aisle with Elliott. All Ryan had to do was offer a little subtle encouragement, toss them together and watch the sparks fly. Elliott had never been worthy of Phoebe and was about to prove it. Ryan was more than happy to give Elliott ample rope to hang himself. Of course, this meant he wouldn't be taking things any further with Kiki, but a week of sun and sand without the sex was a small price to pay to keep Phoebe from making the mistake of a lifetime.

Ryan bit back a smirk and tossed a Jet Ski key to Kiki. "You and Elliott take number twenty-seven. We'll take twenty-eight."

Kiki eagerly mounted the Jet Ski and beckoned to Elliott. "I haven't had a virgin in a very long time."

Elliott climbed on behind and wrapped his arms around her middle. Given their height difference,

Elliot's hands hovered just below Kiki's breasts. Kiki revved her engine.

The steady ocean breeze stirred up a potent mixture of suntan lotion and the fragrance Phoebe favored. What was it with Phoebe today? Was it the allure of the unknown in what he'd always considered a known quantity that had his heart pounding like a teenager on a first date? Once he got used to her new look, he'd be back to normal.

"I'd say Elliott's about one wave away from copping a feel," Phoebe muttered with more than a touch of asperity in Ryan's ear. Her arm pressed against his waist, wreaking havoc with his composure.

Kiki called, "We're out of here. Catch up with us."

Ryan waved her on. "I think you're right about that feel. Elliott's enjoying sitting behind her. And Kiki doesn't seem to mind."

"Do *you* mind?"

"No. I needed a woman to vacation at a couples-only resort. There's nothing between us except a few fun dates." And that's all it'd ever be, because he'd be damned if he'd sit back and watch Phoebe make a huge mistake with Elliott. He knew what Phoebe was like once she decided on a plan.

"Teach me how to drive this thing." Phoebe's lips quirked to one side, her gearing-up-to-kick-butt expression. "I'm going to run circles around Kiki." She gathered her braids together and secured them behind her head. "Okay?"

Damn. Therein lay the downside to seizing opportunities without thinking them through. The last thing he wanted was Phoebe in a head-to-head competition for Elliott. But if he, Ryan, distracted her with a little light flirtation along the lines of lunch today... Hell, that was what he did best. He'd just never done it with Phoebe. He could handle it, and in the end, if it kept Phoebe from marrying Elliott, it was worth it.

"I don't know about you driving, Phoebes. This being your first time and everything." He struck just the right chord with that teasing note, not too suggestive.

Phoebe dug a bottle of sunscreen out of her bag. "Can you get the middle of my back? Elliott was already gone, and I couldn't reach it myself." She tugged her T-shirt off. "I don't want to get burned my first time." She extended the bottle with a sassy smile, "Actually, I don't want to get burned at all."

He stood transfixed. Heaven help him. All over the beach, women wore much briefer, much more revealing bikinis, but none wore them as well as Phoebe. A slow heat burned low in his belly and spiraled through him.

"Ryan?" She waved the sunscreen in front of his face. "Are you going to help me out here or do you want me to ask that guy playing volleyball?"

He snatched the bottle. She wasn't about to ask the guy who'd been gaping at her. "Turn around."

She presented her back to him. He'd always appreciated the feminine lines of a woman's back. Phoebe's took his breath away—the graceful curve leading to the flare of her hips, the slight hollow of her spine. Ryan poured a generous amount of lotion into one hand and passed her the bottle over her shoulder. He rubbed his unsteady hands together. *Get a grip, man. This is Phoebe. Slap on the lotion and be done with it.*

The instant his hands touched her shoulders, he realized he'd severely underestimated the task at hand. His palms, slicked with the warm lotion, glided over the supple silk of her sun-heated skin. That hiss of indrawn breath belonged to him.

His hands and fingertips took on a mind of their own, stroking and massaging her pliant flesh. Which was a good thing, considering his brain damn near ceased functioning, content to relish the fine texture of her skin, the sensual line of her back, her scent.

He splayed his fingers under her bikini strap. She quivered beneath his palm, and a response echoed through him. Careful not to leave any skin untouched, he smoothed the lotion down her spine to the small of her back. Another quiver radiated from her to him. She was so sensitive, so arousingly responsive to his touch, and his hand had only stroked her back.

Ryan quelled an insane urge to slip his hands

beneath the elastic of her bottoms and massage the fullness of her bare buttocks. He'd whisper sweet words in her ear until she willingly sought a secluded section of beach and indulged his earlier fantasy. Perhaps if it had been any other woman, but this was Phoebe.

All she'd asked him to do was put sunscreen on her back, not work himself into some delusional state.

He dropped his hands to his sides and reminded himself she was his friend. *Think friend, not woman,* he instructed his libido, his brain and all the other body parts that suddenly seemed to have minds of their own.

She turned. "I'm ready. I don't want to be a virgin anymore."

His body blatantly ignored his instruction.

PHOEBE CHECKED HER WATCH. Eleven o'clock. After the flight down, the exhilaration of skimming over the turquoise sea with Ryan and the lively discussion over one of the finest dinners she'd ever enjoyed, she ought to be exhausted. Instead she was energized. Restless. Eager.

Despite the hour, the night felt young and brimming with life. In the nearby garden, birds called to one another. The night air carried the perfume of foreign blooms and exotic spices, borne by the ocean breeze. The low murmur of lovers whispered beneath the strident tones of partygoers.

Around the curve of the winding walkway, rawly sensual Caribbean music pulsed from the Jungle Room. Phoebe slid her arm around Elliott's waist, her hips instinctively responding to the music's rhythm. Caught up in the moment, she looked at Ryan and Kiki. "Come on. Let's go dance."

Kiki grabbed Ryan's hand and tugged him along. "I love to dance."

"Then let's find the Jungle Room."

Elliott, with three generous glasses of wine under his belt from dinner, displayed more enthusiasm than aptitude as he swayed down the torch-lined walkway. "Bring on the limbo."

Phoebe laughed with the sheer exuberance of the night.

"I didn't know you liked to dance, Phoebe," Ryan commented as he and Kiki followed them.

Phoebe had realized earlier in the day that, as well as she and Ryan knew one another, there was a whole layer beneath the surface neither knew. While they'd discussed their other relationships over the years, they'd steadfastly avoided any recognition of one another's sensuality. When Ryan had smoothed on suntan lotion, she'd discovered a whole new side to him. And to herself. His touch had turned her inside out.

"Maybe there's a thing or two about me that you don't know." She tossed the words over her shoulder.

Try as she might to keep her tone light, a hint of provocation crept in.

"How long have you two been friends?" Kiki asked.

"Twenty-four years," Phoebe said. The music grew louder as they got closer to the club.

"Don't you ever get tired of one another?"

Ryan was one of the most interesting people she knew. "No."

"No."

They answered simultaneously.

Elliott tightened his arm about Phoebe's shoulders, pulling her closer to his side. "She might not get tired of him, but I do. He's around all the damn time," Elliott groused to no one in particular. "No offense, Ryan."

"None taken." Ryan laughed off Elliott's comment.

"Twenty-four years and you've never..."

"No," Phoebe reassured her, not that Kiki seemed insecure, just curious as if their relationship presented an oddity to be dissected. And maybe on another night in another place, Phoebe might have been offended by her curiosity and her questions. But not here and now. The heat of the night and rhythm of the music invited lascivious thoughts.

Kiki stopped within a few feet of the club doorway. "Come on. Twenty-four years and neither of you ever even thought about it? I'm not buying it."

She'd wondered once or twice on occasion. And since they'd arrived at the island, she'd felt the undercurrent, the subtle flirtation between them, but it wouldn't go any further. Phoebe wasn't willing to share that just to satisfy Kiki's curiosity. She shook her head, laughing at Kiki's insistence.

Elliott waved his hand in the air. "Believe it. They're like brother and sister."

In the flickering torchlight, Phoebe glanced at Ryan. Her breath caught in her throat and her blood raced. She was caught up in the spell of calypso and the look in his eyes that acknowledged he'd thought about her too.

Yes, she'd wondered. And now she knew he'd done the same. On a sane, rational day the thought would terrify her. But there was nothing sane or rational about a Caribbean night. Tonight, the thought excited her.

"I think my *sister's* ready to dance."

They stepped into the dimly lit club. The air hung thick with perfume and aftershave, cigarette smoke, a faint whiff of ganja, the cloying sweetness of rum, and sexual arousal. Couples packed the dance floor. The music, loud and rhythmic, entered Phoebe, became one with her body, precluding conversation, ousting inhibitions. It pulsed in her, through her, a fever. Words were extemporaneous. Primal movement reigned—contagious hedonism at its finest.

The four of them surged into the crush of people

on the dance floor. Phoebe gave herself over to the music's driving beat. Gyrating. Undulating. Her body responded to the music's demand with seductive movements, the music filling her, compelling her to a place beyond her usual bounds.

Within minutes, the crowd swallowed Kiki and Elliott. Ryan, however, was still there, separated from her by a handful of people. He made his way to her. She leaned close, still dancing, her mouth next to his ear to be heard above the music and noise. "Kiki and Elliott?"

Ryan shrugged and shook his head. His lips were warm against the shell of her ear. "Don't know. Doesn't matter."

His mouth, the heat underlying the laughter in his eyes, his hard body against hers in the crush of the dance floor, the music's relentless throb compelled her. Phoebe snaked her arms around Ryan's neck in invitation, her hips seconding the offer. Laughing, seductive, she retreated. Eyes glittering, he accepted her challenge and followed.

A crowded dance floor offered the opportunity to seduce without consequence. Dancing to the wildly uninhibited music, she crossed a line she'd never consider actually approaching. Dance became mind sex.

Dark sensuality wove between them, bound them. Advance and retreat. Undulating. Thrusting. Pulsing. Grinding.

In the heat of the music, the night, the moment, it seemed the most natural thing in the world for Ryan to pull her tight against him. Caught up in the erotic rhythms seething between them, Phoebe crossed the line she'd only allowed herself to fantasize about occasionally. She boldly claimed his mouth. Ryan moaned against her lips, his fingers molded against the sweat-slicked skin of her back. Teasing tantalization gave way to fervent fusion. She closed her eyes as he explored her mouth with his tongue. Murmuring deep in her throat, she suckled him. As if a line ran straight to his erection, she felt him pulse against her. Feverish, thick passion flowed through her. Where did her heat end and his begin? She surged against him, burning up with a fire only he could put out.

He wrenched his mouth from hers. "Phoebe?"

Eyes still closed, still on a sensual high, she licked her swollen lips.

"Phoebe?" She opened her eyes. Ryan's green eyes probed hers, a thousand questions rolled into her name.

What had she done? This was her best friend she was grinding against, hot to the point of madness.

"I'm sorry...I shouldn't have—"

And then, having crossed the line to a place from which there was no return, she did what any self-respecting coward would do.

She ran like hell.

CHAPTER FOUR

THE NEXT MORNING Ryan waited for Phoebe by the pool. Over breakfast, Kiki and Elliott had announced plans to play the slot machines in the lounge, both citing hangovers from the night before, which left Ryan and Phoebe to follow through on the canoeing plans they'd made over dinner the previous evening. Ryan also had a hangover, but his had nothing to do with alcohol. Phoebe and her hot kiss had kept him up most of the night.

"Ready?" Phoebe pasted on a bright smile. He read her determination to ignore the previous evening's activities.

"Sure. This way." Ryan started in the general direction of the beach. "The concierge said the canoes are down here and it's just a short distance to the cliffs. It's supposed to be spectacular."

Uncomfortable silence stretched between them.

"Ryan—"

"Phoebe—"

She cut in with a rush of words. "Listen, Ryan, I'm sorry about last night."

"I'm not." He tried to make her feel better.

"You should be. It never should've happened."

"You're probably right." It probably would've been better if he'd never tasted her passion. It had haunted him all night, and even now he craved another taste.

"I wasn't myself. I just got carried away with the wine and the music and the night. You could've been anyone."

"Is that supposed to make me feel better?" That was a royal slap in the ego.

"I just wanted you to understand where I was coming from. Don't let this come between us, because it really didn't mean anything."

"Fine." He didn't much care for being told he had been just a warm body in the right place at the right time.

"Can we just forget about it?"

"I said that's fine, Phoebe. It's forgotten. Done. History."

They reached the canoes lined up at the edge of the water. An attendant offered them a friendly smile. "It's a beautiful morning for canoeing. The water is nice and calm. You will go around this curve and then you will find yourself next to our magnificient Caribbean cliffs." He pointed to a western point on the shoreline. "Choose whichever boat you like."

Ryan and Phoebe selected the first boat, and the attendant handed them each a paddle.

"I haven't been in a canoe since we were out on the lake in high school," Ryan commented.

"That's right, you missed the trip I took last year. You had that sales meeting. You'll remember everything in no time. What'll make it easier for you? Do you want me in the front or behind?" Phoebe asked.

It was a perfectly legitimate question to pose to someone you were getting in a canoe with. Unfortunately, it stirred erotic images of her undulating before him on the dance floor last night.

"Take the front." He managed a nice even tone despite the rush of desire her words unleashed.

Phoebe positioned herself in the bow. Ryan shoved off from the white-sand shore and climbed in. With fluid, graceful movements, she dipped her paddle into the clear blue water and pulled. Her T-shirt hugged the line of her back and the womanly flare of her hips.

Distracted, thrown off, Ryan chopped the water with his paddle.

Phoebe glanced over her shoulder. "Take your time. Remember—long, smooth strokes. Make sure it's in before you pull through."

She demonstrated her long, smooth stroke for him. "See?"

He clearly saw that it was going to be a long, torturous day.

THAT EVENING, by the end of the second course, Kiki and Elliott had drifted into a discussion of the inner workings of Vanderbilt, leaving Ryan and Phoebe to what amounted to an intimate dinner for two.

Ryan studied Phoebe. In the shimmering candlelight, her skin glowed honey gold, and her eyes sparkled like a fine sherry. How many times had he seen her without really seeing her? How had he overlooked her provocative sensuality? All these years, he'd taken her for granted, assuming he knew her, only to discover she had hidden layers and depths he hadn't begun to discern. She was a complex woman he'd reduced to one dimension.

Canoeing with Phoebe had proved a subtle form of torture. The curve of her back as she paddled had teased him. Her scent drifting back on the breeze, the memory of last night's kiss had kept him aroused.

"You're awfully quiet tonight," Phoebe said. She seemed to have effectively forgotten that shatteringly erotic dance and kiss.

"Maybe you wore me out earlier today." Shit, he had no business flirting with Phoebe.

Phoebe's eyebrows arched above the sweep of her lashes. "I think it was probably your extracurricular activities before dinner." Was she fishing for information on him and Kiki?

"The only thing extracurricular in my room was Kiki's two-hour preparations. They were exhausting to watch." Kiki defined high maintenance. "Have some mango brulée." He nudged the dish toward her. He'd ordered it for her, anyway.

She picked up her spoon. "Maybe just a bite."

Ryan grinned and shook his head. Phoebe and

her parceled bites of pleasure. She raised a spoonful of the dessert to her mouth, her lashes lowering in anticipation. She opened her mouth and slipped the spoon inside, wrapping her lips around it. "Mmm." She opened her eyes as she slid the spoon out.

How many times had he seen her do the very same thing? Savor a bite with deliberation. But never, until now, with such a devastating effect. Ryan damn near choked as his brain supplied a visual of something other than a spoon sliding between her lips. He tried to will away the image. "Good?"

She shook her head, the beads in the ends of her hair brushing against her bared shoulders. "Better than good." Her brown eyes glimmered with sublime pleasure. "Orgasmic."

She'd said it before. This time, though, the word sizzled into his brain, tightened his groin. He reached for his water glass and took a long, cold drink. It didn't do any good.

She dipped her spoon in the dish. "You've got to try this." She leaned forward, proffering her spoon.

"No, thanks."

"You should at least try it." She teased the spoon in his direction, and the neckline of her halter top shifted, offering Ryan a glimpse of succulent golden skin. "Isn't your mouth watering for a bite?"

She was killing him. Hell, yes, his mouth was watering. He leaned slightly forward and then caught himself. He deliberately looked away. "No, thanks."

"Come on. Aren't you even tempted? You're always willing to try something new." Her voice was low and husky, and he wasn't sure if the note of seduction was real or supplied by his licentious thoughts.

But she wasn't something new. Only his way of seeing her was new, and that wasn't what she was offering. Or was it? It wasn't the brulée that tempted him. "I'm not hungry."

"It's exquisite. You'll regret this decision later," Phoebe teased. "See if I offer you any more of my mango." She nibbled at the fruit, then licked the creamy custard off the spoon with delicate precision and a fantasy-inducing attention to detail.

His heart pounded like a jackhammer while an alarm sounded in his head. Kiki pushed a button on her watch, and the alarm stopped. Oh.

"Nine o'clock. I have to check in with the California office before they leave." Kiki stood.

Ryan pushed his chair back. "I'll go with you." It beat the hell out of staying for more erotic mango brulée torment.

Kiki waved for him to stay. "There's no need. I may be five minutes or it could be forty-five. You'll be bored."

"But—"

She pressed him back into his seat. "Stay and finish your wine. I'll meet you guys at the Jungle Room. Besides, I wouldn't mind a little privacy to freshen up."

She offered him very little choice but to stay. "Fine. The Jungle Room. I'll look for you."

"I may be a little late."

"Don't worry, Kiki. We'll take care of him until you get there," Phoebe teased with a hint of provocation. She'd definitely noticed Kiki's monopoly of Elliott over dinner.

Kiki's eyes narrowed, and she dropped Phoebe a wink. "Thanks, Phoebe." She eyed Elliott. "I'll catch up with you all later. By then, I'll be ready to try out the limbo stick and see how low I can go."

Elliott watched Kiki's wiggling behind as she crossed the restaurant. He shook his head in admiration. "She's something else. Refill, anyone?" He reached for the bottle of wine with an alcohol-induced grin. "We'll have a full-fledged Caribbean bacchanalia."

Phoebe held her glass out, deepening her cleavage. "Just a touch, thanks."

Ryan accepted another half glass, as well. God knows, he didn't want Elliott to level off without a drinking buddy. The idea of Elliott passing out nightly suited Ryan just fine. If he was passed out, he wasn't up to bedroom games with Phoebe. Ryan assured himself the idea held such appeal simply because it put Phoebe one step further away from Elliott as a suitable husband.

"Can you believe Kiki knows Dean Whatley?" Ryan had no idea who Dean Whatley was and didn't much care. "They go way back." Elliott refueled with a full glass of wine.

"How does she know Dean Whatley?" Phoebe asked.

It was the only prompting Elliott needed to drone and drink. He polished off the bottle, his speech growing increasingly exact. He enunciated succinctly when he spilled the last of the red wine down the front of his white shirt. "Sod the dog."

Martin appeared immediately, a wet cloth in hand. "Most unfortunate. Let me help." He dabbed at the stain blooming on Elliott's shirtfront. "Might I recommend our most excellent laundry so that you do not ruin this shirt? Shall I send someone from housekeeping to collect this from you?"

"Fine." Elliott pushed to his feet, steadying himself against the table. "Great. Now I have to change my shirt. I'll meet you in the Jungle Room, too."

Elliott huffed off.

Martin nodded sagely. "Ah, the Jungle Room. A most excellent choice."

Ryan's body quickened as he recalled Phoebe's sensuous movements of the previous night.

Phoebe laughed, low and husky. The sound skittered down Ryan's spine. "Is everything always a most excellent choice, Martin?"

"Unfortunately not." Ryan could've sworn Martin glanced toward Elliott's retreating figure. "But I enjoy pointing out the ones that are, such as your hair." He bowed at the waist. "If you will excuse me."

Phoebe turned to Ryan and propped her elbow on the table, resting her chin on her hand. "Am I just being sensitive or have Kiki and Elliott formed a mutual admiration club?"

"You noticed too, huh?" Had she also noticed how close she'd come to killing Ryan over dessert?

"Yeah. I'd have to be dead to miss it." She smiled wryly.

"I suppose you're reconsidering Hot Sands as a potential honeymoon site?" Elliott was a goner. Ryan hoped like hell she'd given up her crazy marriage notion.

"Hot Sands is great. However, I'll be going back to the drawing board on groom material."

Relief filled him. It wasn't the whole wedding, but it was a start. She couldn't have a wedding without a groom. "Damn glad to hear you're dumping Elliott."

"I didn't say I was dumping him. I just know for sure I don't want to marry him."

She was dumping him.

Ryan felt better than he had in weeks. Everything would soon be back to normal. "Want to check out the beach before we meet them at the club?"

Phoebe smiled, the sexy gap between her two front teeth knotting his belly. Her eyes glittered smoky brown in the glow of the candle. "That sounds like a most excellent suggestion."

He stood and pulled out her chair. His hand brushed against the bare satin of her back as she stood. Fire licked through him at the brief touch.

Perhaps *everything* wouldn't be back to normal as soon as he thought.

"JUST LEAN ON ME." Ryan slid his arm around Phoebe's waist as she hobbled along the sidewalk, favoring her throbbing right ankle. She stumbled to a stop beside one of the flickering tiki torches that lent a primal feel to the night. His warm breath stirred against her neck, and his scent wrapped around her in the heat of the night. Laughter and throbbing music spilled out from the Jungle Room and blended with the nocturnal noises of insects and birds and whatever else rustled in the dark tropics, lending an intense intimacy to the right.

She wasn't so sure she'd be able to stop at leaning. She had the most insane, inopportune, politically incorrect, powerful urge to kiss him and see if the passion that had exploded between them last night had been real.

Wouldn't it make for a Kodak moment if Kiki or Elliott happened along while she put the moves on her best friend, who would most likely be horrified that she'd lost her mind and was flinging herself at him? It was one thing to test the waters with mild flirtation at a table for four or on a crowded dance floor, but there was no safety in numbers now.

"Phoebes? You're not about to faint, are you?"

"No. I'm not going to faint." Nor was she about to fall on him like some sex-starved harpy. And her ankle wasn't nearly as sore as her pride. "At least it was dark and nobody saw me fall off my shoe. Whatever possessed me to try and walk in the sand wearing platform sandals?" The offending shoe and its mate dangled from her right hand.

"Maybe because those shoes look hot with that short dress." His words played havoc with her pulse rate and made her long for things she had no business longing for. "At least until you fell off of them."

"I only fell off one," Phoebe amended, a small salve to her pride.

His teeth gleamed in the flickering torchlight. "I stand corrected."

Competitiveness led her to ask, under the cover of the sultry, inky night, "Do you think my legs are better than—"

His grin faded. His face tightened in the torch glow. "Anyone's. Your legs leave a man weak." No amusement lightened the rough cadence of his declaration. "Now either lean on me or I'll pick you up and carry you."

She didn't think so. There was nothing sexy about indignity—his arm wrapped around the back of her thighs, him staggering along the sidewalk beneath her

Amazonian proportions. Coupled with the disturbing realization that she was beginning to crave his touch like an addict needed a fix. "You wouldn't da—"

"Easy, Phoebes." His arm tightened around her waist, and his voice dropped to a husky caress, sliding along her nerve endings like verbal foreplay. She reminded herself of all the practice he'd had at hitting just the right note. "You know I can't resist a dare."

She tried to relax into him. For as long as she could remember, she and Ryan had propped one another up in time of need. The press of his hip and thigh against hers should've been reassuringly familiar. Instead it aroused her, evoking a disquieting ripple of longing that tightened inside her. He'd always been so attuned to her nuances. Could he feel her hunger for him? She pulled away. "I'm fine."

"If that's the way you want to play it." In one swift movement, he scooped her off her feet.

Time slowed to seconds of infinite awareness. Every inch of her responded to him. The brush of his hair-roughened arms against the sensitive backs of her knees and her back, bared by her halter top. The rise and fall of the hard wall of his chest against her right breast. His firm abs against her hip. The frantic beat of his heart against her arm.

His pupils dilated, darkened. Emotions, once so clearly defined between them, tangled, wrapped around them, between them, binding them with thick, sweet cords of promise.

"Put your arms around my neck," he instructed hoarsely.

In some distant recess of her mind, the idea niggled that she should demand he put her back on solid ground. However, the other part of her acknowledged how much she liked being swept off her feet in the beguiling shadows of a Jamaican night and held tight against him. She looped her arms around the strong column of his neck and tucked her head into the crook of his shoulder without a word.

She expected him to stagger forward beneath her weight, shattering their dreamlike intimacy. Instead, he strode forward effortlessly. "Your room or mine?"

The night. His suggestive words. His scent. The rough edge to his question. Phoebe reminded herself this was Ryan and he only intended to examine her ankle.

His room was just ahead. Hers was on the west wing. The sooner he put her down, the better. "Yours. It's closer than mine. And there's a good chance Elliott's passed out." She didn't want to think about Elliott while Ryan's solid strength melted her from the inside out.

He stopped outside his room and fished out his room card, still holding her. A muted giggle sounded on the other side of the door. "Kiki must still be on the phone," Ryan murmured, his mouth mere inches from her ear.

Ryan toed open the door and angled inside.

Unaware of an audience, flat on her back in a tangle of sheets and limbs, Kiki squealed. The door clicked shut behind them.

What the…. Phoebe looked at Ryan. "She's not on the phone."

Kiki's head popped up. Her subsequent squeal echoed the surprise on her face at seeing Ryan and Phoebe. Midway on the bed, Elliott's dark head poked out from beneath the sheet.

All the air swooshed out of her. She had recognized the obvious attraction between Kiki and Elliott, but she hadn't expected *this*.

Phoebe slid down the front of Ryan to stand, one arm still wrapped around his neck. Not only was Elliott in bed, naked, she presumed, with another woman, but given his position, she didn't need Kiki's quantum physics degree to figure out what he'd been doing. Only he'd never been willing to do *that* for *her*.

Ryan raised a sardonic brow. "And he's not passed out."

"SORRY, GUYS. We just sort of hit it off." Kiki delivered the understatement of the year. "Hope you're not too wigged out."

"Come on in." Elliott lifted the edge of the sheet in leering invititation. "Two's a couple, three's a crowd, but four's a party."

And this was the man she'd barely managed to budge out of the missionary position? Phoebe had counted on Jamaica loosening Elliott up. But she wasn't ready for this loose. Ryan wrapped a thick arm about her waist in support. "Thanks, but no thanks," Ryan declined on their behalf.

Phoebe laughed, hoping no one noticed the faint echo of hysteria in her voice. "I'm not much of a party girl."

Kiki shot her an arch look. "Now, Phoebe, I know you're wrong about that. I saw you on the dance floor. Don't be coy. And although you and Ryan denied anything last night, I've seen the way you look at one another when no one else is looking. Why else would two couples head down here together if they weren't interested in a swap and swing meet?"

That had never occurred to her. She wasn't particularly old-fashioned and she didn't have sexual hangups, she simply wasn't a group-sex kind of girl.

"It'll put a little spark back in our relationship, Phoebe," Elliott wheedled.

"It could be a lot of fun," Kiki coaxed. "The four of us. And you did tell me at dinner tonight you'd take care of Ryan."

Just because she'd thought Kiki deserved a little verbal payback for so obviously playing up to Elliott. It hadn't meant she would hop into bed with her best friend. Her hand itched to slap that seductive look off of Kiki's face.

"Fun's a relative issue." Ryan shook his head, his eyes hard despite the studied amusement on his face. "I don't like to share with others."

Elliott blanched.

Although Phoebe felt a bit naive and gauche in view of Kiki's sexual sophistication, this was one game she had no interest in playing. Or at least not by Kiki and Elliott's rules. She wasn't about to be dumped on. She'd set her own rules. A slow smile spread over her face. She turned to Ryan, throwing them into full body contact.

Surprise flared in his eyes. Insinuating her leg between his thighs, she leaned against him and silently willed him to go out for a long pass. A thread of tension wound through her that had nothing to do with their audience. "We obviously don't have to worry about how or when to break the news to them, darling."

Ryan caught the ball and ran with it. He brought his other arm around her, sliding his hand over her hip to settle on her behind. "Most excellent timing, in fact."

For a moment, Phoebe lost herself in the simmering heat of his eyes, the muscular length of his body pressed against her and his marauding hand on her bottom. She was a woman being held by a very sexy man.

"What news?" Elliott scowled from the bed, compounding his lack of good judgment—choosing Kiki over Phoebe—with offense.

"Kiki's right about one thing. Phoebe and I realized earlier today there's something much more intense than friendship between us. Something hot and explosive." Even though Ryan directed his words to Kiki and Elliott, his eyes never left Phoebe's face.

She licked at her suddenly dry lips. It was closer to the truth than he knew. "We weren't sure how or when to tell you." She managed to utter the words.

"I've barely been able to keep my hands off her all evening." Ryan smoothed his palm up her buttocks and along her back until he touched the skin bared by her halter dress. "Now I don't have to."

His touch trailed fire along her sensitized nerve endings. His pale green eyes mesmerized her. For a second, they were all alone in the room.

"Phoebe! How could you do something like this to me? I'm shocked," Elliott protested.

She was pretty shocked herself.

"I'm not." Kiki pouted. "I told you I saw the way they looked at one another earlier."

Damn if these two didn't have some nerve to embrace outrage—while they rolled around naked under the covers together. Apparently the two of them falling into bed together or the four of them cavorting under the covers was acceptable, but Phoebe and Ryan getting together on their own was an insult. Phoebe was doubly glad she and Ryan had turned the tables on them.

"You look as if you're dealing with your shock," Ryan noted with more than a touch of sarcasm. "I think you'll both recover quickly."

Phoebe pasted on a contrite expression. "I'm really sorry, Elliott. This thing between us…" She brushed her mouth against Ryan's, her eyes locked in the green depth of his. Despite her performance for an audience, a shiver crawled over her skin. "It's overwhelming." She glanced at Elliott. "Look at it this way. You're not left high and dry. At least you two get the consolation prize."

Kiki's mouth tightened. "Now, wait a minute, sister—"

Phoebe cut her off at the pass. "I understand you're upset. I'd be upset in your position, as well." Phoebe eyed Kiki in the bed with Elliott. "But there are so few good men out there, you just have to take one when you finally find him." She rubbed her head against Ryan's chin. "Even if he's been there all along."

His smoldering look left her trembling. "I'm ready for some privacy, now that we've got this out of the way." Ryan opened the door and looked at Elliott. "I'll be back in just a minute with your clothes and then I'll get my suitcase."

Elliott pushed the sheet aside, as if to pack for himself. "I don't want my shirts wrinkled."

"Please." Ryan threw up a hand. "Do us all a favor. Don't get up."

CHAPTER FIVE

"I CHECKED AT THE FRONT DESK and even tracked down Martin to see if he could help us out." Ryan tossed his suitcase on the upholstered chaise. "It's a no-go on an extra room. They've got a few empty rooms, but they're under renovation. Everything else is booked. Looks like we're roommates for the rest of the week."

Elliott had surpassed Ryan's expectations. Ryan had thought Elliott would hold steady with some heavy flirting. He'd been damned surprised to find Kiki and Elliott bumping uglies.

Ryan tugged his shirttail free. Things had gone much further than he anticipated. He damn sure hadn't bargained to share a room with Phoebe. Phoebe, who was slowly driving him crazy.

She nibbled at her lower lip and shrugged, failing dismally at appearing nonchalant. "Not a big deal. How many nights have you crashed at my house before?"

That was before he'd touched her as a man instead of a friend. Before he knew the hot, sweet taste of her mouth. Before this throbbing awareness of each other as a man and a woman pulsed between them. And crashing at her place was a far cry from this opulent room with its king-size bed that begged for sex.

"Sure. Not a big deal." He called on all his resolve. "We can handle it."

"Absolutely." She didn't look any surer than he felt. "And it certainly makes our story of newly discovered passion more valid if we're actually in the same room."

Ryan grinned at her wry assessment, "I guess it's a good thing you're quick-witted with a competitive streak a mile wide." He unbuttoned his cuffs. "You need to get off that ankle."

Phoebe ignored him and paced to the French doors and back, her dress hugging her delectable rear. "Can you believe they were in bed together? In my book, it's far better to be the dumper than the dumpee. Even though things were on the down slide with Elliott, there's no way Kiki's going to walk away thinking she stole him." Phoebe planted her hands on her hips, her competitive ire up. "Even if she did. And of course, you didn't fare any better at Elliott's hands."

Ryan read her hurt beneath the bravado. Striking Elliott off the marriage list was one thing. Finding him in bed with another woman was another. In the warm glow of the bedside lamp, she was a stirring mixture of indignity and vulnerability. Just looking at her standing beside the bed filled him with a longing so fierce it left him breathless.

As a rule, he never felt fierce about anything. "That's strictly a matter of opinion. I definitely wound up with the best. Elliott's a fool."

"Spoken like a true best friend."

Was that an affirmation or a reminder? He'd never lied to Phoebe and he wasn't going to start now. And a smidgen of guilt for encouraging Kiki and Elliott prodded him to come clean.

"Spoken like a man." His quiet words hung between them.

Irreversible.

Provocative.

Her eyes held his with an intensity that left him breathless. "Kiki's the fool."

"They have a lot in common." The comfort he ached to give her wasn't what she needed. Ryan stepped toward her. "Get on the bed, Phoebe."

Color stained her cheeks. "Ryan, we can't… I don't think…"

Was that a combination of guilt, confusion and lust clouding her eyes? Or were those his emotions he saw reflected? "You need to get off your ankle."

"Oh. Right." She sank onto the mattress and swung her legs up, shifting over to make room for him. "How's that?"

"Fine." He was living proof that men were visually stimulated because he was so damn stimulated at her stretched out on the bed he could hardly stand himself. Exotic braids, satin smooth skin, legs that went on forever, coral-tipped toenails. She was one dress away from yesterday's beach fantasy.

"Do you want to look at it?" She turned her leg and winced.

Her question twisted him in knots. Her ankle. She meant her ankle. How would he ever last six nights in this room with her?

"Sure. Let's see what's going on." He turned his back to her and leaned on the edge of the bed facing her feet. A man could only stand so much torture. And with the short, tight fit of her dress... Her ankle was the only thing he was supposed to check out.

"Ryan?"

He glanced over his shoulder. "Yeah?"

"When they asked us to join them, were you tempted?"

He turned, carefully probing the tender skin of her ankle with his fingers. What tempted him would send her through the roof. "Were you?"

"I asked you first."

"No, I wasn't remotely interested. You?"

"The truth? I think I'm far too competitive for group sex. I'd be so busy trying to outperform, I couldn't really enjoy myself."

The delicate bones and smooth skin of her ankle were warm beneath his fingertips. He closed his eyes with a silent groan. Images flashed through his head, leaving him speechless and hard. He twisted on the bed and studied Phoebe, the high cheekbones, the dusting of freckles across the bridge of her nose, the faint ridge of a scar beneath her chin, earned when they built their backyard clubhouse at the ripe age of ten. He'd never cared for anyone the way he cared for Phoebe. And he, of all people, knew caring and sex were two separate issues.

"What?" Her voice was breathy. Unsure.

He reached out and smoothed the pad of his thumb across her cheek. "All this time I've known you, I never noticed you have remarkable bone structure." Color washed the high ridge and warmed the skin beneath his finger.

"That's what Martin said." Uncertainty flickered across her face. "I thought he was just angling for a kickback."

"No. Martin was on to something." Was this exotic look a new image for her? "Are you going to keep the braids? When we go home?"

"No. It's an exciting change for a few days, but it would never fit in. I'll go back to the way it was before."

He wasn't Mr. Sensitivity, but he had the distinct impression they were talking about more than just her hair. "Some things may never go back to the way they were." Would he ever again meet Phoebe for lunch at Birelli's and not feel this powerful tug of attraction, like the dangerous undertow of a treacherous tide? And what was wrong with him? He never made cryptic observations.

She squared her shoulders and tilted her chin as if preparing for battle. "Would you have been interested if I hadn't been part of the equation?"

Couldn't she feel the yearning for her that gnawed at him? "You're kidding, right?"

"Do you see me laughing, Ryan?"

No. Vulnerability and intensity shadowed her sherry-brown eyes.

"I don't like to share."

"Oh."

"I prefer making love one-on-one." His eyes held hers. "Undivided attention. No distractions." He could barely think beyond wanting to do just that with her. "But that's just me. And for the record, you were the only part of that equation that held any interest for me."

His raw admission hung between them. Bare. Open.

Phoebe dragged in a deep, shuddering breath. "So, what do you recommend for my ankle, Dr. Palmer?"

He hadn't expected her to launch herself at him, and she hadn't. But with the pretense gone, perhaps they could make it through the week. He read her we-can't-go-there message loud and clear.

"Let's elevate and ice it." Ryan grabbed a pillow. "You should be okay by tomorrow." Phoebe shifted her ankle to her pillow, inadvertently offering Ryan a view of sun-kissed thighs beneath the hem of her short white dress.

He straightened abruptly. A man could only take so much. "I'll go get ice for an ice pack. Why don't you change into your pajamas while I'm gone?" Otherwise he was in serious danger of forgetting those gorgeous thighs were attached to Phoebe. Baggy boxers and a worn T-shirt, Phoebe's standard sleepwear, would, he hoped, give his blood pressure more of a break than her sexy, short dress.

"But it's still early."

"Yeah. And if you take care of this tonight, you should be all better by tomorrow. If you don't, you could wind up blowing the whole week."

"Okay. You're right." She huffed out a breath, and his heart threatened to stop as her breasts heaved against her plunging neckline. "Go ahead and go out without me. I'll be fine here."

No way he'd leave her in the room alone to work herself into a state over Elliott. And it wouldn't be any fun without her, anyway. "Forget it. We're in this together. Anyway, what if I ran into Kiki and Elliott? How can I be out hitting the bars when I'm supposedly in bed with you?"

"Oh, yeah. Right."

He headed for the door. "Ice. Coming right up."

Unfortunately, so were other things.

PHOEBE LIMPED OUT OF THE BATHROOM, determined to regain some measure of equanimity before Ryan returned.

I prefer making love one-on-one...no distractions... you were the only part of the equation that held any interest for me.

Friends. Friends. Friends. She repeated the word over and over to banish the echo of his tempting phrases, the memory of his fingers against her skin and the heat in his green eyes. Awareness rumbled between them like some great beast begging to be unleashed.

He opened the door.

"Ice." He hoisted the ice bucket and crossed the room without looking at her. "Why don't you prop your ankle up on the pillows again while I make an icepack?"

A nervous shiver passed over her skin as she settled on the bed. While he fashioned an ice pack out of a plastic laundry bag he found in the closet, she studied the familiar set of his broad shoulders. Even though he looked the same as her Ryan, this was a different man. Or, more aptly, a different facet of the man she knew. Secondhand exposure to his carnality was vastly different than coming face-to-face with his desire.

She tugged the scoop neck of her tank top up further. Ryan had seen her ready for bed any number of times. But she hadn't packed sweats, boxers or oversize T-shirts on this trip. She'd armed herself with a suitcase of seduction. At Victoria's Secret, they now knew her by name and American Express account number.

Bronze satin tap pants and a matching scooped tank top were the most sedate things she'd brought along. She gave the top another tug. Maybe Ryan wouldn't notice it barely covered her.

He turned, wrapping a hand towel around the ice-filled bag. He glanced up and stopped midstride. His face flushed, and he sucked in a ragged breath.

Her pulse hammered so hard it left her breathless.

He'd noticed.

"Where are your boxers? Your T-shirt?" The low gravel of his voice pebbled her nipples to hard points. "I'll get them for you."

"I didn't bring any." Phoebe wavered between gratification and dismay. Finding Elliott in bed with Kiki had delivered a none-too-subtle message that her ex-boyfriend had found her lacking. Her ego was wide open to a healthy dose of male appreciation. But this was Ryan.

"You're probably cold." Actually, she was very, very hot after seeing the look in his eyes. "Why don't I grab your robe for you? Just tell me where it is and I'll get it." His harsh desperation fanned the flame inside her, heightened her sensitivity to the play of satin against her buttocks and between her thighs, the cling of her stretchy top to her breasts and their aching crests.

"I didn't bring a robe." Her husky tone seemed to threaten his control.

He closed his eyes and clenched his jaw. "I'm going to open my eyes in five seconds. If you know what's best for both of us, you'll be under the covers then."

She was there in three, leaving her ankle out and propped on the pillow, trying to relax between the soft brush of cotton sheets.

Ryan opened his eyes, his expression bland, the fire in his eyes gone. If she didn't know better, she would think she'd imagined the whole thing.

"This should help." He settled the ice pack on her tender ankle and adjusted the pillow beneath her lower leg. His square, capable hands trembled against her skin, giving lie to his composure and destroying hers. The scent of Ryan's cologne wrapped around her. Need coiled between them. Heat rolled through her. She wanted him with an intensity that left her shaking.

She moved her leg away from his touch. "That's fine. Thank you."

He stepped away from the bed, and Phoebe struggled to regain her control.

She laughed, the sound strained even to her ears. "This isn't quite what I planned. Propped up in bed with a bum ankle..."

"Finding your boyfriend with my girlfriend?" Ryan turned his back to her and began to unbutton his shirt.

Wanting him to the point of distraction...

"No, that was definitely not part of the plan." She

watched him in the dresser mirror. Golden-brown hair sprinkled his chest and narrowed to disappear beneath his pants.

He looked up and caught her watching him. Wanting him. Without a word he strode to the bathroom and closed the door.

Phoebe turned out the light and willed sanity to return.

Ryan was her friend. She needed to remember that.

Ryan had a terrible track record with women. She definitely needed to remember that.

Ryan's touch set her on fire. That would get her in deep trouble.

MMM. Phoebe shifted, snuggling closer to the solid warmth beneath her cheek and against her thigh as she drifted out of the depths of a deep, dreamless sleep. A familiar and arousing scent seeped into her consciousness. Layers of sleep fell away. She woke to the of the weight of a male leg thrown over her. The tickle of chest hair against her breast. The hardened length of a man...

Her eyes flew open. Her. Ryan. Entwined. They'd started out on opposite sides of the king-size bed last night. During the night they'd definitely found each other in the middle. Steady, even breathing—thank God he was still asleep.

The sensible thing to do would be to extricate

herself immediately. And she would—in just a minute. What harm could possibly come from a few minutes of sensual indulgence?

She closed her eyes and absorbed the feel of him. The muscular length of his pajama-clad legs tangled with hers. The tease of his springy chest hair against her bared nipple. The ripple of his belly beneath her hand. Ryan's thickly muscled arm pillowed her head. The hard ridge of his erection, confined by his pajama bottoms, pressed against her thigh. His warm breath stirred against the back of her scalp.

Languid, liquid desire flowed through her, filled her. Nestled in his arms, Phoebe realized she'd never truly known desire before now. What she'd thought desire had been mere sexual arousal.

Ryan was her desire.

Ryan was also her best friend.

She flexed her fingers against his flat stomach, exulting in the texture of his skin, his male scent. The feather-light brush of his chest hair against the tight bud of her breast left her wet and aching.

He wanted her as desperately as she wanted him. She'd seen the heat in his eyes, heard the hoarse want in his voice. The easy thing to do would be to wake him by slipping her hand beneath the drawstring waist of his pajamas and wrapping her fingers around him while she flicked her tongue against his flat male nipple.

Phoebe closed her eyes. The realm of friendship

offered safety. She was there for him, and he was there for her. But there was nothing safe about Ryan as a lover. How many times had she seen him go from one woman to another? He'd never intentionally hurt her, but he could devastate her nonetheless.

She'd never planned for this to happen. She didn't have a plan for how to deal with this. But there was a world of difference between the easy thing to do and the right thing to do.

She untangled her leg from between his and tugged her top into place. Moving carefully, she rolled to her other side and inched toward the edge of the mattress. Ryan made disgruntled sleeping noises and rolled over behind her, curling his arm around her neck and across her chest. His other arm wrapped around her from behind, effectively trapping her. Like a homing device, his erection found her backside.

She should move. Jump. Run. Take action. Instead, she instinctively wriggled against him. His right hand slid to her breast, cupping it in his big palm. With lazy, somnolent movements, he rolled her nipple between his fingers. Exquisite sensation arrowed through her. Behind her, his warm mouth nuzzled against the sensitive juncture of her neck and shoulder. A low moan escaped her.

She knew the second Ryan gained some semblance of consciousness. His hand toying with her nipple stilled, and his entire body grew rigid. "Phoebe? Phoebe, are you awake?"

How could she roll over and say yes? Phoebe stretched out of his arms, pretending to wake up. "Hmm? What?"

She avoided looking at Ryan as she catapulted off the side of the bed. "I've got the shower first."

She slammed the door behind her and leaned against it, filled with equal measures of longing and self-loathing.

RYAN FINISHED UP quickly in the bathroom. He'd showered the night before. A long, cold stinging shower before he crawled into bed with Phoebe, his best friend and tormentor. He pulled on his swim trunks and walked into the room.

"Ready for some breakfast?" Phoebe's voice rang overbright and brittle. She hadn't looked at him since she'd showered and dressed.

He ought to feel really, really bad. He'd groped his best friend this morning while she lay sleeping. Unfortunately, he'd enjoyed the hell out of it. He could still taste the sweet warmth of her shoulder against his lips, feel the lean line of her back against the wall of his chest, the tease of her buttocks against his hard-on.

"Breakfast sounds good. How's your ankle?"

Phoebe brushed past him. The brief contact and her freshly showered fragrance left him aching.

She slipped into a pair of sandals and wiggled her foot. "Much better. Just an occasional twinge."

"Are you up for snorkeling this morning? The boat

leaves the pier in an hour and a half. I put us on the list while you were showering."

"Absolutely." Phoebe squared her shoulders. "Now remember, when we see Kiki and Elliott, we need to lay it on thick."

He could still feel the swell of her breast with its crested tip in the palm of his hand. He wasn't sure how much thicker he could handle. "Are you sure you don't want to just let it go?"

"They dumped us and hopped in bed together practically in front of us. How can you even consider letting it go?"

There was no swaying Phoebe when she went into her hypercompetitive mode. "Right. We'll lay it on thick."

Six more days and five long, hot nights. He just needed to remember Phoebe wasn't like other women, she was…well, Phoebe. Although exactly why Phoebe being Phoebe was a problem was beginning to blur for him, lost in the haze of haunting want.

He slung an arm around her shoulders when they left the room, her breast a tantalizing reach away from his fingertips. The sway of her hip against his, the press of her arm about his waist, the brush of her braids against his shoulder, proved sweet torture as they walked to the waterside restaurant.

The translucent blue-green waters of the Caribbean sparkled beneath the clear azure sky. Early morning sunbathers lined up their chaises along the white sand, avoiding the shade cast by the tall palms. A couple, their arms wound about one another, walked along the edge of the surf. Despite the people, spindle-legged sandpipers darted on the wet sand. From the carefully tended garden, the mournful call of doves echoed among the raucous cry of parrots.

"It's another beautiful day in paradise, isn't it?" Phoebe offered quietly, uncannily giving voice to his thoughts as they entered the open-air restaurant they both favored.

Breakfast was an informal affair where they seated themselves. A buffet offering a smorgasbord of breakfast items lined the back rail.

Ryan spotted Kiki and Elliott the moment they entered the restaurant. "Don't look now, but the enemy's at two o'clock."

Phoebe didn't bother to scan the room. She immediately attached herself to him like a limpet.

The same river of desire he'd almost drowned in earlier flooded through him again.

She nuzzled his jaw, her lips mere millimeters from his ear. "Come on, Ryan. You need to look at me as if we just rolled out of bed and you can't wait to get me back there again."

"Maybe that's closer to the truth than you know," he murmured against her mouth, tasting the hint of mint toothpaste clinging to her lips. He slipped his arm around her waist and splayed his fingers against her hip.

They crossed the room, lucking into a table next to the water. Ryan sat next to Phoebe, instead of across the table, as if he couldn't bear to be that far away from her, which was the case. He caught her hand in his, gratified by her swift intake of breath.

Martin appeared with his ready smile. "I regret that I could not be of more service last night. How is everything this morning?" He looked at their clasped hands and beamed. "Ah, it appears you weathered the evening."

"Yes. It's a beautiful morning on your island." Ryan had given Martin the right to inquire by seeking his help last night.

"We actually see it quite a bit. Two couples who come together and leave with the other." He smiled mysteriously. "It is the magic of the island. It casts a spell and brings out the truth of the heart." Martin laughed. "Ah, I see by your faces' expression you do not believe in the magic of Jamaica. Once I did not believe, as well. Until the magic brought me my most excellent wife."

Phoebe leaned forward, interest lighting her expressive face. She was breathtakingly beautiful. "I would love to hear how you met Mathilde. Wouldn't you, Ryan?"

"Absolutely." Ryan personally thought Martin, although a nice guy, was fully capable of spinning a tale or two for the tourists' entertainment.

"Mathilde and I used to play stickball together. We

grew up in the same village. We were friends, but I did not truly see Mathilde's excellence until I spent the season of my nineteenth year working in Negril to prepare for my position here. When I returned, a new man in our village was courting Mathilde. It was then, through the island's magic, that I truly saw her and we came to be married."

Ryan shifted in his chair. Martin's story struck uncomfortably close to home. And look where it had gotten Martin—married. Tied to one woman. It sounded as if Martin had taken action to protect his interest. But if Martin wanted to call it island magic, who was Ryan to disagree?

A hint of panic flared in Phoebe's eyes. Did she recognize the similarities, as well? "That's a lovely story, Martin. What were you like growing up? Quiet? Shy?"

Martin preened a bit and shrugged. "I was quite the lady's man in my younger days. My Mathilde had become disgusted with me. But that is enough about me. May I bring you some of Jamaica's most excellent Blue Mountain coffee? It is on the buffet, but I will bring a fresh pot for you."

"Thank you."

"It is my pleasure. And might I suggest the akee and *pain au chocolat* when you visit the buffet. Both are exceptional today."

Martin went for their coffee. Ryan pushed his chair back and stood. "Wait here and I'll make a plate." He stilled her protest with a finger against her lips. "Rest your ankle. Don't worry. I know what you like."

She settled into her chair. "Okay. Only a crazy woman would turn down being waited on. Thank you."

Ryan quickly returned. He'd filled one plate with chunks of mango and papaya, akee, naseberries, bananas and a pear-shaped Otaheite apple. The other plate held an assortment of pastries.

While he was gone, Martin had brought and served their coffee. The aroma of roasted coffee mingled with the heavy sweetness of ripe fruit and light, yeasty pastries.

Phoebe longingly eyed the pastry plate. "Ryan, you know I can't resist that, but I don't need it."

"It's your vacation, Phoebes. Indulge. Go back to your diet when we return to Nashville." He tore the *pain au chocolat* in half. Dark chocolate oozed from the croissant's buttery layers onto his fingers.

She reached for a chunk of papaya. Before she could bring the fruit to her mouth, he leaned close— until he saw blue sky reflected in her black irises. Ryan offered the morsel before her pink parted lips. Slowly, deliberately, she sank her white teeth into the flaky pastry and rich chocolate. The clink of silverware and the hum of conversation dimmed, lost in the rushing of his blood as she stroked her moist tongue along the length of his finger, licking the chocolate off him. With that one stroke of her tongue, he thickened and lengthened.

"Chocolate and fruit. One of my favorites." The husky cadence of her voice tempted him, as rich and inviting as the chocolate. Her eyes held his as she brought the papaya to her mouth. She closed her lips around part of the pink-hued flesh, its sweet, sticky juice coating her lips.

The hardened points of her nipples poked at the soft cotton of her cover-up. She was as turned on as he was. Ryan groaned, unsure he'd actually live through breakfast with her.

She held the other half of the fruit to his lips, her bite marks scoring the fruit. "Try it," she invited, sliding the ripe tidbit into his mouth. Firm, yet succulent. He savored the juicy sweetness against his tongue. His body throbbed in response.

He'd never dreamed that eating breakfast with Phoebe would turn into a barely decent experience.

CHAPTER SIX

PHOEBE STOOD ON THE SIDE of the boat and checked her mask and snorkel, the sun warm on her shoulders and back. All around them, the sea shimmered like thick-fired glass hued with greens and blues. Below the surface, corals and fronds of sea grass swayed in the current. Reggae played over the boat's speakers.

Beside her, Ryan pulled off his shirt. Phoebe was more than ready to snorkel. Not only was she eager to explore the tropical waters, she was desperate for a measure of relief from this tension binding her to Ryan. They'd always been close, but this was a deeper, primal connection. She still wasn't sure what had happened at breakfast. What had begun as a show for Kiki and Elliott had wound up a seduction of the senses. Even now, every nerve in her body responded to his nearness, the rhythm of his breathing, his scent, the heat of his body. Surely, the water would afford some relief from this aching awareness.

The music stopped abruptly and a high-pitched squeal rent the air as the boat captain, a small wiry man with a sun-weathered face, picked up a microphone.

"Welcome to some of the finest snorkeling in Jamaica. Before you get in the water, it is necessary for us to go over a few things. Remember, do not touch the coral. It is a living thing and you do not want to damage the reef. This is important." He paused to make sure everyone heard.

"Please snorkel with a partner. This is for your safety. Also in the interest of safety, take care not to swim past the orange markers. The reef does not extend past that point, but boats do. Being run over by a boat is a bad way to end your holiday." A titter ran through the small group on the boat.

"We have snacks and refreshments on board for you. Feel free to help yourself. Finally, there is a rumor that Blackbeard sank a Spanish galleon in these waters." He threw his hands in the air, palms up, shrugging. "Should you find any wreckage, please let us know. We will be here for two hours. Enjoy the beautiful treasures of the Caribbean Sea."

"Are you ready? Your treasures await, sea princess." Ryan's ready, easy smile accompanied his banter.

"Just let me put on my clown feet." Phoebe perched on the side of the boat and tugged on her flippers.

He shook his head, the sun glinting off strands of hair already bleached by the bright rays. The banked fire in his gaze slid over her, heating her.

"No, Phoebes. You're definitely a sea princess. An exotic mermaid with a siren's call, luring sailors into your mysterious depths with the promise of exploring your treasures."

Phoebe could barely breathe. The low strum of his voice. The erotic imagery provoked by his words. It was verbal lovemaking on the open sea with the sun on her back and the caress of the wind against her skin.

"Lead on, princess. I'll willingly follow you," Ryan continued.

Not only was she fairly sure she was incapable of speech, but what could she possibly say to that? Silently, she slid into the waiting arms of the water, sinking completely below the surface into the wet embrace. Ryan slipped into the water beside her.

She surfaced and donned her mask and snorkel. "Are you sure you're willing to follow me, sailor?"

"Always."

Phoebe inserted her mouthpiece, took him by the hand and led him to another world below the surface. Viewed from above, it was intriguing, but below the surface the reef revealed its true intensity and vibrancy—a surreal landscape of unsurpassed beauty. Together they explored canyons and caves of bright, vivid corals in a variety of shapes and sizes, swam through schools of vibrant tropical fish.

Ryan directed her attention to the sandy ocean floor. A manta ray stirred, betraying its camouflaged position. Exhibiting grace and speed, it fled its ocean bed and glided past them.

Even when they were surrounded by the water, awareness pulsed between them, enfolding them in their own private world. The hours passed like minutes. Phoebe was astonished when Ryan tapped his waterproof watch, signaling their time was up.

Together they rose to the surface. Phoebe slid her mask off. "That was absolutely fantastic."

Ryan grinned, pulling her to the boat's ladder with him. "It was, wasn't it?"

They climbed aboard, returned their gear and settled on a cushioned seat next to one another. What a special experience, in large part due to Ryan's presence. She wouldn't have enjoyed snorkeling nearly as much with Elliott.

"Thank you." She plucked two towels off the stack supplied by the resort and passed one to Ryan.

He rubbed the thick towel over his chest, dislodging droplets of water caught in the golden-brown hair. "Thanks for what?"

Phoebe stared as a rivulet of water trailed along his tanned, muscled bicep. She longed to lick the wet brine off his fine-textured, sun-heated skin and savor the taste of him against her tongue. Instead, she blotted her dripping braids with her towel, disconcerted by the depth of yearning Ryan invoked in her. She'd never felt this compulsion with Elliott or any boyfriend before him. She might be losing her mind, but she refused to lose her best friend to this. Through sheer will, she marshaled her thoughts. What had she thanked him for?

"For signing us up for the snorkeling. I've never seen anything so beautiful."

He dragged the towel over the flat planes of his belly with mesmerizing deliberation. His eyes darkened and his gaze lingered on her face like a lover's touch. He leaned forward, his mouth only inches from her own. She recalled, with throbbing clarity, the heat of his mouth on hers that night inside the Jungle Room—his taste, the touch of his hands on her skin.

"I assure you, I've never seen anything more beautiful, either."

"Phoebe. Ryan. Over here."

Phoebe glanced over her shoulder. Kiki waved from a poolside deck chair, motioning them over, Elliott by her side. Great.

Phoebe's nerves were already stretched to breaking point. She and Ryan had spent the afternoon on the beach after they returned from snorkeling. It should've been relaxing, soothing, calming. But the easy camaraderie she'd always shared with Ryan had been replaced by seething sexual awareness. Showering and changing for an early dinner had been worse, sharing the confines of a room designed to invite pleasure, both of them ignoring the want that throbbed between them.

"I suppose it's too late to pretend we didn't see them, huh?" Phoebe asked.

Ryan turned in Elliott and Kiki's direction. "So, do you think they'll ask us to join in a rousing round of naked twister?"

"With the two of them, it's a distinct possibility." Phoebe looked at Elliott. No ache filled her heart. Not even a slight tremor. No weak knees or feverish desire. Blast. She would've felt better if she'd had even one of those responses to his dark-eyed visage. No. Like some whacked-out cosmic joke, Ryan struck those chords for her.

Her body went on red alert when Ryan settled his hand against the small of her back, his fingers hot through the material of her dress.

"Hi, guys. We just wanted to make sure there were no hard feelings about last night," Kiki said.

Phoebe wrapped her arm around Ryan's waist. "Are you kidding? We were thinking about sending a bottle of champagne in thanks."

Elliott appeared suitably affronted. "You needn't be so bloody insulting about it."

"Sorry. We're both sort of giddy with having finally found one another. All this time…" Phoebe sighed into Ryan, and he nuzzled her forehead.

"Were you at the beach this morning?" Kiki asked.

"No, this afternoon. We spent the morning snorkeling. It was incredible. You guys should try it tomorrow."

Elliott shook his head. "Not tomorrow. We're heading over to the private island for some nude sunbathing. But then I don't imagine that would interest you. It's a bit uninhibited."

Did Elliott deliberately use that goading tone?

"Really? We might see you there. We're supposed to go, as well," Phoebe said.

"Unless we're otherwise distracted," Ryan amended with a tight smile. "I'm sure we'll see you around."

Ryan hustled Phoebe off in record time, practically hauling her along. Instead of the restaurant, he headed toward their room.

"The restaurant's the other way."

"I know." Anger rolled off him in waves.

In silence, Ryan opened the room door. He wasn't, however, silent for long.

"We're not going to the topless beach tomorrow. *We* are not going at all. If you want to go, you'll have to go by yourself," Ryan exploded once their room door had closed behind them.

His vehemence surprised her. Easygoing, laid-back Ryan didn't lose his temper. "What's wrong with you? Why are you making such a big deal about nude sunbathing? Have you developed some sense of modesty? They're a bunch of strangers."

"For once, can't you just let it go, Phoebe?"

Phoebe seldom—well, more like never—heard that

note of leashed frustration in Ryan's voice. "No. I can't just let it go." She narrowed her eyes as a totally loathsome idea came to mind. "Is it the idea of seeing Kiki and not being able to have her?"

Ryan advanced across the tile floor, every vestige of boyish good humor replaced by hard implacability. Her heart thudded against her breastbone, part trepidation, part excitement. "Let it go, Phoebe."

"I can't."

He stepped closer, his hands clenched at his sides. She refused to retreat, even though she felt caught in a storm brewing in the cauldron of emotion seething between them.

Ryan stood before her. Phoebe was painfully aware of him. The memory of awakening sprawled across him haunted her with painful clarity. "Talk to me," she said.

"Talk to you? You want me to talk to you?" The sliver of space between them pulsed with tension. "Goddamn it, Phoebe. That's the problem. I can't talk to you. I want you so bad I can hardly stand myself. I'll be damned if I'm going to look at you naked on some island tomorrow to prove some idiotic point. I'm not up for more looking but no touching unless Elliott and Kiki are around. And you want me to talk to you? This is about the only talk I'm up for right now."

He jerked her to him and cradled her head in his hands. Inexorably, he drew her mouth to his. A part of her hungered for the taste and feel of him. Another part of her screamed in protest. There was no audience. This was a kiss between a man and woman, a kiss of want and need. With unswerving surety, she knew this kiss would forever change their relationship. But Phoebe had spent the last few days running. And she didn't want to run anymore.

Her breath became his as he slanted his mouth over hers. She plied her lips against his in return, adrift in the taste of him, the feel of him. Drowning desire tugged at her with treacherous, dangerous undercurrents. Slowly she surfaced, gasping for air, her breath ragged.

"Maybe going to the topless beach isn't such a good idea, after all." Phoebe broke the heavy silence.

"This is the part where I'm supposed to say I'm sorry." Ryan dropped his hands to his sides. "But I'm not. I've wanted to do that all day."

"This is my fault. I started this last night when we found them—"

Ryan shook his head. "No. Maybe Martin was right. There is something magical about this place."

This was uncomfortable, but at least they were getting things out in the open. Phoebe, unfortunately, had a few truths to lay out on the table herself. She screwed up her courage. Confession was reportedly good for the soul. "I need to tell you something."

"Do I need to sit down?" Ryan asked with a wry grin.

"Only if you're tired." Phoebe paced to the other

side of the room. "This morning, when you woke up, I wasn't asleep."

There it was, out in the open. Her relief almost outweighed her embarrassment.

Ryan exhaled harshly, the only sound in the room other than the quiet hum of the air conditioner.

"How long were you awake?"

The brush of his hand against her breast, the touch of his fingers against her nipple, the nudge of his erection between her buttocks—how much had she felt? Phoebe was not a woman given to lying—to herself or to others, overtly or through omission. But facing Ryan with this truth was one of the hardest things she'd ever done.

"Long enough." Phoebe fought the urge to weep and lifted her chin. "I know this will always stand between us, but it's better than having it stand between us as a secret, a lie of omission. I knew what was going on. And I *wanted* you to touch me."

"I WASN'T ASLEEP, either, Phoebe," Ryan admitted. He could still feel her soft curves against him, smell her, hear her soft moan. "I'm sorry. It's no excuse, but the only thing I can offer is the truth. I've never wanted another woman the way I want you."

Phoebe stared at him, her eyes dark and smoky, her breathing unsteady. He closed the gap separating them. She turned her head, looking away from him, her silky braids resting against his face. "What's happening to us, Ryan?"

"The only thing I know for sure is that I want you more than my next breath." He leaned back and traced the line of her jaw with his finger. She quivered at his touch. "I don't know. I didn't wake up and decide to complicate my life by wanting you to the point of madness." His finger trailed against the line of her throat to the slight hollows of her collarbone and settled on the frantic pulse at the base of her neck. "But I do."

She caught his hand in hers, stilling his exploration. "This is madness. Elliott was…just Elliott. I'm fine with what happened. But you're my best friend. I'm closer to you than any other human being. You're my confidant. You know me, accept me, warts and all. I can't ruin that by wanting you."

"Do you want me?" He knew the answer, but he needed to make sure she did. The answer was in her eyes, along with panic. Ryan knew how Phoebe felt about change. A shift of this magnitude would obviously terrify her. Hell, he was even a little thrown off. But she couldn't run from this. "Don't lie to either one of us. Do you want me?"

"Yes." She worried the fullness of her lower lip with her teeth. "Yes, you know I do."

"Phoebe, you're one of the most important people in my life. I don't want to screw that up, either. But pretending I don't ache for you doesn't make it so."

He traced the ridge of scar beneath her chin. "This isn't just going to go away if we ignore it. It's a hunger that'll gnaw at us."

She studied his face for a full minute, digesting his words. "All I could think about on the beach today was touching you. Being touched by you." Her words set him on fire. "If we leave things the way they are, the mystique, the temptation, the fantasy will always be there." She paused, then her expression suddenly changed. Ryan knew that look. Phoebe had another plan.

She reached up and started working one of his buttons free. "I think you're right. There's no going back. The only way to deal with this is to move forward," she said as another button gave way. The slide of her fingers against his chest rendered his brain fairly useless. "What we have to do, is to work through this sexual thing between us." Three buttons down. He had no clue how many to go. "You're absolutely right."

Ryan sucked in a deep breath when the back of her fingers skimmed his belly, his entire body vibrating from her touch. "Did I say that?"

She paused. "Didn't you?"

"Does that mean we get to have sex?"

Her fingers lingered above his belt buckle. "Yes, I think it does."

He fell back onto the bed, pulling her on top of him.

"Then that's exactly what I said."

PHOEBE WASN'T TOTALLY CONVINCED their logic wasn't a bit flawed, skewed perhaps, by lust. But an overwhelming sense of rightness, of destiny was there, as well. And quite frankly she didn't know where else to go with this madness that wasn't going to be resolved by denial.

If they were about to debunk the myth, she wanted to leave no stone unturned to torment herself with "what ifs" later.

She tugged his shirttail free of his pants. "I want to taste you." She leaned forward and pressed nibbling kisses against his stomach, inhaling his male scent.

She dipped her head and traced a path against his naked belly with her tongue, along the waistband of his slacks to the indent of his navel, her beaded braids dragging across his erection. There was more than an element of the forbidden in tasting the slight saltiness of his skin while inhaling his familiar scent. His muscles clenched beneath her mouth. "I love the taste of your skin."

"And I love the way you taste my skin," Ryan said. "I think I'm going to learn a new appreciation for your delayed-gratification approach." She moved her head, her beads teasing against his tented trousers. "That is, if you don't kill me first."

Phoebe felt a deeper sense of intimacy and freedom than she'd ever felt with another lover—perhaps because she knew Ryan so well in every other aspect. She laughed softly against the warmth of his midsection as she mapped the contours of hard muscle beneath satin skin with her mouth. She traversed the smooth lines of his side. The pounding of his heart, the echoing rhythm of her own, sounded in her head as she focused on the ridges lightly covered with a smattering of gold-tipped hair. She felt almost drunk from the touch, taste and scent of him.

She flicked her tongue against his flat male nipple and then suckled it. Ryan groaned and closed his eyes. "Oh, baby, that feels so…" She moved to the other nipple, her breasts rubbing against his naked, hair-roughened stomach with exquisite torture. "Yes. Yes." Her body quickened at his appreciation. His obvious pleasure fed hers.

Chest heaving, he impatiently dragged her head up and kissed her, his big hands cupping her head. Phoebe passed the point of rational thought when Ryan suckled her lower lip, then released it and laved his tongue across its swollen surface. He followed the course with his finger, the faint scrape of his callous arousing after the wet velvet of his tongue. "You have the most incredible mouth."

His rough, excited voice scraped along her nerve endings, sending her internal temperature to an incendiary level.

She caught the tip of his finger in her mouth and fondled it with her tongue. His pupils dilated. His eyes darkened. "The better to please you," she teased.

Abruptly, Ryan withdrew his finger and shifted her to her back. "I think we need to elevate your ankle."

Phoebe understood all too well the game of give and take they played. He grabbed a pillow from the head of the bed and propped her ankle on it, the difference in elevation making her legs gape apart.

Ryan paused, his look smoldering as she lay on the bed. She felt wickedly sexy.

He stood, turning his back to her. "Does it feel swollen? Is it throbbing?" His matter-of-fact, almost conversational tone lent the words even more sensual impact. They both knew he wasn't talking about her ankle. He shrugged out of his shirt.

"Yes." She managed to breathe the word. Yes, she was throbbing, swollen. And yes, she wanted to watch him undress.

She finally admitted what she'd denied so long. She'd spent a lifetime looking at the candy bar on the shelf, secretly coveting it. Unaware, until lately, that she wanted it for herself. Now she got to unwrap it. Savor the experience. Even though she knew she didn't need it and inevitably it would prove bad for her in the long run.

Muscles rippled the sculpted line of his back and shoulders as he dropped the shirt to the floor behind him without turning around.

"What are you wearing under that dress? Are you wearing panties, Phoebe? A bra?" He spoke in that same light, vaguely disinterested tone as he pulled his belt through the loops.

Acutely aware of the play of fabric against her hardened nipples, the ride of material between her legs, she shifted on the bed. "No bra. Just panties."

"Really? What kind of panties?" A harsh note flavored his casual question, followed by the sound of a zipper.

"White. A thong." Aroused, she rubbed her palm against the white spandex covering her thighs. Phoebe ached for Ryan's touch.

His entire body stilled. Then he stepped out of his pants. Her breath caught in her throat. He was awesome. Simply awesome. From this angle, everything was tight and hard. Back, buttocks, thighs...

Gripped by intense longing, she instinctively smoothed her dress to the top of her thighs and splayed her legs. "If you want to know what my panties look like, why don't you turn around and see for yourself?"

"If the view gets any better than it is now, I'm not sure I can stand it."

She looked past him. Her eyes locked with his in the mirror. He'd watched her in the dresser mirror. His tight smile relayed just how much he liked what he saw. Heat threatened to consume her. Emboldened by his obvious turn-on, she dropped her legs wider apart. "And I can't stand it if you don't."

Ryan turned and stood at the foot of the bed. He

devoured her with his gaze, a wicked smile revealing his dimple. How many times had she seen him
in a bathing suit? His briefs covered the same area.
The difference must be the raging erection straining
the fabric and the knowledge that before the night
was over. she'd have intimate knowledge of what lay
beneath.

"You are a goddess."

Phoebe thought about the stubborn cellulite that
refused to budge from the backs of her thighs. And
then she looked at Ryan, felt the heat of his gaze brush
against her skin like a warm balmy breeze, recognized
the naked desire in his eyes. He stared at the juncture
of her thighs, at the small triangle of material covering
her. And, oddly enough, she did feel like a goddess—
beautiful and powerful and unfazed by imperfections
he didn't seem to see.

"Want to hear a fantasy?" He dropped to the foot
of the bed, his voice low, dark. He ran his finger along
the top of her foot, the light stroke imbued with an
intimacy that shivered through her.

They'd shared so much over the years, but this took
it to a new level. "Tell me your fantasy." Need lent a
husky quality to her voice.

"Earlier this week, I was on the beach." His fingers
traced the hollows of her ankle. "And I saw a woman
with the most incredible legs." He lightly massaged
her calf in his big hands, his callouses rasping against
her sensitized flesh.

"I didn't know you were a leg man." Phoebe spoke on an indrawn breath. He'd always favored short women with big boobs.

"Neither did I."

"It's good to develop new interests." She dropped her head back. No one had ever stroked her legs with such devastating eroticism.

He gentled her legs farther apart. "This goes far beyond interest." He lowered his head and traced his tongue against the back of her knee, his mouth warm and moist in direct contrast to the scrape of his stubbled jaw.

Phoebe moaned deep in her throat as sensation arced through her. Lying between her legs, he did the same to her other knee. Oh, my. If his mouth felt that good against her knee and she still had all her clothes on… She closed her eyes, savoring the sensation, her muscles clenching, "Yes. That feels so good."

"That's it, baby. Tell me what you like. I want to know." His low, rich voice whispered over her.

She opened her eyes. His broad shoulders filled the narrowing vee of her legs. She skimmed her instep along his waist and over his hip, curling her toes against his tight ass. His muscles flexed against the sole of her foot. "You were telling me about your fantasy," she prompted.

"Hmm. I got distracted." He splayed his fingers on her thighs, his thumbs tracing lazy circles on her inner legs. Phoebe wet her lips as the tension inside her increased. She ached for him to reach higher, past the tops of her thighs.

"So, this woman had these really great, long…" He ran the tip of his tongue from her knee to midthigh. She shivered soul deep. "…luscious…" He stroked a wider path up to her inner thigh "…legs."

He raised his head, looking up the length of her body from the juncture of her thighs. His moist breath gusted through the thin scrap of her thong and met her wet, hot flesh. Closing his eyes, he inhaled deeply. "Ah, honey, your scent makes me rock hard."

His comment made her wetter still. "Ryan…" She arched her hips toward him.

He subtly inched back, keeping her needy. He hooked his thumbs beneath the edge of her skirt and tugged it a few inches higher. "I keep getting off the subject." He rested one hand on her panty, just out of reach of where she ached for him. He trailed hot, moist kisses from her inner thigh to the tender skin between her belly and hip, his cheek and jaw brushing maddeningly against her crotch. He nuzzled and nibbled along the edge of her underwear, teasing yet offering no relief to a tension notched so high, she stood poised on the point of shattering.

She wanted—no, needed—more. His mouth. His hand. Something more satisfying than his warm breath and teasing kisses that promised but didn't satisfy. Driven to the point of distraction, she writhed against him, "Damn your teasing black soul to hell,

Ryan Palmer." She sorely resented the fact she was about to fly into a million pieces and he was so in control.

"Oh, baby, we're not hell bound. But I haven't finished telling you my story yet." He tugged her upright. They faced one another, their chests heaving. He reached behind her and found her zipper. "When I saw this fantasy woman on the beach with the legs that made me ache and these sexy, erotic cornrows, all I could imagine—" cool air kissed her back as he slid her zipper down "—was that woman, naked, beneath me," he caressed up the curve of her back and released the button on the neck of her dress, "me buried deep inside her, with those incredible legs wrapped around me." The neck of her dress fell forward, leaving her breasts almost exposed. Ryan leaned back and watched her. "So, what do you think about my fantasy?"

She thought she was bordering on the brink of madness, and she had absolutely no intention of suffering this deprivation alone. He was far too in control of himself. Phoebe caught the end of her dress and slowly pulled it up past her navel, past her breasts and over her head, her movements deliberate, seductive. She tossed the dress to the foot of the bed. "I think fantasy is nice—" she wrapped her legs around his waist and leaned back, bracing herself with her hands behind her "—but reality may be even better."

RYAN DREW A DEEP, shuddering breath and entertained the notion that reality might, in this instance, with this woman, indeed surpass fantasy. Every other fantasy had been a dress rehearsal, preparing him for this. For her. This went beyond the physical. They had been an integral part of one another for years. Making love to Phoebe, with Phoebe, was the culmination. The end. And a beginning.

"This reality *is* already better." He ran his fingers along her rib cage, finding pleasure in the tactile smoothness. "Your skin is so soft." His thumbs circled below her breasts, building up the tension for her, for him. Her nipples tightened even more, pouting at puckered attention. Easing his hands around to her back, he pulled her forward and up, circling her delicate tip with his tongue. Ravening hunger surged through him, and he tugged her nipple deeper into his mouth. She pushed her wet heat against his erection, and he pressed against her.

Winding her hands around his neck, she arched her back, thrusting deeper into his mouth with a moan. Ryan readily accommodated her request, moving from one breast to the other. Sensation, emotion swamped him. Everything was thick. The air between them resonated with want, need. The musky scent of their arousal mingled with Phoebe's perfume, hung in the air thick and heavy like the nectar of ripe fruit. His blood coursed, thick with desire. His entire body was caught up in her taste, her scent, her texture and the overwhelming drive to be closer to her, to be a part of her.

Ryan enjoyed sex—sometimes more than others—but this, this was different. This wasn't the mere quest for pleasure. This was an urge that bordered on desperation.

With each tug on her nipple, her sex quivered against his hard-on, dampening his boxers with her arousal. He was burning up. "God. You're so wet and hot." He wrapped his hand around the back of her thong and tugged, pulling the material tight against her. "Do you like this?"

She ground against him, her breath coming in short, sharp pants, her hands clenching hard into his shoulders. "Yes. Yes, I like it. What about you?" She reached between them and pulled his rigid erection through the opening of his shorts. "Do you like it when I touch you like this?" She closed her hand around his length and stroked.

Ryan drew in a sharp breath. "Yes. I like it when you touch me like that."

She tugged his mouth down to hers, her sherry eyes glittering with hot arousal and wanton intent. She kissed him openmouthed, her tongue stroking in time with her hand. Stroke by stroke, she melted the glue holding him together. Frantic for more, he buried his hands in the mounds of her bottom, urging her slick, wet heat closer. Just at the point when he thought he would explode, her hand stilled and she wrenched her mouth away from his.

"Ryan. If we don't do this soon, I'm going to lose my mind."

It was a request and a warning.

"Baby, I've already lost my mind." He began to ease her onto her back. She stilled him with a hand to his chest.

"No. Stay just like that."

"Okay." Hell, at this point she could tell him to get down on all fours and bark like a dog and he'd willingly howl at the moon. He was pretty damn close to howling right now.

With a supple twist of her hips, she raised up and tugged her thong aside. "Now, let's go slow."

Ryan grasped her hips and eased her onto his erection. Her legs still wrapped around his waist, she sank down on him with excruciating slowness. Inch by inch, she wrapped her wet heat around him. Ryan closed his eyes, flooded by pleasure as he entered her tight, hot paradise.

For a moment they both held absolutely still as she settled against him, joined as fully and deeply as possible. With no outward sign of movement, she clenched her muscles around him, deep inside her.

"Oh, Phoebe, baby."

She dropped her head back. "Yes. You feel so good." She clenched again, and he pulsed a response. Her nipples stabbed against the wall of his chest, and he cupped her braided head in his hands and kissed her, hard, deep. And then she began a rocking, grinding motion against him, her muscles gripping him, milking him. Unable to thrust in that position, he ground against her in response, picking up her rhythm.

He was so close to coming but he gritted his teeth and held himself in check, unwilling to go there without Phoebe. He felt spasms begin to radiate from her core. "That's it, Phoebe. Let it go, baby."

As they both found a release, Ryan realized what a hollow experience sex had been before. Nothing more than a physical release. Nothing close to the richness of sharing your body with a woman so intimately acquainted with your mind.

They collapsed against the mattress, still joined. Sated, he could stay inside her forever.

Every fantasy he'd ever had paled in comparison to this moment.

CHAPTER SEVEN

PHOEBE'S EYES DRIFTED SHUT. Emotions, thoughts stirred and blew though her like gossamer fabric fluttering in the breeze. Complete. Replete. Making love with Ryan had brought a pleasure, a completeness so clear and pure, it evoked a piercing melancholy.

She absorbed the texture of his skin against hers, the heat of his hair-sprinkled belly, the fine coating of sweat that slicked them both, the fragrant musk produced by their union.

With startling clarity, Phoebe realized she'd always withheld something of herself during lovemaking. An emotional reserve. A part of her that was hers alone, a part of herself she was unwilling to share. Participation without full engagement. But with Ryan, there'd been no holding back. It hadn't been a conscious decision, it had just happened. She'd given all of herself. In return, she'd realized gratification she'd never known before.

Next to her, Ryan moved, his fingers playing along the line of her hip, his breath warm against her cooling neck. "You asleep, Phoebes?"

"No." Eyes still closed, she smoothed her foot

against his calf, enjoying the tactile play of hair and muscle against her arch. One last time. Phoebe opened her eyes, reluctant to deal with the practicalities of their relationship quite so soon. Knowing, however, that she couldn't languish in the aftermath of lovemaking forever. She shifted her leg off his. "No. I'm not asleep."

He dragged his fingers across her stomach, as if he, too, was reluctant to give up the contact. God, they'd just made everything worse. They'd debunked nothing except their own foolishness.

Rolling to the other side, Phoebe put the width of the king-size mattress between them. She tugged the edge of the comforter over her, suddenly self-consciously aware of her near nudity. Thongs didn't count for much in the coverage department. "Yep. Good thing we got that over with." Awkwardness, the aftermath of spent passion and uncertainty in how to proceed, settled between them.

"So, what do you—"

"Want to—"

They both laughed, rounding off the sharp edge of tension. Phoebe made the mistake of looking at him. All of him. Splendidly, rousingly naked. Ryan wasn't just a hottie. He was a one-man, twelve-alarm fire waiting to happen. Even now, her body stirred in response to his nudity and proximity. And that wasn't part of her plan. She'd figured that making love once would dispel the mystique. Only it hadn't. What a disaster. Phoebe trained her eyes on his face, determined to look no farther south than his neck. "Go ahead."

"No. You first."

"You. I insist."

"Okay." Ryan shrugged, and Phoebe swallowed hard. Amazing, really, how many well-honed, sleek muscles tightened and rippled and generally put on a sensual show when a naked man shrugged. "I was going to ask if you were ready to go to bed?" A banked fire smoldered in his eyes.

"Here?" Phoebe closed her eyes, envisioning them wrapped in each other's arms. "Of course you mean here." The idea of crawling beneath the sheets with Ryan, his smell and taste still imprinted on her, didn't seem such a clever idea. She shook her head. "I don't think so. I'm really not tired. In fact, I'm pretty energized."

While she spoke, she employed a few contortionist moves, trying to retrieve her dress from where it lay wedged between the bottom corner post and the mattress while keeping the comforter wrapped around her. "But you go to bed if you want to. I'll be really quiet. You won't even know I'm here."

Ryan looked at her, his eyes caressing the swell of her breasts above the comforter, a predatory smile tugging at his mouth. "I'd give it about a snowball's chance in hell that I won't know you're around."

Her hand holding the comforter in place shook.

And damnation if her nipples didn't peak to hard buds just at his hot glance and suggestive smile. What had she been thinking to get herself in this position with her best friend and playboy extraordinaire?

"Oh." How else was she supposed to respond? It was either that or jumping his bones again, and more bone-jumping wasn't an option.

"Let me help." Ryan reached down and tugged, his head far too near her comforter-covered breasts for her peace of mind. He worked the dress free. "Here."

Instead of the width of the bed, mere inches separated them. Ryan stared at her mouth. Her lower lip tingled from his gaze, as if he'd actually brushed her mouth with his. He held her dress in his fist.

"Ryan…" His name lingered against her tongue.

"Phoebe…." He dropped his head forward, so close she could see the bristles that cast a golden shadow over his jaw, feel the heat of his body. An answering heat unfurled through her like a ribbon slowly coming undone.

This was all wrong. They'd made love once. That should have taken care of this yearning inside her. Frustration welled. She wanted him as much or more than she had before.

God, she would be lost if she didn't put a stop to this madness right now. "I need my dress, Ryan."

"Sure." He handed her the dress but otherwise didn't move.

Phoebe shoved it under her armpits, stretching it

across her breasts like a giant Band-Aid. She backed off the side of the bed with all the poise of a sand crab scuttling for cover. "Okay, then. I'm just going to put on my bathing suit and go for a swim."

She backed across the room to the bathroom. Not too terribly dignified, but then neither was turning around and showing off her cellulite depository. Yeah, she'd been on the beach in a bathing suit, but you just sort of hoped nobody looked too close. That was a far different proposition than turning around and flashing the best friend you just had incredible, once-in-a-lifetime sex with.

"What are you doing, Phoebe?"

Was that a note of exasperation? "I just told you, I'm going to pop in here and put on my bathing suit."

"But why are you backing across the room?"

Now she was feeling altogether foolish and awkward. Why wouldn't he just drop it?

"The, uh, you know…I'm only wearing the butt floss." Infuriated at finding herself in this position, she yelled the last part.

"I've seen you naked, Phoebe," Ryan shouted. "Well, almost naked, except for that butt floss, which is seriously sexy, by the way."

Reaching behind her, Phoebe awkwardly opened the door and edged into the bathroom. "Yeah. Well, I've seen you naked, too." And that was seriously sexy, also. She slammed the door and clicked the lock into place for good measure.

She'd seen him, felt him, heard him, tasted him, smelled him—she'd had the total sensory experience. And therein lay the crux of the whole problem. She wasn't likely to forget it anytime soon.

THIS WAS RIDICULOUS. Ryan pulled on his swimming trunks. He and Phoebe yelling at one another. Then not speaking when she flounced through the room on the way to the pool. And now she was out in that little round pool that was essentially made for lounging and aqua sex, swimming circular laps so fast she was probably dizzy.

He snatched the bucket of iced champagne and two glasses that came with the suite. For all the years he'd known Phoebe, he realized he didn't have a clue as to what was going on in her sexy head right now. But he damn sure intended to find out.

He shouldered the door open, then stepped onto the walled patio, dark except for the moonlight filtering through palms and the swath of light from the French door, still ajar. Phoebe had abandoned her circular laps and floated on her back, her braids spread on the water around her.

"Go away," she ordered without opening her eyes.

"No." He put the champagne bucket and glasses on the tile and slipped into the pool. "We're going to talk."

"I don't want to talk."

"Too bad. I can sit here all night if that's what it takes." What? Did she think she was the only one involved here? The last time he'd checked, he was the other half of the equation. He uncorked the bottle and poured two glasses.

"You are so obstinate."

"Yep. Now there's a nice glass of Cordon Negro waiting on you over here whenever you decide you're ready."

Phoebe crossed the pool, shooting him a mutinous look. She reached for her champagne. "So, talk."

"Why are you angry with me?"

"I'm not."

"Then why'd you yell?"

"You yelled back." She took another sip.

"Phoebe, this isn't getting us anywhere."

"Okay. I yelled because I'm so frustrated I could scream. And yelling seemed a marginally better choice than screaming."

"Frustrated? But I thought…you seemed to enjoy it."

"That's the problem. I did enjoy it."

"Okay." She was pissed because the sex had been too good. That was a first. Actually, it hadn't been just good—it had been incredible. Stupendous. Just thinking about it, he began to thicken, harden.

She upended her champagne glass and held it out for a refill. She rested her head against the side of the pool and looked at the half-moon, a woeful expression on her face. "You know, if it had been lousy, it would've been embarrassing, but we could've just written it off to bad chemistry. Mediocre chemistry." She paused long enough to swig her champagne. "But no. It's spectacular. The best sex of my life, and it has to be with you."

"You wanted to have bad sex?" On a good day, the workings of the female mind were convoluted and somewhat mysterious, which often made it very interesting to have a best friend who was a woman. Except half the time, Phoebe thought like a guy. At least he thought she did. Guys never hoped for bad sex—it just happened sometimes. Nonetheless, he struggled to grasp her point. "So, you're mad because the sex was so good with us?"

"The plan was to sleep together so we could get past it. But it only made it worse than ever. How can I ever be around you without remembering how good it was? Not any time in the foreseeable future, I can assure you." She turned her back to him, propping her crossed arms and chin on the side of the pool.

Moonlight danced across the curves of her back, leaving hollows and indentions he longed to explore. His pulse hammered an acknowledgment. "I know what you mean."

She glanced over her shoulder. "You do?"

Her taste. Her scent. The feel of her clenching around him while he was buried deep inside her. Making love with her had only whetted his appetite.

"I definitely won't forget what it was like with you anytime soon, either."

PHOEBE LOOKED AWAY, a new plan forming in her mind, one born of desperation, an out-of-control sex drive, moonlight and two, maybe three glasses of Cordon Negro. There, she'd blamed just about every factor she could. "You know it couldn't possibly be that good between us again."

She didn't have to turn her head to know he was behind her. She felt his nearness in the shiver that chased down her spine. "It doesn't seem likely, does it?" he responded.

Her heart thundered as she gave voice to her madness. "Probably just a fluke. If we had the courage to try it again, it'd probably be terrible. A real disappointment."

Ryan wrapped his arms around her bare midriff, pulling her against him. Like a match to tinder, heat raced through her. "I'm willing to give it a second try if you are."

His mouth, warm and wet, nuzzled her shoulder and the sensitive skin on the side of her neck. All she could think about was the feel of his mouth on her and the ache to have him inside her once again. She dropped her head to his shoulder, allowing him more thorough access.

"Do you want me to touch you?" His voice, low and rough, raked across her nerve endings. The rigid, thick line of his erection nudged its way between her buttocks. Instinctively she wiggled closer. "Tell me, Phoebe. Let me hear it."

"Yes. Yes. Please." Her voice was ragged with need.

He reached up and slid his hands beneath her bikini top. She clasped his forearms, urging him on. He cupped her breasts in his hands, massaging the undersides, weighing their fullness. She arched against him, desperate for his touch, for the release from the sweet torment plaguing her. Finally, he reached up and touched her nipples. Her entire body convulsed as he alternated smoothing, plucking and rolling her turgid points between his fingertips. She moaned into the night and ground her buttocks against him.

The scents of champagne and Ryan enveloped her as he nibbled at the lobe of her ear. The scrape of his jaw against her neck sent chills skittering across her skin. It was arousing beyond anything she'd ever imagined, the sensation of cool water and chills on the outside while a white-hot heat licked at her inside.

"It's going to be good, again, isn't it?" Anticipation and dread heightened her excitement.

"It feels like it, baby." His heartbeat hammered against her back, his breath harsh in her ear.

She was already wound so tight and ready for him she teetered on the verge of disintegrating. She whispered over her shoulder, low and urgent. "Now, Ryan. I want you now. Like this."

She snatched at her bikini top and skimmed off her bottoms, leaning forward to drag them off.

Ryan groaned as she bent in the water in front of him. "Like this?"

She looked over her shoulder as she pulled her bottoms off one foot. "Yes. Like this."

Moonlight illuminated his face. Desire etched his features and corded his muscles. He devoured her with his eyes while he took off his swimming trunks. Aching for him to fill her, she turned her back to him and grasped the edge of the pool.

His big hands wrapped around her hips. Eager. Urgent. She pushed back against his erection, spreading her legs. With one decisive thrust he filled her. Sweet. Brimming.

His thrusts rendered languid by the water, it was like making love in slow motion. She quivered, gloriously tuned in to each nuance, the weight of her braids against her neck, Ryan's hands gripping her hips, the thick length of him deep within her, the hard wall of his thighs behind her. Ryan laid claim to her with the phrases of a lover. She answered him, whispered snatches of broken words floating in the night air.

Tiny tremors radiated from her core, building in intensity with each plunge. Just as before, there was no holding back. A maelstrom of emotion built inside her along with the physical sensations.

A low keening unfurled from within and rose from her throat as Ryan shuddered within her, matching and urging on the tremors that racked her as they fused and became one.

Ryan sank onto the built-in seat, pulling her down on his lap, his arms wrapped around her. Exhausted and precariously close to incoherent, she settled there, her cheek finding comfort in the solid plane of his chest.

They sat for what could have been hours, minutes, seconds, a lifetime. The cool water soothed them until their breathing slowed and their heartbeats calmed to something close to normal. Phoebe tasted wet salt and realized it was the brine of her tears trickling down her face. She sniffed, desperately trying to suck them up.

Ryan pulled her closer, pressing a kiss to the top of her head.

"Phoebe, honey, why are you crying?" His palm moved against her back in soothing small circles. "Please don't cry, baby. It's going to be okay."

She snuffled against the warm satin of his skin, her tears mingling with the droplets of water caught in his chest hair. She swiped at her eyes and leaned against his shoulder. She couldn't speak past the knot of tears lodged in her throat.

"It'll be all right."

Moonlight gilded his hair to a molten gold. His face reflected an intense tenderness. God, he was so dear to her. He'd been such an important part of her life. Panic clutched at her. What if this destroyed them?

"But what if it's not? What if things are never okay with us again?"

Ryan's mouth found hers. His lips offered comfort and reassurance and she readily took what he offered, his kiss calming her panic. As he started to pull away, his lips lingered a second too long, and Phoebe sensed the shadow of lurking desire.

She pulled away, resting her back against his arm. "Rank the first time tonight on a scale of one to ten."

"I don't think we should do that, Phoebe. It really goes against the grain." He idly toyed with one of her braids, rolling it between his fingers.

"Well, pretend it wasn't me. I mean, not the me you made love to, but the me that's your friend."

Ryan's brows met in a dubious frown.

"Say I was some strange woman you picked up on the beach and had sex with."

"This might be easier to do if you weren't sitting on my lap while we're both naked. You know if you're going to be sitting there and we're talking about this…" He stirred against her hip.

Oh, my God. "Twice in one night? You can't—" She stumbled to a halt.

"Well, hell, Phoebe, you don't have to make me sound like a freak. It seems to have a mind of its own, and you have that effect on it."

Hovering somewhere between gratification and

mortification, Phoebe moved to the opposite corner. As far away from Ryan as possible.

"Okay. I met this gorgeous stranger on the beach and had some of the best sex of my life." Only *some* of the best sex? Phoebe tried not to scowl. That should be good news. Ryan changed the subject. "Do you do this with other men? Rank the performance—cause I've got to tell you, it's a bad idea."

Ryan paused, then said, "Okay. On a scale of one to ten? I'd give it a twelve."

"Of course I don't do this with other men. But this is you. Twelve? Okay. I'd go with a twelve myself. What about just now? A few minutes ago?" Just thinking about a few minutes ago left her hot and needy.

"You're not going to want to hear this." Latent arousal threaded his voice.

"Probably not." She steeled herself. "Go ahead."

Ryan drew a deep breath and huffed it out. "The best sex of my life. At least a thirteen and a half."

"Damnation." They were sunk. Goners.

"I know. What about you?"

"I'd give it a solid fourteen, myself." She rested her arms along the back of the pool and leaned her head against the smooth inlaid pebbles, looking to the star-sprinkled sky for inspiration, determined not to panic over jeopardizing the most important relationship in her life. "We've got to come up with a plan. Plans A and B have been disasters. Any ideas?"

Except for the distant revelry of partygoers, the

faint crash of waves breaking on the shore and the steady flow of water circulating in the mini waterfall, the night was quiet. Although the sky was beautiful, radiant with stars, it didn't offer any fast solution. Neither did Ryan, for that matter. He better not have fallen asleep.

"Ryan?" She lifted her head.

He wasn't asleep. Phoebe realized she'd scooted up, leaving her breasts half out of the water, her nipples barely covered. The lover in her wanted to slide up and revel in the caressing heat of his gaze. The friend in her wanted to sink lower. She sat stock-still, incapable of either.

"Ryan…" She paused and cleared her throat. That low husky voice that resonated like a lover's plea wouldn't do at all. "Ryan…" Yes, that was much better, stronger, firmer. "We need a plan."

"A plan? Can't we just see what happens?"

"I can't do that. You know I can't." She drank in the sight of him across the moonlight-dappled water, her heart contracting.

"Then we'll come up with a plan," her friend promised.

CHAPTER EIGHT

SWEATING FROM AN EARLY-MORNING run, Phoebe slipped the room card into the door. The empty beach and fresh morning sky, coupled with a long run, had given her a new perspective. Things had been crazy. Both of them had been caught up in the sensual magic of the island. But today was a new day. She'd take a nice hot shower and then she and her best friend would have breakfast and come up with a new plan. Today things would be back to normal with Ryan.

She felt upbeat, resolute. Until she walked in the door and Ryan walked out of the bathroom, wearing nothing but sexy, low-slung pajama bottoms and a smile, a towel thrown around his neck.

"How was your run?" He brushed his hand through his hair, his stomach muscles rippling with the movement. A general flutter started low in her belly, dangerously close to shooting her resolve to hell.

"Good. I'm sweaty so I'm just going to hop in the shower." She would ignore this breathless longing and treat him like a friend. She brushed past him, but he followed her into the sumptuous bathroom.

"I said I was going to take a shower," she reminded him.

"I was just about to shave. Do you mind if I shave while you shower?" There was a challenge there, to see if they could get back to a nonsexual footing.

The sane, rational side of her protested that it was a very bad idea. The competitive side of her challenged her to put her money where her mouth was and treat him like a friend.

"That shouldn't be a problem. Just let me get in first." She could do this. She walked over and turned on the water to let it heat up.

She unlaced her running shoes and took them off. It was far more productive than ogling his bare chest. Except it put her at eye level with his naked belly and pajama-clad groin. She straightened abruptly, biting back a sigh.

Phoebe peeled off her socks, careful not to bend down this time.

She tried to ignore the frisson of desire that clutched at her. "Turn around so I can undress."

The air thickened with wet, hot steam, stirred by a provocative awareness that threatened all her clear-headed resolutions.

Ryan turned. His back offered a study in symmetry and grace. The thin cotton of his pajamas outlined his tight butt.

Phoebe stripped, ran to the shower and stepped beneath the stinging spray.

"Are you in?"

"Yes."

"How's the water?"

"Fine."

Phoebe desperately tried to recall some gross, disgusting fact about Ryan to offset her general state of extreme arousal. Unfortunately, nothing came to mind except how very erotic it was, talking to Ryan's bare back while warm water sluiced over her shoulders and streamed down her back, the curve of her buttocks, the length of her legs. Was she destined to spend this entire trip wet, in some fashion or another, and naked or nearly thereabouts?

The best course of action, at this point, was to get the shower over. A quick wash and she'd be done. She looked around for the soap. Great. She was in the shower. The soap was on the sink, next to Ryan. "Would you hand me the soap? Please?"

"Do you need anything else?" His suggestion, low and husky, unleashed all the memories of last night's lovemaking.

"Just the soap."

He handed it around the glass door, taking care not to look. Her fingers brushed his as she took it from him, the simple contact arrowing through her, tightening her nipples to hard points.

"Thanks."

Frustration, exasperation and more than a little confusion welled inside her. She felt the foundation of their friendship shifting before her very eyes, undermined by the attraction throbbing between them. Even now, in the silence that stretched between them, though they were separated by the glass of the shower stall, a thread of sexual tension connected them as surely as if it were woven into the fabric of her being.

Craving sensitized her skin. She sucked in a breath as she dragged the washcloth across her shoulders. Tension coiled inside her. Tight, hot, wet tension.

"Phoebe, this isn't working."

"It's not?"

"No. You in there, naked and wet. Me out here."

How did he know she was wet? Oh, yeah. The shower. "But…"

Ryan pivoted in slow motion. Phoebe stopped in midsentence. Longing etched his face. Through the shower glass, his eyes devoured her. "I want you so badly, I hurt."

The pounding of her heart sounded in her head with the pounding of the water. God, she was swimming upstream, fighting the current of sexual need that threatened to sweep her away. And quite frankly, she didn't know if she could find her way back to where she'd begun. Right now, she was in desperate danger of drowning.

She opened the shower door tugged him in, tired of fighting the current, latching on to him as if he alone could save her. Ryan stepped inside, pajama bottoms and all, his mouth latching onto hers, driving her through the spray until her back and buttocks pressed against the marble wall. She surged into him, desperate to be close to him.

"Oh, Phoebe," he moaned against her mouth, as if he shared her desperation. He captured her wrists in his left hand and raised them over her head, holding them against the wall, pinning her there. It was an erotically vulnerable position that demanded a level of trust. Water cascaded around them, between them, spraying her face, stinging her eyes. He picked up the bar of soap and massaged it in one hand until creamy, white foam dripped from his fingers. The bar dropped to the shower floor with a dull thunk.

Phoebe's breath came in short, hard pants. Anticipation of his touch bowed her body. With exquisite care, he smoothed his soap-slicked fingers down her neck, along her collarbone. Instead of satisfying, his touch fed the hunger that gripped her.

He stroked the hollow of her armpit and she trembled. Her armpit? Good God, she was in serious trouble if he could make her armpit feel good. And he did.

His clever, nimble fingers smoothed down to the fleshy outside of her breast. He lathered the soft underside, his fingers rubbing the crease where gravity had taken its toll. Her nipples tightened and puckered eagerly against the spray, awaiting his touch. His palm smoothed her peak, his touch echoing through her body.

Phoebe closed her eyes and dropped her head against the marble, giving herself over to the sensations drenching her. He mirrored his ministrations on her right side then moved lower, soaping the indentation of her waist, the expanse of her stomach.

"You have the sexiest belly." His finger rimmed and dipped into her navel while he held her wrists captive above her head with his other hand.

It should've been a position of enslavement. It was a position of power, evident in the tremble of his hand, the hoarse note in his voice, the intense heat in his eyes.

He slid his hand to the rounded line of her hips. Instinctively, she shifted her feet wider apart, opening herself to him. Ryan stroked her inner thighs, the back of his fingers brushing against her curls. She couldn't still the moan that floated out into the steam and warm spray. If he'd just move his hand...

"Turn around and let me get your back."

She opened her eyes. He was killing her, touch by touch. "But..."

"All in due time. Be patient. Do you trust me?"

"Yes. I trust you."

"Are your arms tired?"

"No." At any time she could have dropped them if she wanted to. They both knew that. "I like it."

"So do I. Now turn around."

She turned, pressing her cheek and the length of her soaped torso against the wall. She bit her lip as her aroused body pressed against the unyielding marble. Steamy. Slick. Slippery. Wet. Hard.

He massaged and stroked the line of her back, the tight, tense muscles of her shoulders. Each touch, soothing and gentle, coiled the spring inside her tighter still.

She ground against the slick marble when he rotated his thumb down the line of her spine. He cupped and kneaded her too-plump cheeks. His obvious pleasure in her body quieted any lingering self-consciousness. There was no room in this place, with the two of them, for that. Aching for the touch he deliberately withheld, she brought her bottom closer to his hand, bracing her feet farther apart. His fingers intimately delved the margin of her buttocks, pushing her past the point of reason.

She clutched at the marble, sobbing against the wall. Finally, he reached between her legs, separating her folds with two fingers. One stroke. Feather light. His slippery finger against her slick moisture. She shuddered. Her entire body convulsed at the one touch. But it wasn't enough.

He released her wrists. "Stay where you are."

She waited for what was only seconds but could have been hours, racked against the wall with anticipation. He knelt behind her, squeezing her buttocks, separating her.

"I want to taste you, Phoebe." And then his tongue stroked the same path his finger had earlier.

Falling. Soaring. Drowning. Swimming.

"Delicious."

"Ryan…please…don't…stop," she cried against the wall.

His mouth plied her intimately. Lips. Tongue. Stroking. Nibbling. Suckling. Thrusting.

Appeasement of her flesh. Succor to her soul. Relentless pleasure flooded her. Gripped her. Shook her. Seared her.

She slid down the wall, his strong arms banding around her, supporting her.

"That's it, baby. I've got you. Just relax."

Like a marionette without a master, she folded to the shower floor between his legs, spent. Ryan shifted from kneeling to sitting, his back against the other wall, and tugged Phoebe's limp form between his thighs. Warm water surrounded them like a tropical downpour. With his arms wrapped around her from behind, Ryan pulled her against the solid wall of his chest. His hands cupped her breasts, lifting them, the water sluicing away any remnants of soap, the deluge pelting her sensitized nipples. Through the thin soaked cotton of his pajama bottoms, his erection pressed against her.

She leaned back, her head nestled against his shoulder. Content to languish in the warm water, the satisfaction and his solid strength.

"You're incredible, Phoebe. So hot. So sexy. So sweet." She turned her head and Ryan's mouth—warm, wet, musky—moved over hers. Something deep inside her stirred, something beyond physical, although there was that, too.

Maybe she was a deviant. She must be. Because the better the sex, the more she wanted it. The more satisfying, the more short-lived the satisfaction. She'd just experienced one of the most satisfying orgasms of her life, and now she felt the tingle of desire awakening yet again. She knew she couldn't keep falling into these situations with Ryan. But she wanted to give him the same bone-melting, mind-numbing, soul-shattering pleasure he'd given her.

She reached between them and touched him through his sodden pajamas. "I think you could benefit from a little shower therapy."

"Sounds interesting." His eyes glittered as he moved against her hand.

"I think you'll be very pleased." She sat forward and twisted out of his arms, kneeling, the water hitting her back, spray bouncing off her shoulders. "But to realize the full benefit, you need to let me help you out of your pajamas."

Ryan started to stand. Phoebe pushed him back down. "Stay where you are. Just lift your hips."

She rolled the wet cloth over his hips, his hard-on snagging the cloth like a tent pole. Phoebe laughed. Ryan grimaced, laughing as well. "Go ahead. You know what happens when a beautiful woman laughs at a naked man?"

Phoebe laughed again. She dipped her hand beneath the waist of his pajamas and skimmed up the velvet-smooth, rigid length of him. Her breath caught in her throat and her pulse raced as she freed him from the cloth, her smirk fading. "Now you're truly naked. And I assure you—" her finger traced the length of him "—I'm not laughing."

His eyes darkened with arousal. "Neither am I."

She tugged his pyjama down the muscular length of his legs and shoved them into a corner. Turning to the matter at hand, she snagged the soap and worked up a rich lather.

Phoebe straddled his thigh and ran her hands over his shoulders. Hard muscles flexed beneath fine-textured skin. "Touching you is such a pleasure."

"Honey, feel free to pleasure yourself for as long as you like."

Phoebe knew from the odd occasion she'd treated herself to a manicure how good a quick forearm and hand massage felt. She stroked and kneaded his upper arm, his forearm and finally his hand.

"Damn, that feels good. You've got magic hands, Phoebe. I never knew you could do this." Steam swirled around them. Droplets caught in the water-darkened sweep of his lashes.

"Then I guess I'm doing it right." She smiled at his blissful expression.

"Yeah. I guess you are."

"There are a whole lot of things I know how to do well that you don't know about."

"Now *that's* something to look forward to."

Feeling more sure of herself, she moved to the other arm and then up to his chest.

Leaning forward, he captured her nipple in his mouth and sucked. Hard. She clung to his shoulders and drew a sharp breath as the sensation arrowed straight to her womb. Still holding her in his mouth, he ravished the distended point. "Yes…" she breathed into the swirling steam.

He released her and he dropped his head back. "And that is one of the pleasures of having a naked woman bathe you."

She angled her other pouting crest close to his mouth. "And here's the second one."

Obligingly, he drew her nipple deep into his mouth, tugging, his teeth scraping lightly against her tip, the sensation reminiscent of his mouth on her earlier. Oh, God. She closed her eyes. Her low moan bounced off the shower walls.

Ryan released her and she slowly opened her eyes, drawing back. She ran her slick fingers over his flat male nipples. "I think you'll find the benefits get better and better."

"I hope I live that long 'cause baby, you are killing me."

She palmed the flat plane of his belly with small,

concentric circles. Sweeping wide, she delicately massaged the flesh flanking his groin. The closer her hands came to his straining hard-on without touching it, the sharper and shorter his breath was. His excitement fed hers, and she quivered along with him when her hands rubbed the clenched muscles of his inner thigh.

She slid out of the range of the spraying water and allowed it to rinse him. She watched him through the torrent. "You'd like for me to touch you, wouldn't you?"

He couldn't want it any more than she did. He breathed harder still, his erection pulsing at her throaty suggestion. "Yes. I would like that very much." His voice echoed with raw need.

Until that moment, Phoebe had planned to touch him. He had taken her to the other side of paradise. She wanted to please him to that same extent.

Phoebe approached him on hands and knees. Water pounded the back of her head, her shoulders. She delicately stroked him from tip to base and cupped him. He closed his eyes and clenched his teeth. "Oh, Phoebe. Oh, baby."

Leaning forward, she probed his tip with her tongue, thoroughly aroused, as wet as he was hard.

His eyes flew open.

"I like touching you, Ryan. But what I really want to do is taste you." She licked up the length of him, pausing at the top. "As long as you know we're not playing basketball and there's no slam-dunking."

She poised, ready to take the length of him in her mouth.

Ryan braced his hands on the shower floor, a hot, sexy smile on his facc. "I don't even like basketball."

CHAPTER NINE

"THE BEACH IS CROWDED," Ryan observed from the table they'd dined at the previous morning. Had it only been twenty-four hours? So much had changed between them, it could have been a lifetime.

Martin poured cups of steaming coffee, and once again they shared an assortment of fruits and a pastry. Ryan watched the snorkeling boat pull away in the distance. Making love to Phoebe had been like snorkeling. It had revealed a whole new facet of her, full of beauty and mystique to discover and share. He was unabashedly enchanted.

She speared a mango chunk. "I can't think about the beach. We've got to come up with a plan."

Thank goodness she'd abandoned the denial plan she'd walked through the door with this morning.

She bit into the ripe fruit. Juice trickled down her chin.

Ryan leaned in and caught the juice with his finger. The texture of her skin against his fingertip was fine and silky. "Ryan…"

Heat shimmered and danced between them, through them, provoked by memories of the morning.

The shower. The steam. Her hands. Her mouth. Release. Pleasure.

"I know." Hell, yes, he knew.

Ryan drank his coffee, savoring the smooth, rich flavor.

Focus. He needed to focus. And not on her sexy, full mouth. He'd promised to help her come up with a plan and he would. When he could think clearly.

"How did this happen to us?" She'd asked it before, but it still confounded her.

Ryan didn't answer immediately.

He glanced up soberly. He hated the distress in her voice. Unlike him, Phoebe required to know *why* before she could accept any situation. "I don't know, Phoebes. Maybe it's this place. The sun is brighter, the sand whiter, the water clearer, the food spicier. Everything is more intense."

"You're more intense," she noted.

Ryan knew it. Felt it. Lovemaking with Phoebe had shifted something inside him. He'd found more than physical release with her. She was frightened by the changes between them. Things had changed so quickly, so completely. Her insistence on a plan clearly reflected her need to clutch at something familiar in the midst of all the changes.

He sliced a section of *pain au chocolat* and pushed the plate to her. If he didn't push her to enjoy at least a mouthful, she'd want it but never touch it.

She bit into the flaky pastry. "Maybe you're right.

It must be Jamaica." She paused in sublime appreciation. "This is sinfully good. It's so rich I only want a few bites." She paused and snapped her fingers. Relief and excitement chased the desperation off her face. "I've got it. I've got the plan. This thing with us, it's like starting a diet."

"I'm not following you." He supposed it was the creativity that made her so successful at her job, but sometimes her convoluted thought processes confounded him.

"You start a diet. The last thing you need is a chocolate-covered doughnut. But the thing you want more than anything is a chocolate-covered doughnut." She waved her hands for emphasis. "You don't even have to close your eyes and you can taste it. Five seconds in the microwave and it's hot and gooey sweet and the chocolate all but melts against your tongue." Her voice slowed, taking on a hoarse quality.

Ryan's body stirred in response. Her words and her slow, husky drawl had sent him to the edge. He didn't have to close his eyes to recall her hot sweetness melting against his tongue.

"Baby, I hope you get to the point pretty damn quick, cause you've already got me to one."

She drew a deep breath. The look in her eyes told him she was remembering the same thing he was. "Stay with me and I'll explain. You have one chocolate-covered doughnut and it's so good, that's all you can think about. How good it was and how you absolutely shouldn't have another one."

"But you want another one." Just like their first time.

"Exactly. Like every time we make love."

Just hearing her talk about their lovemaking aroused him. He'd never wanted a woman so fiercely, so completely before.

"So, what's the solution?"

"Before you start a diet, you buy a dozen doughnuts and you eat them all. The first one's great, the second one's still yummy. The third one is pretty darn good. But the fourth one is just okay. By the time you're up to the tenth one, you either don't want another one or they've gotten stale. See what I mean?"

"You frighten me when you use female logic." However, having unlimited sex beat the hell out of her previous denial plan.

Her provocative smile knocked him for a loop. "Good. You frighten me when you act like the superior male."

He reached for her hand, twining his fingers through hers. Her fingers, like her gorgeous legs, were long and slender. And when they wrapped around him... "Let me make sure I understand. You're suggesting we gorge ourselves on sex with each other?"

"Exactly. Between now and when we leave." Her fingers tightened around his. Her lips parted.

"I think it's a damn shame we're in a public place.

Otherwise, I'd show you just how much I like your plan by implementing it immediately." He pressed his lips against the delicate blue vein on the back of her slender hand.

"I'm glad you like it." Her breath quickened.

"I don't usually go in for obsessive-compulsive behavior, but for sex with you I'll make an exception. However, I do have one question."

He nuzzled the fine bones of her wrist, her pulse beating like a wild bird against his mouth.

"Hmm?"

Doughnut theory or not, he couldn't imagine a time when he wouldn't want her again. He knew for damn sure that four more days of intimacy with her wouldn't begin to be enough. He didn't think Phoebe was ready to hear that. She had to move one step at a time.

"Why are you so intent on burning this out with us, Phoebe? Why does this have to end when we leave? Why can't we just see where it goes?"

She toyed with a piece of fruit. "Because this needs to end while we're still friends." She looked at him. "Because we both know this won't last."

"How do you—"

"Because the longest you ever dated one person was four weeks." The specter of his past, all the casual, short-lived relationships, stared at him from the depths of her eyes. "At least this way, neither one of us is sitting around waiting for the shoe to drop."

Her voice wavered. "Because our friendship means everything to me."

"But we can…"

She reached over and quieted him with her finger against his lips. "No. Don't say it. Don't even go there. I won't forsake our friendship for a fleeting physical relationship. And joining the Ryan Palmer harem isn't an option."

A lesser man might have been offended, he reasoned wryly. But at least he knew where he stood with her.

PHOEBE HUNG THE DO NOT DISTURB sign outside their door then closed the door. Anticipation strummed through her. Their days had taken on a pattern. A delicious, addictive, hedonistic pattern. Making love in the morning. A midmorning excursion or water sport. Back to the privacy of their room for a siesta. Perhaps an afternoon activity. Dinner. And then the long tropical nights.

In the last three days they'd windsurfed, snorkeled, visited Prospect Plantation with its breathtaking views of the White River Gorge, and just this morning climbed the six hundred feet of Dunn's River Falls' slippery stone steps through its cascading cold mountain water.

She'd lost track of the number of times they'd made love and where—sometimes playful, sometimes serious, always intensely satisfying. Their room, the private patio with its pool, a darkened corner of the garden behind the Jungle Room, a secluded section of the beach at twilight with the warm water lapping over them—their escapades were barely decent and still she couldn't get enough of him. She was no closer to being sated than when she started. One more day until they left. And she planned to make the most of every minute. Tomorrow she would think about… well, tomorrow.

Ryan crossed the room, a decidedly lecherous, lascivious light in his eyes. He slid his broad hands beneath the edge of her dress and cupped her bikini-clad bottom.

She leaned into him, enjoying the feel of her breasts pressing against his chest. "Do you want to go shopping in the market this afternoon?" she asked.

"We could do that." He wrapped his leg around hers, bringing her intimately against his burgeoning erection. "Much, much later."

"I want to look for…" She trailed off, thoroughly distracted as he stroked the underside of her leg. She shuddered as his knuckles brushed the crotch of her bikini. The now-familiar hunger wound through her, tightening her nipples, aching between her thighs.

His sexy laugh reverberated against her skin as he nibbled at the base of her neck. He knew he destroyed her reason. Just as she did his. It was a heady, frightening knowledge. And she'd think about it when they returned to the cold, gray days in Nashville.

She pulled away from his mouth, realizing a fine sheen of perspiration coated her from the midday heat. Unfortunately, she'd never managed to glisten daintily. "I'm sweaty."

"I like it." He kissed a spot below her ear. "It turns me on." Phoebe's laugh trailed into a sigh as his mouth marauded her neck. His fingers bit into the back of her thigh as he drew her closer. "*You* turn me on. So, sue me."

"I've got a much better idea. What I would like is to—" she paused, allowing him to fill in the blank before she twisted out of his arms "—race you to the pool."

Surprise afforded her a head start. She sprinted toward the patio doors.

"You'll pay for that, you little tease," Ryan yelled behind her as he gave chase.

She tore off her cover-up and slipped into the pool, the water cool against her heated skin.

"I won." She crowed as he followed her in.

"The game's not over," he taunted. "Why don't you come here? Unless you're afraid?"

Lazily, she twisted over and dove beneath the surface. Surreal. Distorted. She glided up the muscular columns of his legs, skimmed the apex of his thighs and the flat expanse of his belly, breaking the surface to stand in the circle of his arms.

Silently, of one accord, their lips met. Clinging. Tender. Exploring. The hunger was still there. But it was a slow simmer as opposed to the searing heat of the morning.

She absorbed the texture of his sun-warmed skin through her fingertips, inhaling the scent particular to him. Forever the faint aroma of chlorine on a hot day would remind her of this moment.

He led her out of the pool and up the steps to their room, leaving the French doors ajar.

"I should pay you back for earlier, but I just want to be close to you. Nothing between us." Standing in the slant of sunlight, he undressed them both, leaving the wet suits to puddle on the tile floor.

The sun backlit his broad shoulders, the narrowed line of his waist, the muscular length of his legs. Phoebe trembled with the pulsing need. Whatever tomorrow might bring, for now, for today, he was hers. She wrapped her hands around his neck and drew his mouth down, pulling him onto the bed, taking his weight against her. She explored the warmth of his mouth with her tongue, memorizing his taste. She stroked the smooth, muscular line of his shoulder, imprinting the feel of him.

Ryan lifted his mouth from hers, his eyes solemn, intense, tender. He rolled onto his back, pulling her on top of him. "If I could, I would crawl inside your skin to be closer to you. Does that frighten you?" He splayed his hands against her naked back, pulling her into his chest, flattening her breasts against his hair-sprinkled plane. "It does me."

"A bit. But only because I know how you feel." His heart pounded against hers, the two rhythms blending into one.

Time assumed a new dimension. Rather than minutes and hours, time was measured in the length of a gaze between lovers, the whisper of his lips against her eyelids, the slant of sun across the back of her knees, the low murmur of his voice against her neck.

This was a symphony of lovemaking, a crescendo of flesh and spirit.

Afterward, Phoebe absently watched the shadows of a palm tree float and sway on the ceiling. That's how she felt. Weightless. Complete. Replete.

The even, measured cadence of Ryan's breathing told her he'd drifted off to sleep. She pressed her lips to the strong arm pillowing her head.

Like the lengthening shadows creeping across the ceiling, realization stole through her.

She had fallen in love with Ryan.

She had loved him for a long time. Maybe for as long as she'd known him. She had always loved him. That love had brought joy and comfort and depth to her life, and she trusted it had offered Ryan the same.

He'd been a constant. All the holidays and birthdays and school functions when her parents had promised to visit or pick her up and hadn't bothered to show or call, only to offer a lame excuse at a later date if they offered an excuse at all, Ryan had been there.

And he'd done whatever it took to pull her through her parents' most recent abandonment, whether it was listen, distract, curse or amuse.

But now she had fallen in love with him. An ache blossomed in her heart. Piercing. Painful. She closed her eyes, willing away the realization. But closing her eyes didn't change anything.

She was in the worst possible place a woman could be—in love with Ryan Palmer.

STALLS LINED THE NARROW STREET. A cacophony of sounds filled the air. Some vendors hawked their wares from stalls, some from blankets spread on the ground. All haggled good-naturedly with potential buyers to the accompaniment of the ever-present rhythm of steel drums, punctuated by a chicken's occasional squawk.

Dodging a pothole, Ryan pressed closer to Phoebe's side. "Is there any chance you and Elliott will get back together once we return to Nashville?" Ryan didn't add, *once we're through*. He didn't have to. It stared both of them in the face.

Phoebe stopped in the middle of the market. Her expression plainly said she thought he'd been out in the heat too long. "Have you lost your mind?"

It was a distinct possibility. He knew it was because they were returning home tomorrow. The idea of seeing her with another man had tormented him all afternoon. And he knew it was because Elliott was the only name that came to mind. But there were plenty of other men who'd be willing to participate in her plan.

"You're sure?" He craved her reassurance.

"Why are you asking about Elliott? Are you thinking of seeing Kiki again?" Tension marked the set of her shoulders.

"Hell, no." She visibly relaxed at his emphatic assertion. "I just needed to make sure Elliott was old news. He doesn't deserve you."

"Well, thanks. I suppose."

It was odd to discuss other men with Phoebe while holding her hand, wandering through the market. Hell, it was a strange conversation to have with any woman he was sleeping with. But then again, nothing was normal about the two of them. This ache for her that he carried around constantly wasn't normal.

The idea of another man touching her was intolerable. Even if Ryan got past that, where did this leave their friendship? When Phoebe found a new boyfriend, he might not be so tolerant of Ryan. Especially if he discovered Ryan and Phoebe had indulged in a non-platonic fling. And what happened when she moved forward with her marriage plan—which he knew she fully intended to pursue, with or without Elliott? Where did that leave Ryan?

Strolling through the market, amid street vendors and the throngs of tourists, Ryan had an epiphany. By God, he, Ryan Gerald Palmer, would marry Phoebe.

She wanted a husband. He cared for her. They understood one another. The sex was great. And if he married her, that left no one to object to him.

With a whoop, Ryan caught her in his arms and spun her around. He set her on her feet, then thoroughly kissed her upturned, surprised mouth.

She blinked, laughing at him. "What was that for?"

"Just because." Now was not the time to pop the question. But he couldn't keep from grinning. She'd be so surprised. He wanted the moment to be perfect, just like his idea.

"Hmm." She wrapped her arms around his neck and kissed him, her mouth cool and sweet and faintly redolent of mint. "What are we shopping for?" She pushed her sunglasses down her nose and peered at him over them. Her brown eyes held that slightly dazed expression he'd come to recognize in the last few days. She wanted him.

He cupped his hand around the damp nape of her neck. "Spiced rum for Ted at work, and you wanted a basket and a hat."

"Oh, yeah." Although a slow, sensual smile lifted the corners of her mouth, melancholy shadowed her eyes. She pushed her glasses into place.

"You are breathtaking."

"And you are delusional." Her pleased smile and the faint flush on her cheeks belied her quip. She ran her fingertips along his jaw, sending his heartbeat thundering. "But thank you."

He caught her hand in his. It was there between them again, that quickly. The mercurial, potent head that quickened his blood. Phoebe felt it, as well. The frantic pulse at the base of her neck and the stiffened points of her nipples against the thin cotton of her dress gave her away. "Come on," he said. "Let's find you the perfect straw hat."

"Hey, mister." A street vendor hailed him in a lilting singsong. "Come take a look." She held aloft a handful of coffee bean necklaces. "Come. I sell the finest necklaces in Jamaica. Your woman, she will like this."

His woman. His Phoebe.

And after tonight there'd be no question about it.

CHAPTER TEN

"YOU'RE SURE YOU DON'T WANT to get in the whirl-pool before dinner? It's very good for tension." Phoebe slid her top button open.

Ryan waffled, seriously tempted by her long legs, seductive smile and the promise of pulsating jets of warm water. But he wanted tonight to be absolutely perfect for them, and that meant a little planning and preparation she couldn't know about.

"I'll take a rain check. Maybe you can hold that thought until later this evening." He quickly closed the door on temptation before he lost sight of his plans and crawled in there with her.

He pulled on his pants and willed away the arousal brought on by Phoebe's proposition. He had a couple of things to take care of before tonight. Hell, it wasn't every night that a man proposed.

He let himself out of the room and checked his watch. The first thing on his agenda was to find Martin and enlist his help.

He made his way to the restaurant and sidestepped the placard deeming the restaurant closed. Martin stood folding napkins with two young men at the wait station. He looked up and spotted Ryan.

Martin crossed the room, a welcoming smile lighting his face. "How are you today? Tomorrow is your last day? I trust you have enjoyed your holiday in Jamaica."

"Jamaica's great. I love it. In fact, we'll be coming back on our honeymoon." Ryan didn't care that there was no dignity in the goofy grin on his face.

It must've been catching because Martin got a big goofy grin, as well. "Congratulations. That is most excellent. And might I offer salutations to your lucky bride-to-be, as well?"

"That's why I'm here. She doesn't know yet. Well, she probably suspects since she wants a husband. But maybe she was just trying to get my attention in the first place. And it worked." Actually, that didn't quite seem like a Phoebe-esque thing to do. But then he'd discovered other aspects of her personality he'd never considered before. And, as he'd managed to overlook for almost a lifetime, she was a woman. "I never thought when we came here…"

Martin laughed and shrugged. "It happens. Island magic. I sensed the magic between the two of you from the beginning. It was much the same way for me and my Mathilde."

It had been incredible between them. "I want something special tonight. Can you set us up with a waterside table? Maybe a little secluded?"

"I have just the spot."

"Perfect. And I'd like a bottle of Cordon Negro iced and at the table." Not the most expensive brand, but they'd certainly enjoyed it and each other in the pool. He was forgetting something. "Oh, yeah. And a ring. I can't ask her to marry me without a ring."

"Ah, yes. The ring. My cousin Angelique, she works in the gift shop here, off the lobby. She can show you many rings to choose from. There is a local artist who designs unusual jewelry. She also has choices more in keeping with tradition, such as the diamond."

"Definitely local." Perhaps when they returned to Nashville, Phoebe would want to pick out a diamond. But Jamaica was exotic braids, dazzling white sand, swimming pools at midnight and friends who became lovers. "Thanks for all your help, Martin."

"No problem. I am most honored to assist in such a memorable occasion."

Ryan grabbed his hand and pumped it. "I think it'll be a night we never forget."

"WE'RE A LITTLE EARLY for our reservations. Do you want to have a drink in the bar or a quick walk on the beach?" Ryan paused outside the restaurant, breathtakingly handsome in a lightweight summer suit. Not that it had anything to do with the suit. He'd been equally breathtaking stretched out naked on the bed earlier.

"A quick walk. The beach is practically deserted."

She needed the physical activity. She was all keyed up and definitely melancholy at the prospect of leaving tomorrow. It hadn't helped her general state of mind when Ryan turned her down earlier today. It felt like the beginning of the end with them.

They veered to the path leading to the water. Phoebe stopped at the edge of the sand and slipped off her sandals. "No twisted ankles tonight."

Ryan carried his shoes and socks in one hand and slipped his other arm around her waist. Phoebe's toes curled into the sugar-fine sand, her body quickening at his touch. "I don't know. Everything turned out just fine in the end," he assured her.

They crossed the sand, Ryan's hip brushing against hers, his breath stirring the fine hairs at her temple. What woman would share his warmth and know his touch after tomorrow?

They crossed to the water's edge where the damp, packed sand was firm. Warm water swirled over their feet and lapped at their ankles. A low, thrumming urgency filled her as she recalled making love with him in a similar spot only a few evenings ago.

Arms wrapped around one another, they stopped. Phoebe absorbed the beauty and vastness of the sea stretching before them. "Isn't it beautiful? And it's amazing how constant it is. No matter what's happening in the world, this tide continues to ebb and flow."

Ryan rubbed his clean-shaven jaw against her

temple. "It is beautiful. But the only constant is change. Look. No two waves are ever the same. The one that just broke over our feet is different from the one before and the one after. The tides constantly shift."

"I never thought of it that way."

They strolled along the edge of the surf. The resort buildings fronting the shoreline gave way to lush vegetation. A barely discernable order held the rampant tangle of vines and leaves in check.

Phoebe stopped. "The garden's not as controlled here by the water." Something about the place called to her. This was exactly how she felt. Barely contained. On the verge of overrunning herself. Wild. Lush. "Look. Over beyond the trees. There's a bench tucked in there."

"It's a great view of the ocean and very private. Why don't we watch the sunset?"

Phoebe paused at the edge of the sand and slipped into her strappy heels. Ryan brushed aside a branch, and they sat on the bench. The perfume of the tropical garden hung heavy around them, stirred by the ocean breeze. Faint snatches of conversation floated through the air. A fireball sun sank toward the blue-green horizon. The distant rhythm of steel drums seemed to resonate through the air, announcing their last night together.

How could she appreciate the view when she couldn't think past the press of his thigh against hers?

The hot, achy hunger inside her that begged to be fed? They had so little time. Tomorrow they'd return home, and this would all be just a memory.

"Phoebe?" He breathed against her neck, his voice low and caressing, like the wash of the surf against the shore.

"Yes?"

She traced her fingernail against his cloth-covered thigh. His muscle clenched beneath her nail. That was a good sign.

"Remember the other night on the beach?"

"Yes." His thigh beneath her fingernail trembled, and his breath quickened in sync with her own. "I definitely remember." As if she'd ever forget a minute of this time with him. She wanted to make sure he never forgot, either. This was their last night. In all the years to come, she wanted him to remember making love with her as the best experience he ever had. She knew it would be, because no other woman would ever love him as deeply and fully as she did.

She slid her fingers to his inner thigh. "There's something very exciting about making love in a semi-public place. Don't you think so?"

He swelled and hardened against the back of her fingers even before he answered. "It's very… stimulating."

"If I held on to the back of the bench and you stood behind me with your jacket unbuttoned…" Her voice was low and breathless. Her knuckle traced the hard ridge of his erection. They were both on the verge of exploding.

"Stand up," he directed, his voice hoarse with excitement, his eyes bright.

Phoebe stood and walked to the back of the bench, aware of the sway of her hips, the play of her panties against her wetness. Ryan watched. The heat inside her notched up to inferno level.

She planted her feet apart, knowing her three-inch heels showed off her legs. Bracing her forearms on the back of the bench, she leaned over, her spine straight, buttocks out, and murmured in his ear, "I'm ready when you are." She laved the rim of his ear with her tongue. "Unless you've changed your mind."

"Baby, I'm so ready, I'm not sure I can walk."

"I'll be very disappointed if you can't manage to get up. I really wanted to share this view with you." She bit the lobe of his ear.

He hissed in a sharp breath. "Why don't you tell me just how disappointed you'll be," he instructed in a low, urgent tone.

"I'm all achy and hot and I'm afraid that'll just get worse if you can't join me."

Ryan stood and rounded the bench to stand behind her. Phoebe straightened, resting her hands on the back of the bench. The noise of a zipper and Ryan's harsh breathing sounded behind her. Ryan stepped closer, his stiff erection brushing her backside. Phoebe watched the glowing ball dip in the sky. Her body quivered with anticipation. Ryan eased up the back of her dress, tugging her panties to one side, wrapping one arm around her waist.

"Have you ever seen such a beautiful sunset?" he asked, thrusting into her, filling her.

She gasped. "No. It's spectacular."

His hands tightened on her hips. She leaned forward, driving him farther into her. He surged again and again. She tightened around him, embracing him, telling him with her body what she could never say. Phoebe focused on the sunset until the fiery ball exploded in a dazzling array of color and disappeared into the wet depths beyond the horizon.

"That was…" Words defied her. Her legs unsteady, Phoebe tugged her dress into place.

On the beach only a few feet away, a couple strolled into view.

"Barely decent." Ryan finished her sentence as he wrapped his arms around her and nuzzled her neck, sending shivers down her spine. "And absolutely incredible."

MARTIN GREETED THEM at the door. "Right this way. We have a very special seating for you tonight. A most excellent view."

Ryan guided her with his hand on her back. A flashpoint of fire trailed through her.

This was crazy. This feverish desire for Ryan was consuming her. It was rather like having made the mistake of climbing on a ride at the fair. Caught up in the excitement, you get on and strap yourself in. The instant the ride starts, you realize you've made a mistake. But it's scary and thrilling and you don't have any choice except to stay on until the end.

Martin led them to a table overlooking the water, where a few strategically placed potted plants lent a feeling of intimacy and privacy. "And this table will please you?" Both men looked at her.

A candle flickered in the steady breeze that brushed against her bare neck and arms. Silverware gleamed against the white linen cloth draping the table. Beyond the rail, twilight transformed the stretch of ocean to fluid turquoise.

"Yes. This is great."

Martin pulled out her chair with a flourish. "Very good, then."

Phoebe sank onto the cushion, the rattan biting into her shoulder as she shifted against the high back. Ryan sat in the chair next to her, capturing her hand in his, his fingers twining through hers. Her pulse raced. "Why don't we start with a glass of champagne? Cordon Negro?"

His gaze held hers. Memories stretched between them. Shared intimacies connected them. Phoebe traced her tongue against her lips. "That's fine."

Wasn't she capable of more speech than acquiescence? At this point, she wasn't sure. And what did she have to object to? A spectacular view? Champagne? Ryan offered everything he knew she liked.

As much as she didn't want to think about tomorrow, it kept intruding. They'd need to lay some ground rules for when they went home. She thought it best if they didn't mentioned Jamaica to each other. Let it fade like a dream. Perhaps this was the best time and place.

"Ryan…"

"Phoebe…"

"What? Go ahead." She might as well let him go first.

"We need to talk."

"Okay. What do you want to talk about?"

"I want to talk about us."

Phoebe nearly fell out of her chair. "That's my line." As a rule, men never felt compelled to talk. And Ryan was no exception. He was a man of action.

Ryan ran his hand through his hair. He only ran his hand through his hair when he was nervous. Why was he nervous?

Martin arrived with the champagne, beaming. Ryan smiled tightly at her and tugged at his tie. Definitely nervous.

As she sat through the opening and pouring of the champagne, everything fell into place. The special table. The champagne. His uneasiness. Here it was. The big dump.

Phoebe fought an insane urge to cry. It wasn't

technically a dump because they'd both gone into this with their eyes open. And it was precisely what she wanted to discuss with him. It did, however, hurt a bit that Ryan felt compelled to put on the dog and pony show. For goodness' sake, this was her. Not one of the legion of other women who had come before her and who would follow behind her.

Martin retreated. Sweat beaded in a fine line across Ryan's forehead. "I didn't think this would be so difficult…."

"Oh, for pity's sake, just say it. If you don't, I will." Distress lent a sharp edge to her voice. How hard was it to say that this thing between them needed to end?

Ryan quirked an eyebrow. "I don't think we're talking about the same thing."

"We've been friends for such a long time. I think we know one another almost as well as we know ourselves. I assure you, there's no need to keep hedging around. We're on the same track."

He looked surprised and relieved. Good grief, was he always so uptight about ending a physical relationship?

"Good. So, when do you want to get married?"

"There, that wasn't so hard—" Her mouth stopped moving as she scrambled to assimilate what he'd said instead of what she'd anticipated. She almost laughed. She could've sworn he'd said *married*. Nah. No way had she heard what—well, what she thought she'd heard. "What did you say?"

"Let's get married."

Nothing wrong with her ears. Her life was falling apart but her hearing was fine.

"Married?" Her voice rose several octaves, squawking in the night air. At nearby tables, several diners looked over at them. Phoebe lowered her voice, "Did you say married?"

"Married. Tie the knot. Step up to the plate. Married."

Two weeks ago, he could barely utter the word. Now he was tossing it around the table with abandon. Her stomach roiled in protest. She couldn't have heard him right.

"So, who do you want to marry?"

He laughingly admonished her. "Stop fooling around, Phoebe." His laughter died out, and he peered into her face. "You're not fooling around, are you? You. I want to marry you."

"You and me? To each other?" She wasn't slow on the uptake. It simply didn't make sense. She had obviously misunderstood him somewhere along the line.

"You and me. Us." His expression bordered on smug.

Phoebe contained her rising hysteria. Ryan Palmer had just proposed. My God. A vacation fling was one thing. Long-term commitment was another. And this, coming from Ryan, the king of short-term commitments. "Why?" She barely managed to utter the word. She picked up her glass and gulped the champagne.

"Hey. We're supposed to toast our engagement with that as soon as you say yes." Uncertainty replaced his smugness.

"Sorry. I need a drink now." She drained the glass.

"I thought you'd be excited."

Try appalled. "I'm practically speechless."

"I noticed," he said with more than a note of asperity.

"Why would we want to marry each other?" She tried to keep her tone light, neutral, conversational, as if they were discussing the weather rather than matrimony. But just saying the words made her queasy.

His usual easygoing demeanor gave way to a frown of annoyance. "But you said you wanted to get married."

"Yes. And do you remember the other part? Start a family?"

He waved a hand in the air. "Okay. In a couple of years we'll talk about a kid."

She struggled to make some sense of the incomprehensible—Ryan's proposal and willingness to start a family.

"Why?"

"Damn, Phoebe. Is that all you can say? *Why?* Because you want one."

"You're not making any sense. We can't get married and have kids just because I want to. We're friends." She couldn't allow herself to give in to the temptation of imagining a life with him.

She poured another glass of champagne.

"Now you're the one that's not making any sense. Why can't friends get married?"

God, they were talking in circles, and if they didn't cut to the chase, she was going to make a spectacle of them both by screaming. "Forget about that. I want to know why *we* should get married."

"Think about it. We like one another. We get along great." He lowered his voice and leaned closer. "And the sex is phenomenal."

Even in the middle of a breakdown, he reduced her to hot candle wax with a single touch and a searing glance. Phoebe reveled in the phenomenal sex ranking for just a second before she discounted his reasoning. "You can't marry someone because the sex is good."

"Great."

"Okay. Great. It's still no reason to get married."

"What's going to happen to us, Phoebe? Stop and think about it. Your next boyfriend may not be so tolerant of our friendship, especially after this week. I sure as hell wouldn't. Have you given up your marriage plan?"

"So, you want to get married because my next

boyfriend or possibly my husband will object to our friendship because we've been lovers?"

"Exactly. You're very important to me, Phoebes." Nowhere along the way had he mentioned love or being in love. Up until this point, she'd been somewhat confounded. Now she was simply angry. Of all the high-handed, arrogant maneuvers... "Ah, I see. Protecting your interests?"

"Not exactly. That makes it sound..."

"Selfish? Absurd?"

"I wouldn't put it quite like that."

"Oh, really? How would you put it?"

"Sensible. Reasonable. You're normally so rational—"

"Are you implying that I'm behaving irrationally?" Perhaps a tad tipsy after two glasses of champagne on an empty stomach but certainly not irrational. Nowhere near as irrational as the idea of the two of them marrying one another.

"Don't put words in my mouth."

"I'm not. You're doing a fine job all on your own."

"Dammit, Phoebe, it's a good plan. We understand one another, we care about one another. Why wouldn't it work?"

She'd never been very good in debate club. She detested presenting arguments. Things that made sense to her often lost their impact in the translation. But this was important. She'd try to make him understand.

"Do you have any idea how much you mean to me? Do you know how important our friendship is?" Tears pricked at the back of her eyelids, sprung from the desperation, confusion and frustration welling inside her. She bit her lip. Hard. She would not cry.

"All the more reason to get married."

"All the more reason not to. We'll weather this… this…this fling. We can still come back from this, but a bad marriage would destroy us, and you're too important to me for that." Her bond with Ryan was the only one she'd allowed herself since her parents had abandoned her. She'd often thought how much easier it would've been had they died rather than just dropping her off. Then all hope would've died with them. The thought of losing Ryan was unbearable.

"Why are you assuming we'd have a bad marriage?"

"Marriage is a long-term commitment. You yourself have said how fond you are of changing channels. I won't sit around and wait for you to switch to another channel." Or sit around hoping he'd come back if he did. She didn't exactly inspire those near and dear to stick around.

"That's not fair. This is different. How long have we been friends? Don't you consider that a long-term commitment?"

"Friendship is one thing. Marriage is another."

She didn't want to hurt him, but they'd always been honest with one another and the stakes were high. Even though they sat in the open air, she felt trapped. She couldn't bear to sit at the table another second. "You're the best friend I've ever had. The best friend I'll ever have." She scraped her chair back and stood. "But you're the last man I'd choose for a husband."

CHAPTER ELEVEN

RYAN FOUND HER EASILY ENOUGH, standing alone, silhouetted by the moonlight against the shoreline. He squared his shoulders. She'd sliced through his pride, but he refused to leave things this way between them.

And he really didn't give a damn that she'd left him standing there like a fool. Well, maybe he gave a little bit of a damn, but she couldn't dissuade him that easily.

Sand crept into his shoes as he crossed to where Phoebe stood, her arms wrapped around her middle, looking out over the dark expanse of water. He stood behind her, not touching her. She knew he was there. He felt her acknowledgment of him in the space between them.

She spoke without turning. "I know you're angry. And hurt. I didn't want either one." Emotion thickened her voice. "I didn't expect you to walk down here."

He cupped his hands around her shoulders, her bare skin smooth as silk beneath his palms, and pulled her against him. She held herself stiffly. As if she wouldn't allow herself to lean on him. He stood for a moment, the length of her lightly against him, her braids against his face, absorbing her scent and the emotions that rolled off of her like waves crashing in a storm-tossed sea.

"How could I leave things between us that way? I can't. You mean too much to me."

"God, how did things get to be such a mess between us?" Her voice cracked on the last word, wrenching something deep inside him. The last thing he'd ever wanted was to hurt her.

"It's just different. It's a change. You know you don't handle change well. And this is a biggie. But I'll help you. We'll help each other. Because that's what we do."

He turned her to face him and wrapped his arms around her, drawing her close. He took heart that she allowed him to hold her. Her face was wet against his neck when she leaned into him. He stroked her head with one hand. "Shh. It's okay. It's all going to be fine."

"How?" Her low keen rent the night. "How will things ever be the way they were between us again?"

"They won't." Things would never be the way they were before they'd made love. "They'll be better. Have you thought of it that way?"

He could practically feel the fear surrounding her, prickling her skin beneath his fingertips. "No." Desperation and denial resounded in her voice. "If we just try, we can get back to where we were."

A light went off in his head. She wasn't moving forward when they'd slept together, embracing a new phase of their relationship. She'd been scrambling like hell to get back to where they'd come from. She wasn't going out on a limb, she was running in a circle.

"Listen to yourself. You want to go back and you can't, Phoebe. Life is all about moving forward. Change is a good thing."

"That's the problem. That's why it would never work between us. You can't live your life without change. You're addicted to it. What happens when you get tired of me as a wife? When the phenomenal sex isn't so phenomenal anymore? Do you think we can go back to being friends after that? I'm not one of your women that will hang around in the harem afterward."

Ryan let the harem comment pass. As a rule, his breakups weren't nasty, but he sure as hell didn't have a harem. "So, how do you see it happening now? I don't understand the difference."

"The difference is in the level of commitment and trust. It takes a little more to be a husband than a friend."

He dropped his arms to his sides. "So, you don't trust me emotionally." That hurt. "I've got what it takes to be your friend. And as a lover, you seem fairly satisfied. But I'm not marriage material. Thanks, Phoebe."

"Look at your track record with women."

"There were a lot of fish in the sea, and I enjoyed fishing." That sounded lame even to him. Hell, there'd been a lot of women before her, and unfortunately, she knew about each and every one of them.

"But now you're ready to put away your rod? I don't think so. Those fish are still out there."

"I've never asked another woman to marry me. I've never felt this way about anyone else. And I never will."

A cloud covered the moon, pitching the beach in darkness.

"It's a temporary aberration."

"You're the one that I want. The only one." He could be as damned stubborn as Phoebe.

"Perhaps you should listen to yourself. I may be the one with the reputation for competitiveness, but you're the consummate competitor. Don't destroy our friendship just because you won't allow me to be the one who got away."

Ryan wasn't the best salesman in the southeast for nothing. He knew when to back off. He'd let his pitch rest. "Okay. We'll let it drop for now."

But Phoebe better be prepared. Because he wasn't about to lose the best thing that ever happened to him.

TWELVE HOURS.

Twelve hours until they climbed on a shuttle bus and headed for the airport. Twelve hours until this crazy ride ended and she climbed off.

Tomorrow was another day. Tomorrow she'd think about Ryan's proposal. Tomorrow she'd lose her braids. Tomorrow she'd figure out their friendship.

But for tonight she wanted her lover.

"I know we'd planned to go to the beach party and then the Jungle Room tonight. But I just want to go back to the room."

Quite frankly, she felt far too emotionally raw for either one.

He skimmed his hand along the length of her side and rested it on her hip. "I'm not interested in the beach party or the Jungle Room. I just want to be with you."

Her breath caught in her throat. "That's what I was thinking, as well." They did still agree on *some* things.

Silently they made their way to the room, wrapped in the distant sounds of revelry and the dark of the night.

The door closed behind them, wrapping them in the intimacy of their room. The imminent return to Nashville, Ryan's proposal and Phoebe's refusal all flavored the atmosphere with a hint of desperation and borrowed time.

Ryan dropped to the chaise. He caught Phoebe's hand and pulled her onto his lap.

"Phoebe…" He sounded as urgent as she felt. He cupped the back of her neck, drawing her mouth to his.

She wrapped her arms around his neck and lost herself in his kiss. In the subtle play of his lips slanting against hers. By tacit agreement, it was a leisurely exploration. She gave herself over to his long, slow, drugging kisses.

Phoebe rested her head against his shoulder. Tonight she would say all the things she couldn't tomorrow. "You're a great kisser."

"You are eminently kissable." He captured her mouth again.

Phoebe rimmed the inside of his mouth with her tongue. Deep, satisfying strokes. His heart pounded beneath her shoulder.

"Phoebes…"

"Hmm?" She'd be content to sit here making out with him all night. Well, maybe not making out all night. But a large portion. He kissed like nobody's business. After tomorrow, it wouldn't be her business.

"Is it like this for you with other men?" His eyes were intent.

"You can't ask me that."

"Why the hell not? We seem to be making up our

own rules as we go along. You had me rate our sex together."

"Okay. No. It's not." She'd always considered her sex drive healthy, but making love with Ryan bordered on an obsession. She traced the line of his brow with her finger. "It's never been this way before with anyone else. Only you."

"It's never been this way for me with anyone else, either."

"I don't want to talk." She scattered short, tiny kisses along his cheek, the line of his jaw. "We can talk later."

Later there'd be no sweet, slow kisses on his lap. And she still had enough brain cells left to realize that sexy, seductive Ryan was working her. That was fine. She wanted to be worked.

He slipped her dress off one shoulder. "If you don't want to talk, what do you want to do?"

She slid off his lap and stood before him. Reaching behind her, she tugged down the zipper, thankful the back was low cut and she didn't have to go through any funky contortions to get to the thing. She slid the dress off first one shoulder, then the other, letting it hang for a few tantalizing seconds on her breasts.

Ryan swallowed hard, a feral expression on his face. She let the front drop and shimmied, sending it past her hips to pool around her feet. Standing in front of him, wearing only high-heeled sandals, a thong and a Wonderbra, she didn't think he could possibly be confused as to what she wanted to do.

However, just to dispel any lingering doubts, she murmured, "We have a few of those chocolate-covered doughnuts left, and the diet starts tomorrow."

RYAN STUFFED HIS LAST PAIR of shorts into his suitcase and zipped it. "Ready?"

Phoebe, propped against the doorjamb, staring at the pool, turned. "Sure. I'm ready."

They'd made love off and on all night and then again this morning in the shower. Far from being worn out, they'd been desperate for one another this morning.

The fleeting thought had occurred to him that if they screwed one another to death, they wouldn't have to worry about what happened afterward. However, that hadn't happened. By the time she'd finished packing, Phoebe had surrounded herself with a wall built of distance, mortared by friendly cheer that had him gritting his teeth.

"So, why don't we bring our leftover doughnuts with us? It seems a shame to just leave them here." Hell, it didn't hurt to ask.

She shook her head. "I don't think so." She offered the first real smile he'd seen in the last hour. "But that was a nice try."

Ryan shrugged, hoping he appeared more nonchalant than he felt. "Can't blame a guy for trying."

Her hand was on the doorknob when he did some quick thinking. "Whoa." She turned to face him. "I just wanted to remind you that Kiki and Elliott will be on the shuttle, and we all have seats together on the flight. They'll be watching us."

He'd like to say that he didn't give a crap what Kiki and Elliott thought, but that wasn't strictly true. He didn't want Elliott getting the idea that Phoebe was available. She wasn't. She might consider herself available, but he knew better. After all, it was just a matter of convincing her. And he damn well didn't need Elliott nosing around while Ryan was busy doing that convincing. Plus it gave him a reason to touch her and work on wearing down her defenses.

"I'd forgotten all about them."

It was a small detail, but it offered more than a generous measure of hope when ultracompetitive Phoebe admitted she'd forgotten about the competition.

"Well, let's make this easy on both of us. Let's bring our doughnuts as far as Nashville."

"They get left at the airport."

"At the airport. Gone. Deal?"

"Deal."

"Then we need to take care of this." He braced his hands on the door on either side of her, effectively trapping her. He leaned in, inhaling her scent, breathing in the moist heat of her breath, heartened by the flare of passion in her eyes. "Can't have you looking neglected."

"PHOEBE." RYAN SHOOK HER. "Baby, wake up. We're circling to land."

Leaning against his chest, her head pillowed on his shoulder, Phoebe reluctantly shook off the last vestiges of sleep.

"Uh-huh." She didn't open her eyes immediately. She took a few last seconds to soak up his warmth, the scent of him overlaying his aftershave, the rhythm of his hearbeat, the texture of his skin.

She opened her eyes and sat up. Ryan moved his arm from around her to reach over and click first her seat belt in place and then his. "You slept most of the way. Do you feel better?"

"I didn't realize how tired I was." She had fallen into an exhausted sleep once the plane took off.

"It was all that physical activity. Besides, you didn't get any sleep last night. And not a whole lot the night before." Ryan nibbled along her jaw.

Phoebe caught a movement in the row behind them. Elliott. Eavesdropping.

She nipped at Ryan's mouth with a playful kiss. "Sorry I kept you up all night."

"Mmm. It was a pleasure."

"Yes, it was."

She was pathetic. There was no other word for it. Here she and Ryan were, putting on a show for the benefit of Kiki and Elliott behind them, and she was enjoying her last few desperate moments of intimacy with Ryan. A few suggestive phrases, a tender touch and she wanted him again.

Without considering the wisdom of her actions, her eyes dropped to his crotch. Oh. He was in the same boat she was.

"Phoebe." Ryan's voice was as strained as the front of his jeans.

Caught up in Ryan, Phoebe was quite surprised when the plane touched down and braked along the runway. While the flight attendant ran through her spiel on the intercom, Ryan whispered in Phoebe's ear. "Baby, if you don't stop looking at me, or more specifically *it,* like that, I'm not going to be able to walk off the plane without embarrassing both of us."

"Oh."

They taxied to a stop at the gate. There was the awkward stretch of waiting in front of Kiki and Elliott for overhead bin luggage to be removed and the passengers ahead of them to disembark.

"Well, I have to say this was a different week than I imagined," Kiki offered.

And just what did you say to the woman who'd hopped into bed with your boyfriend, expecting you to join them, the woman who'd essentially started the whole ball rolling? Phoebe smiled. "I never dreamed it could be so good."

Elliott, standing behind Kiki, flushed. Ryan turned and draped his arm possessively over Phoebe's shoulder, "It was the best week of my life."

Kiki smiled at Ryan. "Call me sometime."

Jealousy, white-hot and cutting, surged through Phoebe. For one insane, irrational moment her hand flexed, intent on slapping the leer right off Kiki's gorgeous face.

"I don't think so." Ryan's lack of interest, sanity and a moving stream of passengers saved her from herself.

Phoebe walked down the plane's narrow aisle. *That* was why she and Ryan could never make it as a couple. He was like a pot of honey to a horde of flies. Women liked him. Wanted him. So he wasn't interested in Kiki now. What about later? What about the next woman who hit on him? What about the fifth or sixth woman? It wasn't Ryan's fault that women liked him. And he liked them in return—for a while. Since his first girlfriend in high school, he'd never dated one woman more than a few weeks. He'd set a record a few years ago with a redhead named Judy. They'd dated a month.

She stepped into the chilly tunnel leading to the terminal.

Ryan was right behind her. "Phoebes, wait. I told her I didn't want to call."

Phoebe slowed down. It really wasn't his fault. It was just the way things were. So she did the next best thing to slapping Kiki. She slipped her arm around Ryan's waist as if she had every right to.

They stepped into the terminal, and she pulled him

to one side and wrapped her arms around him, kissing him square on the mouth. Let Kiki take that home with her. His mouth was warm and, after his initial start of surprise, he was a willing participant.

Phoebe lost track of time, place, and wasn't too certain of her name. Kissing Ryan tended to affect her that way.

CHAPTER TWELVE

PHOEBE UNLOCKED THE DOOR to her condo, and Bridgette ran in ahead of her, settling in her favorite spot in front of the couch, obviously glad to be home. Phoebe followed, already missing Jamaica, or more specifically, Ryan.

Nashville was cold and rainy. Even her condo, which always seemed so comfortable, was cool and damp. She dragged her suitcase to the middle of the room and kicked off her shoes. She hit the flashing red light on her answering machine and listened to her messages while she set up a fire to dispel the chill.

"Hi, honey. It's me, Aunt Caroline. You know I hate talking to this thing but I just wanted to say I hope you had a good time. I want to hear all about your trip sometime next week. Why don't you plan on coming by for dinner on Tuesday night? And bring Bridgette with you. We enjoyed her company."

Aunt Caroline and Uncle Frank had been out for their regular Sunday afternoon hike when she'd dropped by to pick up Bridgette. Phoebe felt guilty over how relieved she'd been that they weren't home.

She'd have to practice a travelogue before she went over Tuesday night.

With the fire off to a crackling start, she plopped onto the sofa. She rubbed her toes along Bridgette's back. The dog sighed happily.

Message number two was a mortgage telemarketer promising to save her money if she refinanced with his company. She skipped ahead to number three, a reminder from her dentist's office to schedule a cleaning.

Message four. "Phoebes, I wanted to make sure you got in okay. Call me when you get home." Ryan.

The sound of his voice, rich, smooth, with a hint of a Southern drawl, washed over her like the warm waters of the Caribbean. It wasn't a message from her friend. It was a message from her lover. Just the sound of his voice evoked a landslide of memories and emotions that besieged her good sense and left her breathless.

In the midst of gathering her remaining wits, the phone rang again. Aunt Caroline? Ryan? She almost wished for a telemarketer, which was probably a first in consumer history and just went to show the depth of her deprivation.

"Hello."

"Phoebes." Ryan. Her stomach flip-flopped. "Did you just get in?"

"I was listening to my messages."

"Listen, baby, about—"

"Ryan." She interrupted him, her pulse pounding like those steel drums they'd left behind in Jamaica. "You can't call me that."

"What?"

"Baby."

"Oh?"

"Yeah. It's too…it's not…" How about provocative? Sexy? It brought to mind a steamy shower against a marble wall, champagne in a private pool, a Caribbean sunset she'd never forget. "How about you just don't call me that. Let's stick with Phoebe. Okay?"

"I'll try."

"Try hard." She closed her eyes. Poor adjective choice. Freud would have a field day with that.

"For you, I'll try very hard."

Evil lurked in his soul. Well, evil wasn't exactly the word for it. But she recognized the interest in his voice. He was in the same sorry state she was. His eyes would be narrowed, his face taking on that hard look. He was trying to seduce her over the phone.

"I personally think you're at your best when it's hard." She should've never said that, but good grief, she missed him. It had been hours since they showered this morning.

"Things are very hard for me right now."

"I think we've digressed."

"I think there's another word for it." His sexy, teasing note curled through her.

"Behave."

"You started it."

"No, I…well, I suppose I did. Sorry. It won't happen again."

"I hate to hear that."

"Stop. That's exactly the kind of thing we have to watch."

"Okay, baby—"

"No baby. Remember?"

"Oh, yeah. So, where were we before we wandered down the path of telephone perdition?"

"You were just calling to make sure I got home."

"Oh, yeah." Silence stretched across the line. "I miss you, Phoebes." His voice was quiet and low.

It had been all of what? two hours? She missed him desperately also. "It's Sunday afternoon. Do you want to come over?" There was nothing suggestive at all in her invitation. He usually came over on Sunday afternoons for an early dinner. And what difference would one more day make?

"I could pick up a pizza on the way over."

"Double cheese with anchovies?"

"I thought you'd want light cheese with roasted veggies."

"I'm starting my diet tomorrow."

"Oh." A wealth of meaning came through in that one word. "I'll pick up a box of chocolate-covered doughnuts, as well."

"That's always a good way to start a diet."

"I'll be there within an hour." He hung up before she could answer.

This was the downside to diving into the murky waters of sleeping with your best friend. Who the hell were you supposed to talk to about it? And she desperately needed to talk.

She'd always been very private. And while she had lots of acquaintances she could call up for dinner or a movie, Ryan was her true friend. Bridgette was a decent listener, but not very forthcoming with advice. It was fairly difficult to bounce ideas off a dog.

She supposed she'd have to start talking to herself. She caught a glimpse of her braided reflection in the window. Perhaps that was part of her problem. She was still in the Jamaican mind-set.

"The first step is to lose the braids. Who knows, maybe all the magic was tied up in Jamaica. Maybe things will be just like they were before."

Bridgette lifted her head, then lowered it again, closing her eyes.

Phoebe didn't think so, either.

RYAN BALANCED PIZZA, doughnuts and a six-pack of beer and knocked on Phoebe's door.

It wasn't as if he was desperate to see her or anything. He'd called, and she'd invited him over. Same as every Sunday.

Locks turned on the other side, and she threw the door open. "Hi."

"Pizza. Doughnuts. Beer." He hefted the cartons. "The essentials." God, he sounded pathetic.

She stepped aside. "Come on in."

The door closed behind him and he stood stock-still on the foyer's parquet floor, drinking in the sight of her. She wore faded plaid boxers, an old college T-shirt, no bra—he could see the soft round mounds of her breasts and the outline of her nipples—and her unbraided hair hung in wet rat tails around her head. He'd bet she wasn't wearing any panties underneath those boxers, either. She looked delectable.

While he was looking, her nipples hardened and thrust against the front of her T-shirt. Phoebe was doing terrible things to his blood pressure. She was like his own all-natural version of Viagra.

"Just put it on the coffee table." She gestured toward the other room.

"I see you got rid of your braids."

"I told you I would. That was Jamaica. This is Nashville."

Yeah. He got the message loud and clear. He put the boxes on the table and bent to scratch Bridgette behind the ears. "How are you, girl? How'd you get along with all those cats?" Bridgette licked his hand.

"Want to watch the game?" he called.

"Sure."

He turned on the TV while she rounded up paper plates. "Beer?" she called from the kitchen.

"Sounds good."

She came in balancing plates, napkins, silverware and two beers. Ryan grabbed for the beers as they began to topple. He caught them in the nick of time, his finger skimming her nipple.

"Sorry." His heart thundered like that of an adolescent boy with a girlie magazine.

Phoebe sucked in her breath. "Don't worry about it." She dumped the stuff on the table, the silverware clattering on the glass top. "So, what channel is the game on?"

"Try five." Ryan sat on one end of the couch and lifted the lid on the pizza. He wasn't particularly hungry, but it gave him something to do other than stare at Phoebe and the jiggle of her breasts against the stretch of her T-shirt.

He and Phoebe went through the motions. They bet on the outcome of the game, ate a slice of pizza, each drank a beer and cheered on their respective teams.

No tropical breeze blew in over a sparkling sea. Her ceiling fan didn't work; the motor had burned out in the fall, and she hadn't gotten around to replacing it.

No steel drums pulsated in the background. Twelve men beat the hell out of one another on a field of ice while fans screamed from the stands.

She wasn't wearing high-heeled sandals, a thong and a Wonderbra. Her clothes were worn and old, and her feet were bare.

Her hair wasn't in sexy cornrows. It had dried

pretty much the way it was after she ran a towel through it.

They weren't in exotic Jamaica. They were in cold, gray Nashville.

It should've been just like old times.

It wasn't.

Ryan wanted her so badly he could hardly see straight.

Tension. Awareness. Want. Need. Stretched between them.

"Want a doughnut?" He hadn't meant for it to come out so abruptly.

"I thought you'd never ask."

Neither of them glanced at the box on the table. Ryan reached her in midlaunch. He buried his hands in the damp silk of her hair, his mouth devouring hers. She molded her hands to the back of his head, forcing him closer.

Both panting, chests heaving, they came up for air. He rested his forehead against hers. "Oh, baby. I missed you."

Whatever it was between them may have started in Jamaica, but it definitely hadn't ended there.

PHOEBE ENTERED BIRELLI'S, just as she'd done for the last seven years, for lunch with Ryan on Thursday at twelve-thirty. Over the course of those seven years, she'd arrived elated with good news, depressed with bad news, frustrated with her job, current boyfriend or parents. But until today, she'd never arrived nervous.

She tried to quiet the butterflies in her stomach. This nervousness was silly. Almost as silly as her decision to forgo panty hose this morning in favor of stockings and a flirty garter belt.

Ryan was at the same table they sat at each week. He looked up from a report as she dropped onto the stool opposite him. "Hey. You made it."

"Yeah. So did you." Feeling ridiculously adolescent, she devoured him with her eyes. As if she hadn't seen him a mere four days ago, she noted the sexy quirk of his lips, the hug of his button-down across his broad shoulders, the gleam in his pale green eyes.

Naomi sauntered over with two glasses of tea. "Here you are. The stromboli'll be out in a minute. How was—" She stopped abruptly, glancing back and forth between Ryan and Phoebe. "Lord have mercy. Ya'll did it, didn't you?" She didn't wait for confirmation. Holding her tray in one hand, she pumped the other hand in the air. "Yes! I've won a ton of money. We've had this pool going on ya'll for the last couple of years. I knew it was just a matter of time. Wait until I tell George." Naomi hurried off in the direction of the kitchen and George, the cook.

Great. Phoebe'd obviously picked up a banner proclaiming she'd slept with Ryan Palmer. She smiled tightly at the other customers staring at them. A slow burn heated her face.

Ryan shrugged. "Don't worry about it, baby." He held up a hand. "Sorry, I forgot."

Naomi bore down on them again. "Here you are. One stromboli. One salad with bread sticks. And it's on the house today."

"Naomi, we can't—"

"Trust me, I can afford it today. Thanks to you two." She cut off Phoebe's protest. "Ya'll enjoy."

Ryan sliced off a neat quarter of the stromboli. Instead of transferring it to another plate, he picked it up, stringing the melted cheese along the way. "Here."

She leaned forward and bit into the crusty bread filled with gooey cheese, her teeth scraping against his finger. The laughter in his eyes faded, replaced by a hunger that had nothing to do with stromboli.

They didn't exchange tales about work or coworkers. Instead, lunch passed in a haze of desperation and desire. Phoebe sat across from Ryan, aware of each brush of his trousered leg against her stockinged legs, the scent of his aftershave, the cadence of his voice, the tension enveloping them in a cocoon of intimacy.

"Baklava?"

Phoebe made a pretense of checking her watch. "None for me. I really need to get back to the office."

"We'll skip it today. Thanks, Naomi."

"No, thank you. Both of you." She dropped a wink at them. "Enjoy the rest of your lunch."

They stood. Ryan followed Phoebe, his hand resting against the small of her back, his fingers burning through her suit fabric.

They both paused on the sidewalk. Ryan's hand slid to her hip in a possessive gesture.

"Where'd you park?" Ryan asked, his mouth close enough to her ear to send shivers down her spine.

"Two blocks over, on Thurston. It was crowded."

"I'm right across the street in the parking garage. Why don't I give you a ride?"

They crossed the street and waited silently for the garage elevator. Phoebe took great care not to touch him, not quite sure that she wouldn't come unhinged. How could it possibly be only four days since she'd touched him, tasted him, breathed his scent and marked him as her own? It felt like a lifetime.

The doors opened, and a businessman stepped off, checking his watch. Ryan pushed the fourth-floor button. The doors had barely closed before they fell on one another.

His mouth was hot and hard against hers, just like his body pressing her against the elevator wall. Phoebe ground against him. He dove beneath her skirt with his hands and clutched her.

The elevator bell rang, announcing their stop on the fourth floor. They tore themselves apart. Panting. Frantic.

"Where's the car?"

"Back in that corner. On the other side of that big truck."

"Hurry."

Phoebe practically dragged him along the row of parked cars.

"Passenger side," Ryan instructed as he rounded the car and unlocked the door. He opened it, fell into the seat, then tugged Phoebe onto his lap. He slammed the door closed, killed the dome light and threw the seat into the recline position.

Phoebe hiked her skirt up and straddled him, leaving her thighs bare and open to his view.

If she hadn't been wet before, the look of absolute lust and appreciation darkening his eyes would've done the trick. The garter belt and stockings were a big hit. "Oh, baby," he groaned, one hand on his zipper, the other on the back of her thigh.

Phoebe held his head between her hands and kissed him hard. Her teeth ground against his. Her tongue plunged into his mouth. Ryan fisted his hand in her panties and dragged them to one side. With his other hand, Ryan positioned her over his erection. In one downward surge, she filled herself with him. Hot, sweet emotion raged through her, escaping in a keening moan that he absorbed. Within seconds they both found the release in each other they so craved.

Spent, Phoebe collapsed on top of him, unsure where the pounding of his heart began and hers ended.

God, she loved him.

PHOEBE CLIMBED OUT OF HER CAR, a little perplexed and a lot frustrated. Why Ryan wanted to meet at a municipal park on a blustery day on the tail end of winter was beyond her. She was all achy, and there wasn't going to be much opportunity to assuage that ache here. Of course, making love with Ryan never assuaged it. But it did keep it manageable. She wouldn't even get that today. Unless they found a nice remote spot for the car. Her blood pumped a little faster at the thought.

Ryan waited for her at a bench overlooking a duck pond, his jacket collar turned up against the cold. Only a handful of hardy ducks braved the water this early. The wind whistled eerily through bare limbs with a chill that chased down her spine. Two joggers in winter gear ran along the winding path. A couple of mothers and their bundled children were at the playground.

"Hi." Phoebe shivered into her coat. "It's brisk out here. Why don't we go sit in my car?"

Ryan stood to greet her but didn't touch her. "No. It's too easy to get distracted. That's why I wanted to meet here today. There's not much opportunity for distraction," he said without his customary grin.

Sinking to the bench, she didn't offer a smile, either. She had a very bad feeling about this. Ryan sat beside her.

"Phoebe, we've got to talk," he stated baldly.

Oh, boy. She was growing to really hate it when he said that.

He ran his hand through his hair. Phoebe hoped the primal scream rising inside her wouldn't find its way out. She steeled herself.

"This isn't working."

Her stomach clenched in protest even though she'd known this day was coming. She'd known before the first kiss. She'd known he would leave her. Ryan was a short-term kind of guy, and she seemed to have that effect on people. She checked the date on her watch with a tight smile. "Fourteen days. A bit shorter than I thought we'd last. I was hoping we could go for a personal record with you, a little over a month. But I guess it's not to be."

Jesus. She sounded hateful and bitchy and more than a little spiteful. But it beat the hell out of sobbing like a baby and begging him not to end things, which was what she felt like doing. She absolutely would not beg.

"Dammit. Would you listen?"

"You have my undivided attention." Or what was left that hadn't already died inside.

"We can't keep going on like this. We can't just keep having sex."

"But that's all…"

"That's what I mean. We get together all the time, although calling our encounters dates is a stretch." A hint of bitterness curled his lips. "Sometimes for lunch, occasionally for a movie, always for sex. The sex is great, but that's all we have anymore. The closer we get physically, the further away you slip emotionally. Can't you feel it? This is destroying us."

"Well, that's a unique breakup approach." She felt a searing pain and a horrible hollowness. She knew he was right.

"Every time I try to bring up the dreaded *M* word, we wind up distracted. We're not distracted now. Marry me."

Anything that hurt this bad now would be unbearable in six months or a year down the road.

"No."

Ryan brushed her cheek with his gloved thumb. She could swear she felt his heat against her skin through the black leather. "Phoebe, I've waited all my life for you. All the other women were a crazy attempt to run from what was staring me in the face. You. Don't you see? They were all the exact opposite of you. Of course none of them lasted. It wasn't meant to be. I suppose I'm a little slow, but I've finally figured it out. You're all I've ever wanted. You're all I'll ever want. I love you. I'm so in love with you, I ache."

She had firsthand knowledge of aching. However, emotional cauterization reduced her to monosyllables. "No."

"Phoebe, you love me." He took her hands in his, the desperate tenor of his voice at odds with the children's ringing laughter on the playground. "And I'm pretty damn sure you're in love with me."

Her hands lay limp in his, and she looked at him. She hoped he finished soon. She felt she at least owed him that, but she couldn't stand much more of this.

"Baby, there's always been this connection between us. Since the first time I found you crying in the woods behind my house. Remember Jamaica? Remember looking out at the Caribbean? Our relationship is like the ocean. The tides change. Sometimes it's calm. Sometimes it's stormy. But it's always there."

She'd been waiting for this to come. Waiting for the other shoe to drop. Just as she'd known it was coming with Elliott. She'd known from the beginning he'd walk away from her. "That's a lovely analogy. I wish I could buy into it—and you're a very persuasive salesman—but I can't."

"Phoebes, don't do this to us."

"I'm not the one doing this. You're the one laying down ultimatums. Didn't you say marriage or nothing?" He wanted more than she could give. He wanted her to step out farther on that limb than she could go.

"I've tried it your way, Phoebes. It's not enough. I want to wake up and feel your warmth next to me every morning. I want to grow old with you."

"I just don't think we can have those things."

"You know what I think?" She was certain she was about to find out. She was equally certain she wasn't going to appreciate his opinion. "I think you're so damn scared you can't see straight. When we were friends, that was nice and safe, wasn't it, Phoebes? You can still maintain a comfortable distance with your friends. The men you've dated? No emotional depth there. All nice, safe, distant choices. It didn't really hurt when Elliott defected, did it, Phoebes?"

Anger displaced her debilitating numbness. "How about you? With your revolving-door relationships? Like there's some emotional investment there? Don't make me laugh," Phoebe said.

He nodded, his face hard. "At least I can admit it. You hold everyone at arm's length. Your aunt Caroline and uncle Frank. Me. Your coworkers. Not too long before we left for Jamaica, you told me I was emotionally retarded and you were the enabler. Hell, maybe I am emotionally retarded. But you need to step back and take a good, hard look at yourself. Because you were looking in the mirror, not at me. You know why I'm the last man you'd want to marry? Hide behind my track record if it makes you feel good. But the truth is, you don't want to marry me because you'd feel too damn much, Phoebe."

She held her backbone ramrod stiff, otherwise it'd crumple and she'd die in a pile right before him. "Well, I hope you feel better. I don't."

"It's not about feeling better. It's about saving us."

"So, that's your offer? Marriage or nothing?"

"I don't see any other way."

"I guess there's nothing left to say."

He stood and looked at her. "You know where to find me, baby. Just know that I'm not cheap, free or easy. I come with a high price. You."

His feet crunched on the gravel path as he walked away. Unlike when her parents left her, at least this time she knew he wouldn't return. Somehow it didn't make the hurt any more bearable.

CHAPTER THIRTEEN

Ryan sat at the table in Birelli's, ostensibly reviewing last month's production report. It had been two days since they'd met in the park. He hadn't called. She hadn't called. No take-out Chinese. No hockey games. No sex. No Phoebe.

He'd be lying like a big dog if he said he didn't miss the sex. Just the thought of a parking garage gave him a hard-on. But what he really missed was Phoebe. It was as if he'd amputated an essential body part.

Naomi stopped by the table and checked her watch, "She's late. Where is she? She's never late."

"I don't know if she's coming." Ryan spoke the words he'd avoided facing.

Naomi snatched Phoebe's glass of ice tea, swiping the puddle beneath it. Most of the ice had melted. "She'll be here." She thunked the glass onto the table. "There she is now. I told you'd she'd come," Naomi said.

Ryan spotted Phoebe on the sidewalk through the glass windows of the restaurant. He felt nauseous with relief. He could admit it now. He'd been so damn scared she wouldn't come. But she was here. And together they could work through anything.

Phoebe looked at him through the glass, her expression unreadable. When she reached the restaurant door, she hesitated, then turned and kept walking.

"That was Phoebe. Wasn't that Phoebe? Did she just walk by?" Naomi asked, clearly perplexed.

Ryan grunted. His gut response was to rush outside, haul her stubborn butt home and screw her to the point of exhaustion so she'd agree to marry him. But he'd already tried that, after a fashion, and it hadn't worked.

"Cancel the salad and I'll take the stromboli now." It was pretty damn amazing how calm and composed he sounded when he was dying inside.

Naomi sniffled and swiped at a tear. "Those are the saddest words I've ever heard."

Ryan couldn't agree more.

PHOEBE TURNED HER CHAIR and stared at the Nashville skyline showcased by her office window. This view at dusk, when the city lights flickered like fireflies against the encroaching darkness, always thrilled her.

It failed to thrill her now. She swivelled around. She felt dead inside. Dead and empty. But that was preferable to hurting so damn bad she could barely tolerate the pain. That's what lurked behind her emptiness. The emptiness merely held the pain at bay. But it kept things manageable. She closed her eyes. Was this what the rest of her life would be like? Managed emptiness? Perhaps. She'd felt this way before, every time her parents promised to come get her and had never shown up. It wasn't a new sensation. But before, Ryan had always helped her through. Now there was no Ryan.

Phoebe pulled on her coat, picked up her briefcase and locked her door behind her. Moving on autopilot, she rode the elevator down to the parking garage, found her car and joined the steady stream of rush-hour commuters.

Red taillights stretched ahead of her. It had been five long weeks since she'd met Ryan at the park. Five weeks of feeling as if an important part of her was missing. Was he right? Did she deliberately hold everyone at arm's length? She'd always thought her reserve was a part of her personality. But there'd been nothing reserved about the passion she'd found within herself in Jamaica.

Lost in thought, Phoebe tuned in and realized she was a block from Aunt Caroline's house. In the slow flow of traffic, she'd found her way to the place that had offered her refuge since childhood. She'd produced one reason or another to avoid Caroline's repeated dinner invitations in the last month. She hadn't wanted to discuss Jamaica with her aunt. She'd told herself it was because she didn't want anyone close to her to know about her and Ryan. But maybe only part of that was right—maybe she just didn't want anyone close to her.

She parked her car in the driveway and approached the Depression-era bungalow with a sense of homecoming. She bypassed the front door and wound her way to the back stoop. The familiar clink of metal against stone resounded from the open door of the detached two-car garage that served as Uncle Frank's studio.

Phoebe opened the back door that led straight into the kitchen. Aunt Caroline sat at a corner desk, surfing the Internet, a glass of wine on her desk. Two salads sat ready on the kitchen table, crowded by a stack of magazines and newspapers and junk mail.

"Hi."

Aunt Caroline whirled around, joy lighting her angular face. "Phoebe! We've missed you so. We were beginning to think you didn't love us." She pushed away from the computer and started across the room, her spontaneous smile giving way to a frown of concern, her footsteps flagging. "Sugar, what's the matter?"

Phoebe hadn't planned to wind up here. Nor did she plan to burst into tears and fling herself into Aunt Caroline's open arms. Nonetheless, that's where she found herself. Sobs racked her, rendering her incoherent. Aunt Caroline held her tight against her spare frame, rocking the two of them back and forth in a soothing motion but making no effort to stem the tide of emotion ripping Phoebe apart.

Finally, the storm inside her subsided. Embarrassed, desperately in need of a box of tissues, she pulled back from the comfort of Caroline's arms and tried to stumble through an apology, "I'm sorry—"

Caroline would have none of it. She smoothed Phoebe's hair and pushed her into a kitchen chair. "Don't you dare apologize, my sweet, sweet girl."

Phoebe snuffled and tried to compose herself. Caroline turned from the sink with a damp paper towel. She blotted away Phoebe's residual tears, the paper cool and calming against her heated skin. Then as if Phoebe were six instead of thirty, Caroline handed her the paper towel and instructed, "Blow."

Phoebe blew. And sat there at a loss. She really hadn't planned to come over and she didn't know what to say. She drew a deep shuddering breath. "I didn't mean to—"

Caroline cut her off again, her eyes awash with tears. "Shh. Do you know how long I've waited for you to come to me for anything? I hate it that you're unhappy, but I'm glad you're here. I've waited a lifetime for this." Guilt and sorrow painted her face, "Of course, that's the way it's always been."

"What are you talking about, Aunt Caroline?" Phoebe spoke softly, surprised by the pain etching her aunt's usually cheery face.

"Your uncle Frank and I found out we couldn't have children a few years after we were married."

Phoebe started in surprise. She'd always assumed they didn't want children.

"It probably wouldn't be a big deal today, but thirty-five years ago, they didn't know nearly as much about infertility and we didn't have the money to spend the thousands of dollars to pursue it," her aunt continued.

She paused, closing her eyes for a second as if seeking the words to continue. She looked up. "And then Lynette and Vance had you." Love transformed and softened Caroline's angular face. It took Phoebe a second to realize it was love for her. "You were wonderful. Bright and beautiful, and I tried very hard to be happy for Lynette and Vance." Her voice broke. "They were so careless with you. Living like Gypsies, going wherever their wanderlust led them. So many nights I worried that you didn't have enough to eat or a place to stay."

Even now, sitting in the warmth of Caroline's kitchen, Phoebe instantly recalled going to bed and waking up in the backseat of her parent's car with a gnawing hunger eating at her empty belly. She knew her confirmation would only hurt Caroline. She held her tongue.

"You were so smart. But they never stayed in one place long enough to enroll you in kindergarten or first grade. When they left you with us, Phoebe, I was glad." She spoke with a fierceness Phoebe had never heard in her voice before. "I was ashamed then and I'm ashamed now at how happy I was over something that caused you so much pain. You were a gift to us, a blessing we never expected. I kept thinking that one day, if we gave you enough space and showed you we loved you, you'd come to accept us and love us in return. I'm so sorry, Phoebe, but I thought you were better off with us. I never kept Lynette and Vance away, but I never pushed them to come for you, either. Because I wanted you for my own."

Tears rolled down Caroline's face. Fat, silent tears that picked up momentum. Without giving it consideration, Phoebe pushed away from the table and stood, wrapping her arms around Caroline.

They'd wanted her. All this time, they'd wanted *her*. She wasn't an obligation. She was a blessing. "I thought you all didn't want me but were too kind-hearted to send away a stray. God knows, you had enough strays already."

"Do you remember Boris, the big tomcat that wandered up the spring you got your braces?"

"Yes." Boris had trusted no one and tolerated few.

"You were so like Boris. Do you remember how you'd put food out and watch him eat? Every day you'd get a little bit closer, but he never would let you touch him. But then he and Duchess became friends, and you stopped trying to pet him because he wasn't alone anymore."

Phoebe nodded. She'd desperately wanted Boris to let her near him.

"You were like that cat. Skittish and standoffish, but you and Ryan found one another so Frank and I figured you were okay. Although we never stopped wanting you to let us near you."

Phoebe never realized how much her distance had hurt them. "I'm so sorry."

"Honey, it's hard to learn to trust and open yourself up. It's hard to believe you won't find yourself abandoned again. We probably should've found a therapist to help you deal with everything. But the money was always tight and we thought if we just loved you enough, one day you'd let us love you."

Phoebe felt like a dike with a small hole that couldn't withstand the relentless pressure of water on the other side. Caroline's words crumbled the wall that had surrounded Phoebe's heart for as long as she could recall.

"Why?" One word. So important. "Why didn't they want me, Aunt Caroline?"

"I don't know why." Compassion lit Caroline's eyes. "I've never figured it out. Maybe it's because Lynette was the youngest and our parents spoiled her. Maybe it's just the way she is. But you'll find out as you go through life that often there's no ready answer as to why. Things just are, and we have to deal with them."

"That's not good enough. I need the whys."

"Forget about the why and get on with life. I think you've already come up with your own why, and you're wrong. Look at me, Phoebe, when I tell you this." She cupped Phoebe's chin in a gentle hand. "Your parents dropped you off and never came back. They deserved a horsewhipping for that. And a good flogging still wouldn't cover all the times they told you they'd be there and never were. But the thing you need to know is, there's something wrong with *them*. Not with you. My guess is that some time ago, you decided you didn't care and wouldn't let them hurt you anymore."

"They can't hurt me anymore."

"They can't as soon as you wrestle control of your life from them."

"They have absolutely no control over me."

"Unfortunately, they do. You're still letting them control you. You're still giving them the power. Your fear of abandonment, the fear to let someone get too close to you—that's the power you've given them over your life. If you don't move past that, you'll never realize your full potential. You only get out of life what you put into it. And life can be so good for you. Don't let them cripple you." Caroline paused as if carefully considering her next words, "And don't let them ruin what you could have with Ryan."

Phoebe dropped back into her chair. "What about Ryan?"

"He called us a few weeks ago. He loves you, Phoebe. He's so in love with you he can hardly stand himself. Just like you love him. Frank and I have seen it for years."

"But all his girlfriends—all those relationships…"

"Phoebe, those were never relationships. That was a man doing what a man does best, running scared. If you look beneath all of his easygoing charm, Ryan's a Boris, too. His mother chose to drink herself to death, and then his father flitted from woman to woman and never paid Ryan any attention. That boy was as abandoned as you. He doesn't trust easily, either. But from the day you met, you were the Duchess to his Boris. I've never seen two people more destined for one another and take longer to figure it out."

Phoebe sat for a minute, absorbing Caroline's words. The fear inside her fought them. "Why didn't you tell me this sooner?"

"Because your heart wasn't ready to hear it."

"But what if—"

Caroline laid a quieting hand on her shoulder. "Life doesn't come with any guarantees, Phoebe. All you can do is love like there's no tomorrow and hope for the best."

Moving past the repression she'd spent years perfecting, Phoebe hugged Caroline. Holding her aunt near, she found the courage to give voice to the words she'd never been able to say before. "I love you."

BRIDGETTE FOLLOWED HER as Phoebe dug the cardboard shoe box out of the back of her closet and carried it into her living room. Her hand trembled when she removed the worn lid. It was a time capsule of sorts, she supposed.

She pulled out a dog-eared photo. Twenty-five years ago. A pensive Phoebe stood sandwiched between her laughing parents in a grainy color Polaroid. She remembered that day as clearly as if it were yesterday.

She showed Bridgette the photo. "There we are, girl. We'd stopped at a roadside circus. They were having a great time, but I was tired and hungry." They'd spent the night in their car, and according to her parents, there hadn't been enough money for breakfast. Of course, there'd been money for the circus.

How many times had she wondered over the years, each time she looked at the photo, if they'd left her behind because she wasn't fun enough? Smart enough? Pretty enough? Lovable enough? Had she complained about being tired and hungry too much? Because she had been, quite often.

She'd wondered far more times than she cared to remember. It had become a visible cue for inadequacy. Where had she fallen short of the mark? She consciously stemmed the feelings as they welled up inside her.

Bridgette settled her head in Phoebe's lap, as if to offer comfort, her brown eyes solemn, trusting and full of love. Phoebe looked at her. Why had someone dropped Bridgette off at the pound? Phoebe had wondered for a long time. She'd spent the first several months watching for bad behavior, some clue as to why someone wouldn't want a great dog like Bridgette. And finally, over the course of time, she'd stopped wondering. Bridgette was wonderful, and Phoebe loved her. Thank goodness they'd found one another.

She placed the photo on the couch and pulled out a handful of papers. Poems, notes, unmailed envelopes. Outpourings of her adolescent confusion, outrage, humiliation, bitterness. All on paper. Saved to be presented one day to her parents.

An infinite sadness welled inside her. This had been such a central part of her life for so long, it was hard to let it go. She sat on the floor before the fireplace, the crackling fire spreading heat and light.

Her hand shook as she tentatively fed the first envelope into the fire. As the flames licked and curled across the envelope, consuming it, a tear trickled down her face, and Phoebe felt a release. With each piece of paper, it became easier and the tears flowed faster. Sobbing, she tossed the box and the lid into the grate. The fire whooshed as it greedily devoured them.

Bridgette nuzzled against her and barked at the flames.

The only remnant from the box was the photo. Phoebe picked it up, holding its worn corner between her thumb and forefinger, offering it up, as well.

At the last moment she snatched it back. All the bitterness, all the hurt were gone. But she still needed to remember who she was and where she'd come from. She could look at the photo and know that why was no longer important. Her heart had finally heard the message.

RYAN COULDN'T SEEM TO BREAK himself of the habit of showing up at Birelli's each Thursday. Even though it had been five long weeks since Phoebe had stopped coming. Instead of watching for her, he spent his lunch hour reading reports.

Naomi appeared out of nowhere and sloshed a sweet tea opposite him, a huge grin on her face.

"Earth to Naomi. I already have a drink."

"Yeah. But she doesn't."

He looked up and his heart damn near stopped. Phoebe stood inside the doorway looking strong, yet vulnerable. His eyes never left her face as she made her way across the room. Time had pronounced the hollows beneath her cheekbones and the faint shadows beneath her eyes.

She stopped at the table, tugging on the strap of her shoulderbag. "Mind if I sit down?"

"It's your spot."

Phoebe slid onto the stool. Naomi beamed at her. "I'll be right back with a salad."

"Wait. I'll have the spinach and chicken stromboli."

"But you always have the salad."

"I know. But it's the stromboli that I always want. So, I'll have that."

"Sure thing." Naomi's smile was blinding as she hurried off.

An awkward silence settled between them. Were they friends? Lovers? Uneasy acquaintances? Hell if he knew. The only thing he knew for sure was that he loved her and he'd missed her like crazy. He'd already stepped out on a limb twice and been knocked off. What was the saying about the third time being a charm? Of course there was the three strikes and you're out deal, too. He figured, either way, he didn't have anything to lose that he hadn't already lost. Pride was a small matter these days.

"So, did you come to tell me you want to marry me?"

"Well, as a matter of fact I did," She lifted her chin in defiance.

He needed to know what had changed her mind. "Why?"

"Why do I want to marry you?" She shoved her hair behind her ear with an unsteady hand.

"Yeah. Why now?" Would she see this through or bolt like some wild, frightened animal?

"It's the only way I can get you to have sex with me." She offered a tenuous smile.

"There is that." She'd regained her sense of humor. That was a start.

"I love you." Her words were so quiet, he almost missed them.

"But you loved me before, and it wasn't enough for you then."

She took his hand in hers and brought it to her mouth, her breath warm against him. It was as if she'd brought him back to life after weeks of only existing.

"I'm not scared anymore, Ryan. I'm not scared to love you and I'm not scared to let you love me."

"How do I know you won't get scared again?" A man could only be resurrected so many times. "When I stumbled across you in those woods, twentysomething years ago, you brought me back to life. I had been hurting for months. You made me whole. Being apart from you these last several weeks...I can't go through that again, Phoebes."

"You have to trust me. Just like I have to trust you. I want to grow old with you. I need you. You're the ebb and flow in my ocean. You bring the change to my life that I need."

"Just like you're the sand on my shore, my anchor, my constant."

Ryan reached in his pants pocket and pulled out the small square box he'd brought home from Jamaica and had carried every day since. He felt ridiculously nervous.

She opened the box and found the simply designed ring of two strands of metal, intertwined, unbroken, linked forever. He felt her pleasure in the link that had always connected them. "It's beautiful."

He wrapped his hand around the nape of her neck beneath the silky fall of her hair and pulled her closer, his body thrumming in response to her scent that had haunted him. "We can look for a diamond—"

"No. This is what I want. When did you get it?" Her mouth was tantalizingly close to his.

"When we were in Jamaica. The afternoon before I proposed that night. Martin had a—"

She laughed, her warm breath soothing him. "Let me guess. Martin had a cousin that works in a jewelry shop."

"How'd you know?" She had the most perfect lips.

"I think Martin's very well-connected," she murmured as her hand cupped his jaw and her mouth found his.

It was a fairly chaste kiss of promise that, nonetheless, sent the fire of desire licking through him. Phoebe pulled away, her eyes reflecting the same need he felt. "I have something for you, as well."

She pulled an envelope out of her handbag and

placed it on the table before him. Ryan pulled out two Air Jamaica tickets and a Hot Sands honeymoon suite confirmation.

Private pools. Sunsets. Long hot days and longer, hotter nights. Tension coiled deep inside him. "You were that sure of me?"

She shook her head. "No. I was that sure of us. I wasn't going to give you up."

Naomi stopped by with the stromboli.

"Can we get those to go?"

Naomi picked the plates up with a knowing smile. "Sure thing. Want me to throw in a baklava or two?"

"That's okay. I think we'll pick up some chocolate-covered doughnuts along the way."

EPILOGUE

Three months later

"WELCOME BACK to Jamaica. It is most excellent to see you again." A genuine smile wreathed Martin's face.

"It's lovely to be back." Phoebe was delighted to see him.

"We're here on our honeymoon," Ryan announced. The same way he'd announced it to anyone who'd listen since they'd said their "I do's" this morning.

Martin pumped Ryan's hand and then Phoebe's. "Did you have the wedding here in our lovely gazebo by the sea?" Martin asked.

"No. We got married in Nashville so our families could attend." It had been important to Phoebe to have Aunt Caroline and Uncle Frank present. Both had cried when she'd asked Uncle Frank to walk her down the aisle. They'd skipped, however, the giving away part. She loved her family but she was no one's to give away. "We would have definitely invited you and Mathilde if we'd tied the knot here."

"Ah, it is so romantic." Martin swiped at a tear. "It is the island magic. Just like me and my Mathilde."

Phoebe smiled, her heart full. You had to love a man who was a sappy sentimentalist. She certainly loved Ryan, and he fit the bill.

Ryan rubbed his hand in small circular motions against her back. "How are Mathilde and the kids?"

"Most excellent. I am a very rich man, you know."

She leaned into the hard length of Ryan's body, absorbing his scent and his heat. "Yes, I do know. I've just become a very rich woman."

"It would be an honor if you would allow me to prepare a special table tonight along with a special menu, if you can take a late seating. My cousin, he is now a chef here."

Laughter sparkled in Ryan's eyes as he glanced at Phoebe. "We'd like that. We're definitely not dressed for dinner now, and we'd still like to walk on the beach."

"Ah. You are fond of our spectacular sunsets, then?"

A long look, full of memories and promise, passed between Ryan and Phoebe. Heat that refused to be cooled by the ocean breeze filled her. "Yes, we're both fond of your sunsets. They're quite—"

"Exhilarating," Ryan finished for her. A wicked

smile pulled his dimple into full play and weakened her knees.

"Most excellent. I look forward to serving you then. Enjoy your sunset."

Phoebe's heart pounded in time with the steel drums as she and Ryan left the restaurant and stepped onto the sugar-fine sand. Her simple white dress left her legs bare to the last slanting rays of the sinking sun and the whisper of the ocean breeze. Ryan clasped her hand in his as they walked along the shoreline, the translucent blue water lapping at their ankles. She glanced at him, his green eyes full of heat and promise.

The sun sank lower until it lost itself between the lines of earth and sky, painting both in vivid oranges and soft pinks. On a secluded section of Jamaican beach she'd come to regard as their own, Phoebe lost herself in the warmth of Ryan's arms and the heat of his kiss.

Bathed in twilight and the warm waters of the Caribbean, Ryan eased her down into the surf.

"It's not dark yet," she murmured, more observation than objection.

His hand cupped her breast. His finger brushed her nipple through her dress as he nibbled along her neck. "I know."

"You know what this is?" She tugged his shirttail free and slid her hands against the hair-roughened plane of his belly, her breath coming in short, sharp pants. She wanted him as fiercely as she had the first time. She thought it would always be this way between them—hot and needy and "...barely decent."

* * * * *

THE ONE WHO GOT AWAY

Jo Leigh

To Lawrence: The One Who (Almost) Got Away!

PROLOGUE

To: The Gang at Eve's Apple
From: Taylor
EvesApple.com
Subject: BEN!!!!!

IF YOU'RE LOOKING FOR something soft, you won't
find it in Ben's face. Not at first.

He is all hard lines and sharp angles. The cheekbones, of course. The stuff of dreams. Improbable.
Dangerous. Unforgettable. The cheekbones make you
look at his eyes, give you no choice. They're dark and
knowing. Too knowing. Which makes you look away,
but not for long. The focus shifts to his lips. The upper
is thin, but there. The pouty lower makes up for it.
And when the corners of his lips curve up in that slight
smile, when those eyes take you in from the toes up,
when he flicks his dark, straight, too-long hair back
with a hand, there's nothing to do but surrender. Give
it up. Lie down, whether you're near a bed or not.

That's Ben. My first lover. My best lover. Might as
well have been my only lover. Because it's been ten
years, and I can't get that face out of my head.

Every man I've dated, from that gorgeous Richard Gere–like attorney to that race-car driver from Atlanta has failed the Ben Test. Not that I even realized there was such a thing, but now that I know I'm going to see Ben again, I finally get it. I see what he's done to me.

So, my fellow Eve's Apple Compatriots, my sisters in righteous conquests who seek the perfect Men To Do before we say I Do...I hereby declare that Ben Bowman, the man of the exquisite cheekbones, of the mesmerizing dark eyes, is my official MAN TO DO.

I, Taylor Hanson, am going to spend one week with the aforementioned Mr. Bowman, in, appropriately enough, Las Vegas, Sin City, while attending my brother's wedding. I will, without fail, get Ben "Cheekbones" Bowman into my bed, and then I will see, with my very own eyes, that regardless of cheekbones, of knowing eyes, and wicked smiles, Bowman is just a guy. Like a bunch of other guys. Not a God, not an icon, not the King of the Stud Muffins.

I was only eighteen.

And then, my dear friends, I will come home, and I SHALL BE FREE to find my Mr. Right. My forever guy. Because I will have broken the spell. Damn it.

Love and Kisses,
Taylor

CHAPTER ONE

Only in Vegas.

Ben watched the crowd standing in front of the Wheel of Fortune slot machine as he made his way through the airline terminal toward the baggage claim area. Breathless with anticipation, a dozen or so tourists watched the spinning wheel as it slowed, coming to a shaky stop under the bold 20. A collective groan marked their disappointment, and Ben marveled again at the gullibility of humans.

All anyone needed to do was take one look at the Strip to see that Vegas wasn't in the business of giving away money. But most of the good folk who came to Vegas didn't stop to think about the odds. They came for magic. For the turn of the wheel, the flip of a card that would free them from the daily grind of working for a living. They wanted the dream and no place on earth knew how to sell the dream better.

Not that Ben didn't mind a friendly game of poker now and then, but he had no illusions about windfalls or magic. He believed in hard work and persistence. If luck ever entered the picture it was because he'd made sure to be in the right place at the right time.

He passed the shops selling overpriced leather jackets, gaudy trinkets and T-shirts, finally arriving at the escalator that would take him down to the baggage claim area.

As was his wont, he'd checked in at the last possible moment, assuring that his luggage would be some of the first out of the plane. In fact, this time his bag was the very first. A few minutes later, he was in a cab on his way to the Hard Rock Hotel.

He stared at the vision that was Las Vegas as the cab made its way along Paradise Road. How appropriate. The Hard Rock wasn't on the Strip per se, but two blocks east. Still it managed to be the hippest of the big hotels. He'd never stayed there, but he'd had dinner at Nobu and the Pink Taco. Nice place, if you liked that sort of thing. He didn't. Give him a mountain lake and a fishing pole, and he was all set. Glitz and glamour made him itchy, but this was Steve's wedding, and he'd have gone to the far side of the moon for that.

It puzzled him, however. Steve Hanson had been his closest friend since the fifth grade, and while they hadn't lived in the same town since college, they still got together twice a year to go deep-sea fishing. It made things easier that Steve owned the boats. Five of them, actually, all moored in his and Steve's hometown, San Diego. Steve had eschewed the white-collar life of his father to follow the beat of his own drum. He'd started out with one boat, *The Golden Mermaid,* and had increased his fleet by a boat every other year for ten years. He'd made himself a good life, and as far as Ben could see, he was a truly happy man. What Ben couldn't see was why he was about to change all that.

He hadn't discussed his plans with Ben, or the reasons behind his decision. There had just been that one phone call where Steve had asked him to come to Vegas, to be his best man. He'd said his fiancée's name was Lisa, and that she was the best thing that had ever happened to him. He'd also said that he was going to keep the fleet but move to Kansas, and work for her father at his aerospace company. That was the kicker. The puzzle. Steve hated corporate life, had broken his father's heart by not taking over the family insurance business. So why now? Why her? Why marriage?

The cab turned into the big driveway, underneath the huge guitar that was the Hard Rock logo. The lot was crowded with every kind of vehicle from Hummers to limos to beat-up Chevys. At the entrance, a uniformed doorman tried to help but Ben took his suitcase to the front desk. His room, on the fourteenth floor, was ready and after a long walk through the noisy casino, and another down a silent padded hallway, he reached it.

The parlor of his deluxe room had gold walls, green carpeting, a semicircular couch with a round black coffee table, a wet bar and, behind purple drapes that framed French doors, a fabulous view of the Strip. The bedroom wasn't quite as fancy, but nice. Two queen platform beds with leather headboards, a built-in TV instead of the usual armoire and another spectacular view.

He tossed his suitcase onto the bed, then noticed the light on his phone blinking. He punched the numbers to get the message. It was Steve, sounding chipper, asking him to dinner. They were to meet at the front desk in about three hours, long enough for Ben to have a shower and a nap. The last part of the message was that Taylor would be joining the party, and that she was looking forward to seeing him.

Taylor.

Ben hung up the phone, but he didn't move. She'd been a little kid when he'd first met her: Steve's baby sister. She'd followed them wherever she could, always wanting attention, always wanting to be let in on the fun. They'd ditched her as often a possible, and he could still remember her tears.

But mostly he remembered the last time he'd seen her. It had to be ten years ago, just after she'd graduated from high school. He'd been at his folk's house for their thirtieth wedding anniversary, and had stayed on for a week while they'd gone on the second honeymoon cruise to the Virgin Islands he'd treated them to. Taylor had come by on a Friday afternoon and she'd stayed until Sunday.

She'd grown into a beauty and when she'd come

on to him, he hadn't the will or the strength to turn her away.

The weekend had been one of the most exciting of his life. She'd been a wildcat, and he'd loved every second of it. She'd cried when he'd said goodbye, but he'd known the tears were more about the end of a fantasy than any real heartbreak.

Taylor had been heading off for college, for a whole new life that had nothing to do with childhood crushes. He'd returned to the New York police force, determined to become a sergeant. By the time he'd settled back into his regular routine, he'd felt certain she'd forgotten all about him.

It would be good to see her again. According to Steve, she'd never married. Smart girl.

Ben glanced at the clock, and got up. He didn't want to be late for dinner.

TAYLOR CHECKED HERSELF OUT one last time before she had to leave. Her hair wasn't too horrifying, although she would have to buy some kind of conditioner that would give it some lift. She'd put on her makeup with care, and felt she'd hit the right combination of come-hither and stay there. After trying on every item of clothing she'd brought, she'd ended up wearing a cute little Michael Kors she'd picked up at a ritzy secondhand store. It was black, sleeveless, and skintight, with kicky leather shoulders that made her boobs look much bigger than they were. She'd have to hold in her stomach the entire night, but it was worth it. She wanted Ben's jaw to drop the moment he saw her. She sucked in harder. Realizing that she couldn't go the entire night without a breath, she gave it up.

So she pooched. He probably had love handles.

She got her purse, made sure she had her room key, and headed off to the elevator, her pulse racing faster with each step.

By the time she reached the casino level, she was practically hyperventilating. What had she been thinking? She hadn't seen the man in ten years, she had no idea what his life was like. For all she knew, he could have brought a lover with him. Steve hadn't mentioned anything about Ben being attached, but then Steve was a notoriously bad gossip. He'd had all kinds of famous people on his boats, and had he ever brought home one juicy tidbit? Never. She hated that.

And she hated the butterflies in her stomach. This wasn't going to work. Taylor leaned against a large display case exhibiting stage clothes worn by Shania Twain. The woman had to weigh twelve pounds, the outfit was so tiny. But that was beside the point. Taylor had to do something, and do it now. She could go back to her room, call Steven and say she didn't feel well, but that would only delay the inevitable. She couldn't stay in her room the whole week. What made oodles more sense was for her to forget about her Man To Do plan and just go enjoy her brother's happiness. Forget about Ben and his cheekbones. If he looked anything like he had, there was no way he would be single. No woman could possibly resist him, and living in New York, he was up to his deliciously square chin in stunning babes.

She straightened her shoulders, flicked her hair back and pasted on a smile. Tonight, in fact this whole week, wasn't about her. It was about her brother. For heaven's sake, she hadn't even met Lisa yet, and she was going to be her sister-in-law. With that thought firmly in mind, she once again headed toward the lobby, letting the sounds of bells, coins, music and chatter ease her way.

So what if she didn't get her Man To Do? She had her vibrator, and that was a relationship she could count on.

BEN SPOTTED STEVE STANDING near the Jimi Hendrix display. He had his arm around a tall, slim blonde. She was frowning, but even so, she was pretty. A different kind of pretty for Steve. The women he went for tended to look like Playboy Bunnies. They partied like Bunnies, too. But Ben didn't get that feeling from Lisa. She was dressed in white slacks, a pale blue top and a white jacket, tailored, classy; more Midwest than So Cal. Her hair was neat, not quite to her shoulders, and her shoes and purse were both white and conservative. She looked like she'd be right at home in a country club or on a golf course, not on one of Steve's boats.

Ben kept on walking, shaking off his first impressions. One thing he'd learned the hard way was that looks don't mean squat. He'd judge Lisa for who she was behind the Ralph Lauren look.

Steve turned, and grinned like he'd just caught a two-hundred pound swordfish. "Ben, you old bastard!"

Ben shook his head. Some things didn't change, thank God. "I didn't know they let people like you in here. Where's security?"

Steve let go of his girl and gave Ben a rib-bruising hug. "Thanks for coming, man."

"Oh, right. Like I'd let you get married without me? Someone's got to tell her what she's getting into."

Steve laughed, that big hearty guffaw that was as distinct as his fingerprints. It made Ben feel like he was home.

"This—" Steve said, moving toward his lady "—is Lisa."

Ben met her gaze, liked her smile. Close up, she was attractive, but subtly so. Her blue eyes seemed a little hesitant, judging him. Which was only fair, he supposed. "Nice to meet you, Lisa."

"Steven has told me so much about you."

"Uh-oh. Remember, innocent until proven guilty."

She laughed, then took Steve's arm. "Do you think we should call your sister? I don't want to lose our reservation."

"Let's give her another— Wait. There she is."

Ben turned to follow Steve's gaze. He wasn't in the least prepared for what he was about to see.

TAYLOR SLOWED AS SHE GOT her first look at Ben Bowman. Oh, shit. He'd changed, all right. He'd become the most devastatingly handsome man she'd ever laid eyes on.

Her legs wobbled beneath her, but she focused on putting one foot in front of the other, and not falling on her fanny. She didn't know what to look at first. No, not true, the cheekbones were first, they had to be, and holy mama, they were even more chiseled than she remembered. His eyes seemed darker, but she'd need to be closer to be sure. He still wore his hair long, just past his ears. It wasn't neat or tidy in the least. It didn't need to be. He looked like he'd just gotten out of bed. And she meant that in the best possible way.

Her fingers twitched, itching to run through those dark locks, to see those familiar lips curl up in a wicked smile.

Okay, so she was back to the original plan. Sleep with him or die trying. She could do it. She had to do it. Hell, there was a long couch just this side of the lobby that looked pretty comfortable.

Finally, seconds before she was close enough to actually speak to Ben, her gaze shifted down. His body was every bit as wonderful as her memory had promised. Not the tallest guy on the block, but perfectly proportioned. He wore jeans, well-worn, cowboy boots beneath them. His shirt was white, no tie, his jacket hunter green. Altogether a delicious package.

No way he wasn't taken. Not possible.

"Taylor, hello?"

Startled, she looked at her brother. "Hi."

Steve laughed, shook his head. "I see you remember Ben."

Heat filled her cheeks as she forced herself to forget about Ben and concentrate on her brother and his wife-to-be. After a quick kiss and a poke to his shoulder, she said, "Well? Are you going to introduce me?"

Steve stepped over to the woman in the white pantsuit and put his arm around her shoulders. "Taylor, this is Lisa. The woman who's changed my whole life."

Taylor smiled and moved in for an awkward air kiss. To say she was surprised was an understatement. *This* was Lisa? This preppy sorority sister? Not possible. Taylor glanced at Ben, and from his practiced look, she could tell she wasn't the only one who thought something was screwy here.

But she wasn't being fair. She hadn't even talked to Lisa, so maybe inside those Alpha-Gamma-Delta clothes there lived the soul of a wild woman.

"Everybody hungry?"

Taylor turned to Steve. "Starving. Where are we eating?"

"I thought we'd go over to the Venetian tonight. Eat at The Grand Luxe."

"Great."

He turned to Lisa, his gaze adoring. "I'll go get a cab," he said.

"I'll come with you. Give Taylor and Ben a chance to catch up."

They walked away, leaving her alone with *him* and awkwardness swallowed her whole. She smiled, turned toward the big glass doors with the guitar-shaped pulls.

"It's been a while," Ben said, moving closer to her, ratcheting up the heat in the casino by a good ten degrees. "You look great."

"Thanks. So do you."

His low chuckle made her look. The moment their eyes met, she was lost—eighteen again, fumbling, frightened, drowning in lust.

Ben watched as Taylor's eyes dilated, the pale blue shrinking to a thin halo. Her lips parted, revealing the tops of her even, white teeth. Her cheeks turned from pastel pink to dark, and he thought of her breasts, remembering clearly the shape of her nipples, the color of her areoles matching exactly her blush.

He let his gaze wander to her lips: plump, glistening, inviting, then down her remarkable neck, long and elegant, like Audrey Hepburn's, only Taylor was blond, a real blonde, with long straight hair that flowed down her back, that rippled in the artificial lights of the lobby. Her figure had changed, all for the better. At eighteen, she'd been so slender he'd been afraid of hurting her. Now, her hips had become womanly, her breasts a perfect handful. But she still had the silky skin of a teenager.

That weekend so long ago had rocked his world. Had made him realize what making love could be. Had taken him from fair-to-middling to a pretty damn skilled lover. He'd remembered it from time to time, always with a smile. But he'd never once thought there could be a repeat. Time and life had a way of softening the edges of memories. He had no desire to refocus, to see the inevitable chinks and flaws that ride along with reality.

Oh, who was he kidding. He'd beg if he had to.

CHAPTER TWO

"WE'D BETTER GET OUT THERE," Taylor said. "They probably have the cab ready."

"Right." Ben waited until she started walking toward the front entrance to move next to her, to place his hand at the small of her back. He felt her shiver as he touched her.

She cleared her throat. "So you're living in New York."

"Yep. Manhattan."

"I love that city. Where?"

"What used to be called Hell's Kitchen. Now it's almost as trendy as Tribeca."

"You must hate that."

"I do. But there's nothing to be done. I've got my office in the same building, two stories down. I don't want to move."

"What's it like being a private eye?"

"It's just like in the movies. Smoky bars, jazz playing in the background, fallen women, men with dark pasts and unregistered guns."

"Cute," she said, as they got outside.

The heat shocked him again, like when he'd come

from the airport. Not that it wasn't hot in Manhattan, but here it didn't stick to your skin like wet towels.

Taylor must have noticed his reaction. "It was in the low seventies when I left this morning," she said. "Oh, there they are."

Steve was standing beside a Yellow Cab. "You're in San Francisco, right?"

She nodded. "Right near Lombardi. The apartment is too expensive, but I love riding my bike there."

"Ten speed?"

"Honda Shadow."

He stopped short. A motorcycle? Interesting. "You'll have to tell me all about it."

Before she slid into the cab, she smiled at him. "Oh, I plan to."

He watched her maneuver onto the backseat, which was quite a feat considering the tightness of her dress. She did well, very much the lady. But he had a feeling that was only for show. At least he hoped so.

Steve got in beside her, and Ben got in front. The ride to the Venetian wasn't long. It would have been shorter, but for the masses of tourists. Still, it was better than trying to get through Manhattan on a busy evening.

He'd never been to the Venetian, and was impressed with the high arched ceilings and the frescos on the walls. Even the floor tiles were European and stately, somehow managing to appear subdued and classy.

After a long walk past a lot of high-end shops, through the casino, they arrived at the café.

Steve ushered them inside, past a considerable line, into the large, beautifully decorated restaurant. It also had decked-out ceilings, fancy floors and great leather booths. The bar looked as if it served expensive martinis, but the crowd seemed happy and from what he could see on the plates held aloft by the waitstaff, no one would leave hungry.

A waitress showed them to their booth, and he slid in next to Taylor. It was roomy, which wasn't necessarily a good thing when one was sitting beside a woman in a tiny dress. But he wasn't going to go there. Not yet, at least. Tonight was for Steve.

The happy couple kissed after they got their menus. Steve smiled broadly, Lisa more conservatively, but that didn't mean anything. She opened her menu and studied it carefully, her brows furrowing slightly as if the choice was crucial.

Ben glanced down, only it would take more than a glance to get through the choices in the book they called a menu. He decided on something he could always trust, a New York Sirloin steak and baked potato.

Their waitress took their drink orders, and then it was just the four of them.

"All right," Taylor said, putting her menu aside. "I want to hear it all. Omit nothing. How you met, when you fell in love, why you decided to get married in Vegas, the whole nine yards."

Steve laughed and Lisa gave a tentative grin. But then Lisa was the stranger amongst them, and that had to be hard.

Ben liked Taylor's style. Come right out with it. No beating around the bush. She'd always been like that, since the time she was a little kid, demanding to play touch football when she could hardly hold the ball. The only time she'd been reticent had been that last weekend, but he figured it was the newness of the situation. He imagined that had changed.

"We met on the *Turquoise Mermaid*," Steve said. "Her dad was fishing and Lisa decided to join him and his buddies for the day. She didn't fish, which turned out to be a good thing because we started talking and just kept right on going."

"I hadn't even wanted to go," Lisa said, leaning in to the table, her eyes brighter now that they were on a subject she could dive into. "But my father insisted, although he was with Trent Foster and Cal Peterson. Cal brought his wife, Annie, who is closer to my age than his, so Daddy dragged me along. But Annie got horribly seasick, and she didn't want to talk to anyone, which left me free to concentrate on the wildly handsome skipper."

Steve's grin widened. "I got so involved with Lisa it almost cost her father a swordfish. But we nailed him." He leaned over and kissed her cheek. "Didn't we?"

"We? I got as far away as I could. I had no idea swordfish were so big and so dangerous." She settled back in the booth. "At least we won't have to worry about that anymore."

Taylor didn't like the sound of that. "What do you mean?"

"She means I'm letting Larry take over the management of the fleet," Steve said. "Once we're married, I'm moving to Kansas. Her dad's offered me a hell of a good job in sales and marketing. I don't know much about the aerospace industry yet, but I'm learning. They make seals, connectors, gaskets, that kind of thing. Real high-end stuff, the highest temperature seals in the industry. I'll be traveling a lot. Except for missing Lisa, I think it'll be great. I mean, they have this major air show in France every year. Of course, she'll come with me."

Taylor was grateful the waitress arrived with their drinks so she had a moment to absorb what she'd just heard. Her brother hated working in an office. He'd built his life around the freedom of the sea. This was a complete one-eighty, and it made her nervous as hell. She sipped her Cosmopolitan, glanced at Ben, whose expression mirrored her own concern. "So Larry's going to run the fleet, huh? You're okay with that?"

Steve's grin faltered. "Yeah, sure. He'll do a great

job. He's been with me for six years now, and he knows everything about the job."

"But Kansas?" Taylor leaned in, trying like hell to make Steve look her in the eyes. "No sailing? No fishing? It's what you love best in all the world."

"He won't miss it," Lisa said. "And we'll visit San Diego often enough for him to keep his sea legs. You know how bright he is, though, and it's a shame to waste that on fishing. He has a brilliant career in front of him. I'm sure one day he'll take over the company. My father always wanted a son, and now he'll have one."

"You had no interest in the business?" Ben asked.

Lisa laughed. "God, no. I have my own interior design firm. I've done some of the largest homes in Wichita."

"Really?" Taylor said, her concern deepening by the second.

"Oh, yes. I absolutely love it. My mother works with me, and we have a wonderful assistant, Renee. Right now I work out of mother's house, but when Steve and I build our home, we'll include an office. That way, when we have children, I'll be able to be nearby all the time."

"Wow. It sounds like you've got the whole thing worked out."

"We do," Steve said. "Like Lisa says, it's time for me to grow up. Take on the real world. I can't be

Peter Pan forever." He kissed her again, lightly on the cheek.

The waitress came back to take their dinner orders. Taylor stole another look at Ben, and he wasn't disguising his worry in the least. Lisa seemed like a very nice woman and all, but this was nuts. Steve would be miserable working in sales. He hated that kind of thing, and without an ocean nearby, he'd go stir-crazy.

"It seems like all this happened pretty damn fast," Ben said.

"It all just fell into place," Steve said. He held on to his drink with both hands. "I'd been thinking a lot about my life, what I was doing with it. Sure, it's fun helping a bunch of rich guys catch trophy fish, but, I don't know…"

"My father took to him from the moment they met." Lisa smiled. "Just like I did. He saw the potential in Steve. He's a brilliant salesman. There's no reason on earth he can't use those talents in the real world. He could take Daddy's business to the top."

"It sounds lucrative."

"Oh, yeah." Steve nodded. "I'll be making more than I ever dreamed of."

"I didn't know you dreamed about money." Taylor wished she could say more, remind him of how he'd laughed at all those poor schmucks chasing a dime. But it wasn't the time or the place. She needed to think. If this truly was the direction Steve wanted to go, then who was she to butt in? Although it felt wrong. Seriously wrong.

"Of course I think about money. Who doesn't? I mean, if it was just me, it wouldn't matter. But with a wife and kids... How could I put the time into the boats? You know the life. Living at the pier, away for days at a time, no regular schedules."

"I suppose so," she said.

Ben lifted his glass. "To new roads."

She joined in the toast, all the while feeling like her brother wasn't heading down a new road, but off a cliff.

BEN HELD THE TAXI DOOR for Taylor, unable to look away from the expanse of thigh her short dress revealed. Despite his genuine and deep concern for his friend, a large part of him had been preoccupied with the woman at his side. No matter what was happening with his frontal lobe, the primal part of his brain had locked onto Taylor, her scent, the way her hair cascaded down her shoulder, the curve of her breasts.

His plan was to ditch Steve and Lisa, which wasn't going to be too difficult, as Lisa had already said she was beat, and get Taylor to himself. So they could talk. That's all. Talk about Steve.

Steve paid off the cab, then turned to the small group. "We're going to our room. We have to be up at the crack of dawn to pick up Lisa's mom at the airport."

"When's our mom coming in?" Taylor asked.

"Tomorrow afternoon."

"Do you need me to get her?"

"Nope, we have it covered." Steve kissed his sister on the cheek. "But thanks. Why don't you and Ben go have some fun? Win a little dough."

"Right," she said. "You know how lucky I am with cards."

Steve laughed. "Okay, so don't play poker."

"I still maintain that you cheat every chance you get."

He held his hand up to his chest as if shocked. "Me? Never."

"Yeah, right."

"Thanks for the dinner, you two. We'll catch up with you tomorrow," Ben said.

"Great."

Lisa said good-night, then took Steve's hand. Taylor watched them walk into the hotel. Ben watched Taylor.

"This is weird as hell," he said, as soon as they'd entered the lobby.

"I'll say. Did you have any idea?"

He shook his head. "Last I heard, he was thinking about buying another boat."

"He asked me to quit my damn boring job and come work for him. He said I was a fool for wasting my life," Taylor added.

"So what changed?"

Taylor shook her head. "Love?"

"I don't know..."

Ben wanted to touch her again, as he had on the way out. Gently, palm to the small of her back. He wanted to feel her quiver. Instead, he put his hands in his pockets.

"I want to talk to Mom about it," Taylor said. "Maybe she knows."

"Good idea." He stopped just before they reached the main casino floor. "Are you too tired for a drink? We could go outside by the pool."

She smiled and he thought he detected a slight blush. "That sounds great."

"Good." He took her hand, which might have been better than touching her back, and led her through the youngish crowd. Everyone was on the right side of dressy, trying to look hip. The music, loud enough to make people shout to be heard, was only the coolest rock. Right now they were playing Stevie Ray Vaughn from his second album. Although there were lots of people playing video poker and slots, they were mostly silent, concentrating on whatever voodoo they had to mesmerize the machines. The real hubbub came from the craps tables.

Ben and Taylor threaded through the winners and losers until they got to a hall leading past a couple of high-end restaurants, to the door to the pool. A guard stood at the exit, and they had to show their room keys.

After that, they stepped into a lush, green paradise. The pool area, one of the prettiest in Vegas, had a lot of night swimmers gliding about, mostly by the swim-up bar and the water blackjack tables. But that's not where Ben wanted to be. He led Taylor past the purple lounge chairs and the swaying palms 'til they passed the huge bar. Once there, they climbed a few steps to reach the cabana level. He hoped he'd find one empty, and luck was with him. During the day, the cabanas could be rented for a bundle, but after ten, if you were lucky, you could homestead. The refuse from another party still cluttered the small round table, but that wasn't a problem.

He ushered Taylor to one of the green padded chairs, and he sat next to her. The television in the corner was off, which was what he wanted, and the overhead fan was on, creating a nice breeze in the semiprivate space. He'd like it even better if he could close the curtain, but he didn't want to scare her.

"This is unbelievable," she said. "I haven't been here before, but I'd heard about the cabanas."

"They're not easy to reserve," he said, "although sometimes you can get lucky."

She leaned back in her chair and crossed her legs. It was a sight he wouldn't soon forget. The long stretch of bare thigh, the perfection of her knee, the subtle curve of her calf. To say nothing of the arch of her foot, and the seduction of her high black heel. He felt as mesmerized as a compulsive gambler staring at a royal flush.

It was the waitress that brought him out of his daze. She of the black leather short-shorts, leopard-print vest and perky smile. "What can I get you?"

Taylor ordered a piña colada, he got a scotch on the rocks. The waitress cleared their table, then hustled off, leaving them in the relative quiet. The music, now something by Tom Petty, wafted in along with the laughter and muffled chatter from the group at the bar.

Taylor leaned toward him. "It's good to see you, Ben."

His gaze moved up to her eyes radiating fondness that touched him unexpectedly. "You, too."

"You probably know how horrible Steve is at gossip, so I don't know much of what's happened to you other than you're now a private investigator. Are you happy?"

"For the most part. I like being my own boss."

"That makes sense."

"But I still work with the NYPD a lot. More than I figured."

"Interesting stuff?"

"Occasionally. Mostly it's the kind of footwork that takes a special know-how." He chuckled. "That makes it sound like I'm some Colombo or something. I meant that I do the kind of background checks that don't make it into the NCIC. Paperwork traces, poking into things that might get dicey for the force. That kind of thing."

"I think it sounds fascinating."

"How kind of you."

"I'm more interested in your personal life. Again, according to my brother, you're divorced."

"For two years now."

She ran her hand down her thigh to her knee. Not scratching, just an unconscious gesture that held him rapt. Odd, because it had been a hell of a long time since he'd been spellbound by a woman. Maybe it was the memories. Or the fact that he'd had to get up before God this morning and he was getting punchy.

"I'm sorry," she said. "Was it bad?"

"I can't think of a divorce that isn't. But we're friends. In fact, we still occasionally make a night of it."

Taylor's brows lifted.

"Not that much of a night. Alyson's gay."

Taylor's brows stayed lifted.

"You can imagine how that went over with all my cop buddies."

"Oh, my."

"At the very least. But I don't think I'm too emotionally scarred. I vent my anguish by boycotting all reruns of *Ellen*."

Her laughter hit him low, like a vibration right in the balls. It felt good, too good.

The drinks arrived, and she tried to pay. He used

his best scowl, and gave the waitress too large a tip. Once they were alone again, he sipped his scotch, aware that it was either going to make him drunk as a sailor or put him to sleep. "So what are we going to do about this wedding thing?"

Taylor twirled her drink with her straw. It made the little umbrella spin. "I'm not sure there's anything we can do. Or should."

"Are you kidding? Can you honestly see Steve in a suit and tie, doing aircraft sales in the middle of friggin' Kansas?"

She shook her head. "No, I can't. But maybe he's had some sort of epiphany. Maybe we should honor that."

"Epiphany? Steve? Are we talking about the same guy?"

Her sigh echoed his own frustration. "I know. Let me talk to Mom. I don't want to jump the gun."

"He's getting married in six days."

"Look, the last thing I want to do is hurt him. He's such a puppy. And I know he's lonely."

Ben grinned. "I've never thought of him as a puppy, but I do agree about the lonely part. It's not easy to find a woman who likes to fish as much as he does."

"That doesn't mean he has to go in the opposite direction. I could even understand a compromise. But this…this is nuts."

"I agree."

She sipped again, and he focused on her lips. Glossy-pink. Perfectly formed, ripe for kissing. She'd become an uncommon beauty, and if his signals weren't crossed, she wasn't averse to the idea of making this week quite memorable. However, it wasn't going to be remembered for tonight. The dollop of scotch had gone straight to his head, and if he didn't get up to the room soon, things were going to get ugly.

"Taylor," he said, "I hate to cut the party short, but I'm going to have to bail. I was up way too early this morning."

She put her drink down on the table, and he would swear she looked guilty. Why? He hadn't a clue.

"No problem. I need to get some sleep myself." She stood, smoothing her short skirt down. "Are you going to be around tomorrow? I'll talk to Mom as soon as I can."

He pulled out his wallet, then one of his cards. "Try my room, but if not, I've got my cell."

"Terrific." Her smile made him weak in the knees.

He stood, held out his hand. "Can I walk you up?"

"Thank you, but actually, I need to pick up something at the gift shop. You go on ahead."

Disappointed, he nodded. Leaned over and kissed her cheek. Wanted to do a lot more. But he backed off. What he needed was sleep. He wanted to be on his game for Taylor. Nothing less would do. "Until tomorrow."

She nodded, and as he walked away, he heard that sigh again. It almost made him turn around, but he held the course. Although he made his living interpreting nonverbal cues, he couldn't figure this one out. Either she was glad to get rid of him, or damn sorry to see him go.

He chose to believe it was the latter.

CHAPTER THREE

TAYLOR WATCHED BEN GET INTO the elevator. He smiled at her, not noticing that behind him, a tall brunette in shorts was eyeing him with palpable lust. Or maybe he did know. Maybe he'd grown so accustomed to gorgeous women wanting him that it was old hat by now. The elevator doors closed while she still had her hand up, waving.

She wasn't sure why she'd told him she had to buy something. In fact, she didn't need a thing, and for all she knew the gift shop was closed by now. Instead, she wandered into the circular casino, her gaze shifting from the machines to the gamblers at the tables.

She'd never done much playing herself, even though she'd come to Vegas several times since she'd turned twenty-one. Mostly she liked to hang out at the blackjack tables—the cheap ones, not those with a minimum bet of twenty-five dollars. She wasn't rich enough to squander money like that. And normally, she wasn't an extraordinary risk-taker. Her mother didn't believe that, given her preference for motor-cycles over cars, but it was true. There were only so many chances a person could take in life, and she wanted to make her gambles count.

Like her personal agenda for this trip, for example. Sleeping with Ben wasn't so much a gamble as a last-ditch attempt to get herself back on course. She was twenty-eight, for heaven's sake, and dammit, she wanted to get married. Have kids. Two, to be precise. And she had no intention of settling.

Sure there had been nice guys, and she'd liked one or two a great deal. But it hadn't been enough. Perhaps her friends from Eve's Apple were right: she was too picky. She wanted a fairy-tale hero, not a real-life husband. What Taylor didn't understand was why she had to have one or the other. And no, she didn't feel as if she were reaching for the moon.

The truth was, she liked her life. She didn't sit around and mope because she wasn't married. She had lots of things she loved doing, including her bike, shooting pool in her league, going to flea markets, reading, a secret addiction to the Food Channel. She never felt bored, she always had a full plate, and for the most part, she was happy. All she really wanted was someone to share it all with. And, oh, God, how she wanted to have kids.

The Apple gals had suggested she consider doing that on her own, but Taylor had dismissed the idea. In her opinion children needed a father. Not that women couldn't raise kids successfully solo, but it was tough on everybody. Taylor had gotten along incredibly well with her father, and that relationship had formed her in so many ways. A lot of her independence had come from her father's attitude toward her. He'd always told her she could do anything, be anyone she wanted to be.

She couldn't imagine having grown up without his influence.

So, okay, maybe by the time she was thirty-five, if she still hadn't found Mr. Right, then she'd seriously consider it. But for now, she was determined to go for the brass ring. Being with Ben was an important part of the equation, and she still believed with all her heart that once this week was over, her life would change dramatically. She'd be able to date with new eyes, not always comparing the men she met to Ben.

She already felt better about things. His looks, for example. Yes, it was true he was stunningly gorgeous. But she'd been able to put that fact into perspective. There were lots of gorgeous men, but frankly, she would have been drawn to him even if he wasn't so handsome.

And that was the whole point. By the time Steve and Lisa got married she would have everything about Ben in perspective, and then she would be able to move on.

It didn't hurt that the task was going to be such a pleasant one, either. She grinned, but her mood deflated the next second. Perspective was well and fine, but the end result also meant she was going to lose something kind of special. A long-held fantasy was going to disappear in the light of those new eyes, and that was kind of sad.

He'd been her superhero, her perfect guy for so long, it was hard to imagine that standard falling away. But it had to.

Someone bumped her right shoulder, and she turned to face a nice-looking, white-haired gentleman in a really snazzy tuxedo. He smiled, bowed his head gently and apologized. She nodded, then headed toward the elevator, but stopped just before she left the casino floor. There was an Elvis slot machine which would play a song if you hit the jackpot. She pulled a five from her purse, and slipped it in the slot. Instead of a handle, she pressed a button, playing maximum coins. Nothing.

Nothing the second hit, or the third. In the end she only got one cherry. Her five was gone, and she hadn't heard "Love Me Tender."

C'est la vie. Her real gamble was up in his room, sleeping by now. Dreaming of her?

BEN STARED AT THE CLOCK on the night table, the minutes passing so slowly they felt like hours. Sleep eluded him—due, to a large degree, to his preoccupation with Taylor.

The connection was still there after all these years. He hadn't expected that. She'd been so young back then, and had he had an ounce of decency in him, he'd be ashamed that he'd taken advantage of her youth. Yeah, she'd come on to him, but a stronger man would have said no. When it came to Taylor, however, he wasn't the least bit strong.

Not that he'd always felt that way about her. Back when he and Steve had first started hanging out, Taylor had been a nuisance. She'd followed them everywhere in the tradition of baby sisters, always running to her mother when they'd shut her out of their "big kid" adventures. So they'd had to drag her along when it would have been a lot more fun without her. He hadn't minded too much. As an only child, he'd always wondered what it would be like to have a sibling. He would have voted for a brother, however. A girl was too foreign. Too girly. And he'd wanted to be the toughest kid in town.

Steve had always protected the little brat, no matter what, even though he'd complained about her presence. Then protecting Taylor had become a part of him, too. He'd kept the older kids from picking on the tall, skinny tomboy.

After he'd graduated high school, he'd pretty much forgotten about her. Until he'd come home that last week, just after she'd turned eighteen.

His folks were gone on a trip he'd bought them. He'd liked the quiet and the peace, the time to study. He'd been taking night classes, studying forensics. During the day, he'd been a beat cop, and the toll had been heavy. The week away had been a blessing.

When Taylor had dropped by, making it awkwardly, painfully clear that she'd wanted him to take her, he'd hesitated, sure, but finally, he'd given in.

They'd stayed in bed for damn near three days. Doing everything they could think of, and by God the girl had an amazing imagination. She'd been wild, free, unafraid. The first time she'd taken him in her mouth, he'd nearly had a heart attack. And he could still remember her cries when he'd showed her the pleasure of his mouth on her.

She'd cried when they said goodbye, and he'd felt bad, but he'd explained to her that he was only in town for a short visit. The letters she'd sent him had come frequently at first, always with an invitation for a return visit, but he'd only answered one. There was no future for the two of them. Even if she had ended up at a college in New York, he couldn't have kept up a relationship.

His career had been his whole focus for a long, long time. Back then, he'd wanted to be a homicide detective, and he'd accepted every lousy assignment, volunteered for all the crap no one else wanted to do. He'd eventually gotten his master's degree in forensic science.

But he'd still made it out to California most years to go fishing with Steve. He'd heard about Taylor's adventures at Berkeley, her first apartment, her job as a paralegal.

Steve had also told her that Taylor wanted to marry,

to have kids, to have the kind of life that demanded the suburbs. Not Manhattan. Not with a cop.

But this week wasn't about marriage and kids, at least not for them. It was Vegas, after all. Sin City. They were here to have a good time, to be there for Steve, although not in the way Steve imagined.

Ben turned over, thinking about his friend, what had gotten into him. Lisa represented everything Steve had avoided in his life. His love of his fishing boats, and his freedom, were so important to Steve, and anyone who knew him saw that from the get-go. So what had happened? Why the radical shift?

Lisa seemed nice enough, but there was no way in hell she was going to make Steve forget about his life in San Diego. Kansas was a terrible mistake, Ben felt it in his bones.

Maybe he should just shut up and let Steve do what he needed to. Or maybe, this was what being a friend was all about.

Whatever, he wasn't going to be any good to anyone if he didn't get some sleep.

His hand moved down his stomach until he gripped his length in his hand. Eyes closed, he pictured Taylor sitting across from him in the cabana. That tantalizing stretch of bare thigh.

Before he'd even gotten to the really good parts, it was over. He forced himself to get up, go to the bathroom, but now, exhaustion had taken over full-force.

Once he was back in bed, the minute he'd plunked his head on the pillow he fell into a deep sleep.

TAYLOR DIALED BEN's cell from the pay phone next to the Pink Taco. It rang once, and she heard his sleepy voice growl his "Hello."

"Oh, God, I'm sorry. Go back to sleep. Call me later."

"No, no. I'm up. I just haven't had coffee yet."

"Have it down here. Let's meet at the coffee shop."

"Sure. Give me about ten minutes."

"Okay. I'll get a table."

He hung up and so did she. Damn, even his voice made her twitchy. That low grumble made her want to be there in person when he woke up. She desperately wanted to see his hair tousled, the first smile of the day. Maybe tomorrow.

She brushed her hair back from her shoulder, and went looking for the coffee shop. It was called Mister Lucky's, and there was a small line of people waiting for a table. Almost everyone wore shorts and T-shirts, mostly brightly colored, although more so with the women than the men. Sandals were the footwear of choice, and the accessory of the day was small cameras, equally divided between still and video.

She had chosen her outfit with care. Khaki culottes with a nice leather belt, a pale green sleeveless cotton shirt, nothing spectacular at all, but she felt really comfortable in the outfit which was the important thing. She'd worn her angel earrings, the ones she'd picked up in Sedona two years before. They were kitschy, but she didn't care. They were her favorites.

Her gaze went toward the elevators, but she didn't spot Ben. And then she did.

He had on jeans, well-worn and perfect, with a navy polo shirt. His hair was slicked back, still damp from his shower. Her stomach tightened, and she had the urge to squeeze her legs together. What he did to her had to be illegal in most states. Luckily, Nevada wasn't one of them.

He walked right to her, leaned over and kissed her on the lips, stealing her breath and her equilibrium. She put her hand on the wall behind her to steady herself, and when he smiled at her, she gripped harder.

"Morning."

"Hi."

"I hope this doesn't take long," he said. "I'm a bear before my first cup of coffee."

She cleared her throat and her head, amazed at her reaction. Sure, she wanted the guy, but to flip out completely from a pleasant peck on the lips? What would she do when he really kissed her? She'd have to make damn sure she was lying down.

"What's that smile for?"

"Nothing." She turned toward the café entrance. "It's moving pretty fast. Don't worry."

"Did you speak to your mother?"

She turned back to face him. "Yeah, I did. She's just as mystified by this whole thing as we are."

"Did she have any ideas?"

The people in front of them were led to their seats, and a moment later, a second hostess took them to a quiet table near the breakfast bar. They both ordered coffee, and didn't speak until it arrived. Ben liked his black, which made some kind of weird sense. She wondered what else he liked. Wine with dinner? Sweets?

"Okay," he said, putting his cup down on the saucer. "Where were we?"

"You asked if my mother had any ideas. She did, but she's not sure what to make of it all. About six months ago, they had dinner together, and Steve got real maudlin talking about Dad. He was beating himself up over disappointing Dad by not taking over the business."

"Your dad didn't care."

"I know. But obviously, Steve didn't get it. I think going into business with Lisa's dad is his way of making things right."

"It can't work."

"Of course not. But I don't think Steve's thinking too clearly about that."

Ben drank some more coffee, staring just past her shoulder while he thought. The waitress came by, and he ordered eggs and bacon. She chose a cheese omelet.

After refilling their cups, they were alone again, but Ben didn't say anything.

She waited, not wanting to interrupt.

Finally, he looked at her. "We need a plan. I don't want to alienate Steve, and I don't want to hurt Lisa. But we've got to do something."

She nodded. "I've been thinking about it all morning. What if we just talk to him? Tell him our concerns?"

Ben nodded. "That'll be me. Maybe give him a couple of beers to soften the blow."

"I'd like to talk to Lisa. Find out if she realizes what she's getting into."

"That should be fun."

"Oh, yeah. A real walk in the park."

The food came, and for the first few minutes, it was all business. Ben liked his toast with jam, and his eggs over-medium. She watched him while she ate her omelet, liking the way he chewed. Amazed that he could even make that sexy.

When he'd downed about half his breakfast, he smiled at her. "So talk to me."

"What?"

"Talk. Tell me about your life in the city by the bay."

That caught her by surprise. She had to reshuffle the deck in her head, pull out the cards she wanted to play. "I like my job," she said. "I'd thought about going back to school, getting my law degree, but honestly,

I don't want the headaches. I like the research a lot, which I didn't expect. I work for a major law firm. They pay me well to look up the right statutes, dig on the Internet. I imagine in that way, our jobs are similar."

"Sounds like it. You hang out with attorneys?"

"Not if I can help it. I have a small but eclectic group of friends. I play pool on Thursday nights."

His brows rose. "No kidding?"

She grinned. "We got the league championship last year, and we're gunning for it again. We have a good team."

"Eight ball?"

"Yep. Sometimes nine ball. But mostly eight."

"Maybe we can find a pool hall somewhere nearby."

"Actually, there's a place across from the Rio. It's called Pink-ees. Great place to play. Lots of tables."

"Did you bring your cue?"

She shook her head. "Didn't know if there'd be time."

"Let's make time."

She took a bite of toast to hide her ridiculously happy grin. He liked pool. Excellent.

"So what else?" he asked. "Besides being a pool shark?"

"I ride my bike on weekends a lot."

"You said you have a Shadow, right?"

She nodded.

"What got you into that?"

"A guy I went out with. He was kind of a dick, but he did turn me on to bikes. I got hooked immediately."

"Not afraid you'll get hit?"

"Nope, not really. I operate on the principle that everyone's trying to kill me."

He laughed, and she felt all squishy inside.

"What about you?"

"Yeah, I think people are trying to kill me, too."

"No, I meant what you do. When you aren't being a private eye."

He frowned a little, two lines appearing on his forehead. "I read too much."

"How can anyone read too much?"

"Trust me, it's possible."

"What kinds of books?"

"Everything."

"I doubt that."

He grinned. "Okay, so I'm not real big on romance novels. Or fantasy. But pretty much everything else."

"Cool."

"And I hike."

"Where?"

"Wherever I can. I go out to the Catskills from time to time. And upstate New York. There are some nice places in Connecticut and Vermont, too."

"How strenuous."

"Have to be able to run. Remember, people trying to kill me and all that."

She leaned forward. "Has anyone really?"

"Tried to kill me? Yep."

"Oh, God."

"They didn't succeed."

"Obviously. Why?"

"I was faster. From all the hiking."

"No, why did they try to kill you?"

"I found out stuff they didn't want known."

"Scary."

"Yeah. I try to avoid that kind of thing, but sometimes you get surprised."

"That's not the kind of surprise I like."

"But you do like surprises?"

She nodded. "Love 'em. Especially when there are gifts involved."

He laughed. "Hey, let's finish up here. I'm starting to feel lucky."

She quirked her head to the right, but he was busy with the check. She wondered if his idea of feeling lucky involved a locked door, a bedroom and getting naked.

CHAPTER FOUR

THE CASINO WAS HOPPING, tourists and locals all focused on winning the big one, the one that would change their lives forever. Ben knew the odds of that happening were slim to none, but he didn't care. He wanted to play, and to watch Taylor.

"You like blackjack?" he asked.

She nodded. "The last time I was here, I won two hundred dollars. I spent the whole wad on a pair of shoes that hurt my feet."

He grinned, took her hand. "Let's see if we can get another pair." He led her past the machines, surprised as always at the silliness of the glorified tic-tac-toe slots: Little Green Aliens, The Beverly Hillbillies, Elvis and The Munsters, just to name a few. Then they hit the banks of video poker machines, which was a little more understandable, but still confusing. If he was going to play poker, he wanted to do it with other people, preferably in someone's basement, with plenty of beer, sandwiches and good cigars.

Now blackjack, he liked. The only exception to that was when some obnoxious twit came to the table. He'd walk away before he'd play with a drunk who hit on seventeen, and doubled down on face cards.

They had to pass three tables before they found one with two open seats. He got Taylor in position, then sat on the stool next to her. Rubbing the smooth green felt, he checked out their compatriots. An older couple in brightly colored Hawaiian shirts, a tall gaunt man with a three-day stubble and hooded eyes and a young woman who didn't look old enough to drive, let alone gamble.

The dealer's name was Angel, and her name tag said she was from Tucson. She'd already dealt a hand, and was now going around the table, taking everyone's bets, as she'd hit twenty-one in five cards.

Ben got out his wallet and pulled out a hundred. He laid it down above the rectangle where he'd place his own bet.

Taylor reached for her purse, but he stopped her. "This one's on me," he said. "For luck."

Her eyes narrowed. "Are you sure? I brought fun money."

"You'll have plenty of time to spend it. I promise."

"All right. Thank you."

Angel took his bill, laid it out flat in front of her, so the security cameras could get a good shot, called out, "Change one hundred," for the benefit of the pit boss, then gave him a stack of five, ten and twenty

dollar chips. He split them up, fifty-fifty and gave
Taylor her share.

She smiled again, making him want to give her
all the money in his wallet, then she put a five, the
minimum bet, down to play.

He did the same.

The dealer, taking the cards from the shoe, dealt
the hand, and after the second card, Taylor gasped,
turned over her cards to show a jack and an ace.

The dealer paid her, took her cards, then went on
with the rest of the hand. Ben had a twenty, so he
stayed pat. He leaned over to Taylor, getting a heady
hit of her delicate scent for his trouble. "See, I told
you we were going to be lucky."

She turned to face him, her expression serious, but
with a telltale gleam in her beautiful blue eyes. "You
have no idea."

His whole body reacted to her message, and it was
all he could do not to leave the money, the cards, his
dignity on the table and drag her up to his room. But
he was strong, dammit. He wasn't a teenager, run by
his hormones. Half the fun was the seduction, and he
wasn't about to give short shrift to what promised to
be the best week of his life. He'd wait. He'd play. And
in the end, they'd both win.

The next round went by in a blur, but since the
dealer busted, they both won.

The woman sitting to his left smiled. "Where are
you two from?"

Before Taylor could speak, he nudged her lightly with his elbow. "Home base is London."

"Really?"

He turned slyly to Taylor and gave her a wink before facing his neighbor again. "Yes."

"You don't have a British accent."

"We're trained not to."

She blinked. "Oh."

"I'm James," he said, holding out his hand. "And this is Jinx."

He heard Taylor cough, which he assumed was a cover for laughter. She didn't know that this was a game he played frequently, making up some ridiculous persona when the truth would have done just as well, but less amusingly.

"I'm Sarah," she said. "I live in the Valley. That's in Southern California."

Ben nodded. "Ah, yes. The heart of the pornography industry."

Sarah's cheeks reddened. "I wouldn't know about that."

"Of course not."

"I work for a post-production house. But not that kind."

"Fascinating."

The cards went out again, and until the payout, the conversation ebbed. Taylor took the opportunity to elbow him.

"What are you doing?" she whispered.

"Having fun," he whispered back.

"So you fancy yourself Bond, eh?"

"Hey, I could have called you Pussy Galore."

"I would have decked you if you had."

He grinned. "Hey, she was a real character."

"Only a man would say that was a *real* character."

"Sir?"

He looked up at Angel, waiting for him to hit or stand pat. His cards, a six and five, were a surprise. He doubled down, and she hit him with a king. Twenty-one.

Taylor didn't say anything, just gave him a smile. But as the rest of the hands were played, he felt something at his ankle. It was Taylor's foot. She'd slipped off her shoe, and was using her bare toes to tease him. It worked.

He glanced at her, but the smile had become a sly grin, and her gaze had shifted to Angel, watching her shuffle as if it mattered.

Ben said nothing, just enjoyed the feeling of her toes. He'd never been a foot man, but at the moment, he could understand the impulse. It wasn't easy to stay still, and not touch her thigh and run his hand over that smooth skin. The image of her on his bed, naked, him holding her by the heel as he studied her pink painted nails, took hold of him and didn't let him go until Angel coughed.

He picked up his cards, a ten and a seven, then

slipped them under his ten-dollar bet. He didn't give a damn if he won or not. The only thing that mattered at the moment was the woman next to him.

Just as he was about to suggest they leave, a waitress came by. She was young and pretty, as were all the cocktail waitresses in the hotel. Taylor turned to her. "I'll have a Bloody Mary," she said. "He'll have a martini. Shaken, not stirred."

He laughed. The waitress jotted the orders without so much as a blink, then got the rest of the drink orders. So Taylor liked his game.

He faced Sarah. "Are you here by yourself?"

She shook her head. "I'm with three friends from work."

"And they are…?"

"At the pool. But I burn so easily, it seemed kind of dumb."

"This is more interesting," he said. "You can learn a lot about people by watching them gamble."

"Really?"

"See that man at the Wheel of Fortune?"

She followed his gaze and nodded when she saw the portly fellow standing next to his stool, feeding a bill into the machine. He didn't look as if he was having a very good time. In fact, his heavy brows furrowed to match his scowl, his scalp, bald all the way back to the crown of his head, was beaded with sweat. His light cotton shirt was stretched across his ample beer belly, and there were large circles of sweat under his arms.

He ignored the pull lever, pushing the maximum-bet button with the palm of his hand. As the wheels spun, his lips moved. Probably a prayer, and then a curse as he got nothing, nothing, nothing.

"He isn't having much luck," Sarah observed.

"No, it doesn't appear he is. You know that every time he pushes the button, it's two dollars."

"Oh."

"And since we've been watching him, he's pressed that button what, twelve times? That's twenty-four dollars. He was standing there before we sat down."

"Whoa, that's a lot of money."

"He's not holding a bucket, so no winnings."

"Yikes."

"Indeed. What else do you see?"

While Sarah studied the scene, he turned to Taylor. "You realize, of course," he whispered, "you're not going to get away with this unscathed."

"What?" she asked, batting her eyelashes like the soul of innocence while she inched her toes up his calf.

"Whatever you had planned this afternoon? Cancel it."

Her cheeks became pink and the gaze that met his was full of anticipation and excitement. "I don't know," she said. "I have to meet my mother."

"Meet her later."

"You presume, Mr. Bowman."

He looked at her for a long moment. Then he leaned

over so his lips were an inch from the soft shell of her ear. "I'm going to make you beg for mercy."

She inhaled sharply, grabbed her cards with trembling fingers.

Sarah, to his left, said, "Hey."

He held back his grin as he turned to his young friend. "Yes?"

"He's got a whole bunch of glasses stacked there. And he's kind of swaying," Sarah said.

"Which means?"

"He's toasted. And scared. He's lost a whole bunch of money and he's trying to win it back."

"Excellent."

"Cool."

"It pays to be observant."

It was Sarah's turn to grin. "Like seeing that you two aren't from London at all. That you've been playing footsie for about ten minutes, and that while I'm not positive your name isn't James, it sure as heck isn't Bond."

Taylor laughed. Angel grinned, and it wasn't because she'd dealt herself twenty-one.

"Very good, Sarah. If you ever get tired of post-production, you'd make a good detective."

She smiled, mightily pleased with herself. "Is that what you really do?"

He held out his hand. "Ben Bowman, Private Detective."

She shook his hand, but her gaze went to Taylor. "Are you a P.I., too?"

"I'm a paralegal, which isn't half as interesting."

"Somehow, I doubt that."

"Are you playing, sir?"

Ben realized he'd abandoned his cards altogether. He slipped two five dollar chips into the rectangle, and put another five above it, playing the bet for the dealer.

Taylor and Sarah both straightened, made their own bets, and each of them followed suit in tipping Angel. It turned out well for everyone. Angel busted with twenty-four.

"It's almost noon," Taylor said. "My mother's going to be here in an hour."

He shoved his whole stack of chips toward the center of the table. "Cash me in, please."

Taylor's laughter was as intoxicating as the drink that arrived while he waited for his chips.

"Still want to cash out?" Taylor asked.

"Oh, yeah."

"But our drinks…"

"Are portable."

"Good point."

Sarah sighed. "You guys are so lucky. How wonderful to be in love in Las Vegas."

Ben froze, Taylor cleared her throat and Angel wasn't at all successful in hiding a knowing grin.

Taylor pushed her chips in after Ben got his money

back. "We are lucky, thank you. But we're actually here for my brother's wedding."

Sarah leaned forward over the lip of the table. "Why not make it a double wedding? Or better yet, run off to one of those cool chapels. You could get married by Elvis." She reached frantically into her oversized purse and pulled out a small notebook and a pen. "This is my room number. I'm here for three more days. If you guys do get married, I want to be there."

"I'd be delighted to take your card," Ben said with a bow. "But I've been married. It's not going to happen again. Ever."

Sarah smiled at him slyly. "You never know. Magic things happen in Las Vegas."

He looked at Taylor. "Magic, yes. But some things aren't in the cards." Nodding once more at Sarah, he said, "Hope you win a bundle."

She glanced back at the Wheel of Fortune. The same man was still desperately pressing the max bet button, the only thing to have changed was the number of empty cocktail glasses beside him. "I'll settle for not losing my shirt."

"Good girl."

"I'm ready," Taylor said, and from the high flush of her cheeks, he believed her.

Sarah was forgotten in a flash, as was blackjack, gambling of any sort, the casino, the hotel, the entire city. All that mattered was the woman in front of him and getting her to his room. There was so much to do.

He took her arm at the elbow. "Let's go."

TAYLOR PRACTICALLY HAD TO RUN to keep up with Ben's long strides. He darted and weaved through the crowd, aiming for the elevators. Her drink sloshed as she tried not to step on toes. It would have been smarter just to put the glass down, but there was no stopping Ben. Nor did she want to. She felt like a teenager.... No, like the teenager she'd been with Ben. How she'd loved him! He'd been the only thing in her life for well over a year.

She sidestepped to avoid a woman in a wheelchair, her purse banging into her side, then they were clear of the casino.

Ben looked back at her, and his grin made her toes curl. She didn't know the specifics of his plan, but she was all in favor of the general idea.

Good thing she'd dressed with care this morning; shaved everything that should be, worn her matching pink lace bra and panties. She'd even put a couple of condoms in her purse. Then she'd written to her friends at Eve's Apple, filling them in on the distinct possibility that her Man To Do would be Done before tomorrow. She hadn't really thought it would happen quite this soon, but who was she to complain?

Ben slowed as they neared the elevator, pulling her close enough to slip his arm around her shoulders. "I don't remember," he whispered, "if I told you how beautiful you look this morning."

She shook her head. "No, I don't think you did."

He nipped her earlobe. "You're stunning."

She shivered all the way down to her toes. "Why Mr. Bowman, I do declare."

His laugh added to her shivers. "I didn't know Southern California was part of the Deep South."

Finally, they were at the elevator. The button had already been pushed, but Ben pressed it again. They waited with a family of four, all wearing Las Vegas T-shirts, the adults from Caesar's Palace, the kids from Circus Circus. The littlest kid looked to be about three, and very cranky. He tugged on Daddy's shorts, whining about something named "Snooky."

By the time their elevator arrived, three more people had joined the queue and they all clambered in together, Ben guiding her to the back. He stood next to her, his hip against hers.

As they ascended, she felt a slight tickle just below the hem of her shorts. She jumped, but then realized it was Ben's fingers, brushing lightly against her skin.

With each floor, his fingers moved up the back of her thigh. She felt herself blush even though no one was looking at them. It was an incredibly intimate gesture, brazen, and yet totally discreet.

His fingers kept inching up until he brushed the curve of her buttock. Barely touching her, he swept his finger back and forth over the same small patch, giving her goose bumps everywhere. Driving her crazy.

She pressed back against the elevator wall, trapping his hand. "Stop," she whispered.

"Why?"

"Just wait."

"I don't want to wait."

"There's only one more stop before our floor."

"Then it shouldn't be a problem. Come on. Move."

She shook her head, figuring she'd won the battle.

Wrong. He turned until he was directly in front of her, his body pressed against hers so tightly she could feel his hard length, the sharp edge of his belt buckle. He smiled, his brown eyes filled with wicked intent, and then he kissed her.

Thank goodness the family had gotten off two floors down, because the kiss was definitely not G-rated. His tongue slipped between her surprised lips, exploring, darting, daring her to respond, to forget where they were, that they weren't alone.

Her hands went to his shoulders, trying to push him back, but he wasn't having any of that. Instead, he folded her in his arms, and reminded her what it was she'd loved about kissing.

His mouth opened just enough, his tongue, tasting slightly of gin, teased her into a moan that should have embarrassed her a great deal more than it did.

Then he was gone, leaving her on shaky legs, her mouth still open and moist. It took her a second to realize the elevator had stopped, that the strangers at each corner were staring at her, that Ben had already walked into the hall.

She escaped with seconds to spare.

He grinned again, knowing full well what he'd done, what he'd put her through. "I warned you," he said.

"Okay. If that's the way you want to play it." She didn't wait for his response, she just headed down the hall toward her room.

He caught up to her seconds later, putting that devil hand of his on the small of her back. "Yeah, I think it is the way I want to play it."

"No mercy?"

His pace quickened along with his heartbeat. "No mercy."

CHAPTER FIVE

BEN'S THOUGHTS WENT immediately to the gutter. No mercy. The thought of taking Taylor right to the edge made his body hum with adrenaline and flat-out need.

From the moment he'd seen her last night, he'd spent every idle moment running seduction scenarios. Each vignette was rawer than the last, as the memory of that wild eighteen-year-old spurred him farther.

She wasn't eighteen anymore, but he could still see the girl in her. Made better by the years, and not just because her body had ripened to perfection. There was something whole about her, confident and sure. As if she'd grown into someone she liked very much. He couldn't remember ever thinking that about a woman, and he couldn't even give any particulars as to what had brought on the impression. The way she dressed, the way she held herself. Who cared? It was just hot as hell.

She stopped three rooms before his and pulled out her key card. It took her two tries to get the green light, but once she did, she flung the door open and dragged him in behind her.

Before she let him go, she kicked the door shut, then shoved him against the wall. He barely had time to grin before her hands were on his shoulders and her lips were crushing his.

His eyes closed as her tongue thrust into his mouth. It was her show, and he wasn't about to interfere. Not when she made full body contact, rubbing against him from breasts to hips.

If she couldn't feel what she was doing to him, then something was seriously wrong, but he figured she got the drift. Especially after she gave him the little bump and grind right where it counted.

Taylor pulled back just enough to nip his lower lip, then she was off him, walking toward the minibar.

He, on the other hand, felt like a moth pinned to a Peg-Board, unable to move. "Damn, girl. A drive-by ravishing."

She laughed, and the sound shot right to his groin. After a moment pondering the inside of the small fridge, she brought out a bottle of white wine. "It's not a martini, but would you like some?"

He shook his head. "I already had one. Too early for another."

"I know. Hey, it's Vegas. No rules."

"No mercy, no rules. What have I gotten myself into?"

She put the bottle on the dresser and her hand on her hip. "You're right. If you were smart, you'd peel yourself off that wall and march right out of here."

He chuckled as he complied with the first part, but instead of leaving, he joined her near the dresser. "I've never forgotten you," he said.

"Oh?"

Shaking his head, he moved in closer, not touching her with his hands, but with his body. "That weekend rates right up there with the moon landing and getting my first bike."

"Wow, and I thought you were just humoring me."

"Hey, you needed a guiding hand, and God knows at that age, I was all hands."

"You sweet-talker. I'm all aflutter."

"No, you're not. But you will be." He leaned in then, touching her lips lightly with his own. He wanted to take it slowly this time, learning her with due diligence and patience. They had almost a week, and he planned to milk each step for all it was worth.

She didn't try to rush him. In fact, she simply parted her lips slightly and shared her sweet breath as he lazily ran his tongue over her silky contours.

He thought about moving to the bed, but that could wait, too. For now, the only thing that mattered was her mouth, the way she tasted, the softness and the heat.

Her body, touching him at his waist and slightly below, melted back against the credenza, but she didn't use her hands to steady herself. It was as if they had choreographed the whole scene beforehand. To test his theory he pulled back and she followed effort-lessly, neither increasing or decreasing the pressure of the kiss. Damn. He thought immediately of how the principle would apply when they got to the bed. Like synchronized swimmers without the water. Maybe he should try it now, while the magic was still in the air.

He took her hand and led her through the doorway to the bedroom. She used her index finger to tickle his palm, and his whole body reacted. Who was this woman, and how could she turn him to mush with just a single finger?

He stopped her just shy of the queen-size bed. Smiling to match her devilish grin, he ran his hands lightly up her blouse, barely lingering on her breasts. He undid her top button then pushed the material to the sides, baring a small patch of décolletage. Leaning forward, he kissed the newly bared skin, then licked her as if she'd been covered in honey. It wasn't that far from the truth. She tasted sweet and smelled like summer.

She reached up to his shirt, but he shook his head. "Not yet."

Her hands dropped obediently to her sides.

He moved down to the next button, and as he'd done with the first, he spread the material of her blouse. This time he was rewarded with a view of her delicate pink lace bra, molding her breasts into perfect soft mounds. He could just make out the slight darkness of her nipples. Part of him wanted to rip the damn thing off her, but he held back, enjoying the slow torment. He bent forward and kissed the top of her right breast, then licked his way across to the top of her left.

Her skin changed halfway there, breaking out into a field of gooseflesh. Beneath his tongue, he felt her tremble. He'd been hard since she'd touched him with her toes, but now he felt as if he would burst out of his jeans.

Still, he didn't rush. He unbuttoned her farther, flared her blouse, exposing the fullness of her chest. He knelt a bit and kissed her underneath her bra, but that was a tease. Rising just enough, he put his mouth fully over her right nipple, hidden behind the lace. It wasn't so concealed that he couldn't feel the hardness there. He ran his tongue over the nub, slowly at first and then faster; a little demonstration of what she could expect later and not just on her breasts.

He felt her hands on his shoulders, and for a moment he thought she wanted him to stop, but when he did, she tugged him right back into place. She was simply steadying herself. Good, because he planned on being there awhile.

TAYLOR HAD DIED AND GONE TO HEAVEN. At the very least she was at the gate. Ben swirled his tongue around her left nipple, the lace making the sensation sort of dappled, if that were possible. She didn't care what it was called as long as he didn't stop doing it. His methodology was something he'd clearly learned over the years, because he'd been anything but patient that weekend. This was good. Very, very good. Her head lolled back as she drowned in the ocean of pleasure. It was wickedly hard not to touch him, to stand not so idly by and let him do all the work. But that was just manners talking, and this had nothing to do with etiquette.

No mercy. No rules.

It was everything she'd hoped for and a side of fries. "Oh, God."

His chuckle was more a sensation of lips on flesh than a sound, and she wanted to make him do it again. Wait, no... His teeth captured the tip of her nipple and pulled ever so slightly. Her gasp came from somewhere outside her body, but that was the only thing she wasn't present for. God, his hands were on her bare waist, tickling fingers setting her quiver factor on high.

The tickling stopped so his fingers could work on her button. Since her blouse was open, he undid her culottes. He knelt before her, found the zipper pull with his teeth and slowly pulled it down. She was grateful for the dresser, because without it she would have melted right down to the floor.

He let go of the zipper and spread the opening of her pants. It was unbelievably erotic to have him on the floor in front of her, knowing he could touch her anywhere, do anything. He kissed her, right below her belly button. Her head went back, her eyes fluttered closed and she whimpered in pure surrender. She wanted him to hurry, to rip off the rest of her clothes and throw her on the bed. She wanted him to go slower, to make every sensation last a lifetime.

Just the fact that she let him do this, let him take her wherever he wanted to go, astonished her almost as much as the feelings of need inside her. She never did this, didn't like it when she wasn't the one calling the shots, but not with Ben. Not Ben.

"Oh, God," he whispered, just before he licked the expanse of flesh just above her lace panties.

She nodded. Oh, God indeed. The thought of where he was going, what he was going to lick next, made her dizzy and a little faint. She was no Southern Belle, all swoony over being touched, but this was to "touching" like "Mary Had A Little Lamb" was to Mozart's Requiem.

Ben touched her thigh, and she realized her shorts had dropped. He used both hands, very gently and very lightly to run between her knees and the bottom of her panties. "You taste like sweet cream," he whispered.

She put her hands on his head, ran her fingers through his dark hair. "Stand up. Please."

He looked up at her and smiled. "Not yet."

"But I want…"

He got up from his knees, kissed her hard. Let his

body lean against her and she felt his erection through his soft jeans.

When he finally pulled back, he stared at her for a long moment. "Why did we wait so long?"

She laughed. "We just got here last night."

"Ten years," he said. "I missed too much."

Her hand went to his face where she traced his remarkable cheekbones with her fingers. "I'm here now."

"Amazing."

"Do you want to know a secret?"

He nodded.

"I planned to seduce you. The moment I heard you were going to be Steve's best man."

"Really?"

She nodded. "I never forgot that weekend, either."

His grin turned rueful. "I'm not as young."

"I'm not, either."

"It's not the same."

"Oh, please. You're not over the hill yet." She let her hand fall between them. "And it's clear you aren't having any...problems."

"No, no problems. I just don't have the same stamina."

She kissed his lips, ran her tongue along the crease. "Are you sure?"

"Pretty sure. But I'd be delighted to be wrong."

"I think it's time I wasn't the only one undressed."

"You're not undressed."

She kicked her shorts toward the bed. "Almost."

"Almost only counts in horseshoes."

"And nakedness." She reached for his top button and undid it.

He covered her hand while he shook his head. "Nope, not yet. I want to see you, first."

"That's not fair."

"Sure it is. Next time, you can undress me, and stare all you like."

"Next time?"

"You don't think I'm going to let the rest of this week go by without taking full advantage of the situation, do you?"

"We have work to do, don't forget."

He nodded. "I haven't forgotten. But there'll be time for both."

"Oh?"

"Absolutely. I mean, Steve and Lisa have to sleep sometimes."

"Maybe that's something we need to stop."

"Sleeping?"

"It's not the sleeping part I'm concerned about."

"Ah, you mean the sex."

"Exactly. Maybe that's why Steve wants to marry her."

"You think she's that special?"

She shrugged. "I'm completely bewildered by men's taste in women, and even more flummoxed by what they find sexy."

Ben cupped her breast, rubbed his finger over her encased nipple. "It's not very complex. We men are simple creatures. Food, drink, a soft body between the sheets."

"That's it, huh? Any soft body will do?"

"Oh, no. Not at all. And here I'll stop speaking for all men, and just speak for myself. If I don't find something intriguing up here," he touched her temple, "then I'm not interested in what's down here." His fingers moved from her head to the junction of her thighs.

"Come on, Ben, it's me. I'm a sure thing. You don't have to win me over."

"I'm not trying to."

She smiled. "And you know what? I believe you."

"Thank you."

"So don't you think it's the same thing with Steve?"

His face clouded a bit. "I'm not sure. Steve always did like a good time, but I also know he wasn't a hound dog, at least not around me. The things that most interested Steve were what they had in common. He wanted someone who would help with the fleet, who loved the sea as much as he does."

"Which is why Lisa makes no sense whatsoever."

"Right. Which means she's filling some other role. One he's never expressed before. At least to me."

"Me, neither."

"So in order to find out if this really is the mistake we think it is, we need to find out what Lisa represents to him. What need she's filling."

"You don't think it's just about my dad? About making things up to him?"

Ben shook his head. "No, I don't. I think there's something else going on. We talked about the situation with your dad, and Steve never seemed that upset about it. Not enough to leave the sea."

"Yeah, I know. But if not that, what?"

Ben pulled her close against him. "That's what we're going to discover. But not right this second."

"No?"

He didn't answer her. Not with words. Instead, he kissed her again, slipped his arms around her back and in one of the smoothest moves since Rhett carried Scarlet up the staircase, he undid the clasp of her bra.

While his forward flank teased her tongue unmercifully, his side troops moved into position, which wasn't exactly fair. Of course, she wasn't complaining all that strongly, not when his hands were caressing her bare breasts. Her nipples were so taut they were like little weapons themselves, but she felt pretty darn sure Ben could take care of himself.

He certainly knew how to take care of her.

"Now," she said. "My turn."

"It's all your turn, Taylor," he whispered, his lips a breath away from her own. "What gives me pleasure is to give you pleasure."

Her heart sank a tiny bit. Not that she didn't believe him… All right, she didn't. It wasn't as if she thought he was being intentionally insincere, but come on. A guy who's only pleasure is to give the woman he's with all the goodies? Didn't happen. Not outside of the movies.

"Let me make you happy," he went on, still stirring their breath together as he spoke. "Let me see the rest of you."

"I've seen me. That won't make me happy at all."

He grinned. "Ah, but I bet what I do after I see you will."

"Ah."

He kissed her again. "Come with me."

She leaned back, looking him in the eyes. "You must be good."

"Just wait. You'll see." He took her hand in his, and led her to the bed. Moving behind her, he took her blouse from her shoulders, and while she couldn't see him, she could hear the soft wisp of cloth on cloth as he folded the shirt. Then he slipped her bra off, leaving her in nothing but her panties. He sat on the bed when it was time to remove those.

First, a kiss on her belly, that damn pooch she tried so hard to lose. It would have been so nice, especially at a time like this, being naked and all in broad daylight with a man she'd craved for ten years, if she could have looked a bit more like the girl he'd seen naked before. His smile was nice, and his hunger clear in his gaze, but still, she felt sure he would have been even hungrier if her stomach had been flat.

His next kiss, slightly lower, chased all thoughts of vanity and flat stomachs straight out of her mind. No longer able to stand idle, she found her fingers skimming through his thick, dark hair. She wanted to do much more. Kiss him, get him all naked, see everything there was to see, and then play to her heart's content. But this had its advantages, too.

Like the way his hot breath felt on that little space of skin just above her low-cut panties. Like how he trailed that breath down and down, inch by inch, while his fingers, poised on the sides of her underwear, lowered the lacy material at that maddening pace.

Soon he was past the bare skin, and his lips brushed over her small patch of pale curls. Of their own accord, her legs spread half a step apart, giving him broader access, and herself a stronger sense of balance. She had the feeling she'd need it.

A second later, he kissed her at the very top of her lower lips, and she shivered with anticipation. This was very high on her personal hit parade. A man who knew how to use his mouth for more noble purposes was a man worth knowing.

Turns out, Ben knew. Oh, God, how he knew.

By the time he was finished showing her just how much he knew, she was flat on her back on the bed, arms and legs akimbo, gasping for air, quivering like a harp string that had just been masterfully, patiently, persistently plucked.

CHAPTER SIX

IF BEN DIDN'T DO SOMETHING soon, he was going to be one very embarrassed man. But it was impossible to move his gaze from the vision before him.

Taylor's chest rose and fell, making those exquisite breasts quiver ever so slightly. The sheen on her sleek body, the way she lay so abandoned and free made him think of a colt just back from a long, exhilarating run in the fields. She was a wild creature…still. He smiled, terrifically glad that some things hadn't changed.

His gaze moved back to her face, to the flush on her cheeks and neck, to her parted lips, to her blond hair floating on the bedspread like a cloud. And then his problem reared its head, so to speak. The constriction in his pants was beyond serious, nearly terminal. The last time he'd been so hard without doing anything about it was in college. He'd figured out a way to escape to a bathroom back then, but this was a different type of quandary. He wanted to make love to her, to come inside her. But he'd have to get up, go down the hall to his room, get his condoms, come back, then strip. No possible way he was going to make it off his knees without exploding. Maybe if he stopped looking at her.

His gaze shifted to the bedside table, where he saw the red light blinking on the phone. She must have had a call earlier, because the phone hadn't rung since they'd been in the room. Or maybe it had, and they just had been too involved to notice.

A second later, his hip vibrated and his own cell phone rang. No musical ditty, just a plain ring, which was annoying enough. He ignored it. Until Taylor's phone rang again.

Her head came up off the bed. "What…?"

"I guess they're trying to find us."

"Damn," she whispered as her head flopped back. "I suppose we should answer."

"They can wait."

She turned, opened one eye to look at him. "You're still dressed."

"Yep."

"Why is that?"

"I have no idea." His phone rang again, then hers, the disparate pitches mildly grating.

She crooked one finger, inviting him next to her. He stood carefully, wincing at the painful pressure.

"If I had any energy at all, I'd rip those clothes right off you."

"Aha. So my plan worked." He laughed evilly and waggled his eyebrows.

"What, so you could have your way with me? Too late."

"Oh, yeah." He put one knee on the bed, leaned over and kissed her tummy.

Her hand went to his head and she fingered his hair. "That was amazing," she whispered.

"For me, too."

"And yet..."

He chuckled. Her phone jangled once more, the ring cut off as the caller hung up. Whoever was trying to reach him hadn't been as persistent. "Are you sure you're ready for round two?"

She nodded, although her eyes were closed, and she looked like she was more ready for a nap than lovemaking.

Ben wanted to stretch out next to her, but the issues hadn't been settled. The condoms. He was here, and they were all the way in his room. He should have put them in his wallet, like the old days. But he'd never thought the morning would turn out this way.

"What are you grinning about?"

"Just thinking what a lucky guy I am."

"And here I thought I'd won the prize."

He gave in to the immediacy of needing to touch her and lay down, his head on her hair. He took in a deep breath, smelling the sweet fruity scent, the intoxicating musk from her lower body. "You didn't believe me, did you?"

"Believe what?"

He ran his hand up her stomach until he cupped one of her perfect breasts. "That giving you pleasure is what turns me on."

She smiled. "That's a wonderful philosophy, Ben. Truly."

"But…"

"No, that's all. If that's how it is for you, yippee!"

He chuckled, and took the hand closest to him and guided it to his jeans. "Maybe this will make you a believer."

"Whoa," she said, her voice breathy. "That's got to be uncomfortable."

It only took him a second to realize he'd made a mistake. The problem increased by one hell of a lot. He squirmed under her fingers.

She released him, then turned onto her side. "Stay," she said, as if he were a puppy. Then she undid his belt, and with a look of total concentration, started on his buttons.

Every move was an experience in the pleasure-versus-pain principle. It hurt so damn good. By the time she reached the last button he was ready to explode. Which would at least eliminate the need for the condoms, but would be a definite blow to his ego.

She spread his fly open, then carefully reached inside his jeans until she held him in her palm. He hissed as she pulled him free, giving him one kind of release only to put him into a more complex kind of restraint.

"Oh, my," she whispered. "That's very impressive."

He said, "Thank you," through clenched teeth. He'd grabbed the bedspread in his fists, tried to anchor his body in some way that would keep him grounded, but when she sat up, scooted down, and bent over him, he abandoned all ties to the earth.

Her warm lips hovered an inch away when her phone rang again. His followed an instant later. Taylor looked at him guiltily, and with every ounce of strength he had, he said, "You'd better get it."

She looked down once more, and he saw her frown. But the phones were persistent as hell, and for all he knew, something was wrong. He'd feel like a dog if it were an emergency and he stopped her from getting the message.

"I'll be right back." She grabbed the phone. "Hello?"

Ben ignored his cell and struggled to sit up, then get off the bed. With what little dignity he could muster, he fled to the bathroom to try and get himself together. There would be time for stage two soon enough. If, of course, he didn't die first.

"WHERE HAVE YOU BEEN?"

Taylor looked at the closed bathroom door. "Hi, Mom. When did you get in?"

"Over an hour ago, and we've been trying to reach you ever since. Didn't you hear the page?"

"No, I'm sorry. I didn't. I was in the bath."

"For an hour?"

"Reading," she said, knowing it sounded lame. She had to turn away, to stop thinking about Ben and the state she'd left him in. Poor guy. He looked like he was hurting. She'd make it up to him. That made her smile.

"Well, get dressed and come to my room. I'm in 1012. We have to talk."

"Is everything all right?"

"Aside from the fact that Lisa and her mother are taking us to some mystery location tonight after dinner? We're supposed to be semidressed, whatever that means. And I just found out that her mother's dress is pale blue with white lace, which sounds exactly like my dress, so now I have to go buy another one, and I have no intention of spending the kind of money they charge at the hotels. So you'll have to come with me now so we can get back in time for dinner."

"Me?" Taylor asked, knowing it was a silly question. Her mother hated to shop, never trusted her own judgment. When Taylor had lived with her, she'd had to accompany her mom on all clothes shopping trips, and after she'd gone to San Francisco, her mother's friend Beverly had taken over the task. Normally,

Taylor didn't mind, but she didn't want to leave the hotel now.

Her gaze went back to the bathroom door. Still closed.

"Please, honey, I want to talk to you about this whole mess. And who knows when we'll have time alone."

"Sure, Mom. No problem. I'll be ready in about fifteen minutes, and I'll come by your room. Okay?"

Her mother sighed. "Thank goodness. I'm just so…"

"Get some wine out of the minibar."

"It's three o'clock. What are you talking about?"

"It's okay, Mom. I promise. It'll calm you down. Besides, it's Vegas. No one will think a thing about it."

A quiet "Humph," was her only response, and then the dial tone.

Fifteen minutes and she'd have to face her mother. Which meant she had to get into the shower, pronto. Maybe Ben could wash her back.

No. Fifteen minutes wasn't nearly enough time for that. She'd have to wait until later. Until tonight.

BEN WAITED FOR STEVE at the lobby lounge, debating whether he should drop a few bucks into the video poker machine imbedded in the bar. His beer was cold, he was early, so what the hell? He took out a twenty and fed it to the hungry machine.

He played double-double poker, one of the many variations of the game available on the machine. This one had no wild cards at least, and it was played like regular poker. The difference was in the payout schedule, and since it was highly unlikely that he would win, he didn't give it that much thought.

What he hadn't been able to stop thinking about was his afternoon with Taylor. Good God. He felt as if he hadn't been with a woman in years, not months. And that he hadn't been with a real woman since he'd last been with her ten years ago.

It should have told him something that he hadn't been as excited about sex with Alyson. Maybe he blanked it out, maybe he assumed it would get better. It hadn't. In fact, toward the end, the sex had disappeared completely. Of course, he was the only one who'd done without. Alyson had been with Gail, the woman who was now her life partner. And he hadn't suspected a thing.

Some private dick. Couldn't even tell that his own wife was gay. It did appease him somewhat that she hadn't known, either. Or at least she hadn't admitted it to herself until after they were married. And he did know she loved him. Just not the way a husband and wife should.

There had been women after her, of course. In the beginning, he'd been something of a jerk, proving himself, he supposed. But that had calmed down, and in the past year there had only been the occasional liaison, nothing serious, nothing earth-shaking. Just pleasant conversation, nice naked tumbles, don't let the door hit you on the ass on your way out.

With Taylor, it was anything but pleasant. Or ordinary. And he sure as hell didn't want to see anything hit her on the ass, with the possible exception of his palm.

She'd lit him up like a Roman candle, and they hadn't even done the deed. God, he wished he knew where the women had gone off to tonight. More importantly, when they'd return. He planned to be there when Taylor got back, and he didn't plan on doing much sleeping after.

In the meantime, he had to put all thoughts of the delicious Taylor out of his mind. He had Steve to himself tonight, and he planned to talk to the man. Understand what he thought he was doing. Maybe even get Steve to reconsider. At the very least, postpone.

Ben took another sip of his beer, then hit max play. He had three deuces, which he held. He almost spit when the fourth one hit. That was a damn big payoff for quarters. Maybe his luck was changing. Maybe...

He slammed the cash-out button. That's the kind of thinking that led to overspending, cash advances, trouble in River City. Not for him.

"Hey, buddy. What have you got there?"

"Stevie!" Ben turned and shook his hand the way they always did, brutally. In the old days, they'd try and break bones, but things had improved with time. Now, they just went for bruises.

Steve sat down on the stool next to Ben's. "Barkeep, I'll have one of those," he said, pointing to Ben's beer. "And get my fine friend another."

"So, tell me. What's the big secret with the girls? Why all the hush-hush stuff?"

Steve shrugged as he eyed the others nearby at the bar, his gaze lingering on a tan brunette with a very low-cut blouse. "Don't have a clue. The whole evening was set up by some friends of Lisa's back home. They couldn't make it to the wedding, so they planned this mystery evening."

"But only the women?"

"Probably something at a beauty shop. Lisa can't get enough of having her nails done, or facials or some such nonsense. She roped me into a facial once. Thought it was the most horrible thing I'd ever been through. I'd rather face gale-force winds without a rudder."

Ben chuckled at the thought, wondering again what in hell Steve was doing with Lisa Caton. "So you're giving it all up, eh? The freedom of the seas for a necktie and three-martini lunches?"

Steve nodded, his smile quizzical and his gaze fixed on the bartender. "I know you all think I've gone round the bend, but I swear I haven't. She's really something. Once you get to know her, you'll get it."

"I believe you."

"I mean, she has such a clear vision of her future. Mine now, too, I suppose. And I have to tell you, Ben, I like the picture she's painted. Sure, I'll miss the fleet, but Jesus, what kind of a life was that, I mean, long-term? You know what I'm saying?"

"No."

"Come on. Did you really think I'd be out there fishing forever? That I'd be some old geezer trying to catch sailfish for tourists?"

The beer arrived, and Steve paid for both drinks. He left a five as a tip, then turned back to Ben. "It's a damn hard life, Ben. You've been with me often enough to know that."

"Yeah. I've also been with you often enough to know that you love it. That you've never wanted to do anything but sail and fish."

"For God's sake, everyone's acting like I'm giving up the throne. It's fishing. And I'll still own the boats. I can go any time I want."

"Between selling aircraft parts, you mean?"

"You don't think I can do it?"

Ben held up his hand. "No, man. That's not what I said. I think you can do anything you set your mind to. I was in school with you, remember? You didn't even have to study half the time."

"Yeah, well, that's what I think. I can do it. Make a good living. A great living. I can take care of Lisa, and our kids. Have a life that's worth something."

Ben nodded then stared at the flashing light from

his video poker machine. As if summoned, the bartender came back with his winnings, counted it out and waited somewhat obviously for a tip. Ben obliged. When he turned back to Steve, his friend's face had become sullen and his gaze far too distant. Something else was going on with this marriage thing, but…Steve wasn't about to admit what. Not outright. At least, not on one beer.

Maybe the guy didn't even realize what had compelled him to move so fast. To run as far as he could away from the sea. But Ben wasn't about to let the wedding take place unless he knew, for a fact, that Steve understood his real reasons, and still wanted to move forward.

"So, tell me about Taylor," he said.

Steve grinned, crooked his head in Ben's direction. "Tell you what?"

"What's the deal? How come she's not married with 2.3 kids and a golden Lab?"

"Hell if I know. She's had chances. I know two guys right off the bat that wanted her like crazy. Renny was an attorney, looked just like Richard Gere. He came down to San Diego and tried to get in with Mom. I guess he thought if the family approved, Taylor would cave."

"And, yet, they're not married."

Steve shook his head. "I asked her what it was about him. She told me she didn't like his hands. I know. Crazy. His hands. The guy was already pulling in high six figures. I wouldn't be surprised to see him in politics some day."

"And what about the other one?"

"Oh, shit. Yeah. What was his name? Johnny. Or Jimmy. Something like that. He loved to fish. He caught a couple of world-class barracudas on the *Silver Mermaid*. He was in finance. Arbitrage, I think. Another one who made a fortune, but our girl doesn't seem to care much about that."

"No, I guess she doesn't."

"Who can tell with Taylor? She could be a first-rate attorney herself, but she doesn't want to. She likes being a paralegal. Likes not having the responsibility."

"I admire her for understanding herself so well."

"If she really did understand herself, she'd be married by now."

"Why do you say that?"

"That's what it's all about, right? When you get it, then it all falls into place. The people you need to meet are just…there."

"This from the man who once told me that life was like fishing? Sometimes the net is full and sometimes the net is empty. But you still get out in the trade winds."

Steve burst out laughing. "Yeah, that was me all right. I think we'd been drinking kamikazes at the time, however. Quite a few of them."

Ben smiled. "Oh, yeah. And we met those

twins. Oh, man, what were their names? Helga and Lena?"

"Helga and Leanne. Damn, were they fine, or what?"

Steve chucked him in the shoulder. "Incredible. Amazing stamina."

"They weren't the only ones."

"Was it Helga who had the tattoo?"

Ben nodded. "The snake with the big eyelashes."

"I don't think I'll ever forget where she had that bad boy."

Ben held up his beer for a toast. "Amen." They both took generous swigs, and then Ben signaled the bartender. "The hell with this," he said. "Consider this your bachelor party, buddy. We're getting plowed."

Steve laughed, but made no protest when Ben ordered two kamikazes. Each.

TAYLOR'S SMILE STARTED TO HURT. If the spotlight hadn't been directly on her face, she wouldn't have been smiling at all. The truth was, she was mortified. Not so much for herself, but for her mother.

After all, she'd been to male strip clubs before. And the virtually naked man grinding his butt into her shoulder wouldn't have been so embarrassing if he wasn't, at the same time, giving her dear, conservative-as-tea-and-white-toast mother a sloppy French kiss.

CHAPTER SEVEN

TAYLOR POURED HERSELF another glass of the cheap champagne Mimi, Lisa's mother, had bought for the table. Unfortunately, she didn't think there was enough champagne in the hotel to make her forget where she was, and that her poor mother was dying inches at a time, although she doubted Lisa or Mimi could tell that she despised this kind of thing. The two of them, on the other hand, were having a hell of a good time, laughing, drinking, slipping bills into tiny red thongs and calling out for lap dances.

Except for her attitude toward the strip club, Mimi wasn't a surprise. Looking at her, Taylor could see Lisa in about twenty years, and it wasn't a bad thing. Good skin, light wrinkles around the eyes and mouth, but not at all saggy. Blond hair, not a dark root showing. Her figure was trim, and Taylor could easily picture her on a trendy golf course, or playing doubles at the tennis club. The mother and daughter giggled in the same way, the pitch just shy of outright annoying.

The evening had been courtesy of Lisa's best girl-friends, Tiffany and Cassie. Since they couldn't make it to the wedding, they'd arranged this bachelorette party, ensuring their seats at a round table too close to the stage. Mimi had brought some gifts from back home, and Lisa had opened them quickly, squealing with delight at the see-through nightgown, the glow-in-the-dark dildo and the feather boa.

Taylor chastised herself for her petty thoughts, but the truth was, the festivities were not to her liking, and so far, neither was Lisa.

What did Steve see in her? She'd thought that in this kind of let-your-hair-down atmosphere, she'd be able to see a new side to Lisa, something that would resemble the kind of fun-loving gal Steve had always gone for. But it wasn't so.

When Lisa wasn't whooping it up, she and her mother spent most of the time when one could talk above the music gossiping about people back home. They rarely included Taylor and her mother, and when they did, it was to ask about the wedding plans. Neither had asked any personal questions, but then, perhaps Steve had filled them in. As doubtful as that was, given Steven's penchant for minding his own business, she'd still give them the benefit of the doubt.

What had really made her crazy, however, was an undercurrent between mother and daughter that was highly suspect. Not that either of them said anything that would stand up in court, but they shared looks, secret smiles, the odd raised brow, all of it to do with Steve and the immediacy of the wedding.

One of the things that hadn't set right with her was

this whole Vegas marriage. Lisa didn't strike her as the kind of girl to go for a quickie ceremony. In fact, Taylor would have bet big bucks that Lisa not only had the china patterns picked out, but that somewhere in her bedroom, she owned a large hope chest, filled with a trousseau that would have everything from Egyptian cotton sheets to Grandma's silver.

Mimi had let slip one big clue, something about presents for later. That could mean that friends were going to throw Steve and Lisa a reception once they moved to Kansas, or it could mean that there wasn't going to be one wedding, but two. The Vegas wedding was to get Steve on the hook, the Kansas wedding would be to reel him in and mount him.

Whatever, Taylor wasn't pleased. At least the show was going to be over soon. It had to be. There was a second show starting in less than an hour.

"Honey, do you have any aspirin?"

Taylor's mom had leaned over, and yelled the request in her ear. She'd had to, the music was so loud. "Hold on."

She looked through her purse and pulled out a small bottle. "Here," she said, handing it to her mother. "Take all you need."

Grasping it as if it were a lifeline, her mother, Pauline, shook out three tablets, then gave back the bottle to Taylor.

"It'll be over soon," Taylor said, shouting herself. "I promise."

Pauline smiled weakly, looked around for a waiter, gave up the hunt and downed the pills with champagne.

"Tomorrow, we'll go to the spa," Taylor said. "Get a massage."

"I thought you were going shopping with Lisa."

Taylor frowned. She'd forgotten. Or more likely blocked it out. She'd promised, in the limo drive over, to accompany Lisa on a trip to the mall to find an appropriate bridesmaid's dress. She still didn't see the reason for buying something new, but when she'd described the dress she'd brought, the long silence and uncomfortable looks had made it perfectly clear the simple gray shift wasn't going to cut the mustard.

Pauline had masterfully guided the conversation, somehow making herself unavailable for the trip, but promising Taylor's presence.

At least Taylor knew where the mall was. Her shopping trip with her mother had gone very well, for Pauline at least, and if she'd known, she would have shopped for herself at the same time.

What the hell. She took another big sip of her drink. Maybe it would be the perfect opportunity to talk to Lisa. To find out why she was so intent on marrying Steve.

The men on stage, six of them, all with rock-hard bodies glistening from some kind of body oil, all with pasted-on smiles and enormous bulges in their thongs, gathered for what Taylor prayed was the finale.

They'd begun to boogie in earnest when a picture came to her mind, as vivid as a high-definition screen image—Ben doing the old bump and grind, wearing nothing but...

Nothing.

Her face heated ten degrees, she couldn't even face the general direction of her mother, and when she reached for her champagne, the glass tipped over, spilling the bubbly all over the table and the front of her dress.

It was not her best dress. It was, however, her most conservative dress, and now it was soaked, and she'd have to send it to the cleaners or wear something far more risqué than she should to dinner tomorrow night. No, that dinner, with both families, wasn't until the night after. But still, it wasn't very pleasant sitting there with a wet lap, and very naughty pictures of Ben Bowman doing unspeakable things to her insides.

Her mother, bless her little heart, saved the day when she insisted on taking Taylor to the hotel to get into something dry. They gossiped horribly about them all the way back to the Hard Rock.

It wasn't until she stepped inside the lobby that the images of Ben returned, and she made such a hasty retreat from her mother there were probably skid marks all across the purple carpet.

By the time she got to her room, nothing mattered but Ben. Not the edges of the headache starting to form, not the still wet and sticky dress, not the fact that she was far more tipsy than she'd realized.

This, she'd gathered after trying to open her door for the third time. She finally made it in, tossed her purse on the couch, lifted her dress off in one smooth move as she made a beeline for the bedroom.

Once she was in her panties and bra, a whole new set of images came to her. Ben on his knees. Ben on the bed. She reached for the phone only to stop dead in her tracks when she saw the time.

It was past midnight. She had no business calling him at this hour. He was probably sound asleep.

And if he wasn't asleep, he was probably with Steve, and that was something she definitely didn't want to interrupt. She'd had no luck with Lisa, but perhaps Ben had made some headway. He was so easy to talk to, and Steve had never been closer to another person.

The best thing she could do would be take an Alka-Seltzer, take off her makeup, get into jammies and crawl beneath the sheets. Good God, she needed to sleep, and if she could grab a healthy eight or nine hours, she'd be ready to face whatever came her way. Which, she hoped was Ben. Coming her way, indeed.

BEN WIPED THE TEARS FROM HIS EYES, but he couldn't stop laughing. He bent over the table, gasping for breath and bumped heads with Steve doing the same thing, and that made them both get hysterical all over again.

Jeez, it was great being with the old Steve. He totally cracked him up, always had. It wasn't anything anyone else would understand, which to him was the best humor of all.

Finally catching his breath, he looked around the small bar, just a college pub with some pool tables. It was crowded and raucous, but they had killer fries and a special on vodka stingers that they'd taken up.

God, Taylor had been right about that no-rules thing in Vegas. Back home, he'd have an occasional beer with dinner, and every once in a while, he'd go for some drinks with some buddies. Most of the time, he needed his wits about him, and alcohol wasn't part of his lifestyle.

Every time he'd gone for a week fishing with Steve, though, there was plenty of booze and plenty of laughs. Steve wasn't much on alcohol, either, except for special times, like tonight.

They'd talked about the old days, the great days. In high school, they'd been terrors. Steve was the one with the real smarts, and he could have gone to any college he wanted, but that hadn't been his dream. Ben hadn't done badly, but he'd had to work for it. It used to drive him crazy that even though Steve never cracked a book, he'd still managed to ace even the toughest chemistry tests.

And, oh, the girls. They'd both been jocks, with

Steve, again, outshining his poor buddy. But what the hell, it had gotten them the best damn women on campus. None of them had been anything like Taylor. If he'd ever found someone like her, he would have held on for dear life, but by the time the two of them had connected, he was deep in his life in New York, and there was no way he could have pursued anything. Besides, he'd thought Steve would have killed him if he'd ever found out.

That had been the only secret he'd ever kept from his friend. Nothing else was sacred. The conquests. The failures and triumphs, they'd shared it all. Of course, Steve had his own style of "sharing." He usually waited until whatever situation had long since gone the way of all things past, and then he'd tell Ben all about it. The only exception had been his father's death, and now, Lisa.

Ben was fairly certain there was something missing from Steve's chronicle of his courtship. But good old Steve wouldn't be pushed. So Ben had thrown in the towel and decided to have himself one hell of a night.

"I gotta eat something, man," Steve said. "You want more fries?"

He shook his head. "Don't they make anything else?"

Steve picked up a menu that was directly in front of Ben's face. "I don't know. Let's see."

Ben grinned and opened up the plastic two-page list of snacks. "Wings."

"Oh, man," Steve said, moaning in ecstasy. "Wings. You're a friggin' genius."

"I know. I am."

"Plenty of hot sauce."

"Did someone say hot?"

Ben turned his head at the very feminine voice behind him. Steve's eyes had widened, and now Ben understood why. She was a stunner. Tall, slender, with long red hair flowing over her shoulders. She was dressed in skintight jeans and a T-shirt that looked painted on. It certainly did nothing to hide her prominent nipples.

"Hi, guys. I couldn't help notice you were solo tonight."

Steve gave her a smile that had captured more than one damsel's heart. "We are, sweet thing, but this here's a bachelor party."

Her pink, glistening lips turned down in a fetching frown. "Who's the lucky guy?"

Steve lifted his drink. "That would be me."

Her smile returned as her focus turned to Ben. "So you're not taken?"

Normally, he would have considered the possibilities in front of him, but the poor girl had no idea who she was up against. "Sorry, darling. I'm taken."

Now she pouted outright. "Taken, taken?"

He nodded. "More's the pity."

She sighed, which did great things to her chest, and then put on a happy face. "Well, have fun, and tell your ladies they're damn lucky."

Ben didn't look at Steve until after the waitress had come by for their orders. When he did, Steve's expression told him he was utterly confused, and wanted an explanation, pronto.

"Is something wrong?" Ben asked innocently.

"Well, I'm thinking there's something you haven't told me..."

"Me, naw. I'm in the pink." Ben waved his hand in dismissal.

Steve leaned back, studying him carefully. "Bull. Tell me what's going on. That was a major-league babe. Probably the best damn thing you've seen in years."

"True." Shit. He should have talked to Taylor about this. Did she want it to be a secret? Did he?

"Come on, Bowman. Spill."

He debated for a few minutes, until he figured Steve would brain him if he didn't say something, and then he made up his mind. He didn't want to hide or sneak around. Everyone would deal. "I'm interested in someone."

"What? Who? When?"

"You forgot how and where."

"You've been holding out, man. Come on. Give."

He took another drink, then looked Steve in the eye. "It's nothing. Yet. Except a real strong attraction."

"No shit. This is awesome. I didn't think, you know, since Alyson… Why didn't you bring this woman?"

"I didn't have to. She was already here."

"Huh?"

He leaned forward. If Steve was gonna belt him, he didn't want him ruining the furniture. "It's Taylor."

Steve's face froze. Not an eyelash quivered, not a breath escaped. Finally, after what felt like a millennium, he blinked. "Taylor? My Taylor?"

Ben nodded slowly, watching him as if his life depended on it, which it just might.

"Well, I'll be…" Steve's gaze moved from Ben's face to his own hand. For the length of an entire Nine Inch Nails song, he didn't say another word. And then came one mother of a grin. "You and Taylor, huh? I'll be damned."

"You don't mind?"

"Why would I mind? You're my two favorite people on the planet. I think it's great."

Ben let go a breath he hadn't realized he'd been holding. "Wow."

"I'll say. So has this been going on awhile?"

"You could say that."

"No shit."

"You said that already."

"It bears repeating."

The wings arrived along with a couple of beers. If it had been anyone other than Steve, they would have talked about the situation for a long time. But

Steve figured everyone was pretty much like him, that private was private. What was excellent was Steve's obvious approval. That made things a hell of a lot easier, because even if he'd insisted they stop, Ben wasn't at all sure he would have. Or could have.

After they finished the wings, Steve reached for his wallet, but Ben put a stop to that. Then they headed back to the hotel.

It was just past two when they got there, and Ben wanted to see Taylor. Now. Luckily, Steve wanted to see Lisa. They rode up the elevator together, and when it stopped on Steve's floor, he gave Ben a massive bear hug, then looked him straight in the eyes. "Thanks, man. Best bachelor party a guy could have. I'm glad you're here. And if you hurt my sister, I'll rip your heart out."

Then he walked out and down the hall, whistling.

Ben cracked up, glad they'd been alone. At his floor, he looked at his watch. It was late. He had no business bothering Taylor at this hour.

But when he got to her room, he knocked anyway. Softly, so he wouldn't wake her. When she didn't answer, he knocked a little bit harder. He wouldn't bang on the door though. That would be rude.

HE STOOD AT THE DOOR looking so good she wondered if she was dreaming. Considering the last thing she remembered was hitting the pillow, maybe she was.

"You were sleeping," he said, his voice curling inside her like sweet smoke.

"Yeah, I was."

He turned. "I'm sorry. I'll see you tomorrow."

She grabbed his arm. "Wait. It's okay. Come on in."

He smiled, and it changed his face. He could look so tough, so rugged, and yet when he smiled, his eyes became welcoming and his lips promised wonders. "You sure?"

"Uh-huh."

He leaned forward and kissed her lightly before he stepped inside. She noticed he wasn't all that steady on his feet, and his breath gave her a clue as to how he'd spent his evening.

He made his way to the couch and sort of fell on it, expelling a big gust of air. "Whoa."

"Rough night?"

"Great night. But a little too much of it, if you know what I mean."

"I do." She joined him, curling her feet under her, and spreading her robe demurely over her legs. She'd wished she'd had time to put on a little makeup, maybe brush her hair. "Did Steve say anything?"

"He said lots. Unfortunately, nothing that gave me any insight about his marriage."

"Bummer."

"Yeah. You know him, though. He doesn't believe in spitting it out until—"

"It's too late."

"Maybe not. We still have time."

She sighed. "I hope you're right."

"What about you? What was the secret 'girl thing' you all did?"

She groaned. "Oh, please. It was horrible. We went to a strip club."

His brows rose.

"Guys. Mostly naked."

"Oh?"

"Not my idea of a swell night. At least not while I'm sitting next to Mom, who looked like she was going to pass out from embarrassment."

"Ouch."

"But Lisa and her mom sure enjoyed themselves."

"Well, I'm happy for them."

"I could have lived quite happily without it, thank you. I just get more and more confused about the whole thing. I don't know. Maybe we should just be happy for him."

"He's happy for us."

"Pardon?"

"I kind of told him we were, uh, together."

"You did?"

"He seemed pretty cool about it. Although he did warn me if I hurt you he'd kill me."

"Good old Steve."

Ben's mood seemed to shift as he studied her.

"What's wrong?"

He leaned over and kissed her, taking his time. Letting her get used to him once more. "You know what? I'm gonna go."

"Why?"

He smiled and his eyes told her there was nothing to worry about. "Because I'm tired and I've had too much to drink."

"Okay."

"It's not that I don't want to stay. It's that I want it to be perfect."

"Oh, sure," she said, crossing her arms over her chest. "Disarm me with charm and romance. As if that's gonna work."

He chuckled as he stood. "Go back to bed. Sleep well and dream about me."

She followed him to the door. "As if I could dream about anything else."

One last kiss, a gentle caress of her cheek, her chin, and then he was gone. She closed the door, leaned against the cool wood with her very warm forehead. No way she was going to get to sleep now. She should be furious that he woke her up. And that after he woke her up, he had the temerity to leave. But she wasn't.

The feeling was familiar, even though she hadn't felt it for a long, long time. Her crush on Ben was back. With a vengeance.

CHAPTER EIGHT

To: Eve's Apple
From: Taylor
EvesApple.com
Subject: Arghhh!

HERE'S THE LATEST, KIDDIES: Ben is the most amazing man in the universe. And, no, I'm not exaggerating in the slightest. When we walk together in the hotel, women stop and stare, and I swear I actually see jaws drop. Of course, men look, too, which kind of makes me a wee bit self-conscious, but I can't blame them. He's just so...

Okay, so we fooled around a little this morning. No we didn't go all the way, but I went far enough to see stars. Oh, mamma. He was so intense. God, I get the shivers just thinking about it. Too, too incredible. And then I went shopping with my mom, which was fun. After that, I got roped into this horrible evening at a male strip club, which might have been fun with you guys, but with my mother sitting beside me, I swear I would have rather been at the dentist.

I came home, thought about calling Ben, figured

it was too late, went to bed. Then I was awakened by a knock at the door. You guessed it. Mr. Gorgeous himself. He was so sweet! He told my brother that we were an item. Or item-lite, I guess. Which was amazing, as I didn't think he thought—well, you know. And so I'm all jazzed and ready to continue where we'd left off, and what does Ben do? He tells me he's going to bed. In his room. Alone. Because he's had too much to drink with my brother and he wants our first, uh, I mean second time to be perfect.

Which melted me, of course, but on the other hand, here I am at 2:30 a.m. typing when I should have been having an out-of-mind experience with Mr. Bowman.

What I can't figure out is why he left. Was he telling the truth? Did he get scared? Was I so hideous without my makeup that he's rethought this whole item thing? I have no clues. Any objective comments would be deeply appreciated.

Also, and this is kind of scary, I have to admit to you, and to myself, that the crush of old is back. Only, in the past ten years it's had time to ripen. While this week looks to be one of the best (please, please, please) of my life, I think leaving is going to be hell.

Okay, hope you're all doing wonderfully, and that some of you at least have picked out your MTD! Write me back. Soon.

Love, Taylor

BEN TURNED OVER AND LOOKED at the bedside clock—three-forty-five. Just great.

He punched his pillow a few times, but it still didn't come close to his pillow at home. He'd meant to bring it, but then he'd have looked like a perfect ass carrying it all over the airport. Not that he gave a damn.

Sighing, he closed his eyes once more, and his thoughts went right back to where they'd been a minute ago. Why had he left Taylor's room? He could have stayed. Should have stayed. So what the hell had he been thinking?

She'd bought the line about wanting things to be perfect. Which was partially true. He didn't care for the idea of being toasted when they made love. Not with her. But was that really it? It's not as if they couldn't have had a great, albeit woozy evening, then done it again when he was stone sober.

Something else was going on here and he wasn't sure what. This was a dream week for him, aside from worrying about Steve. No obligations, no commitments, no having to get to know her from scratch. It was ideal in every way, and he was nuts not to take advantage of every second.

And yet, here he was in his own room, way the hell down the hall from hers.

Was it fear? Of what? That she'd get attached? That he'd get attached? That was just nuts. Not in a week. Maybe a few months, but a week? Couldn't happen.

So if it wasn't fear, then what? Performance

anxiety? Jeez, he hoped not. Prayed not, but truth be told, since Alyson, he hadn't exactly been at the top of his game. Not that he hadn't been successful with the few women he'd seen, but something lingered. Why hadn't he seen it? Yeah, yeah, she'd told him a dozen times she hadn't known herself, but that information wasn't helpful. So she'd been in denial. Obviously, so had he. And if he'd been in denial with Alyson, why not with Taylor? Not that she was secretly gay, he didn't think that for a moment. But what if there was something else? Something he should see, but didn't?

Most days he realized Alyson's sexual preference was her own business, and had nothing to do with him. This wasn't most days.

Maybe his anxiety had a completely different origin. Taylor had no way of knowing it, but that long-ago weekend had been spectacular. The clouds had parted, the angels wept. They'd been magic together, and from his brief foray into the mystery of Taylor this morning, they probably would be again. Only it wouldn't be the same. Couldn't be. They were both older. Him, especially. And time has a way of changing even the best of things.

So, all right, he was being a dick. It wouldn't be the same, and so what? It would still be great. Because it would be with Taylor. She was terrific. He felt comfortable with her. More comfortable than he'd been in a long, long time.

He turned over, kicked off the blankets. Enough of this Dr. Phil crap. Tomorrow night, Taylor was his. He didn't give a damn what else happened, he just knew there was no way he was going to spend another night alone while he could be with her.

No more excuses. He'd watch his liquor intake, keep himself sharp and alert. He'd even catch a nap tomorrow, seeing as he wasn't getting any sleep tonight.

And then all bets were off. She wanted no mercy? That's just what he'd give her.

TAYLOR HAD TO ADMIT, the pale pink dress was beautiful. She turned in front of the three-way mirror, scrutinizing her butt in the tight sheath. She also had to admit that Lisa had been really nice all day. Solicitous, sweet and kind. She and her mother, Mimi, had taken her to breakfast at the buffet where Taylor had eaten too much to be trying on dresses, but if she watched herself over the next few days the pooch would be gone. There was a gym at the hotel, and she'd use it. Yeah. Right.

Well, at least she could swim. She liked to swim. The pool at the hotel was so beautiful. Did Ben like to swim?

Thinking about Ben, dripping wet, the water shimmying down his chest inch by slow inch gave Taylor a whole new reason to live.

She laughed at herself. What was she, thirteen?

Yeah, that's just how she felt. Like a teenager in love. Lust. Just lust. Lust was okay. Fine and dandy. Nothing more.

What was it with women? She wasn't the only one who did this, that was for sure. See a nice guy, he shows a little interest, and it's straight to wedding invitations and planning the bedroom suite.

The whole purpose of this trip, aside from the obvious, was to play with Ben Bowman. Play like a cat with a ball of yarn. The cat didn't want to set up house with the yarn. And she didn't want to set up house with Ben.

All she wanted was to get the hell past him. Enjoy, yes, but with clear vision and a clear head. Not the rich fantasy life of an eighteen-year-old with a bad case of Ben-itis. She was a grown-up now, with a responsible job, friends, an apartment, a motorcycle.

"Taylor? Are you decent?"

She turned to the curtain. "Sure, Lisa, come on in."

The curtain squealed as it slid on the rod, and Lisa's gasp could be heard throughout the dressing room. "Oh, my God! You look fantastic! That is the most gorgeous dress I've ever seen. You simply have to buy it. I'm totally jealous, and everyone's going to be looking at you instead of me."

Taylor couldn't help but smile. "Oh, please, Lisa, that's crazy talk. You're a total babe, and in that dress of yours, your gonna be a knockout."

Lisa returned her smile, looked at herself in the mirror. She wasn't in the wedding dress, which was white, on the short side, and yet oddly conservative. It had a beautiful pearled bodice and a slightly flared skirt, and she truly was a picture in it. Now, though, she was wearing a little black number. Smart. Expensive. And it made her look like she was built like a brick house.

"For the honeymoon?"

Lisa shook her head. "Dinner, tomorrow night. Didn't Steve tell you? We're going to Picasso's at the Bellagio."

"That's like the best restaurant in Vegas."

"I know. You can wear the gray dress, right? Or do you want to look at something else?"

"No, I'll be fine. But thanks."

"Honestly, you look stunning in that. Maybe with your hair up?"

"Yeah, maybe."

"We have an appointment for you at the spa, if you want it. We can cancel if you don't, but Mom thought it would be nice to set you and your mom up for hair and nails. I would be grateful for the company."

God, why was she making this so difficult? If Lisa had been a flat-out bitch, no problem. But this nice crap? How was she supposed to combat that? "Sure. It'll be fun."

"So tell me about you and Ben."

Taylor's gaze swung from her own reflection to Lisa's. "Pardon?"

"Steve told me you and he are, um, exploring the possibilities?"

She laughed. "I'll bet fifty bucks that's exactly what Steve said."

"How'd you know?"

"One thing you're going to have to get used to about Steve. He's the worst gossip ever. I mean it. It's as if he missed the whole human-interest portion of knowing people. He talks to them, and unless the conversation is about fishing, it's gone. Out of there. It's amazing."

Lisa ran her hand down her hip, eyeing herself critically. "You know, I think I'm going to sneak over to the shoe department at Neiman's and see if I can't get something a little more kicky for this dress."

Taylor realized her faux pas. "Of course, now that he's going to be in sales, it'll be the same thing. If it's not about the business, you can forget it. He won't know if someone's married, of if they're getting a divorce. Nothing juicy whatsoever."

Lisa smiled again. "That's okay. I gossip enough for the both of us. And I really think you should get that dress."

"All right," Taylor said, reaching for the zipper. "I'll get it. But I have to join you over at the shoe department, because I have nothing to go with this. White sandals, what do you think?"

"Perfect. Let me call Mom and tell her we'll be another hour."

"Great."

Lisa stepped out of the room while Taylor changed back into her sundress. It was pale yellow with little squiggles of green. No bra, but in this dress, it didn't matter—God bless built-ins. She slipped on her flip-flops and grabbed her purse. A quick moment with her hair brush and her lip gloss, and it was off to buy shoes with the woman her brother was going to marry. A marriage that she was supposed to stop. Only, she was having a pretty hard time putting her finger on the reason why.

BEN'S HEAD NEEDED HELP, and the pain medication he'd brought with him wasn't going to do the trick. It was past noon, and somehow he'd managed to shower, shave and dress. Higher thought was out of the question. Luckily, he was in a large hotel with a large gift and sundry shop. He padded across the nice thick carpet to where he'd left his sandals, put them on, then grabbed his key card and headed for relief.

Once he got to the lobby, he realized the Hard Rock wasn't the ideal place to nurse a hangover. Normally, he liked Elvis Costello, but right now it felt like a hammer to the skull.

In the gift shop, he found a bounty of headache cures. He bought three different kinds, not sure which would prove the most beneficial. Now, the key was to get coffee and quiet. The first part was no sweat, but the second? He asked the nice young lady behind the counter.

"Quiet? Sure. You got a room?"

He nodded.

She smiled.

He understood. "Thanks."

"Hope you feel better."

"Me, too." He stopped at a hotel phone halfway to the elevator and asked for room service. He ordered a large pot of coffee, a couple of eggs and some toast. "There's a nice tip if you can get it there in five minutes."

Ben wasn't encouraged by the laughter on the other end of the phone, but at least he had water in the room. He'd start with the fizzy kind of pain reliever and go from there.

Back on his floor, he slowed down as he passed Taylor's room. He thought about knocking, but that was already happening in his head, so he let it go.

His breakfast got there twenty-seven minutes later, and when the last bite was eaten and the last cup drunk, he picked up the phone. Taylor wasn't in. He left what he thought was a witty message, but on reflection, he thought about breaking into her room and ripping out the phone. Oh, well. She'd known him for too long to blow him off over a lousy joke. He hoped.

He walked over to the window, and took a look at

Sin City during the day. Man, he could see heat waves from all the way up here. What did he expect for July? It was supposed to be around 110 degrees today. But at least it was a dry heat, right? Actually, as far as he was concerned, an oven was an oven.

It was pretty damn hot in New York now, too. Which had some pluses. A lot of people left town, and a less congested Manhattan was a better Manhattan. Despite the heat, the humidity, all the crap about New York, he missed it when he wasn't there. The rhythm of the city suited him. He hadn't even guessed at that until he got there, and now he couldn't imagine living anywhere else. Of course a summer house in the mountains wouldn't hurt his feelings. Someday.

He sighed, turned, noticed that his head wasn't pounding quite so intensely. He wondered how old Steve was hangin'. Nothing made a hangover more bearable than someone else's misery.

He called Steve's room, and on the fourth ring the man himself picked up. At least he assumed it was Steve and not a bear.

"Feeling chipper, are we, Steve?" Ben laughed at the very succinct reply, "Get in the shower and get some coffee. I'll come get you in a half hour. We'll go terrorize the casino."

"I don't know…"

"What's wrong?"

"Wait."

There was a considerable silence. Finally, Steve

cleared his throat. "Okay. The girls are shopping. Give me forty-five minutes. I'm gonna need it."

"You have something for your head?"

"I'll have some coffee."

"You know, an aspirin won't kill you, buddy."

"I don't like them."

"It's your funeral. Later." Ben hung up, and pondered his next move. The girls were shopping. He assumed Taylor was involved, which would explain her not answering the phone.

Just the thought of her stirred him. God, he wanted today to pass quickly so he could get to tonight. He hadn't been this attracted to anyone in years. Even in the beginning with Alyson, there had never been a major physical thing between them. Sure, they'd made love, and it had been great, but there hadn't been a lot of passion. He'd respected her mind, liked her sense of humor, and she tolerated him better than almost anyone. About a year into the relationship, it was clear she wanted more, so he'd asked her to marry him. It seemed like the next logical step. He'd been so damn preoccupied by his work, and she'd been completely into hers, that they didn't see each other all that frequently. And then things started to slip. He'd tried to make things right with her, but it hadn't worked. Of course, when she finally told him there was someone else, it had hurt like a mother. But things he hadn't even been aware of fell into place.

They were still friends, and he liked it that way.

She seemed happy with her lady, and she encouraged him to try again. He wasn't so sure about that.

Marriage had been tough for him. Even if Alyson hadn't discovered her preference for women, he doubted it would have worked out. His focus, especially back then, was too much about the job to be fair to a mate. He couldn't count how many cops had lousy marriages. Forget about other private investigators. Only one gut came to mind, Frank Rebar, who had a great marriage, good kids, all the trimmings. So while he'd had to deal with some loneliness and a definite lack of getting some, he figured it was better this way.

Although being around Taylor made the lack of getting some feel a hell of a lot more acute. Damn, imagine having her to come home to.

He walked back to the window. Staring at the bizarre skyline, he realized it was the city talking. Vegas was Neverland for adults. It wasn't the real world, with the stresses and strains of daily life. She had a life in San Francisco, a job she liked a lot. His life was far from normal, with odd hours, dangerous people, nothing like stability.

He turned away abruptly, angry at himself for even thinking such stupid thoughts. This was a week of indulgence, that's all. It would make a hell of a memory, but it wasn't going outside the city limits. He didn't even want it to.

His life worked just the way it was. The important

thing now was to make sure Steve wasn't getting himself in hot water. That's all that mattered.

That, and rocking Taylor's world.

CHAPTER NINE

"HEY. YOU'RE NOT THERE. Oh, well. I thought… Oh, I know. You're out winning a couple million, right? Try not to forget your humble roots. Uh, well, give me a buzz when you come back."

Taylor pressed the button to repeat the message, smiling stupidly as she listened to Ben's silly little message. It was goofy and sweet and wonderful. She fell straight back on her bed, spreading her arms wide, then tossed her flip-flops across the bedroom. Shopping was over, she had no plans to meet anyone from her family until tomorrow, which meant she was free-free-free to play with Ben to her heart's content. "Yipee," she whispered, not that anyone could hear her.

The phone rang and she bolted upright, grabbing the receiver before the ring finished. "Hello?"

"So, how did shopping go?"

Her spirits sank, but just a bit. "Hi, Mom. It went fine. I got a really beautiful pink dress, a bathing suit and an incredible deal on shoes and a purse."

"I'm delighted, Taylor, but I was actually more interested in how it went with Lisa."

"Oh, yeah. You know, the thing is, she was really nice."

"I didn't think your brother would pick out a shrew."

"No, but I'm still not convinced he's doing the right thing. Last night I got the impression that the whole reason for this Vegas deal was so Steve couldn't get away."

Her mother was silent for a long beat. "I know. So what's next? Do we leave it alone? Let him make what might not be a mistake?"

"At this point, I'd just be happy if they would delay things. Give him a chance to think this through."

"See what you can do, sweetie." Her mother sighed. "I'm just going to try to avoid Mimi. At least until dinner tomorrow night."

"Right."

"Do you have plans for dinner?"

Taylor winced. She should eat with her mother, it was the right thing to do. "Yep. I'm booked. I'm meeting Ben and we're going to strategize."

"Is that what you call it these days?"

"Mother!"

"Be careful, Taylor. I don't want to worry about two children."

"Everything's peachy with me, Mom. You order something decadent from room service and watch in-room movies. Or better yet, why don't you go over to the Palace Station and play bingo?"

"I just might. And I suppose I should mention that Ben and Steve are downstairs throwing perfectly good money down the toilet at the craps tables."

"Thanks. Talk to you later." Taylor hung up. She should probably leave Ben and Steve alone.

Fat chance.

BEN SHOOK THE DICE IN TWO HANDS, resisting the urge to blow on them and say "Papa needs a new pair of shoes." Instead, he threw the dice toward the back rail of the craps table and rolled boxcars.

Steve pumped his arm twice. "Awesome."

Ben got the dice back, and rolled again. In fact, he rolled seven times before he crapped out. Both men, and several of the others standing around the table, made out like bandits. Then it was someone else's turn to roll, and Ben started gathering his chips.

"Hey, what do you think you're doing?"

"I thought I'd check up on Taylor."

"Are you kidding? They're shopping. They'll be at it 'til the cows come home."

Ben wasn't so sure about that, but he didn't mind hanging out a little longer with Steve. They could still be young and stupid together, which he missed. Back in New York he was serious all the damn time. Except for his weekly pickup game at the Y, he didn't do squat to have fun.

He let go of his chips and took advantage of the

nearby cocktail waitress, ordering a soda for himself and a beer for Steve.

When he turned back, Steve had been joined by a woman who wasn't Lisa. Joined was maybe stretching it. The woman had come up next to him and turned in a hundred dollar bill for chips. She was a tiny little thing, just over five feet, but perfectly put together. Blond spiky hair looked great with her black rectangular glasses. Ben wasn't a fashion maven by any means, but he knew chic and trendy when he saw it. She had on this really tight white shirt that had no sleeves, but was a turtleneck, and blue cropped pants. The way she looked at Steve made it real clear why she'd stood right there. Then the woman, girl, whatever, looked at him, but only for a second. Her gaze moved to his left. Ben had to look. Next to him was another woman who looked to be the same age and type as the woman next to Steve.

She smiled at him with dazzling white teeth. No glasses, the same clear, pale skin. A brunette, she had squared-off bangs and a blunt hair cut that reminded him of Theda Bara, the movie star from the twenties. Another beauty, and he wondered what they did for a living. He'd have said modeling, but Steve's gal was too short.

"You seem to know what you're doing," the brunette said to him. "I don't have a clue."

"That's a pretty good formula for losing your shirt."

Her smile took on a wicked gleam. "Maybe that wouldn't be so bad."

"Oh, my," Ben said. "I'll show you the little I know about craps, but as far as losing shirts or any other articles of clothing..."

"All right, fine. I'll play nice." She stuck out a manicured hand. "Melinda."

"I'm Ben. And this is my friend, Steve."

She reached across him, making sure to brush her breast across his shoulder. Her perfume was Obsession. "That's Gwinn, we're from L.A."

After the introductions were over, Ben placed his bet, conservative, and sent a guarded look Steve's way. Steve wasn't looking back. He was deep in a conversation with Gwinn, who was eating up his every word.

Not at all like last night, when Steve had turned away the babe in the bar. This was more like watching the old Steve in action. God, he'd been a terror. Not that he was one of those dicks who go through women like tissues, but he'd always had his choice of the finest ladies. Ben had done real well, too, and he figured it was just overflow because he never did as well on his own.

But the truth was, Melinda, as beautiful as she was, had nothing he wanted. Taylor was somewhere in Las Vegas, and eventually, tonight, she'd be with him. Everything else was just hang time.

Steve laughed, loudly, then the waitress came by

with their drinks. Melinda and Gwinn both ordered Bloody Marys.

"So what do you do?" Melinda asked.

He hated this part. Usually made up some wild story, but it seemed like too much trouble. "P.I. out of New York."

"P.I. as in Private Eye?"

He nodded. "And my buddy here owns a fleet of ships."

Her eyes widened as her gaze moved to Steve. Aha, a clue. Perhaps owning a fleet of ships made one automatically more attractive. Perhaps most people knew how being a private investigator was not necessarily the most direct method to millions. Go figure.

"No, like this."

Ben watched the maestro in action: Steve put his arms around Gwinn, bent her over the rail and helped her shake the dice before she threw. Totally unnecessary. Completely flirting. Undoubtedly trouble.

"Ben?"

He smiled at Melinda as she touched his shoulder. "Would you excuse me?" Then he turned to face a very perplexed Taylor Hanson.

TAYLOR COULDN'T BELIEVE how badly she wanted to slap the dark-haired bitch. But she simply smiled. Waiting to see how this little drama would play out. Her gaze moved over to her brother as he unwrapped his arms from the blonde. She'd never seen a darker blush on Steve's face. Not even when she'd walked in on him in his bedroom when he was fourteen and definitely "in flagrante."

"Taylor," he said. "Uh, hi."

"Hello, Steven. Your fiancé is in your room, lucky for you. But I'm quite certain she'd love to see you."

"Yeah, right." He gave a guilty smile to blondie, then after quickly scooping up his chips, dashed toward the elevator. The women gathered their meager winnings and skulked away, leaving her with Ben and a table full of anxious gamblers.

"Hang on," he said, stuffing chips in his pockets until he looked like a very successful thief. Then he put his arm around her and led her in the direction of the Pink Taco. "Did you have fun shopping?"

"It was heaven on earth. Who was that?"

"Her name was Melinda, and she was hitting on me."

"That much I gathered."

He smiled angelically. "She wasn't succeeding."

"I should hope not."

"A bit more worrisome about Steve, though. Last night, same scenario and he was true blue without a blink. Today, he was the old hound dog we've come to know and love."

"I don't get it. He's the one who's been so hot on Lisa. And you know what's funny? She was great today. Funny and nice and I was actually going to talk to you about forgetting this whole thing."

"I think, given this minor incident, the very least we should try is to get Steve to postpone, yes?"

She nodded, then looking away from Ben realized they were at the Nouveau Mexican restaurant. "What's this?"

"Food."

She looked at her watch. Four-fifteen. "Early, isn't it?"

He nodded. "I have plans later."

Her face heated, and she imagined she looked a great deal like her brother, only for very different reasons.

Ben leaned over and nipped her earlobe. "If I'm going to ravish you, I need sustenance. So do you."

A whole different shade of red must be making her face look clownlike and awful. "Food. Yes. Good."

"Unless you'd rather have something else. At the coffee shop perhaps?"

She thought about her fave Mexican dishes. All of them had beans. "Yes, actually. I would." She took his hand and led him back where they'd come from. Then, instead of heading toward the café, she turned toward the elevator.

His brows rose in question.

"Room service," she said.

He pulled her to a stop next to a cashier's cage and put both hands on either side of her face. "Brilliant," he whispered. Then he kissed her, sucked her tongue straight into his mouth.

She nearly lost it right there. No more time to waste. Pulling back, she nipped his lower lip. "I don't want to be down here a moment longer."

"Yes, right." He grinned, then ran. Flat-out ran. With her running right behind him.

INSTEAD OF HER ROOM, they went to his. He'd insisted, although he wouldn't say why. As soon as they walked through the door, he put the Do Not Disturb sign out, then segued into the bathroom, closing the door behind him, and leaving her a bit in the lurch. But, as she'd seen quite often in the past few days, Ben was full of surprises, and that was much more fun than steady and predictable.

His room was virtually identical to her own, so there wasn't much to explore, but she did find the room service menu and gave that a quick peruse.

Before she could make up her mind, Ben was behind her, his hands on her hips, his lips on the back of her neck. "Did you miss me?" he whispered, his warm breath tickling in just the right way.

"Oh, were you gone? I hadn't noticed."

"God, you're cute. Mean, but cute."

She spun around, pleased that he didn't let go of her. "It's true, you know. I am mean. But only when I don't get what I want."

His brown eyes steadied on hers. "What do you want, Taylor? What do you need?"

She grabbed him by the shirt and pulled him tight against her, answering with a searing kiss.

Ben rubbed against her, letting her feel his erection. He kept rubbing, pushing her backward until she was up against the wall.

They stood next to the wet bar, and she had a splendid view of the city out the window, although she had no eyes for anything but the man holding her wrists with both hands.

He yanked them up high on the wall and while she gasped he kicked her legs apart until her dress was tight and high on her thighs.

"Is this what you want?"

If she'd been able to speak she would have said yes, but his mouth was on hers, and she had to explain everything with her lips, her tongue, her body.

Kiss, then gone, then kiss, gone. Teasing, testing, grasping her wrists so tight that it would have hurt if she hadn't been so pumped full of adrenaline, among other things. "Stop," she said, but the word was cut off by his lips. A second later, he was gone again, just that brief taste, that quick lick with his darting tongue.

"Stay," she said.

He shook his head. Then he licked the underside of her arm, one long stroke, making her shiver and gasp. God, he was good at making her do that.

"Tell me what you want first," he said, that mercurial tongue of his rimming the shell of her ear.

"A kiss," she said. "A long one."

"No, try again."

"That's not fair."

"I never said it would be fair."

"You were in control last time."

"I like being in control."

"So do I."

"You like this, too."

She turned her head, knocking him on the chin. "Let me go and I'll show you how much you'll like being on the bottom."

"No."

"No?"

"Try again."

"Why should I?"

He smiled real slow. "Because I'm going to make you lose your mind."

"Too late."

He laughed. She watched his Adam's apple bob, and it was sexier than Elvis on Ed Sullivan.

She lifted her leg, snaking along the inside of his until her knee hit pay dirt. Not hard, of course, because she didn't want to hurt anything of value; just enough for him to understand that while he might have her hands captured, she wasn't without resources.

"Ahhh."

"So, where's my kiss?"

"You want to play rough, is that it?"

"Rough is good. Sometimes."

"Oh? How rough?" He nipped her lip again, this time making her cry out.

"Hey."

"Too rough?"

She smiled. "Am I bleeding?"

"No."

She didn't say anything else. Let him figure it out for himself. Ben was quite clever, and she didn't want to restrict his behavior in any way, although of course she reserved the right to say no if she felt like it. Today, feeling as wild as she did, he'd have to go pretty damn far for her to throw in the towel.

"You know what?" he said, just before he circled her lips with the tip of his tongue. "Foreplay is great. I mean it. Right up there with hot dogs at Dodger Stadium and swimming naked. But you know what's even better?"

She knew, but she shook her head anyway.

He held her up against the wall with his lower body, squared himself with her eyes and gave her the most commanding look she'd ever seen. "Do not move until I tell you to," he whispered, his voice somewhere between a promise and a threat.

She obeyed, holding still, holding her breath, almost stopping her heart, anticipating what was to come.

It became clearer as he released her wrists. Her instinct was to lower her arms, but his cocked brow stopped her dead still. It felt a bit silly to hold her hands up like that, but she didn't particularly care.

His hands moved on to much more useful tasks. Lifting her dress, for one. Slowly, the material rose, exposing more of her thigh, then the crotch of her panties, and still he kept lifting until he'd raised her dress past her chest, her head, her arms. He tossed it behind him, and she didn't give a damn where it landed. Next he reached behind her and undid the catch on her bra. That was discarded somewhere, and as he reached to do the same with her panties he bent his knees until his lips where level with her breasts, quite perky with her hands up in the air.

He kissed each nipple, then used his tongue to make her moan. She felt his fingers grab the edges of her silk thong and rip it away from her body.

There. She was naked right in front of him, standing up against the wall, once again with him fully dressed. She had to do something about this. Next time, dammit, she was going to strip him first, and not get herself into this situation.

Oh, who was she kidding? She didn't care one whit who got naked first as long as both of them ended up there.

Taking her by surprise, he lifted her straight up, his hands under her thighs. Her legs wrapped around him, and she'd been so busy being annoyed that he was dressed, she hadn't realized he'd actually lost his pants. Or maybe just lowered them. Whatever. Because what he did then stole her breath.

He lifted her onto himself.

Just. Like. That.

One second she was standing there, and the next he was inside her, fully, unbelievably. Her head rolled back as she cried out, as her hands flew down from the wall to hold on to him for dear life. She probably didn't have to, as he held her completely steady, but this wasn't exactly a position she was very practiced in, so dammit, she was hanging on.

Balancing her weight on the wall, he was able to pull almost all the way out, then thrust back in to the hilt. She gasped, cried, swooned as he entered her over and over, rubbing her in the most perfect way. Faster than she could have ever imagined, she felt the shiver and tightness that was the beginning of an orgasm. Maybe because so much was happening all at once, maybe because it was Ben and she could practically come just by looking at him, but holy cow, she was on the runway speeding toward takeoff.

"Oh, God," he said as he found her mouth.

The kiss was desperate, just like her own, and she guessed he was riding right next to her on the express to heaven.

"Jeeze, Taylor, what are you doing to me?"

"The same thing you're doing to me."

He buried his head in the crook of her shoulder, bit her flesh and kept on riding.

Then his face shifted to a grimace, but there was no pain involved. Just intensity that she knew too well. He cried out and their voices mingled as she peaked, her hands tearing at his hair, her feet banging on his back.

She had no idea how he was doing for at least a couple of minutes. Then she felt his strength wane as he struggled to regain his breath.

He let her down gently, and while she staggered to the bedroom, he followed close behind.

As she flopped on the gold comforter, she flashed on something uncomfortable. "Uh, Ben?"

He grunted, which she took for a response. He'd flopped down next to her, and somewhere along the way he'd taken off his shirt and his pants, and was as naked as she was.

"We got a little carried away there, didn't we?"

He grunted again.

"Except that we didn't…I didn't…I'm on the pill, but that isn't…"

"I got it covered."

"What?"

He lifted his head and looked at her. "I had it covered. Literally. That's why I went to the bathroom first."

"Oh. Good. But, just in case, I have a couple of condoms in my purse."

His head flopped down on the pillow, his chuckle

low and rueful. "Wish I'd known that yesterday. Anyway, sleep now. Thank me later."

"Okay," she said, but she sneaked in a kiss to his cheek anyway.

CHAPTER TEN

THE EARLY MORNING LIGHT hit Taylor right in the eyes. She turned over, but the damage was done—she was awake. Sore and awake.

Ben slept soundly, his breathing deep and even, his face unlined and perfect even with the dark shadow of beard. He was the most beautiful man she'd ever seen, and watching him made her heart ache. Odd, that tenderness could hurt so, but there it was. She was amazed at this man, at his thoughtfulness, his energy, his incredible sexuality. At the way he made her feel.

She closed her eyes, remembering the night, especially the second time they'd made love. He'd awakened her with a kiss, very gentle and sweet, and she'd opened her eyes to the sight of him leaning on one elbow, staring at her as if she were a thing of wonder.

"What time is it?" Her voice had been gruff with sleep, and Ben reached over her to the bedside table where he picked up the bottled water, gave her a sip, then put the bottle back.

"I don't know. Late."

"How long have you been awake?"

He shrugged his one free shoulder.

"And you've been watching me for how long?"

"As long as I could stand it."

"Excuse me?"

He laughed. "I'm not sure how long I've been staring, and then the temptation was too strong, and I had to kiss you. Even though I knew it wasn't a very nice thing to do."

"Kissing is always nice."

"But you looked so peaceful."

"I'll sleep again. Trust me." She rose until her lips found his. "Just remember, whenever the urge to kiss strikes, you have my permission."

His slow grin made her blush. "Does it matter where I have the urge to kiss you?"

She shook her head.

"Even if it's..." He threw back the covers and leaned over her chest, kissing the tip of her nipple.

She laughed. "Well, that probably wouldn't go over too well in say a restaurant or at the blackjack table."

He kissed her other nipple before coming back up to eye level. "Oh, sure. Just spoil it all, why don't you?"

She flung her arms around his neck and pulled him down. "Don't you go giving me any trouble, Ben Bowman."

"Or what?"

"Or things could get ugly."

He looked up at her. "No possible way. You and ugly don't mix."

She threw her arms back and spread her legs wide. "Take me. Take me now."

"Is that it? The secret to having my way with you? A compliment?"

"Not just any compliment, no. I mean, I probably won't lay down after you've said my chicken casserole is yummy."

"You sure about that?"

She shook her head.

He stroked her side as his head lowered to her neck. She felt his warm breath first, then the edges of his teeth as he nibbled. "I'll have to experiment with this. Try different kinds of compliments and see the various reactions."

"It won't work if I know you're trying to get some."

His head came up again. "I'm always gonna be trying to get some. Who do you think I am, for God's sake? A superhero?"

"There's trying, and then there's *trying*."

"Explain."

"If the compliment is heartfelt with no ulterior motives, then the points are quite high. If the compliment is heartfelt and you're groping me under the table, then the points lower proportionately."

"Lower, but don't get cancelled out."

"No. Not always."

"And what if the compliment is completely bogus, and I'm groping you right out in front of God and everyone?"

"Then there are absolutely no points whatsoever."

"And I don't get any?"

"Depends on how you're groping."

He grinned. "Interesting system you have there, Ms. Hanson."

"It's my playground, I get to set the rules."

"And the same goes for me, right? I get to set the rules?"

She blinked a few times, stared him straight in the eyes. "Are you trying to tell me that any form of compliment, heartfelt or otherwise, would have the least effect on your libido while I was in the process of groping you?"

"No. You're right. You grope, I'm yours. You could even call me names, say rude things about my goldfish, disparage my heritage, and if you're groping, there's no contest."

"The difference," she said, "between the sexes."

"Oh, there are lots more differences than that." His hand moved down her tummy until his fingers trailed through her soft curls to the folds of her sex. "See, you go in—" he demonstrated the principle using two fingers in just the right way "—while I go out." He guided her hand to his very erect and insistent cock. "Big difference. Huge."

"I'll say," she said, giggling.

"See, now there's a compliment that works every time."

She pulled him closer. "Why don't you show me how this works?"

THAT HAD BEEN HOURS AGO, when the night had been dark and the only light had come from the little lamp over the nightstand. She had no recollection of how it had been turned off, so exhausted had she been by their slow, incredible lovemaking.

He'd known exactly how to touch every inch of her, how to make her wait, how to build the tension, how to tease and definitely how to pay off. The truth was, he was everything she'd ever thought he was, and more.

She turned to face the wall, away from the sleeping man, no longer caring if the light hit her eyes. No longer caring about much but the building realization that she was in deep, deep trouble.

Everything she'd believed about Ben was true, and that wasn't good at all. She'd been so sure that she'd exaggerated his prowess over the years, that she'd built him into an icon of romance and sex in the fertile fields of her mind. She'd never really considered the possibility that he was the most incredible lover on the planet. The thought was ludicrous. No one could be as good as she remembered Ben.

Except Ben.

And where the hell did that leave her? How was she supposed to go on from here? Settle for boring sex for the rest of her life? Try every man she could find in the desperate hope she'd find someone as wonderful? Give up sex completely? She wasn't Catholic, but maybe being a nun wasn't such a bad idea. No, she'd have to be a lot more saintly, and a completely different person, so that was out.

She'd loved last night. Every single second of it. Now, as she tried to analyze why, her skin started tingling as she recalled his every touch. That wouldn't do.

Instead she focused only on the facts, the empirical evidence. Why was he so much better than anyone else she'd been with? Better wasn't even the right word for it. Ben was to making love what the Mona Lisa was to art. Way the hell outside the box. But why?

She grabbed the almost empty water bottle from the side table and took a sip, wishing she had some coffee, but unwilling to wake Ben.

On the other hand, the water did nothing for her, barely even quenched her thirst. What she needed to do was get out of there, go somewhere alone to think. Somewhere she wouldn't feel Ben's heat next to her skin. Somewhere she didn't have the overwhelming urge to touch him and start the whole damn process over again.

Slipping out from between the covers, she began searching for her clothes, finding them more or less in the same area. She gathered them all and went into the bathroom. She'd shower in her room. Right now, all she wanted to do was make a clean getaway.

Once she was dressed and her hair would no longer scare anyone she met in the hallway, she opened the bathroom door. Listening hard, she waited a good minute until she was sure he was still asleep. Then she headed for the door. As her hand touched the knob, she realized she couldn't just sneak out without any kind of notice. That would be horrible and while she might not be worthy of nun status, she wasn't a complete rat.

She left the bedroom for the living room, and immediately found a piece of hotel stationary. Now, what on earth was she going to say?

No use overthinking the process. "Dear Ben, thank you for the most fabulous night. I've got a busy day ahead, so I snuck off to get it started. I'll catch up with you soon. Hope your dreams were sweet!"

She almost signed it, "Love, Taylor," but she didn't. He'd figure out it was from her, and then the "L" word wouldn't come into play.

The "L" word. No, no, no. She could not go there. She was in enough trouble as it was.

THE POOL WAS ALREADY CROWDED when she got there. Not as many kids as she'd have guessed, but then this was the Hard Rock, which wasn't really a kid-oriented hotel. But those that were there seemed to be having a really good time.

Mostly, though, there were a whole mess of beautiful women and handsome men, all of them wearing remarkably small bathing suits, some exposing more skin than she liked to show her doctor.

The expanse of flesh on display wasn't her concern at the moment. All she wanted was a quiet lounge chair, a cold beverage and time to write to her buddies while she decided whether she should shoot herself or not.

Because she clearly had wonderful luck when it came to pool chairs, she found a prime spot, spread her towel and made herself comfortable. Before she even had a chance to bemoan her fate once, a cocktail waitress came by. After several seconds of deep consideration, she ordered a Bloody Mary.

Soon enough she was left to her thoughts, and it wasn't pretty. She brought her computer to her lap and opened it up. She had enough battery power for a couple of hours. She couldn't log in, but that was okay because she'd downloaded her emails before she came to the pool.

She had just enough shade from a nearby umbrella to read comfortably. The first e-mail she opened was from Angel, one of the sharpest of the women in her Eve's Apple group.

To: Taylor
From: Angel
EveApple.com
Subject: Re: Arghhh!

Dear Taylor,

Sounds like you might be facing some trouble in paradise. Not that your plan wasn't wonderful, but if you're anything like me, the best laid plans have a way of turning into big, fat, hairy messes before you can say Viva Las Vegas.

So Ben is fantastico, eh? He sure sounds like it. Just don't get carried away, okay? Because from what you've said, this is one week of fun and games. One week. Not forever, not the rest of your life, not even the rest of the year. And, my girl, you have to go home and face the rest of your life, and um, sorry, but didn't you say that wouldn't include Ben?

Maybe I'm crazy, but if you can just look at this thing for what it is—great sex with a gorgeous man— and realize it's like Vegas itself, cool vacation, but not sustainable—then maybe you can nip the obsession in the bud, and just enjoy yourself! That's the point. Enjoyment. Pleasure. Bliss.

Also, in my experience, true supreme happiness with the opposite sex is meant to be temporary. Oh, yeah, they say it's forever in the books and the movies and stuff, but come on. We all know better. So isn't it more sensible to have one incredible, mind-blowing, world-rocking week than to go on forever wondering what could have been?

So you have to come back to reality. Face it, honey, we all do. Life isn't a fairy tale, but if you're lucky, you can be a princess at least for a little bit. And it sounds to me like you certainly have found your (short-term) prince. So enjoy. 'Til it's time to say goodbye.

Love, Angel

The cocktail waitress came with her drink, and Taylor had to mask the tears in her eyes with a hand up for shade, even though she was already under the umbrella. The sympathetic smile as she signed her tab signaled her failure at faking it.

"It's okay, honey," the waitress said. "Been there, done that. There's other fish in the sea."

"Thanks," she said, but all she really wanted was to be alone. To weep. Because she knew that while Angel's advice was right on the money, there wasn't a chance in hell she could take heed.

It was too late. Way too late. She'd gone back ten years, right back to the moment she'd first been with Ben. To the magic that had been that weekend. To the revelation that she would never, as long as she lived, find anyone remotely as special or wonderful as him.

Only this time, it was worse. Because she knew what else was out there. And she knew there wasn't going to be another man for her.

She went on to the next e-mail, this one from Kelly, a biochemist from Seattle who also happened to have been a model who'd graced the covers of *Seventeen*, *Cosmo* and *Vogue*. Kelly was less hopeful than Angel, which was a real pisser, because if someone as brilliant and beautiful as Kelly didn't believe in fate, or true romance, what chance did Taylor have?

Depressed beyond measure, she shut the computer and slid it under her chair. She sipped her drink, perfectly chilled and spicy, and watched the soap opera all around her. Men flirting with women, women flirting with men; giggling, blushing, flaunting. She felt as if she were watching the mating rituals of the flat-bellied sun worshipper.

Everyone seemed hungry and desperate for a connection. The women laughed too brightly, the men smiled with friendliness on their lips and lust in their eyes. Arms were touched, shoulders brushed naked torsos. It made her long for Ben's comforting presence, and horribly sad that what she'd found was so fleeting.

Ben didn't want to get married. He'd made that very clear. Steve had told her, twice no less, that Ben had sworn to never marry again. Steve hadn't said why, but she imagined it had a lot to do with his divorce. She doubted very much he would be interested in living together. His attitude was closed and final, even though she knew he liked her a great deal.

She wasn't even sure she wanted marriage. The way she was drawn to him was unlike anything she'd ever experienced with anyone else. No one made her come alive like Ben, and no one sent her to the moon like he did. But even she wasn't foolish enough to think it was love. It was sex. Fantastic, fabulous, incredible sex. Nothing more. So why the big deal?

She had no idea. All she knew for sure was that she ached for him. She felt empty without him, and complete when he was near. What an idiot she was. It was too soon for feelings this intense. Way the hell too soon.

Just last week she'd been so excited about this unique opportunity. She'd bought clothes, makeup, underwear designed for seduction. She'd figured it would be a romp, but she'd also figured there would be a sad, but sweet ending.

Not this.

She took a long pull on her drink. At least she was familiar with what she would go back to. And it wasn't all bleak. She had her job, her friends, her motorcycle. And the utter conviction that she would never be truly happy.

Maybe that was too dramatic. Love wasn't only about fireworks. There were people she knew who weren't sexually active, yet they still had successful marriages. She'd find someone she could respect, someone who had a good sense of humor. There were good men out there, and now that she understood the score, she'd find herself one. Her expectations would be different, that's all. She'd had the best, now there would be the rest.

C'est la vie.

"Hi."

Taylor looked up, knowing the masculine voice above her wasn't Ben's. What she saw, on any other day would have revved up her pulse. He was one hell of a good-looking man. Tall, blond, built like a champion athlete. His smile seemed warm, and he actually looked her in the eyes instead of letting his gaze roam. "Hi."

"I saw you sitting here alone. I was wondering if you wanted some company."

She didn't. But what the hell. Today was as good as any to start her new life. "Sure. Sit down."

He found a plastic chair and pulled it near her lounge. "I'm Cade Miller." He stuck out a long, tanned hand.

Her own felt dwarfed by his, and if this had been a week ago, she was sure she would have gotten all quivery at the touch. She forced a smile. "Taylor Hanson."

"I'm here from Utah," he said. "Spending a week in this crazy place with a couple of college friends."

"You're in college?"

"Not anymore. But we still hang out. I'm a pilot. I fly out of Salt Lake City."

"That sounds exciting."

"What about you, Taylor Hanson?"

"I'm a paralegal. From San Francisco."

"On vacation?"

She shook her head, took another drink. "Here for my brother's wedding."

"Oh, wow, that sounds like fun."

"I'm trying."

He scooted closer. "I know we've just met, but uh, are you okay? Is something wrong?"

She smiled again, meaning to tell him that now wasn't the best time. Instead, she burst into tears.

"Oh, God, Taylor." He looked around as if he'd been trapped with a crazy lady. Then he moved over to her lounge and put an awkward hand around her shoulders. "Don't cry, okay? Whatever it is, it's going to be all right."

"No it's not. I thought for sure I would get over him." She wiped her eyes with the back of her hands, but the tears kept coming. "It was a great plan, and it should have worked, but he's still Ben, and I still want him so much."

Cade patted her shoulder. "I'm sure he wants you, too."

"No, he doesn't."

"Then he's a fool. Because I can't imagine anyone not wanting you."

She looked through tears that blurred his expression, and still she could see the kindness in his eyes. "That's so sweet."

"It's true. You're very lovely."

"You probably think I'm nuts."

"Nope. I've had my share of moments. And you know what, they all passed."

"This won't."

"You don't know that."

She sniffed, and wiped her eyes once more. "Can I ask you a favor?"

"Sure."

"Kiss me?"

To his credit, Cade didn't run for the hills or call the pool police. "Are you sure?"

"Just once. Just so I can…"

He gave her a lopsided grin. Then he bent down, and took her lips with his.

BEN STOOD BY THE POOLSIDE BAR, hands in his swim trunk pockets, watching as some blond Adonis kissed Taylor. He wanted to turn around and walk back into the hotel. It wasn't his business if she kissed another guy. They had no ties to each other. Just a week of sex and the rescue of her brother. It made no difference if Taylor wanted to sample the buffet instead of ordering from the menu.

On the other hand, Ben was pretty damn sure he could kill the guy without working up a sweat.

CHAPTER ELEVEN

TAYLOR FELT HIS LIPS ON HERS, felt his hand tighten on her shoulder. But it didn't feel like it was her, doing this, kissing this stranger.

She pulled back, her cheeks heating with the flame of embarrassment. "I'm sorry," she said, barely hearing her own voice.

"For what?"

She couldn't look him in the eyes. "I'm a wreck, and you seem like a really nice guy. You don't need to be a player in my little psychodrama."

"Hey, if I can help…"

She smiled, meeting his gaze. "You can't. But thanks."

He turned his head slightly to the left. "Sure?"

She nodded. "There are so many gorgeous ladies here, all of whom would be delighted to meet someone like you. So go. Find fun. It's your vacation."

"I don't want to leave you like this."

She touched his warm, tanned hand. "I'm going swimming now. As many laps as I can without drowning. And then I'm going to sleep. So please, don't fret."

He sighed, looked around the pool, then back at her. "I think that's a pretty good idea. But listen, I'm in room 1202, so if you want to talk when you get up from your nap, don't even think twice."

Glancing at his left hand, she saw no ring, not even a tan line where a ring would be. "How come you're single?"

He laughed. "Well, so much for small talk."

"I mean it. You're gorgeous, sweet, and unless you're a serial killer or still living with your mom, I don't get it."

He stared at nothing for a long moment. The outdoor speakers carried the sounds of Fleetwood Mac across the pool, and someone screeched in one of the private cabanas. When he looked at her again, her cheeks weren't burning anymore, which was good, although she really didn't want to think about actually kissing him.

"I haven't met her," he said.

"Her?"

"The one."

"Ah, but how do you know?"

"Because I haven't wanted to commit to someone. Not for the long-term, at least."

"So there have been almosts? Close, but no cigars?"

"Yep. And there's even been one that got away."

"Tell me about that one."

His smile turned rueful and his gaze moved from

her eyes to somewhere around her ear. "She was amazing. I met her in Hong Kong. We were together for six days, and it was the most incredible experience of my life. We connected on every level. She utterly fascinated me, and I can't remember laughing so often and so hard."

"What happened?"

"I had to fly back to the States."

"Why didn't she go with you?"

"Because," he said, his voice dropping into the whisper zone, "I didn't ask her. I'm not sure why, not even now. But I didn't. I did try to find her again, but she'd left the university there, and I have no idea where she ended up. I even hired a private investigator, but she dropped off the face of the earth. I've never really forgiven myself for that."

"So, if you found her again, you'd want to keep her?"

"Only if she'd want to keep me."

Taylor leaned forward and gave him a gentle kiss on the cheek. "I'm sorry. I hope you find her."

"And I hope you find what you're looking for." He stood up. "I mean it about calling. I'll be here a couple more days."

"Thanks."

He nodded once, then headed toward the bar.

Taylor watched him until he'd ordered his drink, and then she got up. After putting her computer under her towel, she went to the deep end of the pool. There were swimmers and some kids playing with a beach ball, but she had room to maneuver. She dove in, the cool water shocking for only a second or two, then comfortable and safe.

She'd been a water child, and because of her, her parents had built a pool in their backyard. She never missed an excuse to swim, and she remembered many a late night, when everyone in the house was asleep, when she'd tiptoe out to the backyard, and in the dark, she'd take off all her clothes and dive into the cool black water.

She'd done a lot of thinking like that, stretching her mind while she stretched her muscles. Lap after lap, her body in a rhythm that made every part of her calm. Even today, her most sacred rituals involved the pool at her gym, although they frowned on skinny-dipping.

As she carved out her narrow route, she thought about what Cade had said. How he'd found *the one* and then let her go. Fear. He hadn't said the word, but that's what it was all about. Fear of commitment, fear of being trapped, of making a mistake.

Was she afraid? Of course. But of what? Losing Ben? Keeping Ben? Not having the guts to tell Ben the truth? Hell, even if she got past all that, Ben had his own fears. He'd been so adamant about not wanting to get married. It had rolled off his tongue as if he'd said it a thousand times.

She'd seen other couples meet and fall for each

other. It looked so easy. As if they were two sides of the same coin; the key being that they immediately recognized that they were supposed to be together.

All she had with Ben was a shared past, the most incredible lovemaking in the world... She had to laugh at herself. She had been going to stop there, but that wasn't at all true. They had a lot more than that together. She loved his sense of humor, his intelligence, his probing nature. She loved the way he talked to strangers and the way he was with Steve. Then there was his eclectic taste in music, art, books. The truth was, he was the most fascinating man she'd ever met.

She hit the end of the pool and dived under to start another lap. She'd stopped counting at eight and was just starting to feel the strain in her arms, legs and lungs. Five more, at least, and if she could bear it, eight more. She wanted exhaustion.

For two laps, all she did was focus on her body, on moving through the water. Then her thoughts went back to Ben.

It was ridiculous to call this anything more than what it was—a crush. That was it. Infatuation. Memories cascading with reality, making the connection electric and enticing as hell. But he wasn't the one. He couldn't be. He just represented what she wanted in the one. So what the hell did she want?

She didn't have a clue.

BEN'S EYES WERE ON THE FOOTBALL GAME, but his thoughts were out by the pool with Taylor. Watching her kiss another man. Watching another man kiss her.

He felt like crap. And aside from the too obvious ego blow, he wasn't quite certain why. Not that he didn't have every reason to feel bad—he'd made love to the woman for hours last night, and it had blown him into the next galaxy—but the depth of his despair was totally unexpected.

He liked Taylor, sure. More than he'd ever have guessed. She was a hell of a lot of fun, he had strong ties to her background, she made him feel like a total stud, not to mention how good he felt whenever he was with her, no matter what they were up to. Everything he could want in a friend with benefits. And damn, those benefits were beyond world-class. But come on. It wasn't as if she'd left him after two years of marriage. For another woman. This was a no-strings-attached week, and all he could think about were strings and more strings.

So what was up with that?

Okay, so it was back to his ego. He had to admit, it hurt. Wounded him deeply. Man, he'd thought she'd had a blast last night. If that was faking it, the woman deserved an Oscar, a Tony and an Emmy.

No. No one was that good. He'd watched her face, her body. Seen her physical reaction with his own two eyes. Had felt the contractions when she'd come, and no matter how much moaning a woman does, there was no way to fake that. She'd come, and come hard.

So why would she need to play kissy-face with that jerk?

He signaled the waitress, and she came over wearing a big smile and a skimpy outfit. He probably should have done something about her welcoming grin, but instead he ordered a gin and tonic. She winked at him as she moved on to the next customer.

Hey, there was proof. He wasn't a total dog. In fact, experience had told him that women seemed to like his odd looks. Taylor had always acted as if she thought he was pretty hot stuff. She hadn't hidden her sexual agenda at all.

So, if he were investigating this situation for a man checking up on his wife, what would he deduce?

First, that the client had better watch out because something wasn't right. Women who are happy don't stray. Women who are getting it the way they want it don't look elsewhere.

Second, he'd look beyond the obvious. He'd been standing across the pool from the couple in question, unable to read their lips or even read their expressions with any degree of accuracy. Maybe he'd misinterpreted the scenario. Perhaps the guy was an old friend, someone she hadn't expected to run into. Or he could have been an old boyfriend. That would have explained the intimacy.

Almost.

That hadn't been a buddy kiss. Not for tan-boy at least, and Ben hadn't been able to see Taylor that well. That kiss had intent, and the position of his body and his hand around her back confirmed it. However, Taylor could have intended the kiss to be friendly and nothing more, and the jackass had taken advantage of the situation.

Ben hadn't seen her hands. She could have been pushing him away the whole time. And he hadn't stuck around to see the aftermath of the kiss. Big mistake. If it had been a case, he deserved to be fired.

But it wasn't a case, it was Taylor. His anger had eased, but his ego still ached like a wounded puppy. What seemed clear was that there were other explanations for the incident. He'd never go to a client with such flimsy evidence.

The right thing to do was to find out more. Just ask her. Tell her he was down at the pool, and he happened to see her with her friend. Her reaction would tell him everything, and then they could have a laugh over the whole thing. Or not.

But he still would ask. Because he didn't want to keep feeling this way. Not for another minute.

TAYLOR CARRIED HER TOWEL underneath her arm, covering her computer. Damp beneath her cover-up, she had accomplished her goal. She was exhausted all the way to her toes. Physically and mentally. All she had to do was make it to the elevator and down a short hall, and she'd be home free.

But, because she was Taylor and life wasn't in the least bit fair, she never made it to the elevator. Her brother stopped her halfway there.

Not that he saw her. She saw him. And what she saw made her stop.

Steve stood alone, leaning against a cashier's cage. He had a glass of clear liquid in one hand, and his other hand was cupped, holding what she guessed were pills. When he threw them in his mouth and drank down the water after, she figured she had it right.

What was Steve doing taking pills? He didn't even take vitamins. The man was sickeningly healthy, worked out daily, ate like an athlete in training. And he had a thing about aspirin. She'd never seen him take one. Not for a hangover, not for the flu, not even for a broken wrist. He'd always been that way, and nothing and no one was going to change his mind.

He scanned the immediate area with a guilty look, then headed toward the Pink Taco. She wasn't about to let him get away. Hurrying, maneuvering through too many vacationers and gamblers, it took her several minutes to get within shouting distance but she finally caught him by the back of his shirt.

He spun around so sharply she gasped, and then he recognized her, causing the mask of anger to drop from his face. Slowly, he formed a sort of smile. "Hey."

"Hey. What are you doing?"

"Me?" He shrugged. Stared at the towel under her arm. "Hanging. Lisa's getting a massage. I've been wandering."

"Oh."

"What about you?"

She looked down at her damp cover-up. "Swimming."

"Cool. Well, I think Lisa's probably done so—"

"Not so fast, mister."

His lips tightened.

"What were you doing back there?"

"Where?"

She pointed back to the cashier's cage. "Right there. I saw you."

"You saw what?"

"You. Taking pills."

"So?" The word sounded simple enough, but the flush on his cheeks said something different.

"So, you don't take pills."

"I do now."

"What kind?"

"Vitamins."

"Bullshit."

"Hey," he said, as if wounded by the crude word. "Anyway, it's none of your damn business."

"It is so. You're my brother."

"And you're not my keeper."

She could tell from his body language that she'd hit a mighty big nerve. Steve wasn't like this to her. To anyone, really. It wasn't that he didn't have his secrets, but he was always nice to her about not sharing. Always. "Come on. You're starting to scare me now."

"Don't be scared. There's no reason."

"Then tell me the truth."

He shifted to his left, but she grabbed his arm. He stopped, looked her in the eyes. "Don't."

"I care about you."

"I know."

She didn't let him go. Not with her heart pounding and her senses on high alert. "Will you tell me one thing?"

"It depends."

"Does Lisa know?"

"About me taking vitamins?"

She nodded, knowing they weren't talking about vitamins at all.

"Yeah, she does."

Taylor sighed. She really couldn't press anymore. He was a grown man. An idiot, but fully grown. Something was wrong, and it was a sure bet that it had everything to do with this quickie wedding. Her first instinct was to go to her mother, but she didn't want her to worry. So she'd go to Ben.

Ben would help her. He'd find out what was going on here. And she had to see him anyway.

She let go of her brother, but not before giving him a kiss on the cheek. "Go on. Find your Lisa. Just don't forget you've got a bunch of folks who care about you, okay? And we're all here, whenever you need us."

Steve's posture changed, relaxed a little, but she could see he wasn't thrilled about the conversation. He squeezed her hand. "I remember."

"See you later."

He nodded, then walked away from her. She stared after him until she lost him, then turned back to her own path. She should sleep, just for a bit. Then she'd face Ben and tell him about the pills. She wouldn't tell him about the rest of her morning, though. Not about the way she felt. Not about what she wanted. Because she didn't know.

CHAPTER TWELVE

BEN CLOSED HIS EYES on the way up to the fourteenth floor. The elevator wasn't too crowded, just two teenagers checking themselves out in the mirror, giving him the occasional glance, hence the closed eyes. He didn't want to smile or act nice. He wanted to figure out what the hell was going on with him and Taylor. He wanted to sleep. He didn't know what the hell he wanted.

The doors opened, and he walked out. There, standing in front of the second elevator, was Taylor. She noticed him with a start.

"Hi."

"Hi."

They both just stood there, staring at one another, until both elevators closed and went on their way. They were alone in the carpeted hallway, and he could cut the tension with a knife. This wasn't how he'd pictured seeing her again. Hell, he'd expected to see her next to him in bed. The note had been simple but terse, and his suspicions had been aroused. Then to see her at the pool... The night had been one of the best of his life, and then he'd gone down the rabbit hole into some parallel universe where Taylor was with some strange blond guy and he didn't know what to say.

"I was just, uh…" She nodded in the direction of their rooms.

"Me, too."

"Great." She started walking first, and he followed, slightly behind her. He could see the tension in her posture, the way her bathing suit was still damp so her white cover-up clung enticingly to her behind. Despite his concern over what happened, his libido seemed to be in fine working order. His gaze traveled down to her bare legs, slightly tan, perfectly formed, and he wanted to run his tongue down her thighs to taste the chlorine and what lay beneath. He was so engrossed in his trip down erotic lane, that he almost bumped into her when she stopped at her room.

He did something to her because her towel dropped to the carpet with a clunk. A clunk? Then he saw her laptop peeking from beneath the terry cloth.

He bent to get it, and when he rose again, he noticed the blush on her cheeks. He hadn't said anything about wanting to lick her thighs, had he? No. This was about something else. And he had a damn good idea what.

He held out the computer and towel. And before he could stop himself, he blurted out, "So, who was he?"

Her eyes widened and her mouth opened. The blush deepened and went right down to her neck.

He silently cursed himself. That wasn't the way he'd planned to bring the whole thing up. And now she was on the defensive, which was the exact opposite reaction he'd been going for. Damn, damn, damn.

"Who?"

He blinked. Who? Was she kidding? "The guy at the pool." Hell, he'd gone this far already, no use backtracking now.

"Oh, yeah." She turned to the door, struggled with her key card. "You want to come in?"

"Sure," he said, although the thought of running away held great appeal.

TAYLOR FINALLY GOT THE DOOR OPEN, and led him inside the room. He'd seen her kiss Cade. Oh, God. Of all the things she hadn't prepared for, that was the biggie. Her cheeks were aflame, she didn't know where to look, her hands shook, and all she wanted was to blink like Jeannie and disappear into a bottle. Any bottle. Instead, she dumped her towel and computer on the couch and made the quickest getaway she could. "Let me go change. I'm still wet. I'll be back in a minute." She inched her way to the bedroom. "Get something from the minibar. Or room service. Or whatever. I won't be long. I—" Then she was inside the bedroom and she shut the door.

She leaned against the door, cursing her bad luck,

her stupidity, her lack of magical disappearing skills. He'd seen her!

She had to tell him something. Anything. Heading to the closet, she picked out a summer dress, this one sea-foam green, with wisps of pale blue that she'd gotten on sale at Nordstrom's for a steal. To add to her luck, she'd found perfectly matching sandals at a completely different store, days apart. It seemed obvious she'd reached her luck quota with this dress, so she'd be damned if she didn't wear it until it shredded.

Next, she got a pair of panties from her drawer, blue, to go with the dress. Not that anyone was going to see her color coordination, as Ben would now discover that she was a blatant slut that didn't deserve anything but his pity.

She went into the bathroom and took off her clothes, stepped into the shower to rinse off the chlorine and tried to come up with a lie.

Any lie.

Okay, she could say that Cade was someone she knew from San Francisco. Just a friend. A pal. A buddy. No one important or sexual. And the kiss? Ha, ha. That was just a friendly hi. No big deal. So how about them Yankees?

She scrubbed her skin with the hotel soap, hand-milled and smelling like lemons. So if not a buddy, then what? An ex-boyfriend? So why would she kiss an old boyfriend? Because he was dying, that's why.

Yeah, Cade looked like a guy on his last legs. *Come on, girl. You can do better than this.*

He couldn't be a dying ex. But the friend thing wasn't too bad. Lots of friends kiss. They don't usually use tongue, but how close would Ben have had to be to see Cade's tongue in her mouth.

The friend thing would work. It would. As long as she told him in a completely casual fashion. No drama. No blushing! Of course, she was well known for her terrible lying skills. Her boss had caught on quite early, and made sure she was never in any kind of position where she had to so much as fib.

Besides, lying to Ben felt like hell. Worse. He didn't deserve it. All he'd been was wonderful and truthful. And last night was one of the most glorious nights of her life. How did she repay him? By kissing a stranger at the pool the next morning.

Maybe slut was too kind. What was worse than a slut? She didn't want to know, although she was sure that's what she was.

God, Ben. Wonderful Ben, who had the audacity to turn her little fantasy into a world of confusion.

She rinsed off, stepped out and got dry in a flash. Her hair, which she should have washed, she simply left in the ponytail. So what if it was wet. As for makeup? Forget it. He deserved to see her for who she truly was. She wasn't good enough for mascara.

On with her panties, then the dress. Damn, but it was a great dress. Perfect lines, silky material, and it really made her look tan. Which wasn't the point. The point was Ben. Waiting. Deserving so much more than her.

She slipped on her shoes, straightened her back and headed out for the lie-fest in the living room.

BEN CLOSED THE MINIBAR DOOR. Opened it again. Nothing new tempted him. He slammed it shut, making the whole shelf tremble. Cute trick of hers to disappear like that. She had plenty of time to work out a believable alibi, and here he was wandering around like a schmuck, waiting. He should go.

He walked to the door. Opened it. Shut it. This was Taylor, for God's sake. She wouldn't lie to him. Why would she need to? They'd made love. So what? So it was the best he'd ever experienced in his life, but hadn't that been the deal? A week of hoppin' and boppin' and adios, amigo. So what if she had a little tongue action out at the pool. This was Las Vegas! Sin City! He could be getting a lap dance right this second, if he wanted one.

But that was just it. He didn't want one. He didn't have the slightest desire to kiss another woman. He wanted Taylor. More of her. Lots more. And right this second, he was terribly afraid the fun was over.

What had he done wrong? Everything had seemed so right. Almost too right. Like that made sense.

The bedroom door opened, and he froze, as if she'd caught him going through her purse or something. He struggled for a smile, but the struggle was short-lived as he watched her walk into the sitting room.

She was a vision in a pale green dress. Fresh-faced, her hair back in a simple ponytail, completely un-adorned, and looking so beautiful it made him want to drop to his knees and beg for forgiveness. He didn't give a damn that he had no idea what he should be forgiven for. He just wanted her.

His gaze moved down over the curves of her breast to the incline of her waist. Then the flair of her hips did something to his groin that wasn't exactly on the agenda.

"Sorry," she said. "I just hate that feeling of chlorine after swimming."

He nodded, although he couldn't remember the last time he'd been in a public pool. He liked water, but not that much of it. "You're probably tired," he said. "I should get going. Maybe grab some lunch or something."

"No, it's okay. I, uh, you asked about…"

He shook his head as he walked toward her. "Forget it. It's none of my business. Man, you look so beautiful in that. It's a knockout."

She smiled, the first genuine expression except for fear and guilt he'd seen today. "Thank you."

He looked down at his jeans and his vintage Island shirt. It was covered with pineapples and old Chevys for some unknown reason, but he loved the damn thing. Didn't get a chance to wear it often. Next to Taylor, he felt like a little match boy.

He stepped closer to her, wanting to touch her, maybe her arm, her shoulder, before he left. Maybe get a hint of her scent to carry with him.

She touched his arm instead. "Ben, listen."

He hated sentences that started that way. He put his hand up to stop her, but she didn't even notice.

"That guy at the pool? He wasn't anybody. I mean, he was a really nice guy. Sweet. Cute. And he came over to, I don't know, try to pick me up or something."

"You don't have to tell me this."

"Believe me," she said. "I hadn't planned to. Now, I think I have to."

He nodded, not sure he wanted to hear the rest. But if she needed to talk, he'd listen.

"I was really confused about a lot of things. And he was just there. And when he leaned over—"

Ben coughed. That thing about listening if she needed to talk? Bullshit. No way. "Hey, you know what? I really am hungrier than I thought." Walking backward, he prayed he was heading for the door. "I'm gonna go get one of those famous foot-long hot dogs. On the Strip. I saw a whole show about them on the Food Channel. They're supposed to be great."

"Wait."

"Really hungry."

She took a step toward him. "It's about Steve."

He stopped. This he could hear. "What about him?"

"I saw him down in the casino. And he took some pills."

"Pills? Steve?"

She nodded, concern all over her gorgeous face.

"That's weird. What were they?"

"He wouldn't tell me. Actually he said they were vitamins."

"That's a load of crap."

"Which is what I told him."

"And?"

She turned toward the window, to the brilliant sunshine just outside. The searing heat that was just a mirage inside the cool hotel room. "He wouldn't give it up. Although I asked him if Lisa knew he was taking vitamins, and he said yes."

"Vitamins."

"I think it has something to do with all this."

"Knowing his pill-phobia, I have to concur. It doesn't look good."

"I don't want to say anything to Mom. She'd just get worried, and I'm doing that for both of us."

He walked over to her side, put a hand around her shoulder. It was easier now, because he was talking to Steve's baby sister. Who needed his help. "I'll find out what's going on."

"He's not going to be thrilled I told you."

"I'd be shocked if he didn't expect it. For God's sake, we're his family."

"I know. I said that to him. But you know how stubborn he can be."

"Yeah, ask him who got to sleep in the big tent four summers in a row."

"Huh?"

"Never mind. Just know, I'll get to him. Before the wedding."

She faced him now, just Taylor. No swimming-pool men, no embarrassed blushes. His Taylor. "Thank you."

He kissed her then. Those sweet peach lips. The soft honey of her breath. Her scent, unique in all the world. He kissed her and wanted nothing more than to be around her. To feel her skin from time to time. To hear her voice.

"I gotta go," he said, not wanting the moment to be spoiled. "But I'll call you later, okay? See what you're up to?"

"I'd like that a lot," she said.

He believed her. It was enough.

"But I want to—"

He put his lips back on hers, then inched away to whisper, "Shh. Later."

And because he'd been very, very good, she kissed him back. Kissed him like she was his and his alone.

BEN WALKED PAST CAESAR'S PALACE, marveling at the statues and the huge sign for the Celine Dion show. She must be raking it in. He heard it was one of the better shows on the Strip. He'd wanted to see O, too. But he didn't think he'd have time. Maybe he could catch something, a comedian or a magic show. He'd like to take Taylor to see Lance Burton. That was one he'd seen before, and it was a trip.

But he didn't see the sign for the giant hot dogs, and besides, he wasn't really that hungry. He was definitely hot, though.

He stepped inside a small casino, one he didn't recognize. It was cooler by a whole hell of a lot, and for that he was grateful. But it was loud. Really loud.

In some of the bigger hotels, they made sure the slot machines were demure, hushed. In here, it was every bell and whistle they could find to drum up business.

He wandered, his gaze moving from one gambler to the next, their faces blurring into one another. He walked all the way toward the reception desk area where the noise abated to a manageable level.

There, a big red couch sat unencumbered and inviting, so he sat down, sinking into the leather cushion. He took his time looking about. The two people behind the desk, a man and a woman both wearing red blazers with nametags, seemed older than the folks employed at the bigger hotels. He was glad they had work. And that they were laughing.

Across the way was one of those old-fashioned shoeshine stands, but there was no attendant. And besides, he was wearing tennis shoes. A bellman studied his manicure, leaning against his podium. That was the total action, and Ben was most grateful.

He reached down to his belt and lifted his cell phone from the holster, flipped it open and used speed dial. He wasn't sure why he was calling Alyson, but he didn't hang up. She answered after four rings.

"Hey, it's me."

"Hi," she said. "I thought you were on vacation."

"I am. I'm in Vegas, ostensibly looking for a giant hot dog and a cheap beer."

"You must be thrilled."

"Actually, I'm having a pretty good time. Except I'm not sure Steve should be getting married."

"You don't think anyone should get married."

He sighed. "Why did we?"

She didn't say anything for a while. "Are you sure you didn't already locate that cheap beer?"

"No, Alyson, I'm sober as a judge. And I need your help. Why is it we got married?"

"Because we loved each other."

"We did, didn't we?"

"Yes. And in a lot of ways, I think we still do."

"Just not that way."

She chuckled. "No. But you're still one of my best friends."

"Yeah. I know."

"So why are you asking me this? Existential angst? The nearness of someone in love?"

"Both. Neither. I'm here with Taylor. Steve's sister."

"Right, you've mentioned her."

"She used to have a really big crush on me."

"And?"

"I think it might still be there."

"Oh."

"And I think I might have one on her."

"Oh!"

"Yeah. But I'm not sure. About anything."

"Tell you what, Benny. Do me a favor. Give it a minute. Stick with the confusion. I know you hate it, but before there can be any good decisions, confusion has to be dealt with. So don't run."

"I can't run. I'm the best man."

"Good. And here's something else. Do not, let me repeat, do not, let my sexual orientation be your excuse. I'll hate you if you do that."

"I won't."

"Promise?"

"Yeah."

After another long silence where he thought he'd lost her, he heard a gentle sigh. "You're one of the good guys, Ben. As scared as you are of all this love business, I can't think of anyone on earth who deserves it more than you. You're good in love, sweetie.

If it hadn't been for, you know, I wouldn't have let you go for all the tea in China. So hang in there."

He smiled, appreciating the white lie. "You sure this whole lesbian thing isn't just a phase?"

She laughed. "I gotta go. Be good. I love you."

"You, too. And, thanks."

He clicked off the connection and settled back into the soft sofa. Love? It wasn't that serious. God, no. Like? Sure. Lust? Oh, yeah. But not love. He wasn't about to go there with Taylor or anyone.

He simply hadn't realized a person in lust could get so jealous.

CHAPTER THIRTEEN

TAYLOR WOKE UP DISORIENTED, unsure whether it was day or night or where she was. Unfortunately, that lasted only a second or two, then she realized she was in the hotel and that Ben had been utterly present in her fitful dreams.

It had been a long time since her emotions had been this rattled. Years. Not that she didn't have the most normal of lives, with work problems and victories, friends who were all too human, men issues. But it occurred to her that she'd actually designed her life to have very few real problems.

She sat up, pushing the big pillows against the headboard. She didn't turn on the light. The dark was better suited to this line of thought.

Staring into the dim room, she focused instead on the patterns of her adult life, and what she saw was as startling as Ben's cheekbones. She really had built herself a nice little safe nest.

Her job challenged her, but in the end, she wasn't responsible for the individual cases. Someone else, the attorneys she worked for, had their heads on the chopping block. She did research mostly, typed up legal briefs, ran errands. She lived within her means, not getting herself into trouble there, but also not risking anything to get ahead.

Her friends, and she had a comfortable group, weren't the kind she'd had in high school. Back then, it was all about heart-to-heart talks, intimate confessions, deep discoveries. She played poker with these guys, went to movies and plays. Talked about sex.

The closest thing she had to real intimacy was in her Eve's Apple online group, people she'd never seen in the flesh. And all she had to do to bow out of that gang was stop answering.

Sobered and unsettled, she clicked on the bedside lamp. The light made her wince, but it wasn't half as jarring as the glaring illumination on her life.

Come to think of it, Cade had been a perfect example of who she'd become. Nice guy, good-looking, not threatening in the least, but she hadn't been interested at all. If Ben hadn't been in the picture, she might have gone for drinks with him, had a few laughs. Who knows, she might have had vacation sex. But she would have done all that because he didn't live in her neck of the woods. Because he was a vacation guy. Because it meant she didn't have to get involved.

A chill passed through her and she brought the covers up to her chin. Oh, God. What if she had this whole thing with Ben all wrong? What if she'd used him, all these years, as an excuse? Sure, the sex had been great, but was that really it? Or was he just convenient? So she didn't have to think, or risk, or try. Not once, in all those years had she put herself on the line. She'd never loved anyone. She'd never even let herself get close.

And now that Ben was back, were her feelings for him real? Did she even know him? More importantly, did she know herself? What did she really want from him? Ten more years of excuses? Or were her feelings for him genuine, and he hadn't been an excuse at all, but a reason.

She glanced at the clock on the nightstand. In two hours she had to be down in the lobby to meet the wedding party for the fancy dinner Lisa's mother was throwing. Picasso's. Elegant and expensive as hell, she had to look great.

Throwing back the covers, she padded to the bathroom. She'd brought some wonderful lavender bath beads with her, and a mud mask for her face. At the same time, she would do a deep conditioning treatment on her hair, and she might even have time to change her nail polish.

But just after she turned on the water in the big bathtub, she went into the living room and got the small radio from the shelf. Taking it into the bath, she put it on the sink and found a radio station that played the oldies. She didn't want to think.

"HEY, STEVE. CALL ME. We've got some time to kill before dinner, so let's kill it with a vengeance, what do you say? I'm on my cell."

Ben hung up, wondering if Steve really was busy or if he was avoiding him. He'd undoubtedly assumed Taylor had shared about the pill incident. Steve taking pills. The only thing that would sort of make sense was if the pills were Viagra, but that didn't seem likely. To the best of his knowledge Steve had never had problems in that area, but what the hell did Ben know?

He didn't know squat. About himself, about his life, about Taylor. He was a man who was all about digging into other people's lives and avoiding his own.

It was time to leave the soft comfort of the red couch. Hours had passed as he'd observed the comings and goings of the people at this little hotel/ casino. Older folks, mainly, but mixed in with kids he would have carded in a heartbeat. He'd made up lives for many of them, certain that he was miles off the mark, but he didn't care. It was a way to pass the time. A way to stop thinking.

But always, he'd come back to Taylor, and he couldn't make up a life for her, even though he desperately wanted to force her into a safe, comfortable cubbyhole, easily dismissed when he went back to the real world.

Something had happened to him last night. Something he couldn't explain. When he'd been inside her, he'd felt…different.

Damn, he wasn't good at soul searching. Mostly, he was good at bullshit, but what she'd done to him wasn't that. Not even close. She'd made him feel things he hadn't felt before. New territory. He hated new territory.

What it meant, he had no idea. That he cared for her? Yeah, that much was true. He did care. But what the hell did that mean?

He liked how he was with her. The whole time sitting here, some part of him had wished she'd been next to him. He wanted to talk about all the people he saw, share his observations, and more perplexing, hear hers.

Him. The loner. Who preferred dinner solo, who liked the quiet of his apartment, with his fish his only obligation.

Even when he'd been with Alyson, he'd never had this strong a desire for her company. In fact, what made them work as long as they had was their separate lives. They got together, sure, but mostly for the odd dinner, and of course, the bedroom. The demands there had been minimal, and only lately had he admitted that it hadn't bothered him near enough.

Alyson had been more of a buddy than a wife, and when she'd left, he'd been upset, sure, but also relieved. That was the real truth, wasn't it? He'd been glad to have a place to himself. Accountable to no one.

Maybe that's what had attracted him to her in the first place. He could have the comfort of a steady woman, without any of the real work a relationship required.

What did that say about him? That he was a selfish son of a bitch? Well, yeah, that was a given. But there was more. He felt it, he just couldn't pin it down.

And why was he worrying about it now? What was it about being with Taylor that had him questioning his motives, his lifestyle?

He walked into the casino and headed right for a video poker machine. Fishing out a twenty, he played for a while, hitting a pretty good jackpot, four fours with a kicker, early on, so he didn't have to think about much. He just stared at the cards as they came up. He made it a game to see how fast he could hit the buttons without screwing up. The machine took him away, and that's just where he wanted to be. Away.

But not forever. Because between the aces and the kings, there was Taylor. Beckoning. The scent of her hair, the look in those astonishing blue eyes. She pulled at him, tugged at his heart with her gentle laughter.

By the time he was back down to his original twenty, it was late. He only had forty minutes to get back to the hotel, get dressed and meet everyone for dinner.

Whatever else was going to happen, tonight would be interesting. He had no idea what he was going to say to Taylor. Only that he wanted to see her. And he needed to get Steve alone, too.

He cashed out, letting the quarters drop into the white plastic bucket. He'd catch a cab to the hotel. They had to get dressed up tonight. Crap.

THE ROOM REEKED OF CLASS AND MONEY. And gorgeous art. Picassos dotted the walls, real ones. Of course, the restaurant was Picasso's at Bellagio, one of the most elegant venues in all of Las Vegas. Taylor could see it was going to be an experience to remember.

She tore her gaze away from Ben to check out the details of the place, but it wasn't easy. He'd worn this gorgeous dark suit, slim slacks and perfect one-button jacket. Underneath was a slate-gray, distressed silk shirt with a matching matte silk tie. The man was to die for, and every woman they'd passed had proved it.

But, she really did want to look around. The room was huge, although somehow it also managed to feel intimate. The floor-to-ceiling windows with incredible gossamer drapes framed the water show in front of the Bellagio. The dancing fountains were amazing, and she'd made it a point to walk by at least once every visit. Tonight, no matter where they sat, they'd get an unbelievable view. Inside was just as spectacular. On the muted walls were displayed a collection of Picasso's original artwork. She'd seen prints of some of his etchings and paintings but they paled before the spectacular power of the originals.

They were taken to their large table in the back by a smartly attired maitre'd, who wasn't, thank goodness, in the least condescending or snooty. In fact, he looked like someone she'd like to play cards with.

Ben pulled her seat out for her, and when she got in position, he discretely sniffed her neck. Oddly, it was an incredibly erotic moment, and she got a little swept away, but Lisa's mother brought her back into the room, pronto.

"We thought it would be nice to go for the prix fixe menu, although if you want you can get the degustation menu, which is, of course, more of a tasting thing, but I hear it's wonderful. And if no one minds, I'd like the sommelier to help with the wines. Go ahead and order cocktails, though. It's going to be a long evening, so we might as well live it up. Daddy's paying for all this, so the sky's the limit, isn't that right, sweetheart?"

Lisa, who looked beautiful in a classy black dress that showed off her figure and also showed off the exquisite gold necklace around her neck, laughed along with her mom.

Poor dad. She already knew the meal was going to be way up in the hundreds. Oh, well. Steve seemed happy. Kind of.

He kept losing his smile. One second he'd seem joyful and thrilled to be right where he was, and the next second the happiness would simply melt away and he'd be blank. Not morose, not angry. Just nothing.

But that never lasted. Whenever Lisa spoke to him or glanced his way, the smile came right back.

Pauline, seated between her and Steve, seemed slightly bemused by the whole evening. Not that she hadn't been to fancy restaurants in her time. Her mother traveled, especially when she'd been younger. Taylor suspected her distraction was due to her concern about Steve.

Ben had been the picture of attention since they'd met at the Hard Rock lobby. It was as if this afternoon had never happened. He greeted her with a sizzling, if short, kiss, and had been wonderfully attentive and complimentary. He really did seem to like her dress. It was another Michael Kors, which she never could have afforded if it hadn't been at a resale shop. The python print felt daring, and the fact that it was basically a tube dress that hit her about midthigh, helped, too. She'd gone with leather pumps in dark gray to match the dress, five inch heels, no less. Being so tall, she'd worn her hair unadorned so it fell straight down her back. And she'd brought her little purse, the one that wasn't so much a purse as a leather baggie.

The waiter came by with menus, and it took them all a moment to ohh and ahh, but finally, they decided to go with the prix fixe. Which meant they had choices. Taylor started with the warm quail salad with sautéed artichokes and pine nuts. Ben had the poached oysters.

And then it was cocktail time, and she went for a

straightforward martini. So did Ben. She smiled as he finished his request, and when he turned to her, his gaze locked on hers. Her entire body responded. Not just her breath catching, which it did, but her head felt lighter, her eyes as if the rest of the room had dimmed. Her breasts tightened, her tummy did, too. As for what was happening below the waist, she didn't dare dwell on that. She had a whole, long dinner to get through.

"You are the most beautiful woman I've ever seen," Ben said, his voice just above a whisper and completely private. "I can't believe I get to sit with you, talk with you."

She blushed, even while she acknowledged how over the top the words were. She felt the same way. That she was privileged to be with him, that the way he looked at her was a gift.

She leaned closer to him, so her lips were near his ear. "I just want to get something cleared up before we're busy with dinner and wedding plans."

He smiled.

"I'd like to do that thing again tonight."

"That thing?"

She nodded. "You know. That thing we did last night?"

"Oh," he said. "*That* thing."

"Yeah."

He turned so their lips almost met, but didn't. "I'm pretty sure that could be arranged."

"Good."

"Not yet. But it will be."

She placed her hand gently on his thigh. The muscle twitched beneath her palm. "You do know you're driving me crazy, right?"

"Ditto."

"Excellent. I didn't want to be the only one."

"Hey," Steve said, butting right in. "You guys do that hanky-panky junk later. Tonight's for my girl. She's our star, right?"

Lisa lit up. Her sparkling white teeth practically glowed in the candlelight. She kissed Steve on the cheek. "You're such a mensch."

Taylor and Ben burst out laughing. The word, coming from Lisa, was so unexpected and, well, crazy. It actually took them a while to calm down. But she took it like a champ.

"I'm not from another century," she said. "Just another state."

"Sorry," Ben said. He held up his martini, which had been delivered so smoothly, Taylor hadn't even noticed. "To Lisa and Steve. May she continue to surprise you. May he continue to be the same guy we all know and love."

Steve looked at Ben sharply, then toasted along with everyone else. Lisa just looked happy. Her mother had some large mixed cocktail, something red, which she drank pretty quickly while the rest of the party sipped.

"Hey, Steve," Ben said.

The bread course had come to the table and Taylor couldn't wait to try it. It smelled like heaven, and she made no pretense about the fact that she was starving.

"Remember that time that guy from Texas hooked the scuba diver?"

Steve cracked up, and there was something a little different about this laughter. It was the real Steve now, the guy she'd grown up with.

"Oh, man, was he pissed, or what? That Texas dude played him for what, half an hour?"

"Yeah, screaming the whole time, 'It's a whale! It's a whale!'"

Taylor laughed although she'd heard the story a dozen times before. But what she really liked was the idea of reminding Steve about his love for what he did, and what he'd be giving up if he moved to Kansas. "Remember that pregnant woman who caught that huge yellowtail, and she went into labor?"

Steve moaned, leaned back in his chair. "She wouldn't stop. She was screaming, and bending over double. Man, she was huge. But she wouldn't let go of that damn rod. She kept it up for like forty minutes, I swear. Caught the damn fish, and almost had the baby on the deck."

"She had it in the ambulance, didn't she?"

Steve, laughing, nodded. "Damndest thing I ever

saw. And her husband sent me a picture, after? Of the fish!"

They went on like that, Steve and Ben swapping tales, funny, silly, outrageous, and Taylor just leaned back and enjoyed the ride. A glance from her mother told her that she approved of the conversation, too, but not so with Lisa. At first, she laughed, smiled, went along with it all, but after the first course arrived and the boys went on and on, Taylor could see she was getting prickly.

It wasn't fair, but this was serious stuff. Steve without his boats was like a race car driver without a license. He wouldn't be Steve.

She probably should have stopped it, but she didn't. Instead, she ate the most delectable food in the universe. Tiny portions, but oh, God, the most succulent, fantastic flavors. The bread was crispy on the outside and soft and perfect inside. Ben swooned over his oysters, which started another whole round of fishing tales. It wasn't until they'd been served the second course that Lisa had had enough. She stood up, gave Ben a truly hateful look and excused herself.

Taylor felt like the heel she was. She followed Lisa to the bathroom, but when she went over to talk to her, all she got was chipper chitchat. Nothing real. But the evening would have to take another turn, or things would get ugly.

Maybe Ben could catch Steve alone tomorrow. Talk to him. Find out about the pills. About everything. In the meantime, she intended to enjoy the hell out of the rest of her meal, including the sumptuous wine and heavenly sounding desserts. Then she was going to take Ben to her room, and ravish him until he couldn't walk.

No more thinking. No more worrying. Back to the basic plan. Fun. Wildness. Sex and sex and sex. Eventually, she'd figure it out. But she wasn't about to waste what could very well be the last truly incredible fling of her life.

CHAPTER FOURTEEN

THE WHOLE WAY IN THE TAXI back to the Hard Rock, Taylor and Ben had only touched hands. That's all. But what touching it was.

All of Taylor's erogenous zones were on maximum alert, and she felt even the slightest brush of his finger everywhere at once. Mostly in her chest, which had forgotten how to breathe properly, and in her sex, where she finally understood the concept of being in heat. Big time.

She could hardly look at him. Not that he wasn't amazing to look at, but when she did, sitting in that gorgeous suit, his hair mussed and touchable, his eyes smoky and filled with wicked promises, she wanted to yank down her tube dress right there in the back of the Yellow Cab and attack him.

It was only a few blocks to the hotel, she could wait. Or at least she hoped she could.

His thumb rubbed against her wrist, the thin skin feeling nearly as sensitive as her clitoris. At that thought, she had to shift in the seat, cross her legs and squeeze them together.

His legs were crossed, too, with his thigh covering

his fly. She guessed he was having a difficult time of it, given that the two of them sounded like they were in the middle of a ten-mile hike up a steep mountain.

The taxi pulled into the parking lot of the hotel, and it took a frustrating five minutes to get to the front door. Ben had the fare and tip ready, and then the doorman helped her out of her side. Ben met her at the curb, put his arm around her shoulder and hustled her inside. When they got into the casino, he sneaked a glance her way, and they went even faster.

She couldn't help herself, she started giggling in the elevator. There were three other people on board, and one young couple kept their hands on each other's fannies. The single man kept looking at Taylor's chest. She found it unbearably funny, and trying to stifle the laughter made things worse.

Ben turned completely around, but she saw his shoulders shake. Too much juice running through them, she knew, but it didn't help. Something had to give.

Once they were on fourteen, they practically ran down the hall. She got the door open in one swipe, and then they were kissing, and his hands were all over her, and she was peeling back his jacket so she could get him naked, and everything was hot and moist and desperate.

His tongue explored her, plunged into her, dueled with hers. His teeth nipped sharply, and then she sucked deeply, getting him right where she wanted him. The devil pulled back, panting. "Wait," he said.

"Why?"

He smiled. "Get into your bikini. I'll be back in two minutes."

Before she could get the first word of her protest out, he was gone, and she was left breathless by the door, her purse somewhere on the floor, her body shaking with a desire only he could inspire.

Swimming? Now? She wished he would have stopped and told her what he had in mind. She didn't need to get wet. She already was.

But because she was the horniest woman in Nevada, she went to her bedroom and changed in record time. The bikini was the new one she'd bought shopping with Lisa—black and tiny, although it wasn't a thong. She wouldn't wear one of those in public, not for anything. Although when she looked in the mirror, she wasn't going to win any modesty awards. Her boobs looked much bigger than they actually were, her hips seemed curvier and even after the divine meal, her tummy didn't look half-bad. It was the tan, of course. She'd snuck some time in the booth back home before coming out here, just to lay a base. Yeah, she knew it was bad for her, but oh, man, it made everything look so much better.

Which wasn't the issue at the moment. She grabbed her cover-up and slipped on her flip-flops, and she was ready to go. Except for her purse. But she didn't really need one, if Ben would carry her key.

She found the little dinner bag and took out what she needed, then stood by the door. Not for long. He rapped twice and she let him in.

He wore black and dark green trunks, a funky Hawaiian shirt, and dark sandals. He'd pushed his hair back with his fingers, and he looked so good she could eat him with a spoon.

"Come on," he said, holding out his hand.

"Why are we doing this?"

"Because I need to expend a little energy."

"I have a really good way for you to do that," she said. "Right here."

"And I will, I promise. But later. This first."

She took his hand and let him lead her down the hall. "Hold this for me?"

He took her key and put it in his shirt pocket. Then he kissed the back of her hand.

"Are you sure?"

He nodded. "Yeah. I want to take things down a notch before we start up again. And, I want to play with you in the pool."

"Marco Polo?"

"Find the salami."

She laughed out loud just as the elevator door opened. They got in, and they were alone. Ben maneuvered her back against the wall, and he pushed up flat against her. "You look hot in that."

"It's just a cover-up."

"You look hot in everything."

"Ha. You should see me in my old chenille bathrobe at home. I look like someone's grandma."

"Kiss me, Granny," he said, but he didn't give her much of a vote. His lips came down on hers and once again, she lit up like a lightbulb.

Her hands moved down the smooth material of his shirt. He toyed with the hem of her wrap, and then she felt his fingers at the waistband of her bikini.

"What are you doing?" she whispered.

"Exploring." His fingers moved underneath the material until she felt him in her curls.

"Stop. They have cameras in here. I saw it on TV."

"They can't see anything," he said. "I'm blocking you."

"But they'll know."

"Then they'll be jealous," he said. "Let 'em. You're mine tonight. All mine."

Her head went back with a mixture of a giggle and a gasp as his finger slipped inside her.

"What's this?" he asked. "We're not even at the pool, and you're all wet?"

She pushed against his groin. "And what's this swelling? Allergic to something, are we?"

"I do believe the opposite is true. I thrive inside you, Taylor. I come alive."

"Oh, my," she said, just before they hit the casino level.

He pulled away in the nick of time, but she knew she was blushing like a fool. His cheeks were pretty damn pink, too. He grabbed her and led her to the nearest pool exit.

Once they were outside, they laughed again, and Ben loved the sound of it. She was like a kid. In fact, like the kid he remembered her to be. She'd been such a little pest back then, but he'd gotten a real kick out of her stubbornness.

Oh, who was he kidding. She'd worshipped him since the time they'd met, and that hero worship had turned into a major crush, and that hadn't all gone in one direction. Taylor had been an important part of his growing-up years. Easy to talk to, when she hadn't been bratty, and interesting in her own right. He remembered seeing her in a dumb school play. It hadn't been a big part, but she'd knocked the hell out of it, and gotten the biggest ovation of the night. She'd glowed. Loved the attention.

And then there was the night she'd asked him to teach her to slow dance. She was going to the junior prom, and she didn't know how to do the slow kind. Her dad wasn't around, and Steve was pretty much a goofus, so he'd stepped up to bat. Not that he was any Fred Astaire, but it had been nice. Sweet. That night he'd realized she had a crush on him. He'd been flattered. And when, two years later, she'd invited herself into his bed, there was no chance in hell he'd say no.

Which didn't mean he wasn't still confused as hell. That kiss this morning, her odd half explanation, his reaction. Way more than he wanted to think about, especially tonight. Tonight, they were going back a step. To what they did extraordinarily well together.

But first, he wanted to feel that body rub up against him in the pool. He wanted to see her shimmer under the water. He wanted to strip her naked and make love to her, but he figured he could contain himself until they went back up to the room. Then they'd have the pleasure of a hot shower, drying each other off. Then howling at the moon as they turned each other inside out.

Chris Isaac was singing about a bad bad thing, making Ben like the hotel more and more. The fact that the pool wasn't all that crowded helped, too. Just a couple of late swimmers, the usual crowd around the swim-up bar, and the cabanas. That's where he led Taylor.

The first three were full, but the fourth had a lone guy, looking a little down in the mouth. "You here by yourself?" Ben asked.

"Evidently."

"Bummer."

The guy sighed. Ben recognized the sound of a man who'd been stood up.

"There's a whole gaggle of gorgeous babes by the bar."

"Yeah, but not the one I wanted."

Ben placed Taylor just outside the cabana wall. "Hold on." Then he went in and sat next to Mr. Lonely. "Listen, I'm sorry your thing didn't work out. And it's rotten of me to even ask, but I'd surely love to bring my lady back up here after a swim." He reached into his pocket, behind the two room keys, where he'd stashed a couple of hundred dollars. He took one bill out and slid it across the table. "Why don't you get a drink, and when we get back, you could go in and try your luck again."

The guy stared at the bill for a long time, then raised his gaze to Ben's. "Yeah, sure. Why the hell not?" He took the money in his fist. "Maybe I'll win something huge and she'd find me a little more interesting."

"You never know, brother. You never know."

"You want me to order something for the two of you?"

Ben grinned. "You're all right. Sure. A piña colada for her, a scotch on the rocks for me."

The stranger gave him a lopsided grin. "Go on. Get out of here before I change my mind."

Ben stood, clapped the guy on the shoulder. "Excellent karma points, my friend." Then he took Taylor's towel from her hand, waited until she'd given him her cover-up, gulped as he got a load of her in her black bikini, and stripped down to his own trunks. He left their stuff on an empty chair, gave a thumbs-up to his new best friend and followed Taylor to the edge of the pool.

She dove in first, and he followed a few seconds later. He found her leg, her calf to be precise, and hung on until they both came up, sputtering. She dipped her head back, letting her hair smooth from her face, and he did the same. They were at the deep end, so they had to tread water to keep their heads up. He got close enough to touch her everywhere he could.

"It's so beautiful here at night," she said, her gaze moving from the lighted palm trees to the colored lights placed directly in the water. "Like paradise."

"Have you ever been to Hawaii?"

She nodded. "I love it there."

"Me, too. I know a little private beach. We could make love in the sand."

"Ouch."

"True. But there are ways."

"I'll bet," she said, and then she kissed him. Her lips were moist and cool, but inside was the same wet heat he'd already memorized. He loved the feel of her smooth teeth, the way she tasted. He could dine on her forever.

The kiss deepened and then they were both coughing. Making out while treading water wasn't cutting it, so they swam far enough for their feet to touch. Another couple, not too far away, had the same idea, and they were at it hot and heavy. Ben couldn't have cared less. All he could see was Taylor, and the way she glistened in the moonlight.

She ran her hands over his chest until she found his nipple. He jerked when she squeezed him there, but came back for more. His hands were on her back, moving slowly down the length of her. When he hit her bikini bottom, he kept on going until he held the firm globes of her buttocks in each hand.

"Didn't you used to hate swimming?" she asked him.

"Me?"

"Yeah. Steve told me something about that a long time ago. That you could have been a really hot jock on the swim team, but you said you didn't like the water."

"I don't know how hot a jock I could have been, but it's not the water I dislike. It's the whole team thing."

"Then what the heck are we doing here, when we could be in private?"

"I said I don't like team sports. There's no one here but you and me, as far as I'm concerned, and honey, you in the water isn't something I was willing to miss."

She swung around, turning them both as she wrapped her legs around his waist. "What are you talking about?"

"I got this image in my head. This morning, to tell

you the truth. And I couldn't shake it. So I took you down here."

Her whole body kind of deflated.

"Hey, don't go there. I told you. I don't care what happened."

"But I do."

"Why?"

She had her arms around his neck, and he balanced her easily in his hands. She fit like she was made for him. Her head went back for a minute and he simply stared at her neck. So beautiful. He wanted to spend a week licking and nibbling that long column.

Her head came down and she looked him in the eyes. "I'm going to tell you something, and you have to shut up and listen."

"Okay."

"I had an entire plan worked out for this week," she said. "Aside from the wedding."

He grinned. "I figured it out."

"No, you didn't. I mean, you figured out what I was after, but not why."

He wasn't real sure he wanted to hear this.

"You do remember our weekend together?"

He laughed out loud. "You could say that, yes."

"Well, I do, too. I remember it too well. And it's kind of…screwed me up."

"What do you mean?"

She put her legs down, unwound her arms. He didn't want to let her go, but he did anyway. She didn't get far. "That was the most amazing weekend I've ever had," she said, her voice much lower, and younger, somehow. As if she'd gone back to that time ten years before. "You were my first, and frankly, my best."

The bang of her words hit him right in the ego and he felt his chest rise with peacock pride. That lasted all of about five seconds. "And that's a problem?"

"Yes, that's a problem. Come on, Ben. It's been ten years. And what we did that weekend has totally blown everything since off the map. How fair is that?"

She sounded affronted. Indignant. He couldn't help his burst of laughter. She responded by hitting him in the arm.

"Hey," he said, rubbing the pain. "That hurt."

"Well, don't laugh at me."

"I'm not laughing. I'm bewildered. Confused. Not laughing."

"What's so hard to understand? You spoiled it for me, Ben Bowman. Every guy I met after you failed the Ben Test. I mean it, there just wasn't…"

"Wasn't?"

"I don't know. The magic. Whatever."

"Whatever," he repeated. "And your plan was?"

She sighed, as if he was particularly slow. "To have a repeat performance, so that I could get rid of all the crazy ideas I had about you. About us. So that I could bring you down to size. Get a real life."

"Oh."

"What are you all disappointed about?"

"I'm supposed to be happy that I'm not your number one stud muffin?"

"What are you talking about? What do you think the whole problem is? Are you dense?"

He held back a grin. Damn, but she was beautiful when she was completely irrational. "Evidently."

She slugged him again, this time on the chest. And this time, her hand stayed right there, her fingers warm against his cool skin. "Damn it, Ben, it failed. The whole plan. Utterly. That's why I kissed Cade."

"Want to run that by me again?"

"I was confused, because of our night. Because it was even better than I remembered. Because, oh God, now I'm really in trouble, and how in hell am I supposed to get on with my life when I know that when I'm with you, it's like…"

"Magic," he whispered.

She nodded, looking like her heart had been broken into tiny pieces. "I kissed him because I should have liked it. He's like this great-looking guy. And nice. Totally buff."

"But?"

"It was nothing. Worse than nothing. A joke."

"Am I supposed to be sorry?"

"I don't know." She walked a few slow steps away. "I don't know much of anything, except I'm completely bewildered by the whole thing. You were supposed to be just a guy. A regular guy."

"And I'm not?"

She turned around. "Not to me."

CHAPTER FIFTEEN

BEN WENT UNDERWATER, and stayed there for a while. The lack of oxygen was an excellent distraction from the thoughts bombarding his brain. She was upset that he was good in bed? That she'd never had anyone better than him? Maybe he hadn't understood properly. Women had always confused him, and this was just another example of how they were from a different planet. Right?

A hand grabbed his hair and pulled him straight up. Right back into Taylor's face.

"Drowning isn't going to get you out of this, mister."

"I don't know. It seemed like a pretty good option."

"Ben, cut it out."

He folded Taylor into his arms. "I'm sorry, hon. I don't mean to be treating this…thing…lightly. I'm just—"

"Confused. Welcome to my world."

They stood for a while, moving gently back and forth in the warm water. He closed his eyes, letting himself enjoy the feeling of her body against his, so much of her naked. Smooth. Slick.

"I shouldn't have said anything," she whispered.

"Yeah, you should have."

"But now both of us don't know what to do."

He pulled back far enough to look at her. "You're wrong. I know just what to do." He kissed her, gently at first. After her lips parted, he entered her, moving slowly and precisely, in no rush at all.

Her body relaxed into his embrace as she shared the kiss. Music, something by Vanessa Williams, wafted through the palm trees and the water, and somewhere out there he heard laughter. But he didn't want to be out there. Not even an inch away from this warm woman, this incredible woman. He had to wonder, albeit briefly, if his overwhelming reaction to her touch had anything to do with what she'd just told him.

Probably not. He'd reacted this way ever since that weekend, long ago. Since she'd first showed up on his parents' doorstep. When he'd made love to her then, it had been the most shattering thing he'd ever experienced. Until this week.

Damn. No wonder he was having so much trouble with all this. He hadn't put it together, that's all. Being with Taylor was completely different from being with anyone else in his life. Everything was completely different, and if his life depended on saying how, he'd be a goner. It just was.

But it was also just sex. Great sex. Incredible sex. Nothing more. So why sweat it? He had her, here, in his arms. They had a cabana. They had a room. It would be moronic not to do what they both wanted.

He pulled back from her lips and moved slowly down to the side of her neck. She moaned, and he figured they better get out soon, because he didn't want to have any spontaneous emissions here in the very public waters of the Hard Rock pool.

"Come on," he said, turning so his arm was around her shoulder and he was leading her to the steps. "There's a drink waiting for you topside."

"Oh, good," she said. "Get me drunk so I don't have to think anymore, okay?"

He laughed. "It's not the end of the world, Taylor."

"Not yours."

"Not yours, either. We'll figure it out."

She didn't say more as they climbed the steps and headed for the cabana. The guy was still there, but the moment he saw them, he picked up his drink, sitting next to theirs, nodded a sad goodbye and went on his way.

Once they were alone, Ben handed Taylor her towel as he dried himself off. It was far more interesting to watch her than to pay attention to damp spots.

God, she was the most beautiful creature on earth. Her skin was as smooth as satin, and her curves were the essence of what was magnificent about women.

Unfortunately, his little—or should he say big—problem wasn't going anywhere, so he found his seat and put the towel over his lap. It was important not to focus on Taylor at the moment. He'd be much better off thinking of say, Joe Panzer, the thug he'd been tracking back in New York.

Only, Joe was far away, and Taylor was bending over really, really close. He could see the curve of her breasts, and he was lost.

He took hold of her shoulders and brought her down on his lap. "I can't get enough of you," he said.

"Yes you can. You have to. We're leaving in two days."

"I don't want to think about that."

"Me, neither. But I can't help it."

He nibbled her earlobe. "Hey, let's just leap off that bridge when we come to it, okay? This is our vacation, and we're the lucky ones. Did you see that guy who just left? He's so jealous of us he could spit."

"I know. And believe me, I'm happy."

"That doesn't look like a happy face."

Instead of the smile he expected, he got an actual frown.

"What?"

She quirked her head slightly to the left. "Tell me about your day."

"Uh, I woke up without you—"

"I don't mean today. I mean your normal, average day."

"Oh." He really didn't want to talk about his life, but he also didn't want Taylor to move. Every time she moved, even a little bit, she rubbed him just enough to make him go a wee bit crazier. "It's not very exciting."

"Tell me."

"And there really isn't an average day."

She yanked on his hair. Not hard, but enough to smart.

"Ow."

She didn't say another word. But then, she didn't have to.

"Fine. I get up. Normally around six-thirty or so. But it depends."

"On?"

"Whatever I'm working on. If I'm tailing someone who's a night owl, then I have to be a night owl, and I sleep during the day. If I'm doing white-collar investigations, I do the nine-to-five thing."

She settled down, doing that wicked thing with her butt. "That's better."

"I'll say," he whispered.

"Hmm?"

"Nothing. Okay. I have coffee. I like coffee. I grind it myself. It has no vanilla or hazelnut or chocolate in it. It's just coffee. Strong."

"Uh-huh."

"And sometimes I have breakfast."

"Not always?"

"Not if it's nine at night."

"But you try to eat healthy?"

He turned his head for a second. "I try."

She grabbed his chin so he was facing her. "How often do you succeed?"

"At least once a week, I eat something green. That isn't mold."

She sighed. "Okay. Continue."

He closed his eyes and pressed his chin against her bare shoulder. "I work out six days a week. There's a gym two blocks from my place. Nothing fancy, just weights. And I run."

"At the gym?"

"Around."

"Tell me about your place. Is it an apartment?"

"A co-op."

"Big?"

"For Manhattan? Huge. For anywhere else? No."

"Do you have a bedroom?"

"And a small office. Really small. But it holds my computer stuff."

"Go on."

"Actually, I like where I live. I've got a great king-size bed that I spent a fortune on. I can't afford to be down with a bad back, or not sleep well."

"A comforter?"

He nodded. "Navy blue."

"Good sheets?"

He shrugged. "Sheets."

"Hmm."

He looked up to meet her troubled gaze. "Sheets are a chick thing."

"Not after you've slept in Egyptian cotton."

"You want the rest?"

She grinned.

"I have a decent TV. I get cable. I like watching the Sci-Fi Channel. And Discovery."

"No Playboy Channel?"

"Sometimes."

"Your living room furniture."

"I've found some decent pieces. I like old wooden furniture. And leather. I have one of the top-ten great couches."

"What about the kitchen?"

"Great coffeemaker. Excellent knives and pots. I don't cook much, but when I do, I don't screw around."

"Last question about the co-op, I swear," she said, crossing her heart. "What about art?"

"Art?" He was a little distracted by where she'd crossed herself. Real close to the edge of her bikini top.

"On the walls?"

"Oh. Yeah. Nothing fancy. Some stuff I've accumulated over the years. Things that I like."

"Anything I'd recognize?"

"Probably not. I tend to go to small art shows, flea

markets, that kind of thing. No posters by Erte or Van Gogh prints."

"I see."

"So, do I pass?"

"Oh, yes."

"Phew."

She laughed. "You couldn't have failed, you goose."

"So is it my turn?"

"Yes, I suppose it is."

"Okay. What do you want?"

She stilled. Completely. Not the reaction he was hoping for, but he supposed she had expected him to ask about her furnishings. He didn't give a damn about those. He wanted to know what all this meant.

"Tell you what," he said. "Why don't you reach over and get our drinks while you're thinking."

"Great idea." She uncurled her arm from around his neck and reached for the drinks, but she could only reach his. She ended up getting off his lap, and he stole the moment to do something he should have done when they entered the cabana. He closed the curtains. Then he sat down again. This time, he didn't use the towel, although if she looked, she'd see that despite the conversation, his hormones were fully engaged.

Handing him his drink, she took a long sip of her piña colada, and then she climbed on top of his lap again. Once they were settled, he drank, then put the glass down on the floor next to him.

He liked the cabana this way. A little on the dark side, but the candles on the table illuminated them both enough to see what was important. She still pondered his question while he went back to studying the rise and fall of her chest.

"One hell of a question there, Ace."

"I know. But I still want an answer."

"So do I."

"What do you mean?"

She sighed, resting her head on his. "I don't know what I want. Except that I want more of this. What I have with you."

"Are you saying you want to continue this after we leave Vegas?"

"Yes. Maybe." She squeezed his shoulder. "I don't know. All I'm sure about is that my plan went to hell in a hand basket. And now…"

"Now you have to face some things that maybe you didn't want to?"

She nodded.

"Like maybe you weren't rejecting those guys because they weren't great in the sack?"

Her head jerked upright, and she looked at him accusingly. "What?"

"I'm just guessing here, but something tells me this whole thing isn't just about sex."

"It is so."

"Oh?"

She stood and walked over to the other chair, all the way across the table from him.

"Look," he said. "I don't mean to upset you. You're the one that decided you liked this truth business."

"I told you the truth. It is about sex."

"Okay. If you say so."

"Dammit, Ben. It can't be about more than sex."

"Why not?"

As she sat, she picked up her towel and covered herself. "'Cause I don't want it to be."

"Ah, good answer."

"Stop it."

He went over to her side, knelt by the chair and took her hand in his. "Listen, Taylor, I think you're an incredible woman. I can't imagine any man in his right mind not thinking you're incredible. The odd thing here is that you haven't found one that you find just as great."

"It's not that easy."

"No. It isn't. And it's a lot harder when you have a built-in defense mechanism at the ready."

"Who died and made you so smart?"

He laughed. "It's a lot easier to see from over here, that's all."

"So what's your story? Why aren't you blissfully happy with a wife and two kids?"

"Tried it."

"And she was gay. Right. So what about after her?"

He shook his head. "Haven't had a lot of interest."

"In women?"

"In a relationship."

She leaned over, resting her chin on his head. "Oh, Ben, don't you dare tell me you think she went gay because of you. That's not possible."

"I don't think that."

"Good."

"But I also know that her being gay wasn't all that was wrong with our marriage."

She sat back. "Oh?"

He stood up. Not so much because he wanted to get away, but because he was getting a cramp. He walked over and got his drink. "We were always more friends than lovers. We had separate lives. Separate interests. It was like having a roommate, not a wife."

"Do you think that's why you married her?"

"More than likely. And to be honest, if she hadn't decided she wanted a real marriage, I wouldn't have complained. I was happy with things the way they were."

"Oh."

He shrugged. Took a drink. Felt the burn all the way down. Thought about telling her the darker truth that came after the marriage ended. About his doubts, his fears. But she didn't need to hear all that garbage. "I'm not a complicated man, Taylor. I like things simple. And I try like hell to be honest with myself.

I'm not the kind for marriage and all that. I'm good at looking at other people's lives. Not my own."

She didn't say anything. For so long, he went back to his chair, sat down. Drank some more. Wondered if he should have kept his big mouth shut.

Then she stood, so abruptly, he almost dropped his glass. "Let's go to my room," she said. "Okay?" She put her drink down, slipped on her cover-up. "Let's just forget all this and do what we do best." She stood over him. "Please, Ben. Let's just go."

He wasn't about to argue.

BEN TOOK THE SOAP from the little dish on the side of the shower and rubbed it between his hands until he'd built up a fistful of suds. Then he smiled as he sidled up real close to her, with the water hitting her back. He began at her neck. His slightly cooler hands, slick with lemon-scented bubbles, rubbed her slowly, tenderly. She let her head fall back, closed her eyes and let him take her to another world.

The combination of the water sluicing down from the crown of her head, his body rubbing against hers, and the divine feel of his soaped hands massaging her flesh was almost too much to take. She had to steady herself with her hand against the shower wall, especially when he moved down to her chest. She'd had massages before, but no one had ever done this. No feeling had ever come close.

His touch was intimate, reverent. Just below the

slippery soap was a hint of coarseness, of masculinity, that was echoed in the sheer size of him. He circled her skin, taking his sweet time, slowing even farther when he got to her breasts.

One hand caressed each globe. Round and round, but not touching her nipples. Her very erect, taut nipples that were aching for equal time.

She almost stepped to the side to force the issue, but she didn't. There was too much pleasure in the tension.

He moaned, and she pushed her chest out, knowing he couldn't wait, either. His palms cupped her, and the touch, light as the bubbles of soap themselves, made the world spin. Nipples were great, wonderful, but no one had told her they could do *this*.

"Oh, God," he whispered.

All she could do was nod. Just the one time, because she was so damned unsteady on her feet.

His hands moved down her body, killing her with disappointment, thrilling her with anticipation.

She was drowning in bliss as he touched her, rubbed her, anointed her with his healing strokes. As his hands shifted below her waist, he stepped closer, rubbing himself against her belly. His fingers trailed down through her curls until he slipped inside her slippery folds.

As he circled her clit with the pad of his finger, he captured her lips in a kiss that made all other kisses fade. His tongue, like quicksilver, darted, thrust, retreated, tasting everything, leaving her breathless. Her hand went from the wall to the back of his neck as she steadied herself and him while she gave as good as she got.

He never let up with his fingers, teasing her mercilessly. Her muscles tensed from her calves to her thighs, all the way to the back of her neck. She was going to come, soon. It wasn't fair. She should have soaped her own hands, returned the magnificent favor he'd given her. She vowed to do that the second she could focus on something besides the orgasm that shut out the rest of the universe.

Her head fell back with her cry, her hands grasped his neck, his shoulder, squeezing as the wave built and climbed and brought her to her toes.

Somewhere out there she heard his low chuckle, but the bastard didn't let up, even though she was so sensitive the pleasure bordered on pain. But then, the hint of discomfort fled with an onslaught of ecstasy that lifted her beyond anything she'd known. She yelled out so loudly, she drowned out the shower, but she didn't care. Nothing mattered but the sensations, the bliss, the man.

He brought her down gently, as if she were a wild creature who needed to be tamed. His hands, still slick, petted her sides, her hips. His body bolstered her, kept her upright. And then he kissed her.

She opened her eyes, finding he'd done the same. Seeing his gaze, she moved back, even though she didn't want to break the kiss. More important though, was to see him. To be amazed at the emotions so clear on his face.

His hand moved to her cheek. "You're crying."

She wiped her eyes, knowing the moisture hadn't been from the water behind her. "I didn't know."

"I'm hoping they're happy tears."

She laughed. "I think that's a pretty good assumption. My God, Ben. That was…"

"I'm glad."

"But you."

"What about me?"

"I just take and take. It's not fair."

He stepped back. Glanced down. It took Taylor a second to realize that he wasn't rock-hard any more. "You?"

He nodded. "It's all your fault. You're so amazing, I couldn't hold back another second."

"Wow."

He grinned. "I'll say."

"I'm going to need a moment or two here, just to catch my breath, but then, Ben Bowman, it's my turn. You are going to get in my bed, and you're not going to move until I say you can."

"Oh, really?"

She grabbed his hands and swung them around his back. Of course he could have broken her hold in a second, but he didn't. "Really."

BEN GRIPPED THE SHEETS and tried to remember how to breathe. In fact, he was stunned the sight in front of him hadn't stopped his heart. Taylor, crouched over his body, slowly lowering herself onto his cock, her head thrown back in a delicious moan, her hands on her breasts, squeezing her nipples as she rode him with slow, torturous intent. Oh, yeah, he knew she was out to drive him crazy, and she was doing a damn fine job of it.

Thank God he'd come in the shower, because just looking at her naked body, her blond hair whipping around her shoulders, the more than obvious pleasure she was feeling, was enough to send him to the moon and back.

He gasped in a lungful of air as she settled fully on him. When she straightened and met his gaze, the fire in her eyes was as exciting as the way she gripped his length.

"I told you you would like me on top."

He nodded.

"So next time, what are you going to say?"

He opened his mouth, but no words came out.

Taylor laughed. Rose up just an inch. "I didn't quite get that."

"Please," he said, his voice sounding more like Darth Vadar than was comfortable. "Anything you want. Anything."

Her grin turned evil, and so did her laugh. But he didn't care because she was on the move again, lifting her body up until she almost lost him, then hesitating an agonizing minute, only to give him back the will to live as she lowered herself once more.

The only problem with this perfect moment was that he couldn't kiss her. But he wasn't complaining. In fact, he was more grateful than he'd ever been in his life.

Her hands went to his chest. He watched, amazed, as her eyes fluttered closed and her rhythm quickened.

"Come for me," he whispered, praying he'd last until she got off. "Come on, baby. Do it."

If she heard him, she gave no sign. But it didn't matter. Because she was speeding toward a climax and there was no turning back. As for him? He just hung on for dear life.

HALF AN HOUR LATER, Taylor tried to catch her breath while she stared at the sprinkler in the ceiling. The sex hadn't been a fluke. He'd…

What had he done to her? It was as if her orgasms had a password that only Ben knew. Frankly, and she'd never admitted this to anyone but her Eve's Apple group, she normally preferred getting off by herself. Her trusty vibrator had been there through thick and thin. It never tried too hard or crapped out before she was done. It never hogged the covers, or smirked when she wanted cold pizza afterwards. She liked the control, and, unlike most women she knew, she preferred going right to sleep after.

And here was Ben making her feel just plain sorry for her pitiful vibrator. The good old boy had done his best, but it was a distant second to making love to the man gasping to her right.

Three times. She'd come three times, and not just little whoopee orgasms, either. Big old honkin' O's that had hit her so hard she'd nearly blacked out. She wasn't exactly sure how he'd pulled off the feat, but my God, she was thrilled he had.

However, and it was a big however, the really impressive thing about the past two hours was that Ben had made her feel utterly, completely safe. She'd never been so unselfconscious with another human. Her sounds, her positions, her face. She'd given him her everything, warts and all. And loved every second of it.

The lovemaking wasn't *it*. The lovemaking was a result of *it*. So?

"Good God, woman, what have you done to me?"

She grinned. He sounded worse than she did. "I was just minding my own business."

"Like hell." He rolled over, attempting to adjust the hopeless covers, then tossing them to the floor. "You're so…"

"No. We're so…"

He nodded then wiped some stray hairs off his forehead. "And I need water. I think I lost five pounds."

"Honey, if it was that easy, I'd never leave the bedroom."

He pulled her close to him, close enough to nip her shoulder. "It's a deal."

She shifted so she could look him in the eyes. "Ben, this is serious."

"What do you mean? The condom didn't break, did it?"

"No."

"So why is it so serious?"

"Because I don't understand it. Us. This."

He stretched, kissed her gently on the lips. "Stop trying. Just let it be."

"I'm trying. I mean— You know what I mean."

"Listen, I have an idea about tomorrow. About Steve and Lisa. Let's focus on them, okay? Give their situation our full attention. I bet while we're doing that, things will straighten out completely for both of us. Deal?"

She smiled. "I think it's brilliant."

"I think you're wonderful."

"Hey, what's with the hand?"

"Nobody said we can't do this while we talk."

She giggled, and tried to listen. She didn't do a very good job.

CHAPTER SIXTEEN

THE RIDE UP THE ELEVATOR had taken them over fifteen minutes. Not because the Stratosphere was a thousand feet in the sky, but because there were so many people trying to get to the top.

Taylor held on to Ben's hand as they were guided to the line for Project XSky, the newest and scariest of the rides atop the downtown hotel. Along with the roller coaster and the Big Drop, Project XSky was crowded as hell, as more people than she'd thought possible wanted to have the stuffing scared out of them.

Steve had always been a huge fan of roller coasters and scary rides, having dragged her to amusement parks from the time they were kids, forcing her, upon the pain of being branded a "girl" to ride with him, despite the terror involved. Once he and Don had hooked up, she'd been left alone to some degree, but still, whenever he had the opportunity, Steve would make her climb into one contraption or another. She'd never admit to him that she rather enjoyed the thrill. He got too big a kick out of her whining.

Today, though, Steve was just plain excited. Lisa

was far less so. She'd been dubious when Ben had roused them early this morning. Of course, their destination had been a secret at that point.

When the cab took them to the Stratosphere, she'd put up a bit of a fight, but Steve had promised her she didn't have to actually go on any rides if she didn't want to. As far as Taylor could see, she was being a trouper, though. Which was interesting, considering Ben's plan.

Of course Ben knew all about Steve's penchant for dangerous thrills, and Taylor had agreed that it was a part of him that wouldn't please Lisa. So they would take him to an environment where the kid in him could come out and play, and when Lisa objected, he'd have a clear and vivid picture of what he was about to sign on for.

Taylor wished it didn't have to be this way, but dammit, Steve was her brother, and nothing was more important than his happiness. Yeah, he loved Lisa, but what was wrong with waiting awhile? Finding out what the pill business was all about? Giving them a chance to think this through?

"Oh, my God."

They had reached the long line for the XSky, and Lisa had clearly realized what the ride was all about. The thing, and Taylor couldn't figure out a better word to describe it, was like a big ramp off the side of the building. Eight people were strapped in, eight hundred sixty-six feet above the earth, for a ride that would take them twenty-seven feet over the edge. At the end, there was nothing between the rider and the very, very long drop. Except, of course, the seat belts and the contraption itself.

"It goes thirty miles an hour," Ben said. "They use a magnetic braking system, and redundant ratcheting. The whole thing's over in a few minutes, but man, what a rush."

Lisa's face paled a bit more. "No. It's insanity. What if something goes wrong?"

"Nothing'll go wrong," Steve said, his hand squeezing her waist. "They test this thing until the cows come home."

"It's not the cows I'm worried about. I hate this."

"It's fun." Steve turned her around so she faced him instead of the ride. "It's all about the adrenaline. Being scared in a safe environment. You'll never feel more alive, I swear."

"I'm very happy with my current feelings, thank you. And besides, I have so much to do. I mean, we're getting married tomorrow, remember?"

"What else is there to do? Your mom arranged all the flowers yesterday. We have the judge all set up. The clothes are bought." He kissed her on the lips, held her shoulders with his broad hands. "Just hang a little while longer, okay? If you decide not to ride, that's cool. But I don't want you to leave."

"I wasn't planning on going by myself," she said, her tone surprised.

He hadn't expected that. "Oh. Well." Steve cleared his throat, looked at Ben, then back at his bride-to-be. "All right. Sure. Let's go."

Lisa smiled, but as she watched Steve's dejection her grin faded. "No, no. I was just kidding. We can stay."

He lit up like a little kid. "You sure?"

She nodded, but Taylor could see this wasn't turning out to be a good morning for Lisa.

"So you don't care for thrill rides, Lisa?" she asked.

"God, no."

"Oh, man," Ben said. "Steve hasn't told you about his dream, huh?"

"What dream?"

They moved another inch along the ride. Screams wafted through the air, along with the sound of metal on metal as the rides started and stopped. The atmosphere, aside from being Vegas hot, was filled with the spice that always accompanied danger, and Taylor couldn't help but notice that the couples around her were all hanging on to each other.

She'd clung to Ben, wanting him close. The same should have been true for Lisa and Steve, but it wasn't. Steve touched Lisa, but her body language was all wrong. Defensive, distant. She didn't want to be here.

Taylor wanted Steve to see it, but she wondered if he could. Love was sometimes so blind. Even if she pointed out the differences between them, Steve would come up with rationales, reasons. Which wasn't a bad thing in itself, but what did it say for the long-term?

In her heart of hearts she knew this marriage was a mistake. But what if it was an important mistake? What if it was all part of Steve's journey toward the man he was supposed to become? They should just butt out.

Except...

She had to find out why Steve had taken those pills. And what they were for. That wasn't negotiable. "Tell you what, Lisa. Why don't you and I get out of line? I don't want to go on the horrible thing, either. Let the boys have their fun. I want to hear more about your decorating business anyway."

Lisa looked at her with genuine fondness. "That would be wonderful." She turned to Steve. "Okay?"

He folded her in him arms, and hugged her close. Taylor's resolve dropped another notch. God, who was she to try to fix anyone else's life? She could barely manage her own.

Steve gave a jaunty wave as he turned back to the line and Ben. Taylor scoped out a place where she and Lisa could sit and wait it out. There was a small bench near the elevator, which was almost empty. A woman was nursing her baby there, but Taylor didn't think that would be a problem.

Lisa sighed as she sat, checked that she could see

the boys in line, then turned to Taylor. "So, you want to know about my decorating business, right?"

Taylor nodded. "I watch HGTV all the time, but I have no talent whatsoever. You should see my place. White walls, bland carpet, nothing truly original or fun. I have a few pieces I really like, that I found at flea markets. This great Vietnamese dragon carved from teak, and then there's this glass sculpture that makes me so happy, it's—"

"Taylor?"

"Yeah?"

"What did you really want to talk about?"

"Excuse me?"

Lisa scooted a bit closer. "I know you guys aren't thrilled about me and Steve. That you think this marriage is a mistake."

"No, no, not at all." She could feel her cheeks heat and wished like hell she was a better liar.

"I don't blame you. I came out of nowhere. I'm not part of the whole San Diego scene. We've only known each other for a few months. Should I go on?"

Taylor leaned her elbows on her knees. "Okay, so we're…concerned. We love Steven, okay? All we want is what's best for him."

"And I appreciate that. The thing is, I love him, too."

"Do you?"

"Taylor, this can't ever work if you're not going to believe me."

She sat up, rubbed the back of her neck. Damn, it was hot. "You're right. Again. In fact, I do believe you love him. What you know of him. And I believe he loves you. What I can't seem to reconcile is this new life he's leaping into. It's—"

"The opposite of everything he's ever said he's wanted?"

Taylor nodded.

"I know. We've talked and talked about it. I don't want him to be unhappy. In fact, I want him to be blissfully happy. And he says, over and over, that our life together is going to make him happy."

"He's always loved the boats, Lisa. He's lived for those boats. What happened?"

"Aside from me?"

Again, Taylor's cheeks heated. This wasn't going as well as she could have hoped. On the other hand, there wasn't a lot of bullshit happening here, and that was a really good thing.

"I admit, love is a pretty powerful thing. But to give up everything he's ever loved?"

"If Ben asked you to give up your life to go with him, would you?"

Taylor burst out laughing. "Ben? Me? Are you kidding? We're not—"

"Now who's not telling the truth?"

"I admit, we're having ourselves a time, but it's not the same thing at all. Ben and I aren't in love."

Lisa nodded slowly. "Right."

"What is this?"

"Nothing."

"Hey."

Lisa smiled enigmatically. "No, no. My fault. You two are just having a good vacation. Catching up on old times. It doesn't mean a thing."

"It doesn't."

Lisa laughed. "There are no guarantees Steve and I are going to make it. Maybe we'll crash and burn, I don't know. But at least we're going to give it our all." She turned and took Taylor's hands in hers. "We talk. We do. Even though it's not easy for Steve to come right out and speak his heart, he's trying so hard. He wants a family, Taylor, and so do I. We want a secure, good life, something that has roots. He doesn't want to give up the boats. But he wants more. He wants everything he had as a boy, only this time, he wants to be the husband and father."

"I think that's wonderful. I do. Isn't there a way to have all that, and still not put Steve in a suit and tie?"

"You don't think I suggested it?"

That caught Taylor completely by surprise. "You didn't?"

"Of course. I wasn't kidding when I said I want his happiness."

"But—"

"What?"

"Why here? Why so fast? I figured you were

hurrying into this so Steve wouldn't have time to reconsider."

"Maybe we are. Maybe neither of us want too much time. Diving into the deep end, you know."

"Yeah. Kind of."

"It's not a bad way to go. As long as you know drowning's not an option."

Taylor sat staring at the line inching toward XSky. Ben and Steve weren't in her line of sight any longer. In fact, they might already be on the giant fulcrum thingy. She shivered, half glad, half sorry she'd begged out.

"Go with us on this, Taylor. Please. You mean so much to him. He won't say anything. He can't. But he's desperate for your approval. He needs your support."

"I do support him. We all do."

"You know what I think?" Lisa said. "I think Steve and I are going to be great. We're going to grow old together, and play with our great-great-grandkids. And Steve's gonna teach all of them to fish."

"I think, with you, he's got a fighting chance."

"But?"

"Will you please tell me what the deal is with the pills? What's wrong with Steve, and why is he being so secretive about it?"

Lisa didn't answer. Another batch of thrill seekers got off the ride, and Taylor was pretty sure she heard Steve's laugh. When she turned to tell her future sister-in-law that the boys were coming, she realized she'd managed to put her great big foot right in the middle of it.

Lisa's face was pale as ivory. Her mouth had opened slightly, and her breathing was too rapid. She clearly didn't know a thing about the pills, or why Steve was taking them. Not one thing.

BEN COULDN'T FIND HIS BREATH, let alone get it under control. And his guts were still somewhere over the edge of the Stratosphere. It felt like the top of his head had exploded, and the rest of his body had followed shortly thereafter.

"Holy shit," Steve said, leaning against the building, his right hand over his heart. "You think the girls would kill us if we did it again?"

"No, but I might kill you if you don't tell me what the hell is going on."

Steve's expression changed immediately. Gone was the breathless rush from the ride, replaced by the kind of anger Ben had rarely seen in his friend. "What the hell are you talking about?"

"If you don't know, why are you so pissed off?"

"God damn Taylor. I told her it was nothing." He tried to push off the wall, but Ben pushed him back.

"Stop it. Tell me the truth."

"Get out of my face, Ben."

"No. I'm your friend, damn you. What are the pills? What happened to you?"

"Nothing."

"Steve, don't make me beat the crap out of you."

He continued to push Steve against the wall, using his forearm in a modified choke hold. He wouldn't hurt him, but he wasn't going anywhere. "You've got family here, big guy, who care whether you live or die. So tell me what's going on."

"Nothing's going on. I'm fine."

"Bull."

Steve stopped struggling. The air seemed to deflate from his body. "Don't do this, man."

"Why not? Why shouldn't I get all over your ass? You're scaring your sister. And I happen to care about your sister."

"It's not what you think."

"How the hell do you know what I think?"

"All right. Let up. You're choking me."

Ben let go. Hating this. Wishing Steve would just tell him the truth so he wouldn't have this knot in his gut.

"Listen, to me. I'm okay. But I can't tell you."

"What?"

The whole line of people behind them turned to stare. Ben smiled at them, then pulled Steve behind a post. "What?"

"I have to talk to Lisa first."

"She doesn't know?"

He shook his head. "No one knows."

"God dammit, Steve. Just tell me you're not going

to keel over at the ceremony, okay? That I don't have to put 9-1-1 on speed dial."

"It's not like that. Trust me."

"You're not making it easy."

"I know. But you gotta just chill. Don't make this more than it is. I'll talk to Lisa, I swear."

"When?"

"Soon."

Ben shook his head. "Not even close."

"All right. Tonight."

"Fine. Now let's go find them. Tell them what a great ride it was."

"Great, yeah."

Ben punched his friend in the arm. "Hey, you love her, don't you?"

"Lisa? Yeah."

"I mean, really love her."

Steve stopped. "What did you think? I'm not marrying her because of her comic book collection."

"She has a comic book collection?"

Steve slugged him back.

"Ow. Okay, okay. So I'm being a jerk. But jeez, Steve, Kansas?"

"Kansas isn't so bad."

"Not if you're corn."

Steve stopped. "I'm not giving up the fleet, man. I'm just changing directions. I'm doing what I should do. What I want to do. And I want to do it with Lisa."

Ben almost argued, but he didn't. He looked at Steve's face and he saw something he'd never seen before. Whether it was maturity, determination or just a commitment to his course, the man wasn't kidding. "Hey."

"What?"

Ben held out his hand. "Best friend. Best man. Beside you all the way."

Steve took it. "I know you're concerned, but don't be. Just take care of yourself, okay?"

"What's that supposed to mean?"

Steve's hand gripped his tighter. "I see what's happening between you and Taylor."

"And what's that?"

Steve laughed. "Are you kidding?"

Ben pulled his hand back. "This isn't funny, man."

"Oh, I think it's really funny. Talk about pots calling kettles."

"You're out of your mind. Those pills are for psychosis right? Hallucinations?"

"Yeah, that's it. I'm the one that's nuts. Boy, are you in for a surprise."

"Look, there they are." Ben pointed to the girls, sitting on the bench. They look hot. And I mean that both ways."

"Fine. Have it your own way, but don't say I didn't warn you."

"Steve, my man, you're out of your friggin' mind."

"Tell you what," Steve said, pulling him to a stop. "Give me that notebook you hide in your pocket."

Ben didn't like it, but he took out the small pad he used for notes and emergencies. Steve had his own pen. He wrote for a few seconds, hiding his hand so Ben couldn't see what was there. Then he tore out the page, folded it, and handed it to Ben along with the pen. "Initial it."

"What's it say?"

"None of your damn business. Just initial it. In your very best handwriting."

Ben did. But only because he couldn't figure out a way to get out of it.

Steve took it back, and with great fanfare, put it in his wallet. "We'll take a look at this baby just before we go home. And then, my man, if you can't call me a liar, then you owe me a beer."

"I'm not an idiot. And I can already call you a liar. It's not gonna happen."

"Don't say any more. Just wait."

"Steve, I like your sister a lot. But I'm not in love with her. I'm not going to be in love with her. This is a week. It's going to end. No big deal."

Steve nodded, then his grin faded sharply. Ben spun around, but he already knew what was behind him.

Taylor. Lisa. And they both looked as if their whole worlds had come crashing down around them.

CHAPTER SEVENTEEN

LISA WAS THE FIRST TO SPEAK. "Steve?" Her voice sounded small, scared. "Honey, is there something wrong with you?"

Steve gave Taylor a scorching glare, then took his sweetheart to stand in the line for the elevator down. His arm went around her shoulders and he whispered earnestly while Lisa leaned against him.

Taylor, feeling crappy in all kinds of ways, turned to Ben. "So, did you have a fun ride?"

"Yeah. It was great. Scary as hell."

"Did you throw up?"

"No."

"Bummer," she said, then she headed toward the elevator herself, careful not to stand too close to her brother. Ben hadn't said a thing she didn't know, but his conviction had taken her about ten steps back.

She was no big deal.

Golly, she could have gone the rest of her life without hearing that. Because to her, Ben was a big deal. One of the biggest. Growing bigger by the second.

She'd thought the guys were talking about the ride. Kidding around. Certainly not discussing her. When she'd overheard his vehement denial, all her defenses had risen. The nights they'd shared, her own confession to him, she'd thought they meant something. Certainly more than he did.

"Taylor?"

"Yeah?" she said, not looking back to see him right behind her. She sure as hell felt him though. Felt his heat, his pull on her. Why? Why did she give him so much power when he obviously didn't want anything more than the boink-a-thon she'd promised him?

"Hey, I didn't mean anything by that stuff, you know. It was Steve. He was trying to deflect the conversation away from him and Lisa."

Ben slipped in front of her, not giving her a chance to escape or even turn. His hands held her arms steady, directly facing him. But she wouldn't meet his gaze.

"Hey, come on. You know you mean a lot to me."

She raised her eyes enough to see he was trying to tell the truth. "I know. And don't worry, my panties aren't in a twist or anything. I'm just tired."

He nodded, but his concerned expression told her he wasn't buying it. "Let me take you to lunch, and then—"

"No, that's okay. I'm just going to go back to my room to get some rest. We have that dinner tonight, remember?"

"Oh, yeah. Tomorrow is the big day."

She nodded for him to step along with the line.

They should be next to get in the elevator. "So what happened with you and Steve?"

By the time he'd filled her in, they were off the elevator, waiting in another line for a cab. When she'd given her own blow-by-blow of her conversation with Lisa, they were back at the Hard Rock.

"Let me take you to the Pink Taco," Ben said.

"Thanks, but no."

They walked in silence into the hotel, past the registration desk. As always, the casino was hopping, the music was rocking, and everyone seemed to be having the time of their lives. All she wanted was to crawl into a cave. Her bed would do, the bathtub would be better, and figure out what the hell she was doing to herself. This was nuts.

Sure, Ben had been a presence all her life, but she'd never realized how deeply he'd affected her. What was all the more disturbing was what she'd made him out to be. He'd become a symbol, a reason, an excuse, all without his permission.

It was time to get real about Ben. About her life. Today, not tomorrow. She leaned over and kissed Ben briefly on the mouth. "I'm going," she said, "I want some time alone. You go have fun, and I'll see you tonight, okay?"

He didn't look happy about it, but he nodded.

She headed straight to the elevator. Alone.

Ben watched her disappear, kicking himself for his own stupidity. Not simply because he'd said that crock of nonsense to Steve, but because he hadn't been able to get out of it with any grace or dignity. He didn't care what kind of a fool he made of himself, but the last thing on earth he wanted to do was hurt Taylor.

How true that was had become increasingly apparent as they'd taken the journey back to the Hard Rock. He gave a considerable damn what Taylor thought of him, and cared even more that he make her happy.

Which scared the hell out of him.

He'd wanted his ex to be happy, sure. But it hadn't felt like this. Nothing had ever felt like this. Symptoms? An overwhelming desire to touch, to caress, to make love. The inability to stop thinking about her. The completely odd sensation of caring more about her happiness than his own.

He didn't want to go to his room. Too many opportunities to think up there. But he also didn't feel like gambling. Sightseeing?

He tried to think what was real close. Everything. Including the New York, New York. Which had an excellent arcade, or so he'd read.

Yes. He'd buy himself some tokens and go kill dinosaurs or zombies, or throw baskets or darts. He had several hours until dinner, and an arcade was just the ticket.

SHE MIXED HER BATH with jasmine oil and when it was all hot and steamy and smelling gorgeous she slowly sank into the water, two candles lit nearby sitting next to a bottle of minibar wine and a chocolate bar.

Thoughts of Ben, what he meant to her, what was real and imagined, what was pretense and what was in her heart, spun in her head. So many years, so much thought, but how much of it was about the real Ben versus the Ben she'd made up?

Back then, when she'd been eighteen, she'd thought him to be the perfect man. Aside from the whole looks thing, there was more to love about him than anyone she'd ever met. His kindness to her, and to most people. She remembered this one kid that was in her brother's class, who was slightly autistic. Shunned by almost everyone, Ben had befriended the boy—Alec, his name was—and they'd played chess together. Alec had worshipped Ben, and Ben had accepted him completely. Then others had behaved better toward Alec because Ben was also the coolest of the high school jocks.

And not just a jock. He'd been smart, a leader even though he never sought out the role. People naturally had followed him, that's all, because even at that age he was so thoroughly his own man.

Later, in his senior year, he'd driven himself to excel even in areas he'd found difficult. She remembered him struggling through chemistry, hiring a tutor. She'd never forget that because the tutor had been this buxom redhead who was more interested in their personal chemistry than what was in the texts, and Taylor had been swamped by jealousy.

Ben had always asked about her. Sent her these weird postcards from wherever he'd happened to be. Most of them said, "Wish you were here," and she'd believed the cards, if not him. She still had them all, in a small shoebox in her armoire.

He'd been so good for Steven. Encouraging, tough when necessary. And how he made her brother laugh.

When she'd found out Ben had gotten married, she'd been miserable for way too long. Months and months. As if he'd jilted her, even though that wasn't the case at all. She'd felt as if something had been ripped from her heart, and frankly, the feeling had never totally gone away.

Ben belonged to her. That was the bottom line. She'd believed that since the age of ten, and no distance between them or time lapsed could change it.

She let her head loll back and closed her eyes. A life without Ben was incomprehensible. A life with Ben, real Ben, close, together, gliding through days of ups and downs, through the mundane and the spectacular, was quite simply the most perfect idea ever.

Her eyes came open and her breathing stopped. *Oh, God.* Ben hadn't been her excuse. Well, he had, but not for the reasons she'd thought. He'd been her excuse because she was in love with him. Had been in love with him forever. Would be in love with him until the end of her days.

No wonder no other man had had a chance.

No wonder Ben was never far from her thoughts.

No wonder this week was doomed to fail from the start.

Okay. So she knew. She couldn't deny it, couldn't alter it, couldn't forget it.

Now what?

THE FIRST THREE ZOMBIES died from a single gunshot wound to the center of the forehead. The fourth got it right in the heart. And Ben was using his left hand.

He switched to his right, and zombies dropped like flies. The graphics on the game were quite good. Fast-moving, nice mobility, cool dimensionality. Better than the cop game he'd finished a few minutes ago. Unfortunately, the zombie game was one of the most popular, and he was surrounded by a gang of middle-school kids, impressed by his shooting skills, but all wanting their turn.

He finished the game, toting up an impressive score, then headed toward the fairway games. Tossing a basketball felt about his speed. And he could be relatively alone, as most all the crowd wanted higher-tech thrills.

Taylor.

He put the money in the slot, and the basketballs

rolled down. His first throw tanked, but the second was all air.

Taylor.

What the hell? He continued to throw, but paid little attention to the results. What was it about her? And what was it that Steve had seen? That he liked his sister? Sure, yeah, he did. A lot. More than he had anyone in a long, long time. Being with her was exciting, excellent. He didn't want the week to end. So what?

So what.

He put more money in the machine. Started back throwing. Moving his legs a bit, getting fancy. Missing. He went back to a straight free throw.

Back home, he had a full plate. Joe Panzer, the Stigler case, estate hunting for an old woman who lived like she didn't have a dime, but in fact was worth in excess of four million bucks. A psychology course at NYU. Lots of stuff. Fun, fun, fun.

Alone, alone, alone.

He threw the ball so damn hard it bounced out of its protected netting, hitting a teenager wearing huge jeans and a Kid Rock T-shirt.

"Sorry, man."

"Cool it, dude," the boy said, shaking it off.

"Yeah. Okay." He took the ball, put it back on the rack. Headed toward the escalator.

At the casino level, Ben walked aimlessly, admiring the Art Deco decor, the brilliant colors. He had no desire to play any of the machines and no wish to visit the bar. But there was a hell of a nice big leather chair in the lobby with no one around.

He sank into the overstuffed cushion, and it made him think of home. He'd gotten his neighbor, Mrs. Pershing, to feed his fish and take in his mail. Collect his newspapers.

But when he got back, he knew just what he'd find. The same old same old. Life, or at least his own version of life. Making a big deal out of his morning coffee. Reading the *Times* like it mattered. Following up on his leads, wrapping up cases, getting new cases, giving up on the hopeless cases.

Going to bed alone. Or worse, going to a bar, meeting someone he didn't want to know just to have a little human contact.

Was this what he'd signed up for? What he'd dreamed of as a kid? He'd wanted to make a difference back then, and he hadn't been kidding. So what had happened?

He'd learned, early on, to keep his emotions to himself. To guard against caring. People lie. People do bad things. It didn't pay to trust.

And then, with Alyson, there had been moments. Infrequent at best. They'd had the occasional meal. They'd talked about her day, his day, but there had always been a distance between them. Sex had been okay for him, an act for her.

Nothing remotely like being with Taylor.

He closed his eyes, his head running a movie he'd never seen before. Him, having his morning coffee, only this time, Taylor had his *Far Side* cup, while he had his *Get Fuzzy* mug. Her, laughing. Asking him where he'd be, when he'd be home. Could he stop at the market and pick up some milk. Him, going through his cases, only this time, he'd stop at one and make a quick phone call. "Hey, Taylor, how's it going, honey? You got that tort done? Fantastic. See you tonight."

Thinking of her again at four, at the station. In the cells that smelled of all the bad things you can think of, but he had a scent in his head that he could pull on, run with. Her scent.

Stopping at the little grocery on the corner, getting the milk and picking up some fresh flowers because Taylor was crazy about mums. Unlocking his door, a smile on his face instead of the steady numbness. Not even thinking about the tube, or if he'd run out of clean socks.

Taylor, greeting him with a smile and a hug, and her warmth and her love and her passion and her humor. Taylor, giving a damn about his day. Telling him stuff that he wouldn't have cared about except that it had happened to her, and she was his, and everything mattered. Every detail. All the mundane crap, the sirens, the crime rate, the screaming downstairs neighbors, the dentist, all of it meaning something because it was her. Taking care of himself not because he needed to outrun the bad guys but because he wanted to be healthy for as long as possible because life wasn't something to wait out, but something precious.

Taylor.

She could change everything. She could mean everything. But what about her end of the bargain? What would she get?

Him.

Not fair. Not in the least fair.

DINNER WAS AT BARABAS. Amazingly, it wasn't the fanciest or the noisiest restaurant on the strip. It was a cozy Italian place with a decent wine list and the scent of parmesan cheese and tomatoes in the air. The table was large enough to accommodate the whole gang—Lisa, Steve, Pauline, Mimi and then, of course, her and Ben.

He looked so gorgeous. Black jeans, crisp white shirt, bolo tie, black jacket. Hair pushed back, cheekbones for days, his eyes full of signs and wonders.

"You look stunning," he whispered as he pulled the big chair out for her. She adored the simple courtesy of him behind her chair, loved that he didn't use any kind of cologne.

"Thank you," she said as his hands ran up the length of her arms before he circled the table and sat across from her.

Steve and Lisa were on her left, the mothers on her right. The lovebirds looked as if all was well. Steve must have told all to his bride, and she clearly was cool with the prognosis. At least there weren't secrets going into the marriage. And from her seat far off in the bleachers, it seemed like the two of them had a real good shot at making it work. Who was she to question anything about love? In that regard, she was a misguided fool at best.

She talked to her mom, who had been in a perfect frenzy of bingo until all hours for the past few days. She'd won a grand, of which she had about two hundred left.

"Mom, you've spent eight hundred dollars on bingo?"

"And I intend to spend two hundred more before I go home. I'm on vacation. My son is getting married. I can have wine spritzers for breakfast if I want, and there's nothing anyone can do about it."

"You're right. Good for you."

"Thank you. Now, tell me what's going on between you and Ben."

"What?"

"I'm not on the moon. Steve tells me you two are getting hot and heavy."

"Mom!"

She grinned, looking a lot younger than she had at the beginning of the trip. "Spill, child."

"Fine. We're not. Hot. Or Heavy. We're just having a wonderful vacation that's going to be over very shortly. That's all."

Her mother grunted. Something else new. "I don't buy it."

"Buy it."

The waitress came by, and Taylor ordered the spaghetti marinara with a salad on the side. Her mom got lasagna and Ben ordered ravioli and sausage. She didn't hear the rest of the orders and barely heard her mother until she got poked in the side. "What?"

"Why are you so sad? Did he say something? Do something?"

"I'm not sad."

"You're my daughter. I know when you're unhappy. That makeup isn't hiding a thing. You're miserable. It's not about Steve, is it?"

"No."

"Then?"

She sighed. Leaned closer to her mother's ear. "Ben said I'm no big deal."

"Oh."

"So can we just enjoy our meal, please?"

"Honey, I haven't butted into your life for a long time."

"Yeah, weeks, at least."

"Shh. Listen. Don't leave this place without telling him how you feel."

"Why? Because my humiliation isn't on a grand enough scale?"

"No. Because you'll hate yourself if you don't."

"Mom, I love you, but you don't know what you're

talking about. Hey, look over there," she said, pointing at nothing across the way.

"Subtle, darling." Her mother patted her hand, showing off some very vivid red nail polish. "I may not know very much about the world, but I know you. And for once in your life, listen to your mother. Okay? Now, what do you say, let's have a toast to the happy couple."

Taylor picked up her wine, and so did the rest of the guests. Steve stood up. Smiled. "Thanks you guys. For everything." He lifted his glass, looked at Lisa, then back at his family. "The wedding's off."

CHAPTER EIGHTEEN

GUILT, LIKE A HOT KNIFE, sliced through Taylor as the words sank in. She'd meddled, they'd all meddled, and look what happened. Two people who clearly loved each other were calling off their future. She wanted to stand up, take it all back, beg them to reconsider. Instead, she took hold of her mother's hand while Steve continued.

"Let me rephrase that," he said, smiling again at Lisa, then looking back. "This wedding's off. We're still going to get married."

Taylor exhaled, the relief enough to make her dizzy.

"Why?" Ben asked. "Everything's all set to go."

"Because we want to do this right," Steve said. He sat down, leaned in to the table. The spark that Taylor had seen only in bits and snatches was back in his eyes, and he looked like the Steve of old. So maybe this was the right thing. Maybe they hadn't screwed things up too badly.

"We're going to get married in Kansas, so Lisa's dad can be there. So her friends can be there." He covered her hand with his. "So she can say goodbye."

"What?" Mimi, who seemed awfully pasty, blinked several times. She looked as if she'd been mugged. "But the chapel. The judge. The flowers. It's all ready. Tomorrow night, seven o'clock. There's an organist. And a photographer."

"And we'll pay for all that, Mom," he said. "But tell the truth, wouldn't you rather us get married at your church, with all your friends there? We can have the reception at the club, just like you wanted us to do."

"I suppose," she said unconvincingly. She drank the wine in her glass and reached for the bottle.

Ben got it first, and filled her glass. "What was that about saying goodbye?"

"A lot has happened since yesterday," Lisa said. "Steve has something else to share."

Steve kept his gaze on Lisa. "I'm sorry I didn't say something before, but… Anyway, about four months ago I had a heart attack."

Taylor gasped, checked on her mother, whose pallor now matched Mimi's.

"Don't everybody freak. It turns out it was a good thing. I had something wrong with the lining of my heart, but they caught it in time and repaired it. I'm lucky."

"You went through it alone?" Ben asked. "You didn't tell anyone?"

"Larry was there. He took me to the hospital. Just in time, it turns out. But here's the deal. I'm better than ever, now. Honest. They fixed it, and the doc said there's no reason I should have any trouble again. Hey, I figure it could have happened at sea, and then I'd have been a goner. I got a second chance."

"And that's why you wanted to do all this," Taylor said. "Hurry up and get married. Start a family."

"Yeah. Let me tell you, it scared the hell out of me. But once Lisa and I talked about it, and she finished yelling at me, we took another look at the big picture."

Lisa squeezed his hand. "I've known from the first moment I met him that he loved his boats more than anything."

"Almost anything," Steve added.

"Right." Lisa focused on her mother, who was having the most difficult time with all this. "The point is, even though I think he'd do wonderfully at whatever he set his mind to, being a sales rep for Dad's company wouldn't have made him truly happy. And that's all I want for him. Besides, I like the weather in San Diego."

"You're moving?" Mimi asked.

"Yes. I'm sorry, Mom, I know it kind of leaves you in the lurch, but I know you'll do fine. You have so many friends, and there's no reason you can't go on with the business. I'm going to start up something in California. And in the meantime, I'll help Steve however I can."

"We're gonna buy a house, though. That's the first order of business."

Taylor looked at Ben who seemed to be in a state of shock. A happy state, from the looks of it. "What I can't understand," she said, "was why all the secrecy?"

Steve shook his head. "I don't know. According to Lisa, stupidity pretty much covers it."

"Well," Taylor's mom said, "I'm thrilled. I think this is an excellent beginning. A wonderful start to a happy life. You both have my full support. Whatever I can do to help." She lifted her glass to the couple, then turned pointedly toward Mimi.

She wasn't so eager to give her blessings, but she did, after finishing her wine.

The food arrived, and for a while all everyone did was eat. But Ben kept sneaking glances at her, then turning away. He had to be happy with all this. Steve had told the truth, they weren't rushing into an ill-advised marriage, and he wasn't giving up his dreams. And yet, she could tell that something was bothering him. She wished they'd sat next to each other. She'd corner him after dinner, that's all.

Lisa rapped her spoon against her glass to get everyone's attention. "Ladies, don't forget, tomorrow morning we still have our appointments at the spa."

"But why?" Mimi looked so forlorn. All her plans had become so much dust.

"Just because we're not getting married, doesn't mean this can't still be a celebration. Tomorrow night, we're taking you and Pauline to dinner and a show. Celine Dion."

Mimi brightened right up. "How? The tickets are impossible."

"Steve came through. Turns out the concierge loves deep-sea fishing, and he's going to be joining us on a trip to Baja next month. Sorry it couldn't have been tickets for us all."

"Hey, that's fine," Ben said. "I'm sure we'll come up with something to occupy our time."

Steve waggled his eyebrows. "You know, it's not too late to change our minds. Keep the chapel and everything."

Ben looked like he'd been slapped. His eyes widened in panic. Taylor could have killed Steve. It had all been going so well. She coughed, trying to cover her embarrassment and excused herself. The walk to the rest room took a million years, all of which were filled with humiliation and a sadness that went straight to her bones.

She wished like hell Steven hadn't made the joke. Not just for the obvious reason, but because at that second she realized that more than anything in the world, all she had wanted was for Ben to say yes.

BEN GOT THROUGH the rest of dinner, although at the end he couldn't have said what he ate or how it tasted. The mixture of guilt and anger had dulled his senses, and all he wanted was to escape.

What the hell was he supposed to have done? Said sure, I'd love to marry your sister, even though we haven't seen each other in ten years, but gee, the sex is great, so I know it has to work out? What the hell was Steve thinking, making a crack like that? It would have been stupid enough to say it privately, but with Taylor sitting right there?

Ben hardly ever got mad at Steve, but tonight was the exception. Boy, was it an exception. The bastard had put him in a tight corner with no escape routes. Of course he knew Taylor would have laughed him out of the room if he'd even suggested that they jump into marriage like that. She was a sensible girl, and even though she was going through a lot of emotional stuff with him, she hadn't once said she was in love with him.

Even if she had, that wouldn't mean they should, well, get married, for God's sake. Marriage was big. Huge. Important. Forever.

Everyone else was already standing, waiting to leave. He got up, followed them out of the restaurant, making sure he wasn't next to Taylor.

At the curb, waiting for taxis, he gave himself a mental chuck to the head and went over to her. "Hey."

She smiled, but it seemed strained to him. "Sorry about that."

"About what?"

She looked at him as if he was a total jerk. Which was true.

"Oh, yeah. You don't need to apologize. However, I do plan on kicking your brother's ass from here to the hotel."

"He doesn't say much, but when he does, it's a doozy."

"Yeah. I mean, come on. Us? Get married? Tomorrow? What's he, crazy?"

She looked down the street. "Yeah, crazy."

"What are you up to now?" he asked.

"I think I'm just gonna go to bed. I'm pretty tired, and I have to get up early to do the whole spa thing."

"Ah, yeah. The spa thing. What does that include, exactly?"

She still kept an eye out for oncoming cabs. "Manicure, pedicure, facial, hair, makeup. The whole wedding package."

"Well, then, I guess I better get cracking on something special for us to do tomorrow night."

She turned to him finally. "No. I mean, don't bother. You don't have to worry about me."

"Worry about you? Are you kidding? I can't think of anything I'd rather do than escort you in all your glory. I just hope I can come up with something worthy."

She smiled. "Thanks, but really. Don't go to any trouble."

He touched her arm, and she flinched. Not a big old jump backward, but he hadn't imagined it. "What's wrong?"

"Nothing."

He took her by the arms and pulled her away from the others. "Taylor, come on. Talk to me."

"It's nothing. I'm just tired."

"I know you better than that. I think you're upset about what Steve said."

"Well, of course. He's my brother, and he had a heart attack. Naturally, I'm worried."

"That's not what I meant, and you know it."

"Ben, drop it, okay? Please?"

He looked at her hard, wishing he were suave and clever and that he could say a few words that would set everything right. But he wasn't. All he knew was that he cared a hell of a lot about her, and he didn't want to make her sad. "Tell you what," he said. "Let's go back to the hotel, but instead of you going to your room alone, let's us have some fun. There's supposedly a really good dance club there. What say we shake it for a while? Get some ya-yas out?"

She laughed. It wasn't fake or anything, and he felt instantly better.

"I'm really not in the mood for any ya-ya shaking. But you're right. Let's do something fun."

"There's a cool arcade at New York, New York."

"Try again."

"Miniature golf?"

She shook her head.

"How about a drive?"

"In what?"

"Let me worry about that. You go on up to your room, get into something comfy. I'll pick you up, and take you for a spin."

She leaned forward and kissed him gently on the mouth. "The cab is here."

It took him a second to register what she'd said. "Okay, then. Let's move."

TAYLOR PUT ON THE GREEN DRESS. She thought about wearing something different, but she needed to feel good. The dress helped, but just a bit.

Her depression was irrational, she knew that. What on earth had she expected? Just because she loved Ben didn't mean he loved her. She knew he cared for her, but he had a whole life back in New York, and he'd said time and again that he didn't want a relationship.

Even if they could get past that, what would it mean? Trips back and forth between coasts? She had savings, but she was by no means wealthy. Who knew what Ben's finances were like. It would cost a fortune, and besides, long-distance relationships rarely worked out.

She finished in the bathroom, and got her computer from the bedroom. Settling herself on the curved couch, she booted up and went in to check her e-mail. There were several notes from the gang, and one was about her and Ben.

To: Taylor
From: Sandra
EvesApple.com
Subject: Discoveries
Dear Taylor,

I've been following your adventures with Ben, and I've decided to tell you what I've been thinking, and not sugarcoat it. Okay, so it's easier to be brave when it's someone else's life at stake, but here goes anyway.

I think you need to tell Ben you love him. What, you say? You never said anything about love?

Well, here's a news flash girlfriend: You're in love with Ben Bowman, and you have been for ten years.

Now, don't get all huffy. Maybe you can't see it, but damn girl, we can. The whole reason you haven't found the right man out there is because you already have the right man. Ben's been your guy, will be your guy. As far as I'm concerned, it's destiny, and you two just have to work out the details.

But, you say, he doesn't want a relationship! Yeah, yeah, heard that before. Here's another cosmic truth: Men don't know bupkis about what they want. They have to be shown. I'm sure Ben's a wonderful guy in all kinds of ways, but he's still clueless. It's up to you, babe, to show him the light.

Tell him that you love him. Don't wait for him to tell you he loves you back. That may take some time. Just believe it's true, and move on from there.

You've been living a half-life in San Fran. I know you have, because (and don't make me get out old e-mails to show you) you've said so time and again. There's nothing holding you there at all. The job? When's the last time you were passionate about that? Your pals? Just how easy has it been to take a pass at an evening out? Sure, you have your pool league, but guess what, they have pool leagues in New York. Your bike? They have roads in New York, too.

Tell the absolute truth now. If Ben asked you tonight to come live with him, what would you say? I already know the answer. You'd be on it like white on rice.

So don't wait for him to make the first move. You're a twenty-first-century woman. Take the bull by the horns, so to speak, and make your intentions known. I promise, Ben will be grateful.

The bottom line? Ben isn't your Man To Do. He's your Man To Keep.

So put your fears on the back burner, and get cooking. You have a life to live, and you'll never forgive yourself if you chicken out.

But, you ask, what if he says no? Then you're no worse off than you are now.

Why are you still reading? Go on. Go!
Your friend, Sandy.

Taylor didn't even realize she was crying until a big fat drop landed on the keyboard. She wiped her cheek and closed the e-mail.

Sure, it was easy for Sandy, for her mom to tell her to go for it. It was all simple when you're sitting in the bleachers. She was on the ten-yard line, here, and the chances of her getting creamed were damn good.

The truth was, she'd already been as brave as she could be. Braver than she ever thought she could. She'd told Ben about her confusion, about him being her reason, she'd even confessed about Cade. What did everyone want from her? She wasn't a superheroine. She wasn't even Mediocre Heroine. She was just Taylor, who'd been hiding from the truth for years and years, who'd been living in her safe little world, never facing the facts about her heart.

All she had to do was get through two more days. Then she could go back home and do everything in her power to get on with it. Forget about Ben, and all he'd been with her.

Okay, so it wasn't possible to forget about him, but she could put it all in perspective. Go out and meet new people with new eyes. She didn't have to continue to live in purgatory. She could change her life, all by her lonesome.

Oh, God. Lonesome.

The tears welled again, and that wasn't okay. She headed back to the bathroom, afraid of what she'd see in the mirror. She would not be a crying fool when Ben came to get her. In fact, she wasn't going to let him see any part of her emotional baggage. He didn't deserve that.

Ben had been nothing but a sweet pea the whole time they'd been here. All this was on her head. Her own damn fault.

Ben Bowman, aside from everything else, was a friend. A good friend. Someone who cared about her, who always would. She'd be a jerk to let that go because she couldn't have everything she wanted.

She worked some voodoo on her makeup, grateful that she wasn't a swollen mess. And just in time. The knock at the door came a few seconds after she'd powdered her nose. Pasting a big smile on her face, she opened the door to the man she would love forever.

Her heart shattered a wee bit more as she saw the bouquet of roses in his hand. He really was her dream guy. She simply wouldn't let it become a nightmare.

CHAPTER NINETEEN

BEN WAITED WHILE TAYLOR filled the vase with water, and put it on the coffee table. He hadn't meant to make her cry. In fact, he'd wanted her to feel better.

"They're so beautiful," she said, wiping her eyes. "I love roses."

"They're not half as beautiful as you," he said, folding her into his arms. He kissed her, grateful when she sank against him.

For a long moment, all he did was appreciate the taste of her, the feel of her. He'd made such a mess of things, and he wanted to make it right. Tonight, he'd take her to play pool. He'd already made sure he could get a table at Pink-ees. They'd play, have some laughs, and by tomorrow, all would be well.

She pulled back, looked at him with glistening eyes. "I'm sorry."

"For what?"

"For being such a sap."

"What are you talking about?"

She sniffed. "Nothing. Never mind." She slipped away to get her purse. "I'm ready. Where are we going?"

"Well, remember you said you wanted to—"

"Wait." Taylor put her purse down again. "Don't say anything, okay? Just let me tell you what I have to."

"Sure."

She shook her head. "Don't say anything."

He almost spoke, but ended up nodding.

"Sit down."

He obeyed.

She didn't join him. Instead, she walked halfway across the room. Turned to face him. Opened her mouth. Shut it again. Then turned away.

He wasn't sure what to do. But he went with keeping quiet.

She turned back. Her spine was straight as a stick, her head upright, her hands twisting in front of her. She looked as if she was facing a firing squad. "Okay, so here it is. The truth. And you don't have to do anything with it. You don't even have to respond. It's my problem, not yours, so don't feel like you owe me anything."

He opened his mouth, but a hand raised sharply stopped him.

"If you interrupt, I won't be able to do this, so just sit there and listen. I've figured out some things these last few days. A lot of things. And trust me, it wasn't easy."

She walked four steps, turned around, came back the same distance. Only looking at him briefly, then studying the carpet or the wall. "I told you about why I wanted to sleep with you. And how that didn't work out so well. I mean, it worked out great, but not for me, you know?" She shook her head. "No, it was fantastic, better than wonderful... Oh, crap. I'm doing this all wrong."

"It's okay."

She glared at him, and he sank back on the couch.

After a deep breath, she started pacing again. "Bottom line. That's always good, right? The bottom line. Here it is. I love you."

He opened his mouth. Shut it again. Shocked more by the surge of happiness that shot through him than by the words themselves.

"For real. I'm talking love. The kind that changes everything. The kind that makes you want to spend the rest of your life with a person. Only, I didn't just fall in love with you. I've always been in love with you. Since I was eighteen. Or before that. I'm not sure of the date, but it's been a really, really long time, and nothing has changed it. Not living thousands of miles away, not being apart for years at a time, not dating other men, nothing. It's you. It's always been you, and there's not a damn thing I can do about it. But I know you don't want a relationship, and I can accept that. I'll go home and I won't even bother you. I'm not sure how, but I'll get over this thing. Maybe now that I know what's really happening, I'll have a decent chance of moving on."

"Can I say something?"

"No!"

He held up both hands. "Okay."

"I just figured you had a right to know. And I couldn't leave here without telling you because, and here comes another bottom line. You're my friend, Ben, you've always been my friend. From the time I made you teach me to slow dance. From the time I seduced you. From the moment I met you."

She looked at him, a mixture of fascination and horror on her face. "Oh God! I didn't even see it. Until right this second. I've been the one... The whole time. It was me."

"What was you?"

"I tagged after you. I was the one with the crush. I asked you to teach me to dance. Forced you, really. I was the one to show up on your doorstep, begging you to make love to me. It was always me, never you. You were sweet and kind and you never made me feel like I was pushy or obnoxious or anything. But you never made a move. Until I'd asked. Until I'd begged."

Her hands went up to her face. "I'm such a moron. I never... Oh, God."

He'd had enough. He got up, went to Taylor, and pulled her hands from her face. "You through?"

She nodded. Then shook her head. Then nodded again.

"Good, because now it's my turn."

She closed her eyes.

"Look at me, Taylor."

She opened her left eye.

"All the way."

She did. Kind of. She squinted, though. It was good enough.

"I'm not in the least sorry that you asked me to teach you to dance. It's one of my favorite memories. Of course, it doesn't come close to the memory of the weekend we spent together, which, I figured, came about because I'd been very, very good in a past life. I certainly didn't deserve it in this one.

"Every single time you've entered my world, you've made it better. Infinitely better. This week has been a revelation. Do you know what I did yesterday?"

She shook her head, and as she did, her eyes widened, her mouth parted slightly, and her expression became rapt.

"You know how I make up lives? For other people, for myself? Remember James Bond? All that?"

She nodded.

"Well yesterday, that's exactly what I did. I made up a life. My life. And you were there. You lived with me in New York. You had a job. We had coffee together. You had the *Far Side* mug, by the way. And we kissed before I left for work. And I got to think about you while I was out on the streets, and I got to call you when it was lunchtime, and I got to stop and pick up milk on the way home. It was as if I'd never seen the city before. As if I'd never understood my work, my life. Because all through the day, you were there. You were waiting for me. You changed that utilitarian co-op into a home, and me into a whole person, a real person, with a reason and a purpose. And when I came home, you were there, and we talked about the day, and I couldn't wait to hear what had happened to you. How you'd finished a damn tort. And everything I'd done was interesting because you cared about it.

"The best damn part of all was that I got to spend the rest of the night with you. And the night after that. In this universe I made up, you were there, for the good times and the bad. It changed everything. You changed everything.

"And you know what? I was a total jackass, sitting on that couch, making this wonderful scenario up in my head. Because I was too stupid, too afraid to take it out of pretend. To come right back to find you, to ask you— No, to beg you, to come to New York with me. To live with me in my stupid co-op. Because what I have now is nothing. It's a pretense of a life. A meaningless blur of days and nights that are so empty I can't see the bottom of them.

"All the time, you were here. Right here in front of me. I should have known it from the second I was inside you. I thought maybe it was the sex, isn't that a riot? That you had some magic when it came to making love. I think I mentioned I'm not very bright.

Because if I'd had a brain, I would have seen that you and me, we're supposed to be together. But I didn't see. Until two minutes ago, when you said—"

She held up her hand once more to stop him. Took a very deep breath and let it go as the seconds ticked by. His heart beat so fast he thought maybe he was having one of those attacks that were so popular these days, but in truth, he just wanted her answer.

She smiled. "Okay," she whispered.

"Okay?"

She nodded, as another batch of tears came sliding down her perfect cheeks.

"You mean, you'll come to New York?"

"Yes."

"You'll take the *Far Side* mug?"

She laughed. "Yes."

"Well, then," he said. And then he kissed her.

One Year Later...

"YOU WANT MORE COFFEE?"

Taylor shook her head. "I don't want to be late. I've got that Simmons brief to write and Dan is breathing down my neck."

Ben poured himself another cup in his *Get Fuzzy* mug. He sat back down at the dining room table, his gaze settling on the small bouquet of football mums in the blue glass vase. Taylor's touch. There was so much of it now in the apartment, it felt as if he was living in a different place. A much better place. Ever since she'd moved here, his life had transformed into something he barely could have imagined. That one day, sitting in Las Vegas, on that leather couch, had been a clue, but he'd been incapable of visualizing how good it could get.

Who knew Taylor would love the city this much? That she'd find such a great job, only one subway stop away? More than that, how could he have guessed that having her in his life would change him from the inside out. He hadn't known this happiness before, not ever. Looking forward to her every day, making love to her, hearing her voice on the phone. It was better than he deserved by a long shot.

She was happy, too. He saw it in her smile, the way she carried herself, the joy in her voice when he walked in the door. This was the kind of love he'd read about, but never believed was real.

She stood up, looking so fine in her tan slim skirt and her white blouse. Nothing fancy, but her beauty made it spectacular. God, how he loved her.

"Okay, so what time will you be home tonight?" she asked.

"Nine, if I'm lucky."

"Should I wait?"

"Naw. Eat. I'll be fine."

She came over to his side of the table and kissed him. Instead of a peck, the kiss lingered, and he felt himself stir, as always. The woman did things to him. Every damn time.

"I've got to run."

As she turned, he caught her hand. "Wait."

She looked at him, brows raised.

"Didn't you tell me you were getting some time off from that job of yours?"

"Yep. My first vacation. A whole week. Why? Did you have something you wanted to do?"

He nodded. "Yeah."

"Well?"

He pulled her around and lowered her onto his lap. "I was thinking we could go back to Vegas."

He saw the disappointment in her eyes. She'd mentioned Hawaii, and he'd seen the brochures she'd hidden in her bedside drawer. "Oh," she said. "You want to do Vegas again?"

"Well, I figure it would be pretty easy to convince Steve and Lisa to come back. And your mom, of course."

She leaned back and looked at him as if he'd gone nuts. "What are you talking about?"

"From what I understand, they have pretty nice weddings out there."

Her hand went to her chest. "Excuse me?"

He smiled, loving this. Loving her. "What do you say you make an honest man of me?"

"Get married?" Her voice had gone real high, real soft.

"If you'll have me."

Her eyes closed for a long moment, and when she opened them again, they glistened with tears. "Oh, God, yes."

"Whew," he said. "I was afraid you were going to laugh in my face."

She slugged him on the arm then wrapped her arms around his neck. "Never, never, never. I love you, you twit. I've always loved you."

He pulled back, caressed her face with both hands and looked deep into her blue eyes. "Turns out, I love you, too. And I always will."

* * * * *

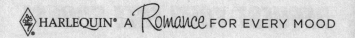

HARLEQUIN® A *Romance* FOR EVERY MOOD

If you enjoyed these passionate reads, then you will love other stories from

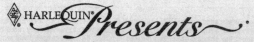

HARLEQUIN® *Presents*

Glamorous international settings...
unforgettable men...passionate romances—
Harlequin Presents promises you the world!

HARLEQUIN® *Blaze*™

Fun, flirtatious and steamy books that tell it
like it is, inside and outside the bedroom.

Silhouette® *Desire*

Always Powerful, Passionate and Provocative

Six new titles are available every month from each of these lines

Available wherever books are sold

REQUEST YOUR FREE BOOKS!

2 FREE NOVELS
PLUS 2
FREE GIFTS!

HARLEQUIN®

Blaze™

Red-hot reads!

YES! Please send me 2 FREE Harlequin® Blaze™ novels and my 2 FREE gifts (gifts are worth about $10). After receiving them, if I don't wish to receive any more books, I can return the shipping statement marked "cancel." If I don't cancel, I will receive 6 brand-new novels every month and be billed just $4.24 per book in the U.S. or $4.71 per book in Canada. That's a saving of at least 15% off the cover price. It's quite a bargain. Shipping and handling is just 50¢ per book.* I understand that accepting the 2 free books and gifts places me under no obligation to buy anything. I can always return a shipment and cancel at any time. Even if I never buy another book, the two free books and gifts are mine to keep forever.

151/351 HDN E5LS

Name _____ (PLEASE PRINT)

Address _____ Apt. #

City _____ State/Prov. _____ Zip/Postal Code

Signature (if under 18, a parent or guardian must sign)

Mail to the **Harlequin Reader Service:**
IN U.S.A.: P.O. Box 1867, Buffalo, NY 14240-1867
IN CANADA: P.O. Box 609, Fort Erie, Ontario L2A 5X3

Not valid for current subscribers to Harlequin Blaze books.

Want to try two free books from another line?
Call 1-800-873-8635 or visit www.morefreebooks.com.

* Terms and prices subject to change without notice. Prices do not include applicable taxes. N.Y. residents add applicable sales tax. Canadian residents will be charged applicable provincial taxes and GST. Offer not valid in Quebec. This offer is limited to one order per household. All orders subject to approval. Credit or debit balances in a customer's account(s) may be offset by any other outstanding balance owed by or to the customer. Please allow 4 to 6 weeks for delivery. Offer available while quantities last.

Your Privacy: Harlequin Books is committed to protecting your privacy. Our Privacy Policy is available online at www.eHarlequin.com or upon request from the Reader Service. From time to time we make our lists of customers available to reputable third parties who may have a product or service of interest to you. If you would prefer we not share your name and address, please check here. ☐

Help us get it right—We strive for accurate, respectful and relevant communications. To clarify or modify your communication preferences, visit us at www.ReaderService.com/consumerschoice.

HB10R

Alaska—the last frontier.

The nights are long. The days are cold.
And the men are really, really HOT!

Can you think of a better excuse for snuggling?

Don't miss the chance
to experience some
Alaskan Heat,
Jennifer LaBrecque's
sizzling new miniseries:

Northern Exposure *(October 2010)*
Northern Encounter *(November 2010)*
Northern Escape *(December 2010)*

Enjoy the adventure!

---

red-hot reads

HARLEQUIN® *Blaze*™

*It's said that you have to lose yourself
in order to find who you really are...*

Three intrepid Blaze heroines
are about to test that theory—

in the sexiest way possible!

Watch for

Shiver by JO LEIGH
(October 2010)

The Real Deal by DEBBI RAWLINS
(November 2010)

Under Wraps by JOANNE ROCK
(December 2010)

*Lose Yourself....
What you find might change your life!*

---

red-hot reads

www.eHarlequin.com

HB79575